Best Laid Plans

Best Laid Plans

MARY A. LARKIN

A *Time Warner* Book

First published in Great Britain in 2003
by Time Warner Books UK

Copyright © Mary A. Larkin 2003

Larkin, Mary

Best laid plans
/ Mary A.
Larkin

F

1589519

A   .
is available from the British Library.

ISBN 0 316 72583 8

Typeset by Palimpsest Book Production Limited,
Polmont, Stirlingshire
Printed and bound in Great Britain by
Clays Ltd, St. Ives plc

Time Warner Books UK
Brettenham House
Lancaster Place
London WC2E 7EN

www.TimeWarnerBooks.co.uk

I dedicate this book to my late dear father
Tommy McAnulty.

Acknowledgement

Grateful thanks to my son, Con, for designing and maintaining my web site, and to his wife, Debbie, for her constant support.

Author's Note

The geographical areas portrayed in *Best Laid Plans* actually exist and historical events referred to in the course of the story are, to the best of my knowledge, authentic. However, I would like to emphasise that the story is fictional, all characters fictitious and any resemblance to real persons, living or dead, purely coincidental.

Chapter One

'I forbid you to go! And that's the end of it!'

They glared at each other across the kitchen table, like arch enemies ready for martial combat. Grim-faced, Alice Maguire thumped the wooden surface with her clenched fist for the second time, to emphasise her words or to try to scare the living daylights out of her daughter, and ground out between clenched teeth: 'Do you hear me?'

'Hear you? I'm sure they can hear you at the top of Springfield Road. You're screaming like a banshee, so you are. But you listen to me, Mam! I'm going, with or without your permission. Only an idiot would pass up the chance to see the Rolling Stones live on stage. It was only by sheer good luck that Agnes got the complimentary tickets in the first place. If her sister's boyfriend hadn't been suddenly taken into hospital with appendicitis this morning we'd be going to the Broadway or the Windsor as usual.'

Alice was now gnawing worriedly at her lower lip. Since threats didn't appear to be having any effect, perhaps an appeal to her daughter's better nature would do the trick. 'Please don't go, Tess. I didn't want to tell you, but I had one of my bad turns today when you were at the wholesaler's.'

Tess had heard these very same words all too often in the past, when her mother wanted to put pressure on her to get her own way. Usually the ploy worked and Tess gave in for the sake of peace. Not today, though. This was the chance of a lifetime and Tess was not to be swayed. However, she did walk round the table and put a sympathetic hand on Alice's shoulder, and the tone of her voice was caring. 'Mam, tell me the truth, now. Did you really have an asthma attack?'

Shamefaced, Alice admitted, 'No. But I'll be worried to death about you going to see the Rolling Stones. And you know that could be enough to bring one on. Remember last year when the Beatles were here? There was near riots that night. The police had to send for reinforcements. Some young girls even finished up in the Royal.'

'That concert was held in the Ritz picture house, Mam. We're going to the Ulster Hall. They're used to live shows there. Think of all the boxing and wrestling tournaments that have been held there and no sign of crowd trouble. Everything will be fine, so it will.'

'Hah! How do *you* know there was no trouble? You've never been to the Ulster Hall before.'

'It would have been in the newspapers, Mam.'

'How often do you read the papers, eh? Your nose is always stuck in those silly romantic magazines you waste your money on.'

'See, Mam? As far as you're concerned, I can do no right. All my friends read magazines. Why should I be different?'

'Because I brought you up to be sensible, that's why! There'll be trouble, you mark my words. Young people today get carried away where these long-haired lads are concerned. Don't go, Tess. Please don't go.'

Aware that her mother could have an attack when it suited her, Tess was urged to action by the peal of the doorbell. 'That'll be Agnes now, Mam,' she said gently. 'I'll have to go, but I'll try not to be too late. And I promise to be careful and stay away from any trouble.' Giving Alice an affectionate hug, she quickly left the room.

Alice heard the outer door slam and hurried to the room at the front of the house they used as a workshop. She stood at the bay window and watched her daughter and Agnes Quinn, heads close together, striding arm in arm down Springfield Road until they were out of sight. Young ones were so independent nowadays, thinking they knew it all. With a swift glance upwards she asked God to look after them, and returned to her chores in the kitchen.

Bubbling with excitement the two girls jumped off the bus at the bottom of Grosvenor Road and turned to gaze at each other in amazement at the sight that met their eyes. Throngs of people were hurrying along Howard Street towards Bedford Street.

Quickening her steps, Agnes cried, 'Do you think they're all going to the Ulster Hall?'

'Where else?'

'We'd better get a move on, then.' Grabbing Tess by the elbow, Agnes almost dragged her friend along. 'Come on, hurry up or we mightn't get in.'

'But we've got passes!'

'If this crowd has its way it will be first come first served, no matter about passes or what not. I've never seen the likes of this in my whole life.' Since Agnes's life, like Tess's own, spanned a mere twenty years, Tess smiled mockingly at her. 'What on earth are you grinning at?'

'Nothing. Nothing at all. But you're right, we'd better get a move on.'

It was absolute bedlam outside the Ulster Hall, the crowd a heaving mass of bodies surging towards the building and then being pushed back. Tess laughed delightedly, her eyes dancing with excitement. This was indeed a new experience for them. Why, if they were on a boat they would be seasick with all this motion. A glance around showed her that some girls nearby did indeed look a bit under the weather.

Clutching their precious passes tightly they slowly elbowed their way towards where the stewards were trying to force the crowd into some kind of order and ensure that all paid their money at the kiosk before being allowed through the doors. After a lot of pushing and shoving, and rejecting extravagant offers of money for their tickets, Tess and Agnes reached a uniformed steward. He gave a quick glance at the passes and pushed the girls none too gently through a door and into the hall, pulling it shut after them.

Inside they came to a breathless halt and gazed around them in awe. There was little order as harassed staff strived in vain to keep control of the ever increasing crowds, amidst loud shouts and whistles. Another steward relieved them of their passes and, tearing them in two, waved the girls into the concert hall. Without further encouragement they pushed their way as close to the stage as they could manage.

Agnes turned to Tess with a rueful smile. 'I feel so guilty, being here, in all this excitement, about to see the Rolling Stones, and our poor Marie sitting in the Royal holding Dennis Sullivan's hand.'

'Why did she not come with you?'

'Well, you know what our Marie's like. She didn't like

to leave poor Dennis. I could see she was tempted, mind you, but she was afraid of something dreadful happening to him. You can die, you know, if the appendix bursts.'

'I know that. You can get some kind of blood poisoning, can't you? Poor Marie. But her bad luck is my good fortune.' Tess gripped Agnes's arm. 'Thanks for asking me along. I'll never forget this! Never!' She gazed around her in awe. 'It's an honour to be here, so it is.'

'Who else would I ask, eh? You're my best friend. Did you ever see so many girls in your life before? They certainly outnumber the men.' Standing on tiptoe she peered down towards the stage. 'I wish we were down there at the very front. Those girls might even get to touch the Stones. Imagine being that close to Mick Jagger.'

'Don't be so ungrateful. We're lucky to be here at all.'

'I know. I'm never satisfied,' Agnes admitted with a wry grimace.

'Anyway,' Tess continued, 'I'd prefer to touch Keith Richards. I think he's gorgeous. That is, if he has turned up. I heard on the news at lunch time that he wasn't on the same flight as the others. There might only be four Rolling Stones here tonight.'

The lights dimmed and Agnes stated the obvious. 'It's about to start.'

Rolling her eyes in exasperation, Tess exclaimed, 'I'm not stupid, Agnes. I can see it is.'

An expectant hush fell as order was called for, the curtain lifted, and the show began.

During the acts that preceded the Rolling Stones, the heat built up and the excitement mounted towards fever pitch, the dancers going into a frenzy as they jumped and twirled on the floor. When at long last it was time for the Rolling Stones to appear, everyone was already in a lather. Sweat rolled down Tess's face and she could see that those around her were also sweltering.

The curtain rose and the crowds were jumping with joy and screaming at the tops of their voices. And there they were, five very ordinary young men – obviously Keith Richards had turned up – that the audience was idolising as if they were some sort of gods. In spite of having warned herself not to go overboard about them, Tess was jumping up and down with the rest of the crowd, screaming and hysterical. The group paid very little attention to their fans and concentrated on their musical instruments, Mick Jagger prancing about the stage singing his heart out.

Near the beginning of the act there was some disruption at the front but Tess and Agnes were too far from the stage to see what the trouble was. The police were there in numbers and managed to keep some sort of control. At one time there were more police and St John's Ambulance men on the stage than musicians, as they tried to remove fans who had managed to climb up from the floor. As time passed, to her amazement, Tess saw girls dropping like flies. The St John's Ambulance crew was working flat out trying to revive them but most were being carried out on stretchers. Some hysterical fans were in such a frenzy they had to be put in straitjackets before being removed from the hall.

Her mother had been right after all. Alice would have a field day tomorrow when she saw the newspapers. Tess glanced at Agnes and saw she was white as a sheet, as if alabaster had replaced the blood in her veins.

'Are you all right?' she shouted above the din.

Agnes nodded but confessed, 'I just feel a bit faint.'

'Well for goodness' sake take it easy. If either of us

gets carried out of here, I'll never hear the end of it. My mam will make sure of that.'

All too soon it was over. They were hoarse, and limp as wet rags, when after many encores the curtain finally fell for the last time and the group could be seen no more. It had truly been a wonderful experience for the girls.

Tess and Agnes hung back as the crowd now turned its attention to leaving the hall. Most of them, carrying souvenir programmes, were intent on getting to the stage door to try to get the group's autographs. The two girls had no such intention, so they dallied to let the eager ones get ahead. Even so, they were pushed and buffeted as they tried to make their way out of the hall, and eventually in all the confusion they became separated.

Tess stumbled, keeping her feet with difficulty in the crush and looking around vainly for her friend. When a tall young man placed an arm across her shoulders, cushioning her from some of the mad confusion, Tess quickly glanced up at him, decided he was harmless and allowed herself to be propelled in the direction of the exit.

It was a great relief to get outside and she stood for some moments, hands on hips, gulping in great mouthfuls of warm night air. It was far from fresh, but better than the smog and stench of body odours inside the concert hall.

The lad looked at her in some concern. 'Will you be all right, now?' Tess shot him a tremulous smile and nodded. Still looking concerned he said tentatively, 'I'll have to go and look for my mate.'

Tess gazed around her in dismay. 'I'll never find my friend in this crowd,' she wailed. Afraid he might think she wanted him to remain with her, she hastened to add, 'But don't let me keep you any longer. I'll manage. And thanks! I'd be still in there if you hadn't rescued me.'

'Where do you live?'

'Up the Springfield Road.'

He laughed. 'Well, that settles it! I live off the Falls Road, so I suggest we make our way round to the bottom of the Grosvenor Road. If we do that we can't possibly miss our friends, unless they decide to take a short cut and I can't see them doing that.' Struck by a thought, he inquired, 'That is, assuming your friend lives up there too.'

'Tess! Where on earth did you get to?' Breathless, Agnes arrived at her side and cast a suspicious look at her companion. 'Is he annoying you?' she asked protectively.

'On the contrary, when we got separated, this young man . . . excuse me, I don't know your name? . . . helped me to get out of that mad house.'

With a slight bow he introduced himself. 'I'm Jack Thompson.'

'I'm Tess Maguire and this is Agnes Quinn.'

Just then another figure approached them and Jack said, 'And here is my best friend Tony Burke.'

Since they were all going in the same direction it seemed only natural that they walk home together. Tess found herself paired off with Jack.

They got on like a house on fire, debating the state of the country, unemployment and sport, and giving their versions of how the world could be put to rights if they were in charge. All too soon they arrived at the junction of the Falls and Springfield roads.

Tess's heart missed a beat as Jack smiled down at her. 'I've really enjoyed your company. Would you care to come out with me some time?' he asked tentatively.

Unable to hide her delight, she beamed up at him and readily agreed to meet him the following Wednesday. After good nights were exchanged, Jack and Tony made off down the Falls Road and Tess and Agnes continued on their way.

With a sideways glance, Agnes said, 'You look pleased with yourself.'

'Jack has asked me to go out with him,' Tess confessed.

'And are you going?'

'Yes.' Suddenly doubtful, Tess asked anxiously, 'Didn't you like him?'

'Come off it, Tess. I hardly exchanged two words with him. But he's nothing to write home about, is he?'

Tess shrugged. 'Well now, Agnes, I'm no oil painting myself, am I?'

'You're a businesswoman, Tess! You could do well for yourself if you put your mind to it.'

'Hah! I'm only a glorified dressmaker.'

'You know you and your mam are very good at what you do and are doing very well in your little business. I only wish I was in your shoes. I can assure you, I wouldn't go jumping at the first guy that came along. I'd pick and choose, so I would.'

Tess looked at her friend's blonde curls, big blue eyes and pretty elfin face. 'You'll have no bother making a good match. I'm surprised Tony didn't ask you out.'

'He did. But I'm not exactly over the moon about it, like you. They're just two ordinary lads, after all. And remember, we know nothing about them. They could both be married for all we know.'

Tess laughed at the idea. 'Don't be silly. Are you going out with him?'

Agnes shrugged. 'I might.'

'When?'

'I'm supposed to meet him on Tuesday night.'

The thought of what might happen if Agnes stood Tony Burke up hit Tess like an icy blast. 'But you've got to meet him! You've just got to,' she wailed.

A bewildered frown was bestowed on her. 'I don't have to do anything of the sort, Tess Maguire!'

Tess gripped her arm. 'Don't you see? If you don't turn up he will probably tell Jack and maybe Jack won't come to meet me, in case I'm as fickle as you. Please, Agnes, go out with him at least this once. Do it for me, please.'

Seeing her friend was in a really agitated state, Agnes reluctantly gave in. 'All right. All right. Don't get your knickers in a twist. I'll meet him this one time, but I'm not making any promises further than that.'

The next six weeks were heaven to Tess. Jack took her out at least once a week, sometimes twice, and she was in her glory. How her mother never guessed she was seeing a bloke was a mystery to her, as she worked alongside her in a happy haze. But alas, it ended all too soon.

It wasn't hard to remember their last date. It coincided with the riots that flared up that particular night in September and would be for ever etched in her mind. They had been to the pictures on Royal Avenue and were waiting at the bottom of Castle Street for a bus when the news came, via word of mouth, that no more buses would travel up the Falls Road that night as there was rioting in Divis Street. They were advised to take an alternative route home.

Nodding her head wisely, Tess said, 'We'd better go up the Grosvenor Road.'

'Are you not in the least bit curious to see what's going

on?' Jack gasped, disbelief written all over his face.

'It could be dangerous. We might get caught up in it.' Tess was apprehensive; if people had any sense at all they didn't go anywhere near situations like this, she thought.

Gripping her by the shoulders Jack shook her gently and urged, 'Let's live dangerously for a change, eh, Tess? Just this once, let's take a chance.'

As she gazed up into eyes alight with excitement, some of his fever rubbed off on her and, pushing away thoughts of how her mother would react if she ever found out about her daughter's stupidity, Tess eagerly agreed. 'All right. Let's go for it!'

'Good girl! Don't worry, I'll look after you.' Tucking her hand under his elbow Jack pressed it close to his body and started walking briskly up Castle Street, Tess skipping and running alongside to keep up with him.

Long before they arrived at Divis Street they were aware that things were bad. The RUC seemed to be out in force and they were being attacked with stones and bottles. Why? What on earth had started all this? Determined to find out, Tess and Jack stayed on the fringe of the mob. After a conversation with a young man who he thought might be a reporter, Jack explained to her the apparent reason for the riots. It appeared that the RUC had forcibly removed a tricolour from the window of the Republican office and had actually broken down a door to do so. Word of this had quickly spread around the adjoining streets and a small crowd of stone-throwing youths had soon snowballed into a full scale mob.

'I'm sorry now I talked you into coming up here, Tess. It was irresponsible of me. This could be very nasty. Let's make a detour and get you home.'

They backtracked to Hamill Street and cut across to Durham Street and eventually reached the Grosvenor Road.

Glancing at Tess, Jack saw how white she was and placing an arm across her shoulders hugged her close to his side. 'Are you all right?'

'I am now, but I was really frightened back there, so I was,' Tess confessed. 'It's hard to believe the removal of a silly flag could cause such anger.'

'It's not actually the removal of the flag that's the trouble, Tess. That flag has been in the window since the Republicans took over that shop as offices, to prepare for the elections, weeks ago. So why target it now? Believe me, there's more to this than meets the eye. Who sent the RUC in to get it? They certainly didn't take it down off their own bat! You wait and see. All will be revealed. It'll be in the papers tomorrow morning.'

Tess could tell Jack was agitated and restless and respected his silence for the rest of the journey until they arrived at the corner of Malcomson Street. There she stood on tiptoe to kiss him on the cheek, her usual form of good night. 'Don't you worry about it, Jack. It will probably be all over tomorrow.'

To her amazement and joy, he drew her into his arms and pressed her close. 'Tess, I'm in a bit of a quandary. I need someone to talk to.'

'Well, I'm here. Talk to me,' she urged.

Whether or not it was the emotional state the riots had raised in him Tess didn't know, but there, on the corner of Malcomson Street, for the first time ever Jack had cradled her in his arms and held her clasped to his chest. Overcome with joy she had nestled against him. They cuddled and kissed and it all came pouring out, punctuated by dry sobs, and urgent kisses: his distress that he was secretly meeting his mother without his father's knowledge.

Bemused, and not really understanding what he was going on about, aware only of the pressure of his body crushed against hers, she had gripped him tighter still, whispering words of encouragement and comfort, her arms willingly enfolding him, her lips feverishly returning his kisses. Even when his kisses became fierce and demanding and his hands explored her body she had not rebuffed him as a decent girl should. No, she, fool that she was, had exulted in the emotions that were carrying them along on a wave of passion such as she had never dreamed existed and allowed him to touch her up.

With hindsight she was mortified at her actions that night, in plain view should anyone pass by. Oh, it was quite dark in the shadows where they stood. But still . . . to behave like that in public. At the time all she knew was that she wanted him to kiss and touch her; wanted the moment to last for ever. It was her first encounter with sexual pleasure and she revelled in it.

He was the first to recover some composure and had gently put her from him, apologies tumbling from his lips. 'I'm sorry. So very sorry, Tess. I had no right to do that. I don't know what on earth I was thinking of. I'm afraid I got carried away. Can you ever forgive me?'

Believing that this was the beginning of their love affair she had waved his apologies aside and tried to draw him close once more. He had resisted her efforts and, saying he would be in touch soon, had hurried down Malcomson Street, head lowered, a shamed hunch to his shoulders. Although she wasn't aware of it, he was walking out of her life.

*   *   *

The Republicans had pledged that if the tricolour, removed on Monday night, were not returned, another one would take its place on Wednesday. Tuesday passed without incident but with no flag. On Wednesday, true to their word, the office staff displayed another tricolour in the shop window, and young people who a week ago hadn't even noticed there was a flag there gathered in Divis Street to admire and if necessary defend it.

Tess and Agnes met on Wednesday evening and, worried that Jack had not contacted her on Tuesday, Tess surprised her friend by suggesting that they take a walk down to Divis Street and see if everything was quiet.

'Why shouldn't it be?'

'You amaze me, Agnes. Do you not know about the riots on Divis Street on Monday night?'

'Of course I know all about them. They've talked about nothing else in work these past two days. The RUC removed a tricolour from a wee shop in Divis Street and were pelted for their trouble. They're hardly likely to make the same mistake again. Now are they?'

'I don't know about that, now. I was there. It was an awful experience, so it was. I was terrified. We had to make a detour to get to the Grosvenor Road because we couldn't get past the rioters in Divis Street.'

Agnes's eyes widened and she gasped at the glow in her friend's eyes. 'Let me get this straight. You say you were terrified, yet you want to go back? Are you daft? You're better staying away from anything like that, unless you want to end up in hospital, or even jail. Your mam would just love that, wouldn't she?'

'I know, but it was also exciting, Agnes,' Tess confessed earnestly. 'Besides, we don't have to go right down. We can go as far as Albert Street and see how things are. We needn't go any further if you don't want to.'

Agnes dithered. It didn't seem right to her to go seeking trouble; she had been brought up to avoid it, if possible. So to appease her conscience she compromised. 'Tell you what . . . we'll dander down to Victor's for an ice-cream, but if there is any sign of trouble whatsoever, we turn back immediately. Okay?'

'That's fine by me,' Tess eagerly agreed. She was secretly hoping to see Jack. He had been enthralled by the riots on Monday night and she had a gut feeling he would be down again tonight. She had been uneasy about the abrupt way he had left her. Had she disgusted him with her display of passion? Was that why he hadn't been in touch the night before?

They arrived at Albert Street and from there onwards as far as the eye could see the road was black with people. The rioting was intense. Police were being driven back by a barrage of bottles and stones and anything else the mob could lay their hands on. Some petrol bombs were also being thrown, the fumes and smoke permeating the air and catching one's throat. In the distance a trolley bus was blazing furiously.

In spite of their good intentions, curiosity got the better of Tess and Agnes, and in no time they were caught up in the midst of it. They were flung this way and that and would have fallen had there been room to do so. Frightened, and gasping for air, Agnes cried in alarm, 'This is awful! Let's get the hell out of here.'

They had left it too late. They had been dragged into the centre of the crowd and now all possible avenues of escape were cut off by armoured cars parked at the entrances to the narrow streets, their headlights picking out the dense mass of rioters. Rain spattered over them and Tess was thankful, hoping it would cool down the tempers. Only when the water lashed against her, almost lifting her off her feet, did she realise that it wasn't rain but a water cannon the police were using to quell the mob. The sound of breaking glass and sirens was deafening yet some of the mob were trying to make their voices heard above it all as they sang Republican songs, and swore and jeered at the police.

The RUC, wearing steel helmets and using bin lids as body shields, battled their way to the front of the shop that held the offending tricolour. This time the Republican offices were barricaded against them and resisted their efforts at entry with crowbars, so they smashed the window to remove the flag. The crowds were enraged at their audacity and all hell broke loose as emotions soared completely out of control. More stones and bottles were thrown at the RUC. They retaliated with baton charges and the fighting intensified. The girls were in tears and shaking with fright when at last they managed to struggle free from the angry mob.

Looking down at her sodden clothes Agnes cried wrathfully, 'I hope you're satisfied now, Tess Maguire! Look at the state of us. This new skirt of mine is ruined and it's all your fault. The next time you want to go chasing after a cheap thrill, do it on your own. I've had enough to last me a lifetime. My mam bought me this skirt for my birthday. It cost a wee fortune, so it did. She'll kill me when she sees it.'

Mournfully Tess agreed with her. 'I'm sorry. You're right, it's all my fault for encouraging you to come down here and I'm sorry about your skirt, Agnes. Come home with me and maybe my mam will be able to sort something out.'

'I doubt it. Your mam will be angry too. She'll be too

busy venting her wrath on you to be bothered with the likes of me.'

'She will help you. I know she will,' Tess replied with more confidence than she felt.

Alice went berserk when Tess eventually arrived home, hair plastered to her head and clothes soaked. She surmised that somehow her daughter had been involved in the rioting she had heard about on the radio. 'In the name of God, have you no sense at all, girl?' Seeing Agnes was in a similar condition, Alice urged, 'Get you two up the stairs and out of those wet clothes before you catch your end. You did right to come here, Agnes. Your mam would hit the roof if she saw you like this.'

Agnes wholeheartedly agreed with her. Her mother was a bit of a snob and she would be furious if their neighbours saw her daughter come home in this condition. Agnes was glad of the opportunity to make herself presentable before going home. 'Thanks, Mrs Maguire. I appreciate this.'

In the bathroom the two girls gazed at each other and burst out laughing. 'You'd think we'd been through the wars,' cried Agnes.

'In a way, I suppose we have,' Tess agreed ruefully and threw her friend a towel. 'Let's get our hair dried and into some dry clothes. It's just as well we take the same size.' She lifted Agnes's wet skirt and grimaced sightly. 'Then I'll get Mam to take a look at this. Actually, I think a good pressing just might do the trick.'

Alice had pulled a small table close to the fire and a tray containing a pot of tea and a plate of sandwiches awaited the girls when they descended the stairs.

'Oh, how lovely, Mrs Maguire,' Agnes cried. 'You're an angel.'

'I don't feel like an angel, believe me, Agnes. I feel like banging your two heads together. When I heard on the radio that there was trouble in Divis Street I was sure you would have enough sense to steer clear of it. This could become very nasty, you know, if it's not nipped in the bud.'

'We realise that, Mrs Maguire, but I can't see it continuing. People are too sensible to go on fighting over a wee flag. It will blow over. You'll see.'

Alice sighed. She wasn't so sure about that. But then, how could she expect them to understand? They had grown up during the forties and fifties when, although after the war there had been rationing and a shortage of material things, everything in Northern Ireland was relatively peaceful. She herself remembered her own young days when things hadn't been so good.

Taking the offending skirt from her daughter, she said, 'This is wool. Hard to work with. See . . .' She pointed to the label inside the waist band and read, 'Dry clean only. But I'll do my best.'

In the kitchen, spreading the pleats on the ironing board, she covered them with a damp cloth and carefully pressed the skirt. As she did so, the past came back to haunt her. When she was a young schoolgirl her mother and father had taken her down to Royal Avenue one Twelfth of July to watch the Orange parades. The footpaths had been crowded and they had had to walk some distance along the road before they found a gap near North Street and settled down to watch the marchers go by. To her young eyes it had been a wonderful spectacle.

Each lodge was heralded by a large banner followed by a band dressed in colourful uniforms and there were all kinds of instruments: bagpipes, accordions and flutes.

Her favourite had been the drums. She had been mesmerised by the way the drummers swung the drum sticks, throwing them in the air and catching them without missing a step. The Orangemen looked grand in their fine bowler hats and orange sashes as they marched proudly in step with each other, but it was the young boys striding in front that caught her attention; boys no older than herself, twirling their long staffs into the air and catching them with little effort.

Alice was enchanted, and sighed when the end of the procession came in sight and she knew that soon they must return home. Suddenly loud cracks rent the air and she had thought it was fireworks going off, but to her amazement the marchers scattered in all directions and the next thing she knew her father had swung her up in his arms and grabbing her mother by the arm had sought shelter in a shop doorway, protectively shielding their bodies with his own.

Somehow her father had managed, by taking them into Smithfield Market and cutting up side streets across to Townsend Street, to get them away from the trouble. Eventually they reached the safety of their own home. Although her mother was tearful and shaking like a leaf, her parents had played down the severity of the incident for her benefit. However, for weeks afterwards nightmares about the event had caused her many sleepless nights.

That was the start of the rioting in July 1935 and it had continued for some time. Was the same thing about to happen again? Carefully spreading the skirt over a chair she went to tell Agnes the good news that her birthday present was as good as new and she could face her mother without fear, but her thoughts were still troubled.

The next week showed that her anxiety was unfounded. To everyone's relief the rioting in Divis Street was quickly over and somehow or other there were no apparent consequences. An uneasy peace returned to the city.

Tess paused, breathless, at the top of Spinner Street and chastised herself. Why was she in such a big hurry? Probably only bad news awaited her anyway. She stood for some moments outside the Dolphin chip shop until her breath had settled to a steady rhythm before turning the corner and slowly walking down past the row of terrace houses, some of them still with just the basic kitchen, scullery, and small room downstairs and two bedrooms upstairs. She had been in Jack's home once before and was aware that he and his father lived in just such a house. You couldn't blame them. Two men living together wouldn't worry too much about the latest mod cons.

The terraces had been built years earlier to lure workers from rural areas to seek employment in the nearby linen mills. Her eyes scanned the red brick walls and high narrow windows. She smiled as she observed, by the light of the street lamps, the well-looked-after front steps and scrubbed semicircles of pavement outside a lot of the front doors. Caring women must surely live in these particular houses. They were obviously their owners' pride and joy.

Would Jack Thompson be annoyed at her for coming, uninvited, to his home? No matter. She had to know where she stood. It was almost two weeks since he had been in touch; long days of yearning for the sight of him. What if he was ill and unable to get word to her? In her heart she knew she was deluding herself.

Although private telephones were, as yet, rare in this district, there was a public pay phone in the Clock Bar at the top of Lower Clonard Street. If Jack was unable to get out at all, surely his father, if asked, would have phoned on his behalf.

She was halfway down the street when she was startled from her musing. To her dismay she saw Jack coming out of his house at the bottom of the street, ushering a young girl before him and turning to lock the door. In a panic, she stepped into the nearest hall, thankful that, unlike the road where she lived, the occupants of these houses when at home left their outer doors open. What if Jack and his companion came up the street and saw her? It didn't bear thinking about. He would know, only too well, that he was the only reason she was likely to be in Spinner Street. She whispered a short prayer that God would not let the owner of the house where she now stood, shaking with nerves, become aware of her and open the door into the hall.

Tess prayed in vain. First the net curtain on the half-glass vestibule door leading to the kitchen was twitched aside and then the door itself was pulled open. A small, dark-haired woman suspiciously eyed the stranger standing in her hall. What would she be wanting here? She didn't know her from Adam. 'Can I help you?' she asked, in a not too friendly tone, looking as if she was ready to slam the door in Tess's face and retreat for assistance if need be.

The name of an acquaintance came to Tess's mind. Stella Mullen lived in one of these streets. 'Does Stella Mullen live here?' she asked in a trembling voice.

The woman's demeanour softened. 'Oh! You've got the wrong street, love. Stella lives in Lower Clonard Street.' Stepping into the hall, the woman forced Tess to retreat backwards before her and move out on to the pavement. The woman pointed down the street. 'Just go to the bottom of the street here, and turn the corner. It's one of the houses facing you on Lower Clonard Street.'

Thankfully aware that Jack and his companion had, before her forced exit, passed by without so much as a sideways glance in her direction, Tess, with a sigh of relief, thanked the woman and continued on down Spinner Street, anxious to put as much distance as possible between herself and Jack Thompson.

Blinded by tears she turned the corner at the bottom of the street and walked quickly up Lower Clonard Street. Near the corner, passing the Clock Bar, she was brought to an abrupt halt when the tall figure of a man suddenly exited the pub, causing her to collide with him. He gripped her arms to prevent her falling and when he spoke she recognised Dan Thompson's voice.

'Whoa, there.' Jack's father peered into her face and she smelt the whiskey on his breath. 'Why, it's young Tess! Why the big hurry, love?'

She tried to smile through her tears but failed miserably.

Putting a comforting arm round her shoulders, he said, 'I was trying to coax myself to go into the Dolphin for a fish supper, but I hate eating alone. Will you join me?'

She sniffed. Was he blind? Couldn't he see she was upset? How could she go anywhere the state she was in? 'It's very kind of you, Mr Thompson, but I'm not in the least bit hungry.'

'Have a Coke, then, Tess. Go on, keep me company. I really do hate eating alone.' He was not hungry either, but this young girl was obviously upset about something. He had an idea that his son was the cause of her distress and felt compelled to help her.

'No. I'm sorry . . .'

'Please? I'm feeling a bit down and I don't want to go home yet. I'd be glad if you'd come,' he said persuasively.

She was about to refuse again, but realised that in the circumstances she might just perhaps find out who the girl with Jack was. After all, she might be a cousin or a family friend. Against her better judgement she found herself agreeing to accompany Dan. 'All right. If you're really that hard up for company, I'll join you.'

They crossed the street and walked the short distance to the Dolphin. It was too early for the second show in the Clonard picture house to be over and the shop was practically empty.

The proprietor, Johnny Reid, gave them a friendly wave and continued shaking the chips in the wire basket, whistling cheerfully away as usual. Johnny was well liked and his fish suppers were delicious. According to Johnny the batter on the fish was prepared from a closely guarded family recipe handed down through the years, and it was certainly always light and crunchy. Dan escorted Tess to one of the boxes along the far wall and when they were seated he leaned across the table towards her. 'Tess, I insist you have something to eat.'

The strong aroma of the fish and chips teased her nostrils, making her aware that she had eaten very little since lunch time. 'I'll have a fish, then, if you don't mind. No chips, thank you.'

'Mind? I'm delighted. You're getting far too thin, you know. A few chips wouldn't do you any harm either. Are you sure you won't have some?'

'Just a fish, thank you,' she reiterated.

Dan went up to the counter to place his order and his heart was heavy. Hadn't he warned his son that Tess might be reading much more into their friendship than he intended? But Jack had laughed at the idea, saying, 'Come on now, Dad, Tess is a big girl. Me and her are just good friends. Nothing more. And she knows it. She's great to talk to, discuss current affairs with, and she even knows a fair bit about sport too, but I'm just not attracted to her in the other way. That's why I stopped seeing her. I didn't want her getting the wrong idea.' Colour had burned in his cheeks as he recalled his last meeting with Tess. He felt a cad. She had every right to think he was interested in her, the way he had behaved that night. What on earth had got into him? He had ruined a good friendship with his carry-on. And who knows how things would have gone if Colette Burns hadn't come into his life? But she had, and he had fallen for her, hook, line and sinker.

At Dan's look of contempt his voice had trailed off. His dad was no fool. He'd be well aware that Colette had changed things as far as his son was concerned. Colette with her thick black hair and sultry brown eyes.

Dan stole a sideways glance towards where Tess sat. By the look of that poor soul she had expected better from his son.

However, when he returned to the box he found Tess more composed. 'What upset you, lass?' he asked tentatively, not wanting to become too involved but feeling the need to show some concern.

Wearily she ran her fingers through her bright auburn curls and confessed, 'Oh, this and that. You know how it is? Some days nothing seems to go right no matter how hard you try.'

'You can say that again. I've had plenty of those days myself. But, believe me, they do pass, love. Can I be of any help?' His look took in the big green eyes that would put emeralds to shame, and her hair was lovely, a mass of red highlights. Could his son not see she had her share of beauty? With that hair and those eyes she would soon be snapped up.

Tess gazed back at him, seeing only compassion and caring in his dark eyes, and longed to question him about Jack. Her mouth contorted into words that would not emerge. 'Not really,' was all she could manage.

Johnny gave a shout to let them know their order was ready and Dan went to the counter to collect it. When he returned Tess saw that Dan also had only a fish on his plate. 'I thought you said you were hungry? Or are the chips not ready yet?'

'They are ready and I am hungry, but I must watch my weight.' He patted a non-existent tummy and dared to bring his son's name into the conversation. 'My Jack had better watch his weight as well. He's drinking far too much these days if you ask me.'

'He misses his mam,' Tess said softly, remembering the feel of Jack in her arms when she had consoled him.

'It's time he put all that behind him,' Dan said abruptly.

A hand reached across and patted his in sympathy. 'Have you heard from her at all?' she dared to ask quietly, thinking that perhaps, unknown to Jack, Anne Thompson had also been in touch with her husband. Jack was in such a state because she had contacted him and not his father. She must be a cruel woman, making Jack promise not to tell his father that she was back on the Falls Road. But at least it had brought Jack into Tess's arms for comfort and for that she was grateful. On the other hand, by returning his affection that night, letting him see how much she cared, had she scared him off? She dragged her attention back to what Dan was saying.

'No. Not a single dicky bird. I suppose our Jack has told you all about it. If she'd told me just how unhappy she was, we might have sorted something out. But no, she just upped and packed a few things and went off with some guy from work. The coward's way out,' he said bitterly.

Since meeting Jack, Tess had, from different sources, heard various accounts of why Anne Thompson had left her husband and son but it was none of her business, so she held her tongue. He had yet to touch his fish, and Tess felt the need to apologise. 'Look, I'm sorry I brought the subject up. Please eat up. Don't let me put you off your meal.'

He smiled grimly. 'I will, lass, if you'll eat yours.'

She forced herself to take a forkful of fish and place it in her mouth. It was delicious and she savoured the fine-textured cod and crispy batter. After a short pause, Dan followed her example. They ate in silence, Tess trying to think of some way to inquire about Jack's companion, and Dan trying to avoid opening a flood-gate of tears. Her back was to the door and she didn't see Jack enter. Dan did and, with a glance at her bent head, gestured to try to warn his son off.

Apparently not understanding, and looking app-rehensive, Jack approached their box. 'Hello, Tess. Are you keeping my old man company tonight?' he asked tentatively.

Her cheeks coloured slightly as a young girl joined Jack and smiled at them in a friendly fashion. The second house in the Clonard picture house must have recently finished because a surge of noisy teenagers at that

[26]

moment entered the shop, saving her from having to answer him.

Jack glanced over his shoulder as the boxes filled up. 'Can we join you?' he asked his father.

Knowing that Johnny Reid, understandably, would expect every available space to be filled now the picture house was out, and aware that someone would eventually be sharing their box, Dan nodded reluctantly. Rising to his feet he politely gestured for the girl to sit down facing Tess.

'Tess, this is Colette Burns, a friend of Jack's. Colette, this is Tess Maguire.'

'Hello.' White teeth flashed in a Mona Lisa face and a hand was thrust in Tess's direction. 'Jack has told me all about you.'

Tess shook the proffered hand and nodded a greeting. She felt betrayed that Jack had discussed her with this stranger. Just what had he told her? She picked at her fish now, afraid each morsel would choke her as she forced it down a throat constricted with nerves. A glance at Dan revealed the pity in his eyes and unable to bear it she rose abruptly to her feet. Why should she sit here being patronised?

'Forgive me, Dan, but I did warn you I wasn't hungry.' She glanced across at the girl. 'Excuse me, Colette, but I must go. My mother will be wondering where I've got to. Nice to meet you.'

Jack was leaving the counter after placing his order and he gazed in bewilderment at Tess's back disappearing through the door. He looked askance at his father. Muttering angrily that he would speak to him later, Dan excused himself and, bidding Colette good night, followed Tess. He caught up with her at Dunville Park and grabbing her arm brought her to a standstill.

'Here now, slow down, girl.' He was dismayed to see tears pouring down her face. 'You mustn't upset yourself like this, Tess. No man's worth it.' He thrust a clean white handkerchief into her hand.

She mopped the tears away and blew her nose. Grimacing at him, she said apologetically, 'I'll wash this and get it back to you,' before pushing the handkerchief into her coat pocket.

He wagged a hand to show it didn't matter. 'Don't worry about it. Come on, I'll walk you home.'

He turned to walk up the Falls Road and she cried in dismay, 'There's no need. I'll be all right.'

'I want to see you safely home,' he said stubbornly, and reluctantly she fell into step beside him.

They walked in silence until they reached Springfield Road. For the life of him, Dan couldn't think of anything to say that wasn't an inane cliché.

Tess was ashamed of her behaviour. She should have stayed and put on a brave face; tried to show she didn't care that Jack had dumped her for a new girlfriend. But she had been too upset to put on an act and now here she was completely tongue-tied. Mr Thompson would think her a fool.

She stopped and faced Dan. 'There is really no need for you to come any further, Mr Thompson.' She nodded up the Springfield Road. 'This is a well-lit road. Besides, it's still early and there's plenty of people about.'

'I'll see you to your door.' She tut-tutted in frustration and he reiterated firmly, 'I'll see you to your door.'

To her dismay, when they arrived at her home her mother was watching from the big bay window, and before Tess could say good night to Dan and send him on his way the door was thrown open.

'I've been worried sick about you, so I have,' her

mother cried shrilly, her eyes taking in the big feller from his thick dark hair and rugged face to his well-polished brogue shoes. What on earth was her daughter doing out with this middle-aged man?

She intended finding out. 'Come in, the pair of you. I'll put the kettle on.'

Dan flashed Tess a glance to gauge her reaction to this request but she was staring abjectly down at her feet and failed to notice.

Having recognised the woman standing in the doorway, he said tentatively, 'If you're sure it's no bother?'

'None at all. Come on in.'

Resigned, Tess climbed the steps to the door and Dan followed. Now her mother would find out she had been dating a young man and would want to know why Tess hadn't mentioned it to her. An inquest would be held.

In the hall, Tess introduced them. 'Mam, this is Mr Thompson, a friend of mine.'

Seeing a puzzled frown gather on Alice Maguire's brow, Dan was quick to intervene.

'Your daughter is a friend of my son's, Mrs Maguire.'

'Oh, I see.' But she didn't. If that was the case where was the son and how come she'd never heard tell of him? 'Show Mr Thompson into the living room, Tess. I won't be five minutes.' Alice headed towards the kitchen at the back of the house. Slipping out of her coat, Tess hung it on a rack in the hall.

'Would you like to take off your coat, Mr Thompson?'

He eyed her apprehensively. 'I realise now that I shouldn't have come in. Would you like me to beat a hasty retreat?'

In spite of her misery she laughed at the idea. 'Too late for that now, I'm afraid. Here, give me your coat and prepare yourself for the third degree.'

Alice was deep in thought as she put the kettle on for the tea. There was something familiar about this man, but then she had probably seen him about the road. It was a busy thoroughfare and he was handsome enough to catch any woman's eye. She carried the tray into the living room and Dan was quickly on his feet to relieve her of it.

Alice was using her best china. Pouring the tea, she handed Dan a cup on a matching saucer, and inquired with a reproachful glance in Tess's direction, 'I'm surprised my daughter hasn't mentioned you, or indeed your son, to me. Have you known Tess very long, Mr Thompson?'

'Dan. Please call me Dan. You too, Tess. We've just known each other a matter of weeks.' Then Dan dropped a bombshell. 'I recognise you from way back, Mrs Maguire. Me and your husband were mates for a time before he left Ross's mill. I even remember dancing with you a few times at the Gig.'

Alice was gazing at him open-mouthed, loath to admit that she had ever frequented such a lowly place as the Gig, and had apparently been held in this man's arms; not just in his arms but probably crushed against his body, the Gig being so small and always packed to capacity, she recalled. 'I'm afraid I don't recognise you at all,' she admitted weakly.

Wide eyed, Tess sat taking all this in. He had never mentioned knowing her mother. But then she had only met him briefly when Jack had forgotten his keys one night and they had returned to his home to collect them.

Dan winked at her while Alice poured another cup of tea. 'Probably not. I was run of the mill, but you . . . well.' He shrugged, not willing to imply that she had thought herself better than the rest of them, a bit of a snob in fact. 'You had class,' he finished lamely.

Mollified to learn that he had apparently recognised her worth even back then, Alice asked, 'Where did you live in those days, Mr . . .' At his raised brow she quickly said, 'Dan?'

'Not far from here. I lived on Cavendish Street.'

'My, but isn't it a small world?'

'Indeed it is.' His face became solemn and he said gravely, 'I was very sorry to hear about Tommy's death. I attended the Requiem Mass, but I didn't go to the cemetery. It was a shame he died so young. Is Tess your only child?'

'Yes, and a great comfort she's been to me.' Alice looked fondly at her daughter who sat gazing into her cup, anxiously awaiting her mother's interrogation of Dan Thompson. 'I don't know what I'd have done without her.'

Relieved that his cup was almost empty and if he made a quick exit there would be no time for questions, Dan drained it and rose to his feet. 'I'll have to be going now.' She hadn't given him permission to call her Alice but he did so nevertheless. 'Good night, Alice, Tess.'

To Tess's relief, before her mother could gather her wits about her, he was in the hall and shrugging into his overcoat, and then he disappeared out the door.

Chapter Two

Dan slowly retraced his steps down Springfield Road, his mind alive with long-forgotten scenes from the past. It had never dawned on him that Tess might be Tommy Maguire's daughter. She didn't resemble either of them. Her mother had been a beauty in her day and half the men in town had chased after her, himself included. Everybody had been surprised when she had chosen brash, loud Tommy Maguire to be her beau.

Of course his job as a buyer in Ross's mill had appealed to her, and soon she had got rid of his rough edges. She also had him speaking properly in no time.

Dan remembered ribbing Tommy about his new posh Belfast accent, but he also recalled feeling a bit jealous. Tommy was an only child, and his parents had insisted on his staying on at school. He had achieved good qualifications, too good for working in the mill, really, albeit in the office, and Alice had great plans for him. He had stayed in the mill because he wanted to remain one of the lads, didn't want to outclass his mates too much. Alice had soon convinced him otherwise. Without any bother he had acquired a position more appropriate to his qualifications, as a quantity surveyor in Farrans of Dunmurry.

For a time Tommy and Dan still had the odd night

out but Alice never deigned to meet Dan socially. Then when she and Tommy got married they bought a house on the outskirts of Belfast to be near his work and the two friends had eventually lost touch with each other. A shame that, but Alice had still thought herself a cut above Tommy's mates and had put a stop to his going out for a drink with them. Dan had often wondered if she had allowed Tommy to keep in touch with his parents, who had since died.

Dan's house at the bottom of Spinner Street was on the bend and faced the Falls Road. Even from the top of the street he could see that his son was at home. The blind was down and the light was on. The question was, was he alone? When Colette Burns had come to stay with her grannie in the house next door to them, Dan had encouraged his son to show her around, little thinking he would drop Tess in the process. But Colette was a pretty little thing and had apparently won his son's heart. Tess would really be a far better match for Jack but young ones wouldn't be told; they thought they knew best. Colette lived with her mother and stepfather in Omagh and worked in one of the banks there. She had been just on a visit to Belfast, but now had apparently got herself a job in the Northern Bank in Belfast city centre and intended staying here. Her and Jack were very close. It looked serious between them.

The outer door was locked and Dan rattled his key with unnecessary force before he entered the small hall. He heard shuffling in the kitchen and delayed a few seconds before opening the vestibule door and entering the room. Jack and Colette were sitting suspiciously far apart on the settee.

'Hiya,' he greeted them and continued on into the

scullery, saying over his shoulder, 'Who's all for tea?'

'Not for me, Mr Thompson. I'd better get in next door before my grannie comes looking for me.'

He turned in the doorway and appraised her. Her hair was tousled and the buttons of her blouse were wrongly fastened. 'I think I'd be worried too, if my seventeen-year-old granddaughter was out this late.'

Colette followed his gaze and quickly adjusted the buttons. With a wry grimace at Jack, she bid them both good night and quietly left the house. The two men were silent until they heard Mrs Burns's door open and close.

Jack rose to his feet and faced his father. 'What was that all about?'

'It's twelve o'clock! That young girl should have been in bed an hour ago.'

'Says who?'

Dan stabbed a finger in his chest. 'Me! This is my home and there'll be no hanky-panky in it while I'm about. Okay?'

Tight lipped, Jack said tersely, 'We were doing no wrong. Just a few kisses.'

'Look, son, I'm not over the hill yet. I'm still young enough to remember where a few kisses can lead.'

'Pity you didn't give Mam some more then and keep her at home.' The words came out on a sneer.

Dan's jaw dropped and he stepped threateningly towards his son. 'You'd better watch your tongue, young fellow!' he growled.

Jack straightened to his full six feet and eye to eye with his father glared at him. 'Or?' His voice was softly dangerous.

Resisting the urge to punch his sneering face, Dan turned his back and entered the scullery.

A few minutes later Jack passed him in the narrow space and opened the back door. 'You could at least have got an inside toilet built. That might have helped.'

Because there was truth in what he said, these words rankled and when Jack returned from the yard Dan rounded on him.

'Look you, when we were lucky enough to get the key to this house, your mother and I were over the moon. Granted, it was far from perfect, but we were living in rooms at the time and glad to get a place of our own. You were a baby in your mother's arms and I was determined to make it into a home your mother would be proud of. You think this is bad?' A wide sweep of an arm embraced the kitchen. 'You should have seen it then. At that time, it was lit by gas mantles. There was an ugly big cast-iron range along that wall' – he motioned to the kitchen wall where a Devon grate now held pride of place – 'for cooking, and the floor was rough flagstones. Your mother near died at her first sight of it, but it was ours and we were enough in love to overcome all the hardships. I worked my fingers to the bone to have it as nice as it is today. It wasn't easy, you know. These things take time but she got fed up meanwhile. Everything else would have followed, but she couldn't wait any longer. There was no pleasing her. No one could have worked harder or done better. Even if I do say so myself.'

'Huh! You call this nice? Well, obviously your best wasn't good enough or she wouldn't have left us.'

Wanting to wound his tormentor, Dan cried, 'I don't know why you're defending her. After all, she left *you* behind.'

He had touched a sore point. How many times had Jack wondered about that selfsame thing? Why had his

[35]

mother left him behind? Was he so unlovable? Now he cried defensively, 'Only because she couldn't afford to take me with her.'

'Hah, that's a gag! The only reason she didn't take you with her was because she didn't care enough.'

'No, you're wrong. She wanted to! But I was only twelve at the time, remember, and this guy she run off with wouldn't allow her to take me with them.'

A puzzled frown gathered on Dan's brow. 'What makes you think that?'

'She told me. So there!' The words spewed out before Jack could stop them. He was behaving like a wee child. Head bowed with shame, he awaited his father's wrath.

Dan stared, uncomprehending, for some moments then gasped, 'You've seen her! Haven't you?'

Jack wished he hadn't opened his mouth. In his heart he knew his dad had made the best of a bad job and had looked after him well. Until he himself reached seventeen, his father had had no social life worth talking about to call his own. 'A few times,' he admitted.

'And you never said?'

'She asked me not to.'

'Why, you ungrateful bastard . . .'

'Don't you dare call me that.'

'Why not? You would have been one if I hadn't married your mother.' Then, at the horrified look on his son's face, Dan cried in anguish, 'Ah, son, I'm sorry. I'd no right to call you that.'

'Hadn't you?'

'There was no need for you to know and I'm sorry I opened my big mouth. You took me unawares, son.' He reached out a hand pleadingly.

Pushing it roughly aside Jack snarled back, 'Go to hell.' He thumped up the stairs two at a time, and his bedroom door slammed with a resounding bang.

Dan stood still, his thoughts in turmoil. His son had always blamed him for his mother's leaving them and perhaps he was right. Dan and Anne had drifted so far apart he hadn't realised how unhappy she was. Heaven knows, he had worked hard to make this house into the kind of home she wanted and he was getting there. He'd given up smoking and spent the money on things she wanted done. He'd thought he was succeeding; had been gobsmacked when he arrived home from work one night and found a letter telling him Jack was with a neighbour and that she had gone to live with someone else.

To be truthful, his first emotion had been one of relief. No more coming home to bickering and unrest. No more listening to her gripes and jealous comments. Then anger had consumed him when he realised she had taken the brand new TV set. They were so expensive they couldn't really afford one but she had plagued him and he had bought one on the never never to please her, had still owed a lot of money on it when she had upped and gone. Tearing the letter to pieces he muttered, 'Good riddance at any price.' Whoever the guy was, he was welcome to her.

It was only when he collected his son from the neighbour's house that the whole sorry mess really hit home. Jack, through no fault of his own, was the one who would suffer most. How could any woman do that to her son? Why was it always the innocent children who suffered?

Alice Maguire was also remembering the past as she washed and dried, and carefully put her precious tea set back in the china cabinet. She could not really recall dancing with Dan Thompson, but then there were so many lads wanting to dance with her in those days and, to be truthful, she had cultivated only the company of a chosen few.

Oh yes, she had been very particular in her day. Only lads whose fathers owned pubs or shops or who were businessmen of some kind or other got her attention.

Then Tommy Maguire had captured her heart. Not quite what she had hoped for but she had been unable to resist the magnetic pull that was constantly there between them; the need to be with him, to hold his hand and gaze into his eyes. No other man had been able to capture her imagination the way Tommy did.

He had been putty in her hands; her wish was his command. Tears filled her eyes when she recalled how handsome he had been. She had been so proud to be seen out with him. The big house outside town that she had set her heart on was quickly acquired and her cup was full to overflowing. Their marriage had been bliss-fully happy, and when they were blessed with a beau-tiful baby girl their happiness was complete.

The tragic accident that had taken his life at the early age of twenty-nine had almost destroyed Alice as well. She knew in her heart that Tommy's parents, although they had tried to hide it, blamed her. If she had left well alone and let him stay in Ross's mill he might be alive today. But no! There was no prestige working in the mill and Alice had felt that it was in their best inter-ests to talk him into seeking a better appointment. Unfortunately, Tommy had died in a freak accident, struck by falling masonry while crossing from the offices to the work site. He had neglected to wear a safety helmet and compensation was reduced accordingly.

Alice was inconsolable, and wanted to die herself. Only the thought of her daughter had kept her going. Now she went in search of that daughter. She must get to the bottom of this affair. She found Tess in the workshop at the front of the house. Alice had been trained as a milliner and the bay window was used to display her handiwork. She was very good at her trade and her creations were soon snapped up. Coloured posters also advertised her daughter's dressmaking designs, and between them they had built up a small but prosperous business.

They had worked hard and, with the little money left over after purchasing their house, had built up the business from scratch. Now people came from near and far to get wedding dresses and ballroom gowns and suits made to order.

Alice designed hats to match the outfits her daughter made and the clients were so impressed that the Maguires were seldom left with any spare articles on their hands. All in all they were a good team. When she left school at fourteen Tess had started work in the Belart stitching factory, renowned for its beautiful children's clothes. It was there she discovered that she had a flair for dressmaking. She loved Belart's exquisite children's designs and had, in time, created some patterns of her own. Now she designed exquisite flower girl dresses and page boy outfits for weddings.

The door was open and Alice stood for some moments unobserved, contemplating her daughter at work. Rich auburn hair fell forward like a curtain and the bright electric light picked out the highlights. Alice knew better than to speak while the scissors were sliding across the table, but when Tess stopped to adjust the material she warned, 'It's too late to start cutting now. The skirt of that wedding dress is on the bias. One wrong snip and the lot will be ruined.'

Tess turned wearily from the table. 'Mam, go to bed

and let me get on with it. I haven't made a mess of anything yet, have I?'

'No. But there's a first time for everything and I can see you're not yourself at the moment.'

'Please, Mam. I'm all right. I just don't feel like sleeping. Leave me alone.'

Sensing her daughter's misery, Alice said softly, 'Would you like to talk about it, love?'

'There's nothing to talk about. Jack Thompson and I went out together a few times. That's all there is to it. It was nice while it lasted. Short and sweet.'

'How come you never mentioned him to me?'

Tess smiled grimly. 'Because you would have been hearing wedding bells, frightening him away before it got off the ground.'

Annoyed at her daughter's tone, Alice thoughtlessly retaliated. 'So somehow or other you managed to do that yourself.' Then sadness engulfed her at the stricken look her daughter turned on her.

'That's right. I didn't need any help from you.'

What had gone wrong, Alice wondered. 'But you had hopes, didn't you?' she queried gently. Tight-lipped silence greeted this remark and Alice continued. 'Did you like him very much?'

'Quite a lot,' Tess said curtly. 'But now he has a new girlfriend, a very pretty girl, and he hadn't the decency to tell me to my face. So what does that tell you? Whoever said looks don't count didn't know what they were talking about.'

'Look, Tess, love, you're gifted and talented and there's plenty of time to meet someone who'll appreciate your worth.'

Tess had heard all this before. 'All right! No need to go on about it!'

'It's true, love. Just wait and see.'

Placing the scissors to one side Tess brushed roughly past her mother, and headed for the stairs. 'I'm away to bed. You've put me right off the notion of working. Good night.'

Alice watched her climb the stairs and her heart was heavy. Why had this to happen to her daughter? If only Tommy had lived things might have been different. Had she done the wrong thing selling her beautiful house and moving back to the city? She had bought this house to be near her mother, so that Tess could at least have one living grandparent to visit. Unfortunately her mother had died shortly after their moving to Springfield Road and the only relative Alice now had in the world was her brother Malachy, who lived in Carlingford. Some years ago he had bought a small farm-holding and now he worked hard to make a living out of the land, and they rarely saw him.

What if she died? Tess would be alone in the world. Sometimes Alice wondered if she should make an effort to remarry. Give Tess someone to turn to if in need, but the idea didn't appeal to her. Besides, who would have her? She was no young beauty any more and the only man to have shown any interest in her lately was a widower, the owner of a shop further up Springfield Road. He was enormously fat and the very idea of being held against his body filled her with revulsion.

Finding no solution to her immediate problems she sighed and, covering the satin material with a dust sheet, left the room and began to lock the doors and windows. It was as she climbed the stairs that the memory of Dan Thompson's handsome face entered her mind. Now, what made her think of him? Wasn't he a married man?

*   *   *

Alone at last, Tess lay on top of the bed, tears streaming down her face. She had thought that Jack cared for her. Obviously he didn't. And why would he? In spite of what anyone else said she knew she was as plain as a pikestaff. And didn't this prove it? Still, she really had thought Jack cared and now she felt betrayed. They had been getting along so well! Not that he had made any promises. Ah no, she couldn't say he had encouraged her. Why, the evening he had broken down and confided in her that his mother had come back was the only time he had shown any physical attraction to her, and he hadn't backed his actions up with any reassuring words. Still, didn't they say actions spoke louder than words? And that night his kisses and hands had implied that he cared.

Tess rose from the bed and went to the long mirror on the door of the wardrobe. Examining her reflection, she decided she wasn't all that bad. She was passable; thick auburn hair, bright green eyes and slim figure. After all, everyone couldn't look as lovely as her mother, or Colette Burns, for that matter! And besides, Jack Thompson was no Errol Flynn; he was just an ordinary run of the mill lad who had managed to arouse passion within her. She realised she wasn't anywhere near as attractive as Colette, of course, but passable. Her mother said when she met a man who really cared for her things would be different.

But would they? She had thought Jack cared but now he had a new girlfriend, which proved her wrong. A very pretty girl, Tess reminded herself, and felt bereft. Slowly she undressed and without looking at her image again returned to her bed. Burying her face in the pillow, she sobbed soundlessly. Would any man ever want her? Indeed, would any other man do, the way she now felt about Jack? She very much doubted it.

*　　*　　*

The atmosphere was strained as father and son ate breakfast next morning. Jack worked in the Silk & Rayon factory in Waterford Street and when on the late shift, as he was today, it was his duty to clear the breakfast dishes away. He gathered the plates up and headed for the scullery where a kettle was already bubbling away on the stove ready to wash them.

Returning for the rest of the dishes he hesitated beside the table and apologised for his behaviour the night before. 'Dad, I'm sorry if I upset you. I didn't mean half the things I said. You know that, don't you?'

Glad to receive the olive branch, Dan said, 'Likewise, son. We were both out of order. Still, I do wish you had told me about meeting your mother.'

'To be truthful, Dad, I didn't think you'd be interested. You don't seem to care one way or the other about her.'

Dan turned these words over in his mind. He mustn't give Jack false hope by letting him think he might take his mother back. Too much water had passed under the bridge for that to happen. 'I don't care, if by that you mean wanting her back. Not any more,' he admitted. 'For your sake, I would have considered letting her return at the beginning, but as the months passed and she made no effort to even see you, not even when she wrote asking for a divorce, I realised how heartless she was.'

'I explained why she couldn't do that.'

'And you believe her? Come off it. Surely you aren't that naive, eh, son?'

Jack sank back down on to his chair. 'It was better than believing she didn't love me,' he confessed sadly. His father's words belatedly penetrated his misery. 'I didn't know you were divorced,' he gasped, seeing any hope of a reconciliation fading.

'We aren't. As you well know, Catholics can't get divorced. I warned her anything she achieved would be under her own steam. I heard no more about it, so I assumed she didn't pursue it further.' Dan's heart was wrung with pity at his son's unhappiness and he warned himself to go carefully and not shatter the lad's fragile pride. 'You know, she did love you, Jack. She loved you very much. It was me she couldn't abide. But we did manage to get along fine without her, didn't we, son?'

Jack's shoulders rose in a negative shrug. Who knew how things would have been had his mam stayed? Seeing his father's face fall, he hastened to reassure him. 'Of course we did, Dad. You've been a great father to me.'

Aware it would be better not to know, Dan found he could not let the matter drop, and asked tentatively, 'Tell me, son. Did you just bump into her in town or something?'

'She was waiting for me outside the factory one night.'

Dan jerked to attention. 'Outside the Silk & Rayon? When was this?'

'A few months ago.'

'How did she know you worked there?' Jack shrugged and Dan continued, 'What reason did she give for being there?'

'At first she just wanted to talk to me. It was a bit awkward, you know – we were like strangers. But later she suggested we should share a flat.'

Dan was dumbstruck. 'I can't take this in. What about "his nibs" – the guy she couldn't live without?'

'It seems he moved on some time ago.'

'Hah, I see! And she thinks she can just come back into your life as if nothing had ever happened?'

'She is my mother, Dad, and I must say I'm tempted.

A flat or even a house with all mod cons? It would be a dream come true.'

'You can have all those things without joining ranks with your mother, son,' Dan cried in frustration. 'If you had said you wanted to live away from home I'd have helped you.'

'That's just it. I don't fancy living alone, Dad. Besides I couldn't afford to. Not on the money I earn.'

'Well, you've no one to blame but yourself about that. I tried to get you to stay on at school, but you wouldn't listen to me. If you had you'd be earning good money today.'

'I know, Dad. I know you did. And to be truthful I was content enough here until she put these ideas into my head. You've got to admit, it would be nice to come home to a warm house and a hot bath at night. Especially you, working out in all kinds of weather. Does that idea not appeal to you at all? It's all right during the summer months, but in winter, to tell you the truth, I dread getting up to a cold house every morning.'

Dan, hardened from boyhood to getting up to a freezing house and, when young, having to fetch water in from outside to see his mother through the day, was staring at his son in amazement. 'Why didn't you say?'

'I didn't realise what I was missing until Mam pointed it out to me. We are quite primitive here, with an outside toilet and no hot water. Mam says a lot of our neighbours already have these basic mod cons.'

It was the gentle way his son said 'Mam' that made Dan aware his estranged wife was using her wiles to win back Jack's affection.

'How would she know?' he cried furiously.

'She visits Lily Brady, so she does. She knows more about our neighbours than we do.'

Dan couldn't believe his ears. To think Anne was so close at times, just a few doors away. She was probably checking up on him and he hadn't even known. 'Do you see her often?' he asked fearfully.

'Not really. Every now and again she'll be there, waiting outside work.'

A glance at the clock brought Dan to his feet. 'Good God, look at the time. I'll have to run or I'll miss my lift. Can we talk about this tonight, son?'

'Sure, Dad. See you then.'

On the building site, Dan found himself working like someone possessed. He was a dedicated craftsman and was given all the important brickwork to do. At the present time he was working on an ornate surround that would house a huge door to a luxurious office block. Small coloured bricks of odd shapes intertwined in a beautiful pattern. No matter how tricky a job might prove he could practically do the work with his eyes shut. Today, however, he had to stop every now and again, step back and take note of how his work was going; once he even had to rectify a mistake.

Lunch-break was a happy release for him. It was a cool dry day and, declining to join his mates in the Portakabin used as a site canteen, he sat outside.

Anne's face was haunting him. Not yet ready for marriage, he had been shocked beyond belief to find out that she was pregnant. Anne had been annoyed at his reaction, had wanted to know if he doubted it was his. That had been a bad time in his life: the rushed wedding leaving them skint, honeymoon put off till another day. A honeymoon that had never taken place. How could it, when there was always something or other needed for the baby or the house? Still, Anne had held it against him; she had expected miracles. When she had talked about getting a job he had encouraged her, thinking the extra money would keep her happy. Look where that had led! To the break-up of their marriage.

He was also remembering the good times when they had worked together to make the house a worthy home for their young son. The times when they lay in bed locked in each other's arms and planned the future. If only she had been patient; given him more time. To be truthful, he had to admit that he had slacked off a bit. Eleven years should have seen this house looking like a wee palace but things had gone wrong. Anne had met someone through her job who could give her more than he could.

Still, they had been happy together once. Could Anne possibly be hoping he'd take her back? Had she discovered the grass was by no means greener on the other side? He shook his head in despair. There was no way he could ever forgive her betrayal of him and especially Jack. Besides, she would have approached him, not Jack, if that were the case. No, it was only her son she wanted. He would just have to make sure that she didn't succeed in winning Jack over.

Chapter Three

Life did go on, Tess found, even with a broken heart. Admittedly, some days she was surprised to find that she was too busy with her work to even think of Jack Thompson and other days she found it hard to cope with the sense of loss that threatened to overwhelm her. She thought it strange how things had worked out. There was Agnes, who hadn't wanted to date Tony Burke in the first instance, yet she was still going out with him, and although she insisted he wasn't Mr Right she seemed to enjoy his company, and here was Tess, nursing a broken heart over the loss of Jack.

When Agnes heard that Tess's romance, if you could call it that, was over, it bothered her to see her friend so unhappy. Unknown to Tess, she tried to coax Tony into arranging a foursome, to try to patch things up between Tess and Jack. Tony wouldn't hear tell of it, saying that if he did so it would probably be Colette Burns that Jack would bring along and then what would Tess think of them? He knew Colette was now the one in Jack's life and he would not be swayed in spite of his own deep feelings for Agnes and his desire to please her. Agnes saw his point of view right away and agreed with him, although her heart was sad for her best friend.

Tess hadn't set an eye on Jack since that night in the

Dolphin chip shop. She had however met Dan a few times; had even joined him once, on the spur of the moment, for a drink in the lounge of the Clock Bar. What an experience that had been!

One of her regular customers who was poorly and temporarily confined to her home had received an unexpected invitation to a wedding in two weeks' time. She had phoned Tess in desperation, asking if she could possibly make her a suit for the occasion at such short notice. Tess had assured her that, as a valued customer, she certainly would somehow be fitted into her busy schedule. That very same evening, armed with samples of material and tape and pins, the tools of her trade, she ventured forth.

It was a bad night to be outdoors, the November weather being atrocious, but Tess wanted to show Nell Montgomery some patterns and discuss the choice of fabric for the suit as soon as possible. On her way home, cowering under her umbrella against the elements, she had been unaware of Dan until he fell into step beside her at the top of Albert Street where it joined the Falls Road.

Peering in under the umbrella, he said, 'I thought it was you, Tess! What on earth brings you out on an night like this?'

She raised the umbrella to cover them both and, smiling up into his face, said, 'Work has me out tonight, that's what. There's no rest for the wicked, you know. Mind you, only something worthwhile would tempt me out in this awful weather. I was measuring up one of my special customers for a suit. What about you? What's your excuse for being out on an awful night like this?'

Glad to see she didn't, outwardly at least, appear to be pining away because of Jack, Dan suited his step to hers and gestured to the umbrella. 'Protect yourself with that. I'm already soaked through. I've been down to Cullingtree Road to see an old work mate who's a bit poorly. It beats sitting in the house alone. Anyway, how are you keeping these days?'

'I can't complain. I've plenty of work in hand to keep me busy for the next two months. In fact we're thinking of taking on a machinist to help out. Someone to train in our ways of working.'

'Expanding the business, eh? That's wonderful news. It's nice to hear someone is doing well.'

She laughed. 'Well now . . . there's well and there's well, but every little counts. What about yourself? Anything different since I last saw you?'

Realising it was really Jack she wanted to know about he shook his head and said gently, 'No. My wife has yet to persuade Jack to leave home and he is still dating Colette Burns.' They were approaching Spinner Street and he turned to leave her, a farewell on his lips, then paused. 'I don't suppose you'd care to come into the Clock Bar with me and let me buy you a wee hot whiskey to warm the cockles of your heart?' he asked tentatively. 'It would do you a world of good, on a foul night like this.'

Tess couldn't believe her ears. Her cheeks reddened with mortification. He was inviting her to go into a *public house* with him! What kind of girl did he think she was? According to her mother only loose women went into those places of ill repute, as she called them. Did Dan think her loose? Of course he didn't, she quickly assured herself. It was just that her mother was old-fashioned. Dan was only being kind to her. She had once questioned Alice as to what the inside of a pub looked like, only to be informed that her mother had no idea whatsoever, as she had never been inside a public house and had no intention of ever doing so. But, she warned her daughter, she had heard all about those dens of iniquity; even knew some hussies who frequented them. They were most certainly no place for a Christian girl to be seen in.

Curiosity aroused, Tess had questioned her mother. 'What! You mean to tell me that you know some scarlet women, then?' she asked, her hands clutched at her breast in feigned amazement, and wasn't surprised when her mother couldn't come up with any names.

'Well now, not exactly,' Alice blustered. 'But I did once hear that Molly Connelly, for instance, a girl about the same age as yourself, goes into different pubs every weekend. Her mother should put a stop to it. And furthermore she drinks *gin and tonic!*' The horror of this revelation made Alice's voice quite shrill. How did she know all this, Tess wanted to know, only to get a vague 'I heard talk about it' for an answer. Tess warned her mother in no uncertain terms to be careful about repeating such things outside or she could be up for slander. Alice had laughed and pooh-poohed the idea. Dan watched Tess closely as all these thoughts passed quickly through her mind and from her expression wasn't surprised when she refused his offer.

'Mam would be scandalised if she ever heard I went into a pub,' she explained. 'Besides, ugh!' A grimace distorted her mouth. 'I wouldn't thank you for a whiskey. It's horrible. Even the smell of it turns my stomach. But thanks all the same for asking me, Dan. It's very kind of you.'

'I wish I felt as you do about whiskey, but unfortunately I don't. It's one of my few vices. You, my dear, can have a brandy and lemonade if you like.'

Sensing his loneliness she hesitated, tempted. After all, why not see for herself what it was like inside a pub? Not that she would have a brandy, oh no, but it would be nice to get in out of this rain for a while and get a bit of warmth. Still, it didn't seem right to go into a public house, especially with this man who was old enough to be her father, but she knew that Dan had no ulterior motive for inviting her; she trusted him.

He smiled wryly as he observed the mixed emotions flitting across her face again. 'There is a small lounge, you know. There will probably be other women present at this time of night,' he assured her. He gave a slight laugh as with hands spread wide he acknowledged the elements. 'Although, mind you, on a night like this we could very well have the place to ourselves.'

The rain seemed at that moment to get heavier, bouncing off the umbrella with a loud staccato rhythm and splattering to the ground, soaking her feet. As far as Tess was concerned that settled the matter. 'Right! Let's go in.'

With a delighted chuckle Dan took her by the elbow and escorted her along to Lower Clonard Street. What a girl Tess Maguire was. His son needed his head examined. Colette Burns seemed like a wee child in comparison.

Leading her to the side door of the pub, Dan took the umbrella from her and shook it free of excess water before he closed it. Then he thrust the door open and ushered her inside. He was wrong. The lounge was full and a hush fell as all eyes took in the newcomer accompanying Dan Thompson. A girl young enough to be his daughter, no less. Most of the people greeted him by name and it was obvious he was a popular figure in here. They were probably wondering who she was, Tess thought, as eyes full of speculation examined her from head to foot. Uncomfortable under their scrutiny, she glanced around, surprised at how small the lounge was. Why, you couldn't swing a cat in here. There were already three couples seated around the walls on benches, facing small round tables on which their drinks rested, which took up most of the floor space.

The occupants, whilst smiling knowingly from her to Dan, obligingly moved round and made room for Tess to sit down. Not wanting to drink in close proximity with these strangers Tess turned to suggest to Dan that they go elsewhere. To her dismay he was ignoring her, his attention focused on one of the women. A very attractive woman, with natural blonde hair worn shoulder length in soft curls. With a vague wave of the hand Dan indicated that Tess should sit down and went to the small hatch that served the lounge from the bar. She heard him order a double Black Bush and a brandy and lemonade.

Conversation had started up again and the woman Dan had shown interest in turned to Tess in a friendly manner. 'It's a terrible night out there, isn't it, dear?'

'It sure is,' Tess agreed. 'It's really pelting down now.' She was relieved when Dan's arrival with the drinks saved her from further conversation. She moved along so that Dan could sit down between her and the woman, but he chose to remain standing, elbow propped against the wall.

An amused laugh escaped the pale pink lips of the blonde and, tossing her head, with a mischievous look in her eye, she asked innocently, 'Are you not going to introduce me to your friend then, Dan?'

Aware that they were being covertly watched by the others and that sly smiles tugged at the mouths of the women, he turned a glare on her and said abruptly, 'I don't think that will be necessary.'

Her mouth opened to protest but her companion, a man much younger than herself, placed a hand warningly on her arm. Light blue eyes framed with thick, dark lashes met his and an unspoken message passed between them. She patted his hand knowingly where it still lay on her arm and his fingers turned and entwined with hers. She apparently forgot all about Dan's existence as she leaned closer to her companion, giving him all her attention.

Tess watched closely. The woman was quite young – late thirties, maybe early forties, Tess surmised – and she obviously took care of her looks. Carefully applied make-up emphasised a smooth forehead with darkened arched brows, and pink rouge threw high cheekbones into relief. The only noticeable lines were faintly etched around a wide sensuous mouth.

Sipping at the brandy Tess grimaced in distaste and decided she didn't like it; not one little bit. It was her first and, she vowed, her last taste of alcohol. She hadn't had a chance to tell Dan that she would prefer a soft drink. He should have asked me what I wanted anyway, she thought indignantly, but he had been preoccupied. In dismay she watched Dan down his whiskey in a couple of gulps and returning to the hatch order the same again.

When he placed another brandy and lemonade in front of her he caught her look of reproof and, leaning forward, whispered, 'Sorry about this, Tess. We'll leave after this one. Drink up, lass.' Dan was annoyed at himself for letting his estranged wife get to him. It was just so unexpected seeing her sitting there with a lad young enough to be her son.

Another few tentative sips of brandy and Tess was surprised at how the liquid really did warm her all the way down to her stomach, sending a glow throughout her body. But she'd never be able to drink two of them. Never in this wide world, she told herself. How wrong she was. When one glass was empty she reached, without hesitation, for the second glass and started sipping away.

There was nothing else to do. She was disappointed in Dan. He stood silent and sombre, dark head bent, not even meeting her eye, let alone engaging her in conversation. She got the impression that he was watching, and eavesdropping on, the blonde and her companion. And here was she, sitting like a fool in the midst of all these strangers, sipping brandy as if it were a regular occurrence. None of them seemed inclined to start up a conversation with her, except the one she thought Dan wouldn't want her to talk to, and even she was now preoccupied.

The minutes dragged and eventually the other two couples, who had been talking quietly among themselves, drained their glasses, bade the rest of them good night and left the pub. Dan motioned Tess along the bench and, sitting down beside her, deliberately turned his back on the other two, who were getting quite amorous.

His glass was empty again and he gestured towards hers. 'Another one?'

'Oh, no! I've had more than enough already.' Her glass was still more than half full but, not wanting to delay any longer, she quickly drained it and stood up with a shudder of distaste, the sudden movement sending sharp pains to her head. 'Let's go,' she said in a voice that shook.

The woman, although her friend strongly objected, followed them outside to the covered doorway. Placing a hand on Dan's arm she said urgently, 'We've got to talk, Dan.'

He roughly threw her hand off and growled, 'Away back to your toy boy.'

She smiled triumphantly. 'I do believe you're jealous, Dan Thompson.'

'Of that wee whipper-snapper in there? Don't flatter yourself. I would have thought you'd have done better than that.'

Tess felt invisible standing there. They were so engrossed they appeared to have forgotten that she existed. Well, she vowed, she would soon put an end to that nonsense! Whether it was inconvenient or otherwise they would just have to remember her presence.

'Dan!' Her voice came out loud and high pitched and she covered her mouth in confusion for a few seconds before finishing lamely, 'If you'll be so good as to put that umbrella up for me, I'll be on my way and leave you two to it.' Instantly she had his attention.

'Tess, forgive me, dear.' He struggled with the catch of the umbrella and at last had it open. Placing an arm across her shoulders he held the umbrella aloft and, ignoring the woman, said, 'Come on, let's get you home, lass.'

Aware that they were still being watched, Tess waited until they were round the corner out of view before angrily shrugging off his arm and striding ahead. At least that's what she intended to do, but, to her dismay, without his support she began to weave back and forth across the pavement. What on earth was wrong with her? Her legs were behaving as if they didn't belong to her. She felt light-headed.

[56]

Once again Dan's arm was around her, gathering her close to his side and piloting her in a straight line. 'You're tipsy, love. I'm sorry. It's all my fault entirely. Brandy should be sipped, not gulped, and to crown it all you get good measures in the Clock. To be honest, I shouldn't have got you that second drink. I just wasn't thinking straight. Will you come down to the house with me and have a cup of strong tea to help you sober up before you go home? Alice will never forgive me if you arrive back in this state.'

'It's late, Dan. Mam will be worried about me as it is, without me being any later. Besides, I don't want Jack to see me like this.'

'Just as you wish, Tess, though you needn't worry about Jack. He won't be there. He's gone to Omagh for a couple of days with Colette to meet her folk and collect some of her belongings.' She swayed unsteadily and he argued, 'Mind you, a cup of tea will make a big difference.'

Thinking of her mother's face if she were to see her now, Tess agreed, if somewhat ungraciously. 'Oh, all right, then. But it had better be a quick one.'

Her legs felt rubbery and she clung tightly to Dan's arm for support as they retraced their steps and walked the length of the street. Once inside the house Dan led her to the table and she sat clasping her throbbing head while he busied himself in the scullery brewing tea. After what seemed like an eternity, a mug was placed in front of her. The house was freezing and she curled her hands gratefully around the welcome heat of the steaming mug. 'Thank you.'

One mouthful of the brown liquid, however, and her stomach turned over. 'I don't take sugar,' she gasped. She tried to control her heaving stomach but the strong sweet tea going down on top of the brandy proved too much for her. She rose abruptly to her feet, hands pressed tightly against her mouth.

'Here, this way.' Dan motioned her into the scullery. She reached the sink just in time and retched and retched. Where on earth was all this water and bile coming from? An empty stomach, she lamented inwardly. In her hurry to go and see Nell Montgomery she had neglected to eat anything, assuring her mother she would get something when she returned. Now look at her! She was ashamed of herself; ashamed that Dan was seeing her in this drunken state.

Dan turned on the tap and pushing her cuffs up her arms made her hold her wrists under the freezing water. Then he gently dried her hands and wiped her face with a towel. 'You'll feel a lot better now.'

Pushing roughly past him she returned to the kitchen and sank down on the end of the settee. 'Better! I feel worse.'

'Have you never drunk spirits before, Tess?'

'Never! Just a sip of whiskey once when I had a bad cold and it was enough to put me right off, I can tell you. You should have asked me what I wanted to drink,' she cried accusingly, putting the blame at his door. She started to shiver uncontrollably. 'It's awfully cold in here. Or is it just me?'

'A bit of both. It is cold but you feel it more because you've been sick.'

'Sick! I think I'm going to die,' she wailed.

He sank down on to the settee beside her and taking her hands in his tried to rub some warmth into them. Shame was eating away at his conscience. What in the name of God had he been thinking of? He should have realised that a young girl like her didn't drink spirits.

And she was right. He should have asked her her preference. The sight of his estranged wife with that young lad – why, he was no older than Jack – had driven everything else from his mind.

'I'll have to get you home, love.'

'My mam will kill me.' Tears overflowed at the very thought of facing her mother. She would never be able to explain it to her. What excuse could she offer? What's more, her mother would never trust her again.

To her relief, Dan assured her, 'Don't you worry, I'll explain everything to Alice. You see, Tess, that was my wife in the pub. She has never been in before and I was gobsmacked when I saw her there tonight.' He shrugged. 'On the other hand maybe she's a regular. You see, I hardly ever go into the lounge, so I don't know how the land lies. I know Jack and Colette go in there now and again but he has never mentioned seeing his mother there. Not that he'd tell me anyhow. In fact, maybe that's where they meet,' he confessed bitterly. 'She's a sore point between us at the moment.'

A loud knock on the door brought him to his feet. 'Who the blazes . . .' He was amazed to see Anne standing outside on the pavement. 'What do you want?' he asked abruptly.

Holding out a handbag towards him she said drily, 'Your friend left this behind in the pub.'

'Oh. Thank you.' At a loss for words, he gazed bleakly at her in silence.

'Can I come in? It's wet out here, you know.'

He pulled the vestibule door closed as she stepped into the hall. 'You can't come any further. Tess isn't feeling too good. She'd only be embarrassed.'

Her brows rose in surprise 'She's still here? I thought you were seeing her home. Surely you're not taking advantage of that young girl, Dan Thompson.'

'Don't be silly! Even so, it's none of your business what I do. Where's the toy boy?'

Pleased that he sounded jealous, Anne smiled. 'I sent him home to his mam.'

She moved closer and he smelt her perfume, and was surprised to find her proximity stirring emotions he had thought long dead. He tried to put some distance between them but the hall was too small to do much manoeuvring. She swayed towards him, her lips parted invitingly. Abruptly he turned his head aside to avoid them. There would be none of that nonsense here. She could save her favours for the others. Her face was a study of hurt bewilderment. He gaped at her. What did she expect? That he would take her in his arms and smother her in passionate kisses, and all would be forgiven? Some hope!

The inner door was pulled open and Tess stared at them open mouthed. What was that woman doing here? How come she was standing so close to Dan? And why was Dan encouraging her? Hadn't Jack said that his father hated his mother? So why didn't he tell her where to get off?

Shamefaced, but glad of the respite, Dan at last made the overdue introductions. 'Tess, this is my wife. Anne, meet Tess Maguire.' He held the bag up. 'You left this in the Clock Bar. Anne was good enough to bring it down here.'

Tess stared at the bag, then, in confusion, at him, shaking her head in disbelief. Forgot her bag? It was unheard of. Oh, how she wished she was at home in her comfortable, warm bed; just to get this day over and done with. One thing was for sure, she would never enter a pub again. 'I didn't even miss it,' she admitted.

With difficulty she focused her attention on Anne. 'Thank you very much.' Turning to Dan in despair, she cried, 'Dan, I must go home now. My mam will be off her head with worry.'

'How do you feel?'

'Awful! But I can't see me feeling any better for some time to come, so I'm going home now,' she added defiantly, almost in tears in her anxiety to get away.

'Right! Don't worry, Tess. We'll go now. Will you excuse us, please, Anne? I must see Tess safely home.'

These words produced a harsh laugh from his wife. 'Safely? I wonder what her mother will think about that when she sees the state she's in?'

'Will you two stop talking as if I'm not here!' Tess bellowed, increasing the throbbing in her head. Clutching a hand to her brow she muttered through clenched teeth, 'Dan, thank you all the same, but I'd rather go home alone. Besides, the rain seems to have stopped and the cold air should help clear my head.'

'Tess, much as I dread your mother's reaction when she sees you like this, I insist on seeing you home.'

'Mam will be worse if you're with me. She'll hit the roof, Dan. There's no telling what she'll say or do. I've never been drunk before, you know, so she's sure to blame you.'

'Can I make a suggestion?' Anne ventured.

Dan turned warily to her and growled, 'Are you still here?' although he had been very much aware of her presence.

She just smiled and said, 'Why don't I come with you? It won't look so bad, so it won't, if the two of us take her home. Mm?'

Dan pondered her words. She was right, of course. Alice wouldn't react so badly if Anne came with them,

[61]

especially if she thought they had been together all evening. With a slight shrug, he agreed. 'All right, let's go.'

'Before we go, let's tidy you up a bit, Tess.'

Without further ado, Anne brushed past Dan and entered the house she had called home for twelve years. A quick glance round showed her it looked exactly the same. She grimaced. It shouldn't be too hard to coax her son to leave these surroundings. But did she really want to come between father and son?

With a sigh she turned her attention to Tess. 'Have you a comb with you, Tess?'

Tess motioned to the bag Dan still held. 'In there.'

Since Tess was no different from most other women her large handbag held just about everything except the kitchen sink. After some rummaging, Anne produced a comb and proceeded to tidy Tess's hair, remarking on its lovely colour and texture. Next she produced Tess's compact from her bag so the girl could powder her face, and at last she seemed satisfied by the result. Standing back, she eyed her charge. 'There now, you look much better already.'

Dan had to agree. Having got rid of the booze and with her hair combed and nose powdered, Tess looked more like her old self.

'Thanks,' he acknowledged, with a nod in his wife's direction. Extending a helping hand to Tess, he said, 'Let's go, lass.' He ushered the two women out into the street and locked the front door.

Miraculously the rain had stopped and an icy breeze fanned their faces. They walked three abreast, arms linked, Tess in the middle, grateful for their support and the cold air on her face. The dark grey clouds were thinning out and a moon was trying to lighten the shadows.

The air was soothing on her hot eyelids but did little to ease the pain in her head. They all remained locked in their own thoughts until Tess's home was reached.

They had no sooner arrived at the steps than the door was thrown open and Alice bounded out. Frantic wasn't the word to describe the state she was in. She was beside herself with worry, her hair standing on end where she had obviously dragged her hands through it more than once.

'Where on earth have you been, Tess?' she cried, tears spurting from her eyes in relief at seeing her daughter safely home. 'I've been at my wits' end with worry. I was just about to go down to the police station, so I was.'

'Alice, it's my fault she's so late. Anne – my wife here – and I invited her into the Clock Bar for a drink and then she came down to the house with us for a cup of tea.'

Alice glared at him suspiciously, then as his words penetrated her brain she rounded on her daughter. 'I don't believe it! After all the warnings I gave you, you went into a public house? How could you be so fool-ish, girl?'

Glad that Anne had made her look at least half present-able, Tess heard her mother out in silence and hung her head in shame. After all was said and done, her mother had been proved right. Look how wretched and sick she felt through entering a pub. If only she had obeyed her mother and steered clear of that 'den of iniquity' she wouldn't be feeling as if she were about to die.

Getting no response from her daughter, Alice turned her wrath on Dan. 'As for you . . . what were you think-ing of? You're old and ugly enough to know better. You ought to be ashamed of yourself . . .'

Moving closer to Alice, Anne interrupted softly. 'It

was all my fault, Mrs Maguire. Dan and I met Tess just outside the pub and I wanted so much to meet your daughter that I suggested we go into the lounge for a drink. It was pouring out of the heavens and it seemed like a good idea at the time. I'm sorry. I didn't mean any harm. It was all quite respectable, I can assure you.'

'Huh! That's as may be, but you had no right to take Tess with you. She's far too young to go into places like that.' Her eyes raked Anne from head to toe. 'If you don't mind my saying so, you don't look like someone who would frequent pubs.'

'You're right, I don't often go into them,' Anne lied through her teeth. 'But as I said, it was pouring down and I knew my son used to date Tess. Jack has spoken often of her and I did so want to meet her. I'm sorry about the pub. It won't happen again. I can assure you it was a one-off and she was quite safe with us.' Big limpid blue eyes asked for understanding.

Mollified, Alice allowed her demeanour to change. 'Oh well, since she doesn't seem to have come to any harm I'll overlook it this time. Would you like to come in for a cup of tea?'

'No, thank you, Mrs Maguire. It's not long since we had one.'

Having made a few attempts to speak and been ignored, and feeling that her legs wouldn't hold her up much longer, Tess at last made her voice heard. 'If you'll excuse me, Anne, Dan, I'll go on in. And thanks for everything.'

'You do that, Tess. We'll be getting back now. Good night.' Dan watched, breathless, as Tess carefully picked her way up the steps. She entered the house safely and, relieved that everything had gone so well, he smiled at Alice. 'Good night, Alice.'

'Good night, Dan. It was lovely meeting you, Mrs Thompson. Good night.'

'Likewise, Mrs Maguire. Good night.'

Dan smiled wryly at his estranged wife as they retraced their steps down the Springfield Road. 'Man, but you can certainly spin a good yarn. You almost had me believing you back there.'

She smiled slyly at him through lowered lashes. 'I thought you wanted to keep Tess in her mother's good books.'

'That's true.'

'Well then, stop complaining.'

'I wasn't complaining. Just the opposite if you must know. So Jack told you all about Tess, did he?'

'Yes. He was dating her when I first approached him.'

All the old rancour came to the fore at these words and he glowered at her. 'What do you hope to gain from pestering him? Eh? He'll never leave home for you!'

'Tell me something, Dan,' she asked. 'What have you done to make that house a better place to live in since I left eight years ago?'

Thrusting his face towards her, he growled, 'Forget the house for a minute! I fed and clothed our son. I wiped his tears and consoled him each time he cried for want of you. I saw he went to school and helped him with his homework. All that was far more important to me than decorating the house.'

This was something she felt guilty about, her son not furthering his education, and she was glad Dan was giving her the chance to gripe at him about it. 'You should have made him stay on at school,' she cried indignantly. Then she backed away from him, such was the anger radiating from him as he glowered at her.

Was the woman daft? 'I tried. God knows I tried! But he wouldn't listen. He wanted to earn money right away.'

'But why the Silk & Rayon, of all places?'

'It was either that or the mill.'

'Don't be silly! You're well known in the building trade. Surely you could have at least got him an apprenticeship?'

'Again, I tried. I set up interviews for him but he didn't want to know. He just didn't bother turning up. If he had listened to me he'd be an electrician or a joiner today.'

'You should have made him go to those interviews! I would have.' Her anger matched his now.

He eyed her through narrowed lids and replied in a low, menacing voice. 'Ah, but you weren't at home, were you? No! You were away flying your kite. Gallivanting about all over the place with your fancy man!'

'If I had only known,' she lamented. 'I wasn't all that far away. I might have influenced him. Talked him into seeking an apprenticeship.'

'You should have kept in touch with him. You broke the lad's heart. We'd no idea where you were, what you were up to, until you asked for a divorce. Then, although I didn't mention divorce to him, I could at least tell him that you were still in Ireland. As far as we were concerned, until then you could have been in America or Australia. Anywhere in the world.'

'I thought a complete break was for the best all round. I didn't want to upset him more than was necessary.' She laughed ruefully. 'Do you know where I was living? Whitehouse!'

'Down the Shore Road?' he cried in disbelief. 'I don't believe it! I passed through there every day for a couple of years when I was working in Jordanstown. Where did you work?'

She sighed deeply. 'I didn't have to work. Jimmy is high up in Greeves mill, and isn't short of a bob or two. I thought it would be great to be a woman of leisure for a change.'

'What went wrong, then?'

'I got bored. Jimmy didn't want any children, said he was too old and I suppose he was right. I didn't realise he was so set in his ways.'

'The story of your life, eh, Anne? Never satisfied with what you've got.' They had reached the top of Spinner Street and he came to a halt. This was as far as he wanted her to come. 'I'll bid you good night. And thanks for your help with Tess. I really do appreciate it.'

A hand on his arm stayed him and she moved closer. 'Dan, I made a terrible mistake when I left you.'

He snatched his arm away. 'Here, pull the other one. You're just one selfish, discontented bitch that no one could ever please no matter how hard they tried.'

'That's not fair! I tried. You don't know how hard I tried. But you'd lost interest in everything. Your efforts on the house had come to a standstill and Jimmy was filling my head with talk of this big house he owned in Whitehouse. He even took me to see it one day at lunch time and I couldn't get over the grandeur of it. You could even see Belfast Lough from the upstairs windows.'

All this had been going on and he had been unaware of it. He must have been blind! The disgust he felt came to the fore. Disgust at himself for not noticing and at her for being so easily tempted. 'And you left a wee twelve-year-old boy because of a big house?' He sounded every bit as flabbergasted as he felt.

Her head was bowed in shame. 'I admit I was weak, but don't make me pay for the rest of my life . . . please.'

He gazed down at her and, in his opinion, her crocodile tears. 'As far as I'm concerned you can go and rot in hell.' With these words he strode off down the street.

Her pleading voice followed him. 'Dan, wait, hold on a minute.' When he kept walking, she shouted, 'I'll take Jack away from you, so I will.'

'Just you try!' he threw over his shoulder, defiantly, but kept on walking.

She followed him down the street and he swung round and stepped threateningly towards her. 'Get away home! Or wherever you're staying at the moment. You're not wanted here.'

She glared at him. 'You watch yourself, Dan Thompson. I've every right to be here. I'm staying with Lily Brady, if you must know.'

He was bewildered. How had he missed her coming and going if she was lodging in the same street?

She read his mind and said, 'I just moved in today. It's only until I get a place of my own. A place for me and Jack,' she added daringly.

'Stay out of my way, Anne! And leave our Jack alone,' he warned. 'Or I won't be responsible for my actions.'

He strode off and she watched him, anger eating away at her. She shouldn't let him get to her like this. After all, she didn't care one way or the other what he thought. Or did she? Wasn't the old attraction trying to raise its head? Did he feel it too? Is that why he was so objectionable? Was there a chance that he might take her back? Would she be willing to go? Nothing was any different from the way it was before, after all was said and done. Still, perhaps it was worth giving it a try. According to Lily Brady, there hadn't been any other woman on the scene since she had left him and with his handsome looks he must have had his chances. Perhaps he did still care a little.

Alice was dismayed to find Tess had retired for the night when she entered the house. That was quick. Had that woman upset her in any way? It had come as a surprise to find that Dan and his wife were still together. She hadn't liked to show any interest in his affairs by questioning her daughter about him, but somehow or other she had got the impression that they were separated. Now what had given her that idea? And why did she feel sad about their reconciliation, if that was what it was? Had she actually fancied him? Surely not!

Tapping on the bedroom door she asked softly, 'Tess, are you awake? Can I come in for a minute, love?'

Tess pulled the bedclothes tighter around her ears and willed her mother to go away. There was no way she could hold a rational conversation tonight. So far her mother had been duped, but once she got close enough and smelt the brandy on her breath all hell would be let loose. Her mother would be assuming that she had been on soft drinks. Any whiff of alcohol she might have noticed at the door would have been put down to Anne and Dan. Dear God, make her leave me alone!

After what seemed an eternity, she heard the squeak of a couple of loose treads as her mother descended the stairs, and blew out a long sigh of relief. She admitted that she had got off very lightly. All thanks to Anne!

Would Anne and Dan get back together again now the ice was broken? It would please Jack so much if they were to be reconciled. But then, why should she care whether or not Jack was pleased? Look at the way he had treated her! What was it Dan had said about his son and Colette? Tess delved into her mind but everything was fuzzy. She would never get drunk again if this was the condition it left you in.

Ah! Dan's words came back to her. He had said they were away to Omagh to collect some of Colette's things. It looked as if it was serious between the two of them. Hot tears escaped from her eyes and she let them flow freely. She hoped it would make her feel better. It hadn't before, but perhaps this time they would ease the pain of rejection.

She fell into a troubled sleep and in her dreams Jack was running away from her. At last she caught up with him and grasped his arm. He turned and to her dismay it was a stranger's arm she was clinging to. The man tugged his arm free and she was left feeling desolate. Next morning she awoke with smarting eyes and cheeks still wet with tears.

Christmas was fast approaching and Tess and her mother were kept very busy. Christmas Day was on a Friday this year and they wanted all their work squared up and out of the way at least a week beforehand.

At breakfast one morning Alice squinted at a letter with an Irish postage stamp and recognised the handwriting. 'Huh, imagine that! It's from your Uncle Malachy,' she gasped in surprise and quickly knifed it open. 'What do you think? He wants to join us for a few days over Christmas.'

They usually spent Christmas and the New Year alone and a wide smile split Tess's face at this news. 'That's wonderful! It will be great to have some company for a change, especially family.'

'There's a snag. He wants to bring a friend along.'

'That's even better! The more the merrier. We've plenty of rooms.'

'It's a woman friend.'

'Well, I'm glad he's met someone at last. Perhaps they'll get engaged while they're up here.'

'I hope he doesn't expect me to let them share a room, that's all I can say,' Alice said piously. 'There'll be no hanky-panky under my roof while I'm alive.'

Tess tut-tutted in disgust. 'Oh, Mam! Stop being so sanctimonious and stop taking all the pleasure out of them coming. I'm delighted, so I am. And it's none of your business, or mine for that matter, what they get up to while they're here.'

'In my house it is!'

Resisting the urge to start an argument, Tess rose, pushed her chair away from the table and started to noisily clear the breakfast dishes. Her mother's holier than thou attitude annoyed her at times. She could take the joy out of everything without even trying. You would think she was the only one that mattered; the only one without sin. As if!

'Malachy's taking it for granted he can come. He says we're not to buy a turkey as he will bring one with him and a leg of lamb as well. Isn't that great? That wee farm of his must be doing well at last. All that snow last year nearly ruined him, you know. It was well he was insured. But just think, all we'll have to buy is a roast of pork and all the other smaller bits and pieces.' Alice lifted the remaining dishes and followed Tess into the kitchen. 'I'll have to buy a fruit cake,' she said mournfully. 'I know it won't be nearly as nice as my own, but it's too late now to bake one. Oh, I wish he'd given us a bit more notice. We could have been better prepared.'

'You can bake some of your lovely mince pies and

make a big trifle,' Tess consoled her. 'You know every-one loves your trifles.'

Alice relaxed. 'You're right, of course. I don't suppose he'll notice. After all, one fruit cake doesn't make a Christmas.'

Tess put her arms round her mother and twirled her around the kitchen. 'I've a feeling this is going to be the best Christmas ever, Mam.'

Alice looked at her daughter's laughing eyes and smiling face and vowed it would indeed be a happy time if she had anything to do with it. She would turn a blind eye to her brother's shenanigans if his stay enabled her daughter to put her troubles behind her. She would do all in her power to make this festive time a happy one.

Chapter Four

Malachy and his friend arrived on Christmas Eve. Early in the afternoon a Land-Rover pulled up at the front of the house and Tess, who had been eagerly watching for them on and off since morning, rushed out to help them disembark, shouting a warning over her shoulder to her mother that they had arrived.

Malachy gripped her close. 'My, but you've grown!' He then held her at arm's length and cried, 'You look a picture! Doesn't she, Rose?'

'She does indeed,' his companion agreed, with a slow appraising look.

Tess was flustered; but they did sound so sincere. 'Ah well, now, I don't know about that.'

'Take my word for it.' Her uncle drew the woman forward. 'Tess, this is my dear friend Rose Donaghy, and Rose, you'll have guessed that this is my lovely niece, Tess.'

As they shook hands, Alice came down the steps in a rush, almost tripping in her haste. Malachy reached forward and stopped her headlong progress. 'Hey, steady on there. We don't want to spend Christmas visiting you in hospital, do we?'

Lifting her face for his kiss, Alice apologised. 'I'm sorry about this. I was checking that everything was all right in the kitchen. I don't want to give you a burnt offering on your first day here.' Her eyes were on the woman as she spoke. Malachy made the introductions and his sister said, 'You're more than welcome in our home, Rose. Come inside. It's cold out here.'

The two women climbed the steps and Tess smiled at her uncle. 'I can't tell you how pleased I am to see you, Uncle Mal.'

'And I you! I've a lad working for me now and he offered to look after the stock till I get back. Never one to look a gift horse in the mouth, I accepted right away. Mind you, there was motive in his madness. His girl-friend will be staying with him while I'm away.' He gave Tess a knowing wink and a nudge with his elbow and she burst out laughing.

'I hope you have the good sense not to tell Mam all that or she won't be able to enjoy Christmas for worrying about what they might get up to.'

'I know my sister better than you think, Tess. I know where to draw the line. I only hope she can see her way to letting Rose and me share a room.'

They had emptied the Land-Rover and were lifting cases and boxes up the steps and into the hall. Tess stopped in her tracks and eyed him with something akin to horror.

Malachy threw back his head and laughed at the expression on her face. 'Do you think I'd be that daft, Tess? No. Besides, there's nothing like that between Rose and me. She lost her husband a few months ago and I persuaded her the break would do her a world of good.'

'How sad.'

'Well now, he wasn't the best of husbands, mind you. Not by any means. But of course now he's gone she can only remember his good points.'

'As far as I can make out that's always the way. They're all saints once they go. What about you, Uncle Malachy? Is there any woman in your life yet?'

'Nobody would have me, Tess.'

Tess examined him and silently disagreed. A bit portly in build, he was nevertheless tall enough to carry the weight. He still had a good thick head of brown hair and mischievous brown eyes laughed at her as he returned her look.

'I find that hard to believe, Uncle Malachy.'

The laughter left his face. 'Although my farm is at last paying its way and I'm quite comfortable, it's no life for a woman, Tess. I couldn't expect anyone to share it. It's all hard graft, especially in the dark winter months.'

'But if she loved you?'

He shook his head. 'To be truthful, I don't even get the chance to meet any eligible women. All my friends and acquaintances are already married to each other.'

Big sad eyes regarded him. 'I'm so sorry,' Tess whispered.

'Hey! Don't get me wrong, I'm not complaining. I'm very contented with my lot. Now, let's get these things inside before your mother comes looking for us.'

They all went to midnight Mass in Clonard Monastery and Rose was enthralled at the beauty of the church and the Christmas service, especially the choral singing.

Back at the house they had a glass of ginger wine and some of Alice's delicious mince pies. Thus fortified, Rose and Tess settled back in comfortable easy chairs and listened raptly as Alice and her brother reminisced over their early years. Alice had never complained about her childhood and Tess was surprised at just how hard a beginning she had apparently had. According to Malachy, their father had been a tyrant who had ruled his home with a rod of iron. He had expected his daughter to pull her weight and quite literally work like a man.

Looking fondly at her brother, Alice confessed, 'Malachy did most of my work as well as his own and many a time took a blow that was meant for me.'

Embarrassed, her brother was quick to deny it. 'Here now, sis, we'll have less of that. Don't you try to make me out to be some kind of Sir Galahad. If I ever took a blow meant for you it was because I deserved it in the first place.'

Sadly Alice shook her head. 'Hark at him! I suppose it was your fault the day Dad discovered me behind the shed with Tom Mitchell? Remember him?'

'Yes, that was my fault! If I hadn't brought him home from school with me you'd never have been tempted. Besides, you were doing nothing wrong. I'm sure it was just an innocent peck on the cheek. You were too good-living even then to commit a sin. You know, you're very like me dad in some ways, Alice. There are no grey areas in your mind. Everything is in black and white.'

Alice laughed aloud. 'Don't you believe it! I was just a curious schoolgirl, and like my friends I was tempted. We never did anything really bad but we felt we were being daring if we egged the boys on. Anyhow, you must have been worried, because you never brought any of your schoolmates home after that. But it did give me an idea of what it felt like to be admired and desired and after that I longed for the company of the opposite sex.'

'Admiration was something you always had plenty of, Alice. Everybody who came to the house thought you were beautiful. You still are,' Malachy gallantly assured her.

Flushed with pleasure at all these compliments, Alice's eyes sought her daughter's face. If only . . .

From past experience, Tess could guess the drift of her mother's thoughts. Why couldn't her daughter have inherited her good looks? Well, she hadn't. So, tough! She rose abruptly to her feet. 'If you'll excuse me, I'll go on up to bed now.' She kissed both visitors on the cheek. 'I'm so glad you're here. See you in the morning. Good night, Mam.'

There was silence for some moments when she left the room. It was Malachy who broke it. Shifting uncomfortably in his chair, he asked tentatively, 'Did I say something to offend Tess?'

With a sad shake of the head, Alice admitted, 'I'm afraid Tess has never come to terms with the fact that she didn't inherit my good looks.'

Malachy's mouth dropped open. 'But she's lovely,' he cried. 'Oh, she hasn't got the conventional Irish rose beauty, but with those eyes and that hair, she's beautiful. She would put Greer Garson to shame, so she would.'

'Do you really think so?'

He could see Alice was taken aback at his outburst and said, 'I hope you haven't been putting the wrong ideas into her head by making her think she's plain, just because she doesn't have your looks?'

'No, no,' she hastened to reply. 'I've always assured her that one day a man will come into her life who will realise her worth.'

That said it all as far as Malachy was concerned. Poor Tess, he thought.

Rose had taken all this in in silence. Now, not wanting Malachy to say something he might later regret, she pretended to smother a yawn. 'If you'll excuse me, it is getting late, so I think I'll also retire for the night. It's been a long day. Good night, Alice, and thanks for having me.'

Malachy rose to his feet, stretched his tired muscles and groaned. 'Me too.'

He stifled a laugh as his sister hurriedly assured them, 'I'll be right behind you. I've just to check the windows and doors.'

On the landing, outside the room allocated to Rose, Malachy turned her round to face him and placed a hand on each of her shoulders. 'Will you be all right?'

'Of course I will. The room is lovely and comfortable, and I'm so tired that I'll probably drop off the minute my head hits the pillow.'

He smiled at her and stretched his neck to look up the second flight of stairs. 'It's as well we're just good friends. Alice certainly intends keeping us apart.'

With a slight push and a laugh Rose sent him on his way. 'Away you go and don't give your sister any cause for concern. Good night, and happy Christmas, Malachy.'

He turned towards the other stairs. 'Good night, Rose, and a happy Christmas to you too.'

She watched him for some moments before entering the bedroom. Chance would be a fine thing, if a man like Malachy could ever take a fancy to her. She certainly wouldn't be holding her breath on the off chance.

Christmas Day for Tess was like a fairy tale come true. After a late breakfast, they gathered in the sitting room to open their gifts. Malachy had bought his niece an exquisite gold bracelet, studded with tiny diamonds.

Open mouthed, she gazed from the bracelet to him and back to the bracelet, then threw herself into his arms. 'Oh! It's beautiful, Uncle Malachy. But far too expensive. You shouldn't have!'

'It's not quite as expensive as it looks, but it is a good one nevertheless. I haven't bought you much over the years, Tess. To be truthful, I couldn't afford to. But from now on I intend spoiling you with nice presents. After all, you're my only niece.' He opened his parcel and exclaimed in delight at the thick Aran pullover she had bought him. 'Wow! Just what I need, love. Thank you very much.'

He had bought his sister a beautiful stole in soft cashmere wool. Crocheted, it was like a mass of cobwebs. She was so quiet when she opened it that he asked tentatively, 'Don't you like it, Alice?'

She pressed its softness to her cheek and assured him, 'It's lovely. Thank you.'

However, he saw her eyes returning to the bracelet that Tess had by now put admiringly on her wrist, and frowned. Surely his sister wasn't jealous of her own daughter?

Rose had bought perfume for the two women and received gloves and a scarf in return. She was embarrassed when they apologised for not buying something more original, saying the gifts were lovely and would come in useful. And sure, hadn't she been in the same boat, not knowing what to buy them?

Malachy was then persuaded to take Rose out for a drive, to show her some of Belfast's famous landmarks, while Alice and Tess put the finishing touches to the Christmas dinner.

As Alice fussed about making sure everything was just perfect, Tess set the table with their best linen tablecloth and napkins. The Waterford crystal glasses sparkled against the pure white of the linen and their best cutlery reflected the glow from the overhead chandelier. It was great to have someone to go to all this bother over. Alice was in her glory that all her precious things were on show at long last.

Tess smiled at her fondly. 'Mam?'

'Mm?'

'Were you annoyed at Uncle Malachy giving me such a valuable present?'

Alice kept her attention fixed on the floral display she was preparing for the centre of the table. 'Why should I be annoyed?'

'Maybe you think he should have given it to you.'

'And when would I ever get the chance to wear something as grand as that, tell me, eh? It would probably end up like everything else I have of any value. Hidden away in my bedroom dresser never to see the light of day again.'

Tess shrugged. 'You'd have as much chance as me. But that's not the point. Do you mind Uncle Malachy giving it to me?'

Slowly Alice lifted her gaze to meet her daughter's eyes. She grimaced slightly and confessed, 'I suppose I was a little bit jealous. No one ever bought me anything as expensive as that. Not even your father. He promised me the world but he died before he was in a position to spoil me.' A tear trickled down her cheek and she brushed it roughly away with the back of her hand. 'But he would have, you know. If only he'd lived longer. But give over! I'm glad my brother intends spoiling you. He couldn't spoil a nicer person.' Alice fondly gathered her daughter close. 'I just wish I could afford to shower gifts on you.'

'Oh, Mam, you know I want for nothing. Thanks to you, I've all my needs.'

They smiled tearfully at each other, then Alice pushed her gently away. 'Doesn't the table look wonderful?'

'It sure does. You'd think it was the queen coming for dinner instead of Malachy and Rose,' Tess replied with a smile. 'We should use all these grand things more often, not keep them locked away, gathering dust.'

'I was just thinking along those very same lines myself. Meanwhile, let's get this meal ready before they return, and remember, Tess, I love you dearly.'

The day passed in a cheerful atmosphere and they were relaxing in the evening, drinks in hand, when there was a knock on the door.

'Are you expecting anyone, Mam?' Tess asked with a frown as she rose slowly to her feet to answer it.

'No. Maybe it's that boy you know, or his father.'

'No chance,' Tess threw over her shoulder with a baleful glare as she left the room. She was surprised when she threw the door open to see Agnes and Tony standing on the top step. They cried in unison, 'Happy Christmas,' and holding high a sprig of mistletoe Tony stepped forward and planted a kiss on Tess's lips. 'Happy Christmas,' she replied.

They had been invited to come up on Boxing Night to meet Malachy and Rose and now Tess cried in disappointment, 'Does this mean you can't come tomorrow night? It's all arranged.'

'No, never you fear, we'll be here tomorrow night,' Agnes said. 'I just couldn't wait to show you this.' She pulled the glove off her left hand and extended it for Tess to view.

There, on the third finger, glistened a solitaire diamond ring. A bit put out, Tess grabbed her friend's hand and pulled her into the hall. 'What am I thinking of, keeping you standing out there in the cold.' She beckoned to Tony. 'Come in, Tony, and close the door while I get a good gander at this rock.'

Her mind was in a turmoil as she examined the ring. 'It's beautiful, Agnes. Congratulations. You too, Tony. I hope you will both be very happy together.' There was a questioning look in her eyes as she grabbed her friend to hug her close. 'This is a surprise. You never let on,' she whispered.

'I was surprised and all,' Agnes admitted. She gave Tony a wide smile. 'He just produced this ring out of the blue earlier today, and asked me to marry him.'

'Come on in and show it to Mam. And you can meet Uncle Malachy and his friend while you're here.'

As a result of the big meal and a couple of glasses of sherry, Alice was heavy-eyed as she rose unsteadily to greet them. 'I thought it was tomorrow night you two were coming?'

'It is, Mrs Maguire. I just wanted Tess to know I got engaged today.'

Tess introduced her uncle and Rose and they all gathered round to admire the ring.

'Have you time for a drink?' Malachy asked. 'You can't go without a toast to celebrate the big occasion.'

Tony nodded his approval. 'Just one, mind. We have other people to visit and break the news to.'

'I'll just nip up to the loo,' Agnes said with a glance in her friend's direction.

Tess followed her up the stairs into the bathroom. Making sure the door was closed and they couldn't be overheard, Agnes said, 'Well, what do you think?'

'I don't know what to think, Agnes. You always said he wasn't Mr Right and I believed you. Now you land in here telling us you're engaged. I'm gobsmacked, so I am.'

'To tell you the truth, so am I. Tony just landed into our living room earlier on today, and getting down on one knee he produced this ring and asked me to marry him. Right there in front of everybody. I could see that they all thought we'd planned it that way. What could I do but say yes?'

'How did your mam take it?'

'Oh, she smiled and pretended to be pleased but I could see she wasn't too happy at the idea. But what else could she do? Marie and Dennis have set the date. They're getting married at Easter and Dennis's parents are at our house at the moment. They've been invited over to celebrate and discuss the wedding arrangements. I had to get away from all the questions. Sorry for bursting in on you like this.'

'Don't be silly! I'm glad you came. I just don't understand. What are you going to do? You can't just marry him because he bought a ring. He should have asked you first.'

'Tony says if he had asked me first I'd have made all kinds of excuses. This way I had to give him an answer one way or the other.'

'He took a chance, didn't he? What if you had said no?'

Agnes shrugged and spread her hands wide. 'I suppose he knew I wouldn't embarrass him in front of everybody.'

'Still, it wasn't fair of him to put you on the spot like that.' Tess eyed her friend closely. 'Do you love him, Agnes?'

'That's just it. I don't know. What is love? As you know, he's my first real boyfriend. I admit we get on great but I've no one else to compare him with.' She sighed. 'Anyhow, for the time being I'm engaged. Now let's get back downstairs. We're going over now to break the news to his family.'

She sounded so despondent, Tess put her arms round her and hugged her in sympathy. 'Never mind. Engagements can be broken.'

'Do you think this one will?'

A slight uplift of the shoulders accompanied Tess's reply. 'How can I tell? Come on, Tony's waiting. We can talk about it another time.'

Amidst more congratulations and best wishes the couple left. As they settled back in their chairs and reached once more for their drinks, Alice admonished her daughter. 'You never said it was serious between Agnes and that young lad.'

'I didn't know anything about it. Agnes always maintained that they were just good friends. He just landed in with the ring and proposed to her in front of her family. She said yes to save him any embarrassment.'

'Not a good recipe for a happy marriage,' Rose said softly. 'What kind of work do they do?'

'He's a plumber and Agnes works in a typing pool.'

'Well, those are two good jobs so they should be all right moneywise, and that always helps.'

'But surely there should be some magic there as well?' Tess queried.

'I've found that's not always the case, but if a marriage is worked at it will probably last. Mine did,' Rose added absentmindedly and then turned bright red at the realisation of her admission.

Malachy jumped to her rescue. 'But then, Rose, you're an exceptional person.' He then changed the subject, to Rose's obvious relief.

The following evening Agnes seemed totally resigned to the idea of becoming Mrs Burke and Tess looked at her in wonder. Twenty-four hours had certainly changed her attitude. Could an engagement ring, even a beautiful solitaire, really make so much difference? Getting her friend alone in the kitchen for a few minutes, she questioned her.

'So you've decided it's all for the best, then?'

Agnes shrugged. 'Who knows? Only time will tell. We're having a bit of a do in our house on New Year's Eve to celebrate. Just a small gathering. You will come, won't you?'

Tess's thoughts immediately turned to Jack. 'Will Jack be there?'

'Nothing's been said, but he is Tony's best friend, after all, so I imagine he will be.'

'You'll have to excuse me then, Agnes, but I couldn't bear to be in the same room as him and Colette.'

'You're my best friend, Tess Maguire! You must come. There won't be many there. Just family and a few close friends. I'm going to ask your mam to come along as well, so you'll have to accompany her.'

'That's blackmail, so it is!' Tess gasped.

'Ah, come on now, Tess. You'll have to get used to seeing them together sometime.'

'Why? Tell me why? I haven't set eyes on Jack for months. Belfast is big enough for both of us.'

Tears glistened in Agnes's big blue eyes. 'I thought I could depend on your support. I thought we were best friends.' A tear escaped and slid down her cheek.

'Okay, okay. For heaven's sake give over. I'll come.'

'Thank you. I owe you one.'

'Oh, Agnes, I hope you're doing the right thing.'

'So do I, Tess. So do I.'

'Promise me you won't rush into marriage, sure you won't?'

'No fear.'

'And you'll be careful, won't you?'

A bewildered frown plucked at Agnes's pale eyebrows. 'I don't know what you mean.'

'I'll spell it out for you, then. Make sure you don't get pregnant or then you'll have to get married, like it or not.'

Agnes's mouth fell open at the insinuation. She quickly snapped it shut. 'That's not likely to happen. We don't do things like that. Tony respects me too much for any of that kind of caper, so he does. Why, we hardly even kiss, just in case we get carried away. A ring isn't going to change our morals overnight, I can assure you.'

Somehow, instead of reassuring Tess, this dismayed her. Surely if two people were planning to marry they should at least feel the urge to show each other affection? Look how she had responded to Jack Thompson. Who would have believed she could be so blatant? But she had cared deeply for him. Would it be the same with every man she dated? Was everyone different?

The appearance of her mother curtailed further conversation. 'Are you two going to stay in here all evening or are you going to join us in the living room?'

Agnes gave her an apologetic look. 'We're coming in now, Mrs Maguire.' She was glad to escape her friend's interrogation and gladly left the kitchen.

To the surprise of all concerned, Alice and Rose got on like a house on fire over the Christmas period. After cautiously sizing each other up on that first day, they discovered that they had all sorts of things in common and chatted to each other for hours on end. Alice, not being too fond of animals, and with a great dislike of farmyard smells and muddy fields, had only occasionally ventured to her brother's farm for a few days at a time during the summer months. Now she was actually promising Rose that she would visit him at Easter so that she and her new friend could renew their acquaintance. And perhaps, if they hadn't too much work on, she might stay a few weeks if Tess was able to manage without her.

It was Monday morning and they were loading the Land-Rover for the couple's return to Carlingford when this conversation took place. Malachy and Tess exchanged startled glances at Alice's promise. Tess was quick to intervene. 'You know we always have a quiet spell after Easter, Mam. Of course you must go! You deserve a wee break. It will do you good to get away for a while.'

'Well, if that's the case . . . then why not?'

'Why don't you both come?' Malachy suggested.

'Well now, Uncle Malachy, we don't close down completely at Easter. You see, some customers get their orders on credit. It's the only way to do business these days and it works out fine for us. However, it does mean that Mam or myself has to be here every Friday and Saturday to collect the money.'

'Ah, I understand perfectly. But you will come later in the year, won't you?'

Tess laughed aloud. 'Do you want me to put the blink on you again? Remember last year when I promised to visit? It snowed fast and furious. It was like living in Siberia. Why, we were up to our knees in snow and slush for many a long day. Would you like that to happen again?'

He joined in her laughter. 'I would not! Nor will I ever forget it. It almost wiped me out, so it did. It was lucky that I was insured. Some of the other farmers weren't so lucky when the thaw came and with it the floods. Some of my fields never fully recovered their true richness, either. They're still unsuitable for most crops, but I'm working at it. But do you know something, Tess? Somehow or other, I don't think it was your fault.'

'Even so, let's play it by ear, eh? Just to be on the safe side. I'll not make any promises. We'll wait and see what the weather is like. Okay?'

'Whatever you say. But I would really like you to come down. Bring a friend along and then you won't be bored.'

'I'd never be bored in Carlingford. There's too much to explore, what with the lough and the Cooley Hills. Your farm is situated in a lovely spot, Uncle Malachy, the way it overlooks the water.'

'I couldn't agree with you more. I never tire of the views. Especially in the spring and summer months. So, I can expect to see you sometime next year?'

'You can count on it. I just wish you and Rose could stay to see in the New Year with us. Is there no chance?'

'I'm afraid not. Duty calls. A working farmer can't afford to take much time off, you know, Tess.'

Impulsively, Tess gave him a quick hug. 'Thanks for coming. I can't recall a better Christmas, and I promise to visit you sometime in the summer.'

Chapter Five

New Year's Eve had arrived and it was with trepidation that Tess accompanied her mother along Violet Street to the big parlour house where Agnes lived. She dreaded the evening lying in wait for her; dreaded having to watch Jack and Colette together as a couple. What if they took this opportunity to announce their own engagement? How would she be able to face that? Worse still, how would she react in front of everyone?

She was glad when her mother broke into her troubled thoughts. 'It was nice of Agnes to invite us along. Do you think she will like the wee present I've bought her?' Alice whispered as they came up to the door and awaited a reply to their knock.

'I think most people are grateful for any kind of gift for their bottom drawer. Not that yours is *wee* by any standards.' Tess repressed a grimace at the size of the parcel her mother clutched in her arms. A bedside lamp! It would be some bottom drawer that that fitted into. At least her Irish linen tablecloth wouldn't take up much room.

The door was thrown open and Ted Quinn thrust out his hand in welcome. 'Come in, come in. My daughter will be down in a minute, Tess. I hope you are well, Alice,' he said cordially.

'Is Tony upstairs with Agnes, Mr Quinn? Or can I go up to her?'

'Oh, no. She's alone all right. There'll be none of that carry-on in this house just because she's got a ring on her finger. His place will be down here. *You* can certainly go up to her. Here, Alice, let me take your coat. You too, Tess. You go on into the sitting room, Alice, and my wife will look after you.'

The first person Alice saw when she entered the room was Dan Thompson, looking very handsome in a cream pullover over an open-necked shirt and brown trousers. A quick glance round showed no sign of his wife, though that didn't necessarily mean Anne wasn't there. She could be in one of the other rooms.

Dan caught her eye and advanced to meet her. 'I'm sure you were as surprised as I was to get an invitation here tonight?'

'I was indeed, and what's more, I was told it was a small gathering of friends.' Alice gazed around the crowded room in bewilderment.

Dan laughed. 'These things are inclined to run out of control. Still, as far as I can make out, bar the prospective groom and his parents, I think you and Tess are the last to arrive.'

'You know something? I thought Tess was going to renege. I don't know what's got into her. She made all kinds of excuses not to come. She's here under duress, mind you, because I wouldn't come on my own.'

Dan looked uncomfortable; he could well imagine what was wrong with Tess. His son had a lot to answer for. 'Can I relieve you of that parcel, Alice? All the gifts are in the dining room.'

Gratefully Alice relinquished her hold on the lamp. 'Thank you very much, Dan.'

He made his way from the room with the parcel and May Quinn arrived at Alice's elbow. 'Can I get you a drink, Alice?'

Alice eyed her closely and decided she looked far from being the happy hostess. 'That would be very nice, May. I suppose you're overjoyed at the idea of having two weddings in the family?'

'Far from it, I can assure you. I've warned Agnes that she will have to wait a year or two until we get over Marie's wedding. Everything is so expensive these days. Why Agnes had to rush and get engaged just as Marie and Dennis finally set the date, I'll never know. Still, that's all in the future. What will you have to drink, Alice? Gin, wine, sherry?'

'A glass of white wine would be lovely, thank you.'

It was Dan who returned with her drink, a tall lad and a small dark-haired girl in tow. 'This is my son Jack and his girlfriend Colette.'

So this was the young man Tess was breaking her heart over. The reason for her reluctance to come here tonight. Alice's eyes ranged over the tall gangly lad and found him wanting. Tess could do a lot better than this, surely!

'Pleased to meet you, Jack. Tess has spoken of you.' She nodded at his companion. 'You too, love.'

Sensing he had been found wanting, Jack teased, 'Not all bad, I hope.'

'No . . . but could you blame her if it was?' Alice's gaze rested on his companion.

A slight frown puckered Colette's brow as she gazed back. 'I don't understand.'

Quickly Jack interrupted. 'Dad, a friend of mine has just arrived and I promised to introduce him to Colette. Will you excuse us, Mrs Maguire?'

Dan quirked a brow at Alice. 'I think Jack did the

[91]

right thing there, don't you, Alice? Tess wouldn't have liked you intervening on her behalf. Now, would she?'

'Mm . . . I suppose you're right.' She raised her glass. 'Cheers.'

Upstairs Tess sat on the bed and watched Agnes put the finishing touches to her make-up. When at last she turned from the mirror and faced her friend, Tess said sincerely, 'You look lovely.'

'Thanks. Has Tony arrived yet?'

'I didn't see him. But then, I came straight up here. Is Jack coming?'

'I'm afraid so.' Putting her hand on Tess's arm, Agnes said earnestly, 'Colette's nice. You'll like her.'

'Huh! That's a great comfort to me, so it is.'

A sad smile puckered Agnes's lips. 'Shall we go down and face them all?'

'I don't know what you're so worried about, for heaven's sake. It's *your* engagement party! You should be full of beans.'

'Ah, but I'm not. That's why I'm worried,' Agnes confessed with a rueful grin. Nevertheless, there was a bright smile on her face as she trooped down the stairs with Tess trailing behind her.

Alice hailed her daughter. 'Tess, look who's here.' She indicated Jack and Colette, who had returned for their drinks.

Reluctantly, Tess joined the group in the corner. How could her mother be so insensitive? 'Hi, Jack, hi, Colette. Did you have a nice Christmas?'

'Very nice. Very nice indeed.' Jack bestowed a fond smile on Colette. 'Colette cooked the dinner and her grannie joined us. The meal was delicious and the four of us had a lovely, lazy day.'

'Your mother wasn't with you, then?' Alice was quick to note.

A wry smile twisted Jack's lips. 'No, she had already made other plans.' He had no intention of letting anyone know that his father had refused to let his wife join them.

'Oh? How odd,' Alice said softly.

Afraid she would pursue the matter, and push her nose in where it wasn't wanted, Tess flailed about in her mind for something to change the subject. To her relief the young man in charge of the record player suggested that it was time to take partners for a dance. The music that had been playing softly in the background intensified and Jack excused himself to gather Colette close and shuffle across the floor with her.

At that instant Tony and his parents arrived, obviously flustered and full of apologies. 'Sorry we're late. We couldn't get a taxi. They're like gold dust tonight and Mam refused to walk in her new shoes,' Tony explained.

The small plump woman who was Tony's mother indicated her husband and son. 'They were mad at me, but I'd have been crippled, so I would, and it would have spoilt my night.'

May Quinn was quick to accept the excuse. 'You did right, Maeve, not to walk here in new shoes. We understand perfectly. Here, let me take your coats and Ted will get you all a drink.'

Tess, being without a partner, found herself alone during some of the dances. Dan Thompson was paying a lot of attention to her mother and danced with her every chance he got. He also danced with Tess a couple of times and Tony and Ted Quinn gave her duty dances.

Covertly watching Jack and Colette, Tess could see

they were very much in love by the way they obviously savoured each other's closeness, kissing each other's cheeks and necks at every opportunity. On the other hand Agnes and Tony danced with daylight between them. Fears for her friend rose in Tess's breast and she felt fiercely protective of her.

It was almost midnight when Jack approached Tess and asked her to dance with him. She wanted to refuse but pride made her smile and join him on the floor. After all, she surmised, he probably was just as averse to dancing with her but had been sent over by Colette to do his duty.

He smiled down at her, a strained, embarrassed smile, and she thought perhaps he had read her mind. 'Don't look so worried, Jack. I won't bite.'

He laughed and relaxed a little. 'Tony's a dark horse. He never even dropped a hint that he was thinking of getting married,' he declared.

'He was playing it safe in case she turned him down. Which she might have done, if he hadn't put her on the spot by asking her to marry him in front of every-one.'

Jack looked surprised. 'You can't seriously mean that. Surely she must love him to have agreed to marry him, no matter what the circumstances.'

Hastily Tess agreed with him. 'You're probably right, Jack. I don't know when to keep my big trap shut. What about you? Are you planning any surprises?'

'No. At least not for some time to come.'

She felt as if a hand had squeezed her heart. *Not for some time to come.* So marriage was on the cards, then. Well, hadn't she guessed as much from the antics of the pair of them on the floor?

A quick glance at her watch told Tess it was a few

minutes to twelve. Soon the New Year would be welcomed in. 'Good gracious! It's almost twelve.' She gave him a gentle push. 'Away you go, Jack, and greet the New Year in with your girlfriend.'

'I didn't realise it was that time.' He was uneasy, not wanting to leave her coming up to midnight. 'Where's your mother?'

'Don't worry, I'll find her. The house isn't all that big. Away you go.'

She watched him thread his way to where Colette was standing. Saw Jack take the girl in his arms and glance in Tess's direction. Felt the pity radiating from Colette.

Blinded by tears she turned away. If only things had worked out differently and she was the one in Jack's arms tonight, how wonderful life would be. Her dance with him had made her aware that she was still very much attracted to him. Her mother and Dan sought her out just as the doors, front and back, were thrown wide to the peal of church bells and the blare of sirens as Belfast welcomed in 1965. 'Happy New Year' was on everyone's lips and neighbours first-footed with their pieces of coal, bread and small silver coins to bring happiness and prosperity to the household.

After the wave of excitement had died down and everyone was exchanging kisses and good wishes, Tess whispered to her mother, 'Mam, I'm going to slip away. I'm sure Dan Thompson will walk you home.'

'What?' Still tingling from the feel of Dan's New Year kiss on her lips, Alice blinked at her daughter in bewilderment. 'You can't go home alone! I won't hear tell of it. I'm coming with you.'

'You'll do nothing of the sort.'

Arms encircled Tess and she twisted round to find it

was Dan. 'Happy New Year, Tess. I hope you get your heart's desire.'

His lips were gentle on hers and she gazed at him pleadingly. 'Dan, I want to leave now. Will you see Mam safely home?'

'Of course I will. But must you go? What about the buffet?'

'I couldn't eat a thing. I just want to get away from here.'

'If that's what you want, love. I'll look after your mother.' When Alice would have insisted, Dan said, 'Let her go, Alice. She knows what she's doing.'

Throwing him a grateful glance Tess went to seek out Agnes and Tony, to bid them good night. She wished them all the very best in the New Year and made her way upstairs to retrieve her coat. As she left the bedroom she came face to face with Jack coming from the bathroom.

Plastering a smile across her face, she cried gaily, 'Happy New Year, Jack,' and proffered her cheek for his kiss.

Roughly gripping her jaw, he turned her face up to his and claimed her lips. To her shame, all the longing of the past months surfaced and she hungrily returned his kiss, all the while reminding herself that he was drunk and didn't know what he was doing. She, on the other hand, was quite sober and knew very well that she was making a fool of herself. He gripped her closer still and how she wanted to give in to his silent demands. There was no one about. She might never get another chance. However, good sense prevailed and she pushed him away. 'Colette will be wondering what's keeping you.'

'Tess, I'm sorry things couldn't be different. I honestly didn't mean to hurt you.'

Pride lifted her chin high. 'And what makes you think you have? After all, what do a few kisses matter? Nobody got hurt. It was a pleasant interlude, that's all.'

With these words she left him and literally ran down the stairs and out into the cold night, glad of the breeze that fanned her burning cheeks.

'How dare he!' she fumed. 'How dare he patronise me like that. Who the bloody hell does he think he is anyway?'

Her mind retaliated. 'What did you expect? Didn't you nearly eat the bake of him back there? You'll have to learn to control your emotions, girl.'

As she walked up the road to her home tears of self-pity rolled down her face. Some Happy New Year this was! Would she ever have a man of her own?

The Maguires were always glad of the quiet spell after Christmas and the New Year. It gave them time to give the work room a good clearing out and pay attention to those things that needed doing, like painting and decorating. It was also at this time of year that the whole-salers were making room for new stock and Tess haunted the warehouses and factories looking for quality remnants at bargain prices to renew her own supplies.

Tess had all her materials in when in the middle of January there was a ferocious storm. Gale force winds, gusting up to almost eighty miles an hour and accompanied by torrential rain, swept across Belfast, lifting slates off roofs and causing a lot of structural damage to many buildings.

Tess and Alice stood by the window of the workshop as the rain lashed against it in a cold fury. Abating and then intensifying, and all the while howling like a banshee, it threatened to break into the house. They watched in awe as the road outside took on the appearance of a river, sweeping all debris before it.

Alice almost wept as she thought of the vagrants out on a night like this. 'God help anyone without a roof over their heads tonight. It must be dreadful to be out there and have nowhere to go.'

Tess was more practical, however. 'I'll tell you this, Mam. There's bound to be floods after all this rain. In the morning I'm going shopping again to see if there is any water-damaged material around. One shouldn't look a gift horse in the mouth, you know.'

Alice bestowed a reproachful look on her daughter. 'It seems wrong to benefit from someone else's misfortune.'

'Don't be silly, Mam. Someone *will* benefit and it may as well be us as the next one. They'll all be well insured against storm damage, and some will be claiming for a lot more than they're entitled to. They'll be jumping on the bandwagon, if I'm not mistaken.'

'You've very little faith in human nature, Tess.' Struck by a sudden thought, she said, 'I wonder what it's like in Carlingford? I hope your Uncle Malachy isn't getting it as bad as this.'

This did cause Tess some concern. 'I sincerely hope not,' she exclaimed. 'After all that carry-on last year, he could certainly do without any more flooding. Maybe we should get in touch with him and find out.'

'That's a good idea, love.'

Next morning they learnt on Radio Ulster the full extent of the damage caused by the storm. Among other things, the newsreader reported that St Brendan's Church on Connsbrook Avenue had collapsed and the *Royal Ulsterman*, a steamer, had struck an oil tanker at

Sydenham oil refinery causing untold damage.

Undaunted, but pausing long enough to say a wee prayer for those in need, Tess ventured out next morning. It was still raining but nothing like the night before and the winds had abated a great deal. There were plenty of signs of the destruction caused by the storm, she noted as she made her way down to the city centre, but it was not as bad as she had anticipated, after the ferocity of the winds and rain the previous night.

Broken slates were strewn across footpaths with warning notices to take care pasted in prominent positions. Some areas were cordoned off to protect pedestrians and Tess felt quite safe as she made her way to her favourite haunts in search of bargains. Her quest was not in vain. About lunch time a jubilant Tess returned home in a taxi, two bolts of material wedged between the seats and a box with buttons and zips and fancy dress trimmings on her knee. She had purchased them at rock-bottom price and knew that they could be easily salvaged. The old saying was indeed true; it was an ill wind that didn't blow somebody good. There was no angering her the rest of the day.

'I'm home, Mam.' Alice came to the top of the stairs and Tess paused at the bottom to impart her news. 'What do you think, Mam? The taxi driver told me that Sean Lemass – you know, the Republic's premier – arrived at Stormont to meet Terence O'Neill a short time ago.'

Slowly descending the stairs, Alice gazed at her daughter, eyes wide with surprise. 'I don't believe it!' she gasped. 'I never heard a word about it on the news. Just imagine! The Taoiseach up here in Ulster. Whatever next?'

Not so sure now, Tess said, 'Well now, it was the taxi driver who told me and he sounded pretty sure of his facts. Of course I can't swear to it being the truth.'

'If it is true, it could do a lot of good, but O'Neill is taking a big chance. There'll be those who won't like it one wee bit, you know.'

'You're right. Come to think of it, it doesn't sound possible. Terence O'Neill wouldn't take a chance like that. The driver must have been talking a load of rubbish.'

Alice reached for her coat and headed for the door.

'Where are you going, Mam? I want to show you the bargains I got.'

'They can wait. I'll see them later. I'm away up to the monastery to light a candle that everything will be okay. This could be history in the making.'

'Mam . . .' Tess was talking to herself. Alice was already out of the house.

As it turned out, the historic meeting between O'Neill and Lemass did indeed take place at Stormont and had been so secret that even cabinet ministers had not been made aware of it until that morning. The meeting was held in an effort to promote better community relations and economic strategy between north and south. Whether or not it would do any good remained to be seen.

Tess and her mother turned their attention to the orders in their books. If any wedding outfits had to be made between now and Easter they were to be given priority over everything else. This year there were three wedding dresses and bridesmaids' outfits on order for Easter weddings. The Maguires toiled over them for long hours each day and had them ready for final fittings in record time. Then, before they knew it, the Easter rush was on. It was late this year, Easter Sunday falling on 18th April. A few mothers, hoping for good weather, wanted suits for themselves and pretty dresses for their daughters with matching Easter bonnets.

The orders came rolling in. Careful of her mother's health, once the wedding outfits were ready, Tess insisted that Alice worked no more than six hours a day, but she herself worked far longer. It was late one evening in March when a knock caused her to lay aside the flower girl dress she was hand-hemming and go to the bay window to ease the heavy curtain aside and peer out into the night. To her surprise Jack and Colette stood on the top step peering back at her. She acknowledged them with a nod and, pulling the curtain back into place, went to open the door.

What on earth did they want here at this time of night? What else but a wedding dress, she fumed inwardly. They must have decided to get married after all. Well, there was no way she would make this girl's wedding dress. How tactless of them to even consider asking her. Successfully hiding her emotions behind a bland exterior, she opened the big outer door and stood aside to admit them, along with a great blast of cold air.

'My, but it's bitter out there,' Jack declared and gave her a timid smile as he sidled past her and entered the hall behind Colette. Guilty conscience there, Tess surmised, and closing the door she ushered them into the sitting room.

'This is a surprise,' she managed to utter pleasantly enough, then, without inviting them to sit down, waited to hear what had brought them up here on such a bitter cold night. After all she could be wrong; not everyone wanted Tess Maguire to make their wedding dresses.

Marie Quinn, for instance, was going to a top designer in the city centre, according to Agnes.

She looked inquiringly at them until Colette broke the silence. 'I'm sorry for disturbing you so late, Tess, but I was wondering if you would consider making my wedding dress?'

The silence stretched as Tess digested these words. At last she managed to find her tongue, excuses dripping from her lips. She was glad she could voice them truthfully. 'I'm very sorry, Colette, but we're swamped with orders at the minute. We couldn't possibly take on anything else until after Easter . . .'

Colette interrupted her. 'Oh, not for Easter. It will be August before we marry. We were just passing by and saw your light on, and knowing how popular your dresses are, and how busy you always are, I suggested to Jack that we call in and book early so as to avoid disappointment. Jack thought that in the circumstances you might not want to make my dress, but I said business is business. No one turns good money away these days. Please say you'll make it, Tess.'

Resigned, Tess casually waved towards the settee. 'Please sit down and I'll fetch the order book.'

She was leafing through a big, well-thumbed register when she returned. 'August, you say?'

'Yes,' Colette said enthusiastically.

'We can fit you in, but, mind you, I would want to start on it early. No last minute rush. I like to get everything just right and that means at least two fittings before the final sewing.'

At these words Colette dived into her handbag and withdrew a pattern. 'It's just a simple design. I've been carrying it about with me ever since I discovered it on a stall in Smithfield market.'

Tess grunted as she took the pattern and examined it. In her experience simple designs were usually the trickiest to follow. However, one glance at it and she said, 'I've made this dress before. Last year, in fact. It's tricky, all hidden lines, you know, but beautiful. Well worth the bother. What kind of material have you in mind?'

'I was hoping you would advise me.'

Tess sat back in her chair and examined the girl who had stolen Jack from her. For the moment, all animosity was gone. All she saw was a new customer with exceptional looks, and she knew just the material that would best suit her.

Getting to her feet she said, 'Come with me, please.'

Jack remained seated but Colette rose eagerly and followed her from the room. In the workshop Tess walked along a row of material piled almost ceiling high against one wall. At last she stopped and turned to Colette in frustration.

'Just my luck. Wouldn't it have to be one of the top ones?'

'I'll fetch Jack to give us a hand.' Colette turned and made to leave the room, but with a raised hand Tess stopped her.

'That won't be necessary. I'm used to managing on my own.' She pulled a stepladder forward and proceeded to climb. 'They're not heavy. I'll ease it out and hand it down to you.' She carefully lowered the bolt of material to the floor and Colette grasped it. 'Just stand it upright against the others.'

Tess descended the ladder and gently caressed the soft ivory material with the back of her hand. 'Feel that,' she suggested. 'Isn't it beautiful? So different from anything else I have. I was lucky to get it. It's from a top designer house. Excess to requirements, according to the manager. I jumped at the chance to buy it on the cheap.'

Tentatively Colette stroked the fabric. She looked a bit put out. 'It's beautiful but . . . I hope you don't mind . . . I had white in mind.'

It was Tess's favourite material and she thought it just right for Colette's colouring. If only this girl knew how honoured she was. A bit disappointed, she nevertheless assured Colette, 'Everybody to their own taste. I've plenty of white material. Silk, brocade, satin, et cetera. You name it, I have it.' She reached for a bundle of material squares. 'Here, there's plenty of samples to choose from. In fact you don't have to make up your mind right now. So long as your name is down in my book you can take those samples home with you and bring them back another time. After Easter will do fine. Of course, you can buy your own material if you wish and bring it to me. I don't mind one way or the other.'

'Thank you very much, Tess. My grannie will be delighted to browse through these with me. It will make her feel important. As if she's part of the show.'

'What about your mother? Won't she want to help you choose?'

'Well, you see . . .'

Tess tensed. She sensed that she was about to hear confidences and this she wanted to avoid; the less she knew about Colette Burns the better it suited her. 'I expect with your mother being so far away it will be difficult to let her see them,' she said hurriedly. 'But you can borrow those samples again any time you like.'

'Thank you, I'll remember that. However, I may as well tell you. Jack and Mam didn't exactly hit it off. You see, she had big plans for me. She worked hard to put me through school and she thinks I'm wasting my time on the likes of Jack. That's one reason I want to be married in white. Mam always thinks the worst. She thinks Jack and I are practically living together and nothing I say convinces her otherwise. If I choose ivory she would be convinced that she is right and I'm not a virgin any more.'

Tess nodded in understanding. 'I'm sorry to hear that. Jack is a fine lad.' She led the way from the work room.

When they were leaving, at the outer door Colette offered Tess her hand in farewell. 'Thank you for agreeing to make my dress.' She held up the bag now holding the samples. 'I'll bring these back as soon as me and Grannie agree on which material I should go for.'

Tess sat for some time after they had gone, fingers entwined in her lap, thoughts working overtime. So much for her determination not to make Colette's wedding dress, but somehow it hadn't mattered. She had suddenly realised that being in Jack's company no longer set her pulse racing. It was the memory of her antics towards him that one night at the corner of Malcomson Street that filled her with shame and made her want to avoid his company. How she wished it had never happened; then she could look him straight in the eye. If only she hadn't been so stupid!

She was glad that she now saw Colette as just another customer and not a rival in love and hoped that Jack would not accompany her to the fitting sessions. And, by the sound of it, if Mrs Burns had her way the wedding might never take place, Tess mused. Now there was food for thought! A few weeks ago she would have been over the moon at the idea that Jack and Colette might part. Now the notion left her completely unmoved. She couldn't care less, one way or the other.

Tess had offered them tea but they had declined and she was glad. She wanted them long gone before her mother arrived back from visiting a friend, knowing Alice would be far from pleased at her agreeing to make the dress in the first place. Hearing the outer door open, Tess quickly gathered the flower girl dress on to her lap and proceeded to sew as if she had been at it all night.

Alice stopped at the work room door and eyed her daughter in dismay. 'Are you still at it, love? You make me feel ashamed. Here's me gallivanting about and you sitting there toiling away.' She entered the room and shrugged out of her winter coat. 'It would skin a fairy out there tonight, so it would. I wouldn't be a bit surprised if we wake up to snow in the morning.'

'Surely it's too cold for snow?'

'You're probably right.' Alice returned to the hall and hung her coat on the stand. She appeared nervous, her eyes darting about until they caught sight of the ivory material. 'What's that doing down?'

Tess gave a start of surprise. So much for wanting to keep quiet, for the time being, about Colette's visit. She had completely forgotten about the material. Her mother was no dozer. Better to tell the truth and get it over with.

'I was showing it to a prospective customer.'

'Your favourite material?' Alice sounded scandalised, bringing a smile to Tess's face. 'Who? Must be someone special. Has Marie Quinn changed her mind, then?'

'Afraid not, Mam. There's no chance of Marie changing her mind. Mrs Quinn wants only the very best for her daughter.'

'Our dresses can hold their own against the best in town,' Alice cried indignantly.

Tess shrugged indifferently. It was no skin off her nose

where Marie chose to go. After all, it was the bride's prerogative. Just because Tess and Agnes were close friends didn't mean Agnes's sister was obliged to ask Tess to make her wedding dress. She was kept busy enough as it was, and certainly didn't need or indeed want Marie's custom. If she had been chosen to make Marie's dress, Mrs Quinn would have been breathing down her neck every chance she got. May Quinn was one of those people who looked for faults where there weren't any. If there was such a thing as a professional nitpicker, she'd fit the bill perfectly. That was something Tess could definitely do without. 'If you must know I was showing that material to Colette Burns.'

She smiled as she watched her mother swallow convulsively before gasping, 'Colette Burns? The cheeky bitch! Did she ask you to make her dress? I hope you told her we were too busy?'

'I certainly did. However, she doesn't want it until August. So what could I do but agree?'

Alice ducked her head to peer into Tess's face. 'I can always tell her to take her custom elsewhere if you like. How do you feel about it, love?' she asked quietly.

'What do you mean?'

'You know very well what I mean!'

'Funnily enough, I didn't think of her as Jack's future wife. Simply as a customer. So much so that I showed her my favourite material. What do you think of that? But she wasn't in the least bit impressed with the ivory. She took away the white samples to pick from.'

'Mm . . . I must admit she would look good in that ivory shade. She's got the right colouring for it.'

'That's what I thought, but everyone to their own taste.' Tess looked thoughtfully at her mother. There was something different about her. A slight smile played about her lips and there was a dreamy cast in her eyes. 'What are you looking so pleased about?'

'What? . . . I don't know what you mean.'

'Mam, I can read you like a book, so out with it. Why all this suppressed excitement?'

'Don't be silly. I'm not in the least bit excited.' Alice drifted about the room and, sensing there was more to come, Tess maintained an expectant silence. After a short pause, Alice casually continued, 'Dan Thompson was at the confraternity in Clonard tonight and we just happened to bump into each other, so he walked down the road with me. Hardly anything to get excited about, is it?'

Uneasy now, Tess muttered, 'Well, well!'

Colour brightened Alice's cheeks and she confessed shyly, 'He has asked me out for a meal next week.'

Tess set her sewing to one side and, rising to her feet, led the way from the room. She would have to tread very carefully here; not get her mam's back up. 'Come on. Let's have a cup of tea and you can tell me all about it.'

Alice fluttered aimlessly about the kitchen, stopping to gaze vacantly into space, getting in Tess's way and generally acting like a teenager in love. Really perturbed now, Tess gave her a gentle push in the direction of the door. 'Look, Mam, you're not much good in here, so you may as well go and sit down and I'll bring the tea in to you. Poke the fire and get a bit of heat into the house.'

By the time Tess carried the tea into the sitting room, Alice had put some more coals on the fire and it was burning brightly, throwing a warm glow around the room. They sat side by side on the settee and, clasping her mug in her hands, Tess challenged her mother. 'Come on, now. Tell me all about it.'

'I've already explained. He asked me out.'

'And you, of course, knowing he is a married man turned him down.'

'Well . . . not exactly.'

'What do you mean, not exactly? Surely you can see there is no alternative, Mam?'

'He was so nice I didn't want to appear too prudish with him, so I told him I would think about it.'

'Mam!' Tess cried in exasperation. 'I'm surprised at you, so I am. You, of all people, contemplating going out with another woman's husband. I just can't believe my ears.'

'Ah now, hold on a minute . . . it's not as if they're living together. He says they're separated.'

'What difference does that make? Eh? There can never be a divorce. You know that. And you, Mam, of all people are not the kind of person to live in sin. Or even, for that matter, have a fling with a married man.'

'Oh, for heaven's sake, Tess, we would be just going out for a meal! He hasn't asked me to move in with him.'

'And what if you get to like each other and he does suggest something like that? What will you do then?'

Alice's nose wrinkled in distaste. 'Live in Spinner Street? You've got to be joking.'

'So you'd invite him to move in here, then? Is that the idea?'

'He knows better than to suggest that. You're way off the mark, girl. It would be purely a platonic relationship. He's lonely and you have to admit it will keep me out of your hair. Give you a chance to meet some suitable young men.'

Tess frowned. 'Why are you suddenly worried about me meeting suitable young men, eh? You were never bothered about it before. Was that Dan's excuse, then? Did he play on your sympathy?' Distressed now at the idea of someone feeling sorry for her, Tess wailed, 'How dare he pity me! And tell me this, how is you going out for a meal with Dan Thompson suddenly going to change my way of life? Eh?'

'Ah, Tess, now, don't get yourself all upset. Of course Dan doesn't pity you. He thinks the world of you.' Realising she was fighting a losing battle, and her daughter would not be swayed, Alice cried in frustration, 'Anyway, why do you always have to go and put a damper on everything I do?'

Tess gaped at her open-mouthed. '*Me*, put a damper on *you*? I'm afraid you've got that arse about face!' she cried angrily. 'I'm only trying to save you from making a laughing stock of yourself. There's no future in what you're contemplating.'

'All right, all right! Let's not make a song and dance about it. I've got the message loud and clear. When he phones I'll make some excuse to say I can't make it. Will that satisfy you? Are you happy now? And another thing, madam. Don't you ever use that kind of language in this house again. Now, I'm off to bed. Good night.' Lifting her empty mug, Alice left the room with an exaggerated flounce. In the kitchen she rinsed the mug under the tap before thumping upstairs in a temper.

To say that Tess was amazed at her mother's attitude would be an understatement. Alice was so good-living she considered it a sin to stay in the company of anyone who made rude remarks. And remembering the way Dan had danced attendance on her at Agnes's engagement do, Tess was sceptical of the outcome. Alice was deluding herself if she thought Dan Thompson could just be her friend. That he fancied her, there could be no doubt . . . and what about her mother? Didn't the signs all point to her liking Dan more than just a little?

As she locked up for the night, Tess vowed to do all in her power to persuade her mother not to become involved with Dan Thompson; it could cause nothing but unhappiness. And . . . God forbid, it could throw herself and Jack together and she didn't want that any more. She preferred to bury the past, get on with her life, and forget her wanton actions towards him. How could she do that if her mother and Dan became close friends? Or . . . lovers? It didn't bear thinking about.

Alice sat at her dressing table and examined her image in the mirror. Turning her head this way and that she had to admit that she found it easy to agree with Dan. She was still an attractive woman, she mused. Dan had taken her hand when he had paid her this compliment earlier that evening and a shiver of excitement had run down her spine at his touch.

She recalled how flattered she had been when he had shown so much interest in her on New Year's Eve, but when he had failed to follow it up by getting in touch with her she had suppressed her disappointment and put all thoughts of him from her mind. After all, she reminded herself, he was a married man and she would be foolish to let her thoughts dwell on him.

Tonight was their first meeting since the New Year. He had been approaching the corner of Dunmore Street as she walked past and had called out to her.

She had been completely unaware of him but the very sound of his voice sent a tremor through her body. She stopped and waited until he joined her on the Springfield Road.

[111]

Gazing down into her eyes, his expression was warm and welcoming. 'Long time no see, Alice.'

'Hmm.'

Her look of reproof brought a hurt look to his face and he replied to the implied criticism. Reaching for her hand he had said, 'You're a very attractive woman, Alice Maguire, and I thought it better to give you a wide berth.'

She was aware that her hand was trembling in his grip and tugged to remove it. 'Oh, indeed?'

He gripped her hand tighter and, smiling, leaned closer. 'Yes, indeed. You know why that must be, don't you? I'm not a free man.'

She managed to release her hand and started to walk slowly down the road. He fell into step beside her. 'Of course, I can't see it doing any harm, us going out now and again.' He slanted a sideways glance at her. 'Can you?'

'What about your wife? Is she still in Belfast?'

'Unfortunately, she is, but we've been separated a long, long time now and, believe me, there is no chance of us getting back together.' His lips tightened on these words. Anne was proving to be a right thorn in the flesh.

'Are you sure there is no chance of a reconciliation?' Alice countered.

'Quite sure. Too much water has passed under the bridge for that. So how about coming out for a meal with me?'

'It would give rise to unnecessary gossip if we were seen out together,' she replied with a grimace. 'You know what people are like round here. They can't mind their own business.'

They were passing the Blackstaff factory and he drew her into the gateway. Talk or no talk he wanted her to go out with him more than ever now. He enjoyed her company; admired her good looks; was aroused and excited in her presence. It was now or never. He needed to convince her before they arrived at her door and, maybe, find Tess at the window watching out for her. He was aware that mother and daughter were very protective of each other.

'Listen, Alice, let's give it a try, eh? I'm sure we can be friends. It would be nice to have someone attractive to go out and about with.'

Inwardly she agreed wholeheartedly with him. It would be nice to have a male companion to share outings with. But could they be just friends? She dithered and he urged, 'No strings attached. Honest!'

'Well, I suppose we could at least give it a try . . .' she ventured.

Relief flooded through him. 'You'll come for a meal with me at the weekend, then?'

'Oh, no! Not the weekend. Give me a ring and we'll arrange something for during the week. Okay?'

He knew not to push his luck; she would only run off and it would be over before it had begun. 'All right. I'll phone you.'

They continued down the road to her home and seeing that the curtains were drawn across the bay window he risked a kiss on her soft cheek. 'See you soon, I hope.'

Breathless, she had watched him stride off down the road and out of sight, thinking what a handsome man he was. I'd be a fool not to take him up on his offer. Just for companionship, she assured herself.

Now, after Tess's reaction, she considered the wisdom of her plans. Her daughter was right, of course; she was treading on forbidden ground. It was so long since she had felt these emotions, they were frightening her. Why, she was behaving like a lovestruck young girl, but she must not let her emotions rule her head. It would be better if she didn't start something that she couldn't finish. When he phoned she would tell him it would not be in their best interests for them to meet.

It was the following Monday when Tess answered the phone to find Dan Thompson on the other end of the line. He greeted her cordially. 'Hello there, Tess. I trust you are well?'

'Yes, very well, thanks. How can I help you?'

Her voice was clipped with disapproval and he grimaced but dared to continue. 'May I speak to your mother, please?'

Dan heard Tess's frustrated, if not exaggerated, sigh and then, 'Hold on, I'll give her a shout.'

A shout was unnecessary; Alice came from the living room like a greyhound out of the starting trap, asking breathlessly, 'Is it for me, Tess?'

'As if you didn't know.' A hand covering the mouth-piece, Tess whispered, 'Please be careful, Mam.'

With an angry toss of the head, Alice took the receiver and stood silent, waiting for her daughter to make herself scarce, although she doubted she would go out of earshot.

Tess didn't move too far away. From just inside the living room door she strained her ears, unashamed, to catch her mother's side of the conversation.

'Hello, Dan.'

A pause and then, 'Well now, I've been giving your suggestion a lot of thought, Dan, and I'm having my doubts. Do you think it would be wise for us to see each other?'

Another pause, 'I'm inclined to agree with you but Tess thinks it would be foolish of me to put myself in a compromising situation.'

After another short silence Alice cried indignantly, 'Of course I don't let Tess or anyone else for that matter tell me what to do, but you are a married man and it could start a lot of tongues wagging.'

A longer pause this time and Tess guessed that Dan was pleading his case.

'I suppose you're right. One date can't do any harm. Yes, Thursday night would be lovely. Seven o'clock? I'll be ready and waiting.' Replacing the receiver, Alice said resignedly, 'You can come out now, Tess.'

When her daughter slowly entered the hall Alice eyed her defiantly. 'Well, did you hear all that?'

'Enough to know you intend seeing him on Thursday night.'

'Oh, don't look so disapproving! We're only going out for a meal, for heaven's sake!'

With a shrug, Tess said, 'On your own head be it then. Just don't expect any sympathy from me when things start to go wrong. And they will, Mam. You mark my words.'

'Tess, please don't take all the pleasure out of this for me,' Alice said wistfully. 'It will probably only be the one date, you know.'

To her consternation Tess saw a tear ripple down her mother's cheek. Alice turned away and hurried towards the stairs, unwilling to let her daughter see how much this date with Dan Thompson meant to her.

Tess beat her to the staircase and barred her escape. Taking her in her arms she said, 'Mam, I don't mean to spoil things for you. Surely you know I'm only concerned because I don't want you to get hurt.'

'Can't you see, Tess?' Alice pleaded. 'If I don't go out with him, I'll regret it for the rest of my life. I'll always feel that I've missed out on something.' She was silent for some moments then added, 'I do think it will peter out. I'm getting far too old for all that old nonsense. You know what I mean? So if Dan should have anything other than friendship in mind he's in for a big disappointment.'

'You're far from being too old, Mam, but I know what you mean. You've missed out on so much with Dad dying so young. I only wish that Dan Thompson was a free man and then there wouldn't be any problem.'

Alice eyed her daughter hopefully. 'Does that mean I have your blessing for just one date with him?'

Hugging her mother, Tess smiled. 'Oh, I suppose so.'

Alice's radiant smile was reward enough for her daughter.

Chapter Six

Thursday dawned frosty with a weak sun painting the sky a pale shade of pink. As they worked side by side Tess couldn't help but notice her mother's suppressed excitement and worry gnawed at her. God knows, not for one minute did she begrudge her mother any pleasure she might be lucky enough to find in life. She deserved all the happiness she could get. But . . . where would it all end?

She was brought out of her reverie by a hand placed lightly on her arm. 'I know what's going through that mind of yours, Tess, but believe me, I know what I'm doing. I'm a big girl after all,' Alice chided.

Covering the hand with her own, Tess squeezed it. 'Just be careful, Mam. I don't want to see you getting hurt.'

'I'll take care, Tess. I promise. Now stop worrying about me.'

Easier said than done. Some hours later Tess rose from the big factory sewing machine, and stretched her aching back. 'I'll have to try and learn to sit more upright in front of that machine before I give myself a bad back,' she groaned. 'Anyway, since you will be eating out tonight let's have a snack now. I might even go out myself to the pictures tonight. There's a good film on at the Broadway. Agnes couldn't get away last night so perhaps she'll come with me tonight.'

Marie Quinn's forthcoming wedding was putting a lot of pressure on her family. The preparations for it seemed far-reaching and had already eroded the few hours Agnes shared with Tess. Her friend saw very little of her these days. She was overjoyed when Agnes agreed to accompany her to the cinema, saying that the wedding plans were on hold at the minute as far as she was concerned and Tony was putting in some overtime while it was available, so she was free to go out on her own for a change.

Delighted to have something to look forward to, Tess prepared a snack for herself and her mother with a light heart. After all, as her mother had pointed out, she was a big girl and could look after herself.

Promptly at seven o'clock, Dan arrived at the door. Alice took a final look at her reflection in the hall mirror, making final adjustments to her hair that were totally unnecessary, and hastened to admit him.

His eyes took in her appearance with a sweeping glance and he said sincerely, 'You look lovely, Alice.' A taxi was parked at the kerb, its engine idling away. 'I told the driver to wait, so if you're ready, let's go.'

Tess, who had followed her mother into the hall, sighed and looked from one to the other of them. It was obvious they were very attracted to each other. 'See and enjoy yourselves.' Her voice was sincere and Dan flashed her a grateful smile.

'I'll see no harm comes to your mother while she's with me, Tess.'

'Good night, Dan.'

Tess watched as Dan handed her mother into the taxi

and then climbed the stairs to finish her own preparations to go out. She was calling for Agnes at half past seven and needed to get a move on.

Agnes must have been on the look-out for her. Before Tess could knock, the door opened and her friend joined her on the pavement.

Slipping her arm through Tess's, Agnes hugged it close. 'I can't tell you how pleased I was when you phoned. It's great to be going out with you again. I've been so bored lately I could scream my head off.'

Tess flashed her a worried look. 'That sounds ominous. Are you and Tony not getting on, then?'

'Oh, we get on fine. It's just that there's so much to do for Marie's wedding, and to crown it all Tony is planning ahead for ours and is taking all the overtime he can get.'

They left Violet Street and hurried along Cavendish Street. 'Tell me all about it,' Tess urged. 'How many bridesmaids will there be?'

'Just me and Dennis's sister Joan, and her three-year-old daughter will be a flower girl.'

'Come on, Agnes, for heaven's sake. Out with it. Anyone would think it was a hush hush affair the way you're getting on. Don't have me dragging every wee detail out of you.'

Agnes laughed. 'I forgot. It's been a while since we've been out together. Well . . . Joan and I will be in primrose and young Amy will be in white. What else do you want to know?'

'The last time we were talking you said Tony might be best man. Is he?'

'I'm afraid that fell by the wayside and he's very disappointed. Remember I told you Dennis had a brother in Florida?'

Tess nodded. 'You said he hadn't been home for about ten years and was a kind of black sheep of the family.'

'That's right! Well, he has decided to grace us with his presence and has agreed to come home and be best man. What do you think of that?'

'The question is, what do *you* think?'

Agnes shrugged. 'It makes no difference to me. He's to arrive a week before the wedding in time for the church rehearsal. He will be home for two months but once Dennis and Marie are married I imagine our family will see very little of the Sullivans. They're not like Dennis at all. Whereas he's friendly and down to earth, the rest of them are inclined to be a bit on the snooty side. To be truthful, I don't envy our Marie her in-laws.'

'But . . . I thought they lived on Mackie's Height?'

'They do.'

'Hah!' Tess showed her disdain. 'I wouldn't have thought anybody up there had anything to be snooty about. Why, they're no better off than we are.'

Agnes shrugged. 'I know, but Mr Sullivan has a good job. He's high up on the council and he and his wife seem to think that puts them a cut above everyone else.'

They had passed down Oakman Street and along Beechmount Avenue out on to the Falls Road. The queue for the Broadway picture house was slowly shuffling into the foyer and they hurried across the Falls Road to join it. Soon they were settled in the back stalls and all further information about the Sullivans was shelved as the lights went out and the big picture started.

Blowing her nose noisily into her handkerchief as they left the cinema, Tess admitted, 'I really enjoyed that! I love a good old cry at a film, and *An Affair to Remember* was certainly a weepy.'

'Actually I didn't realise that was the film on tonight. I saw it in the Windsor some time ago,' Agnes admitted, 'but I enjoyed it again. I thought he was never going to discover that Deborah Kerr was crippled.'

'So did I. Isn't Cary Grant a real smasher?'

'He sure is. You know, I think Dan Thompson looks very like him.'

'Don't be daft,' Tess retorted. 'Did I tell you me mam is out with Dan at this very minute?' A quick glance at her watch and Tess amended her words. 'I'm sure they're home by now.' She could feel Agnes gaping at her but pretended not to notice her surprise.

'You know damned well you haven't said a word about your mam and Dan,' Agnes said reproachfully. 'When did this all start, then?'

'Tonight is their very first and, I hope, their only date. I think he bulldozed Mam into going out with him.' They were crossing the Falls Road and Tess asked hopefully, 'I suppose you wouldn't fancy catching the bus down to the Dolphin for a fish supper?'

'Oh, I'd love one,' Agnes cried enthusiastically. 'Tony would consider it a waste of good money to go into a chippie. To tell you the truth he gets on my nerves at times the way he keeps on counting the pennies.'

'Great! We'd better put a spurt on. That bus is ready to go.'

The bus was packed and they caught it by the skin of their teeth, hanging on to the platform pole for grim life. There was an exodus at the stop at the bottom of Clonard Street and the girls discovered that everybody seemed to be in the same frame of mind and intent on visiting Johnny Reid's chippie.

They joined the growing queue and as they waited Agnes whispered in her friend's ear. 'How do you feel about your mam going out with Dan Thompson, then?'

With a furtive glance over her shoulder, Tess hissed back, 'Hush, for heaven's sake! This is not the place to talk about it. You never know who might be listening. Look.' She nodded towards the far end of the counter. 'Johnny has a helper on tonight doing the takeaways and that queue is moving quicker. Shall we join it and eat ours on the way home?'

'Yes, that's a good idea,' Agnes agreed and in no time they were outside and heading for the Springfield Road, digging into a feast of crispy cod and chips.

'Do you know something, Agnes? I didn't realise how hungry I was. We didn't have a proper dinner today, just a snack, because Mam was eating out. This fish is delicious.'

Stuffing a chip into her mouth, Agnes mumbled, 'So are the chips.' Then silence reigned as they did justice to their food.

As she screwed up her greasy paper into a ball to take home, Tess confessed, 'Now that's given me a thirst. Come up to our house for a cup of tea, Agnes.'

'I can't. Tony said he would call in after work and he'll be fuming if I'm not there. After all, I didn't even know I was going out. He'll probably be sitting there twiddling his thumbs trying to keep a conversation going with my dad. They haven't got very much in common, you know.'

'You may as well be killed for a sheep as a lamb. Go on, coax yourself. God knows when I'll see you again.'

Agnes didn't need much coaxing. She gave in straight away. 'Okay, you've twisted my arm. Let's go.'

The light was on in the kitchen, casting a faint glow

into the hall, and Tess stopped at the foot of the steps in dismay as she saw it shining through the fanlight above the front door. For a short time she had completely forgotten about her mam and Dan. It was obvious her mother was home, but was Dan with her? She fervently hoped not.

Dashing up the steps, Agnes cried impatiently, 'Hurry up, for heaven's sake, and open the door. I haven't all night, remember.'

Sorry now that she had invited Agnes back, Tess reluctantly unlocked the front door and stepped into the hall. The house was very quiet. Had her mother forgotten to switch off the kitchen light and retired for the night? Removing her coat she hung it on the hall stand and invited Agnes to do likewise, all the while straining her ears for the sound of voices.

'It's not worthwhile me taking my coat off. I'll have to run as soon as I finish my tea. That's if you ever get round to making it.' Agnes gave Tess a slight push in the direction of the kitchen just as Alice came through the door.

'I thought I heard voices out here. Hello, Agnes. I've a pot of tea ready, but you'll enjoy it better if you take your coat off and sit down.'

'Thanks, Mrs Maguire.' Agnes pushed open the living room door and stopped abruptly. Over her shoulder Tess could see the reason for her surprise. Stretched out in the armchair close to the fireside, toasting his stocking feet, Dan Thompson looked very much at home. Very much at home, indeed!

He had obviously been unaware of their arrival and quickly rose from his seat in embarrassment. 'Hello, Agnes. Hi, Tess. I didn't realise you were home. Was the film any good?'

'It was smashing, Mr Thompson. A real weepy.'

'It wouldn't have suited me at all then, Agnes. I've enough to cry about in real life. I'd rather have a good old western any day.' Seeing Alice hovering in the hall with a loaded tray, he hastened over to relieve her of her burden. 'Here, let me take that.'

Tess stood speechless; the shock of seeing Dan so much at home had stunned her. Alice looked at her daughter anxiously. What on earth was the matter with her? Surely she hadn't expected her to say good night to Dan at the door? If so she was being rather childish.

Not in any hurry at all to leave now, Agnes removed her coat and placed it over the arm of the settee.

'You sit down, Mam. I'll pour the tea.'

When she handed her mother a cup, Tess received a reproachful look. Agnes was perched on the edge of the settee, eyes agog, not missing a single thing. Why on earth had Tess asked her back? She might have guessed Dan Thompson would be here. The conversation was general and when Agnes could delay no longer she rose reluctantly to her feet.

'I'll have to be going now,' she said regretfully. 'They'll all be wondering what's happened to me.'

Dan slipped his feet into his shoes and quickly tied the laces. He could see that Tess was sitting tight lipped and sullen, looking down into her cup. Alice and he had had a wonderful time and he didn't want to spoil it by a confrontation with her daughter, the mood *she* was in. It was time to leave while he was still ahead. 'I'll walk down with you, Agnes.'

Leaning close to Alice he said softly, for her ears only, 'Thank you for a lovely evening. I hope we can repeat it soon. I'll give you a ring.'

*   *   *

Agnes slanted a sideways glance at Dan as she trotted along trying to keep up with his long strides down Springfield Road. He was so engrossed in thought he seemed unaware of her presence or her efforts to keep pace with him. She confirmed in her mind that he did indeed resemble Cary Grant. The same straight nose, dark brown eyes and cleft chin. Not much older than Cary, he was a very handsome man. Strange that Jack didn't in the least bit resemble him. He must take after his mother.

Suddenly aware of her covert scrutiny, he turned a rueful smile on her and slowed down. 'Sorry, Agnes. I was away in a world of my own there.'

'Don't worry about me, Mr Thompson. I need the exercise,' she joked. 'I'm sure you have a lot on your mind,' she added daringly, with a wise nod of the head.

A grin split his face and his eyes twinkled. 'Now I wonder what you think I have on my mind? Mm? Pray tell me.'

They had arrived at the corner of Violet Street, and, glad to be reprieved, Agnes said, 'Thanks for walking me home. Good night, Mr Thompson.' With a wave of her hand she scurried off down the street.

As he continued on down the road, Dan let his mind return to his immediate problem. Tess had been annoyed when she saw him in her home tonight. Very annoyed, in fact! But he and Alice weren't youngsters. They couldn't be expected to say good night at the corner when they both had homes to go to. Not that he wanted to invite Alice into his house – in the warmth and comfort of her home he realised how primitive his own house really was – but he had no intention of standing at a corner as if they were a pair of teenagers.

He was also very much aware that he wanted Alice, and not just as a friend. She would be the ideal partner to spend the rest of his days with. If he sought a divorce from Anne would Alice agree to marry him in a register office? Anything but marriage would be out of the question, but he couldn't see her consenting to marry him outside the Catholic church. Perhaps given time, and with a bit of friendly persuasion, he could wear her down. The biggest stumbling block would be Tess.

As he approached his house he could see light showing through the blind and expected to see Jack and Colette when he opened the vestibule door. To his surprise, it was his wife who sat facing Jack by the fireside. Before he could recover from the shock, Colette's voice called from the scullery.

'Would you like a cup of tea, Mr Thompson?'

'No. No, thank you, Colette, I've just had one.' His eyes were still fastened on Anne's face. 'What are you doing here?' he snapped.

Jack sprang to his feet and said warningly, 'Now, Dad, I invited Mam in.'

Anne smiled sweetly at Dan. 'We met in the Clock Bar and they told me they plan to marry in August, so I came down with them to discuss the wedding arrangements.'

He wondered if her toy boy had been with her in the pub, but refrained from asking. 'What's them getting married got to do with you?'

Anne collapsed back in the chair in a show of mock surprise. 'Don't act silly, Dan. I'm Jack's *mother*, after all is said and done.'

'You forgot that for a long time, didn't you?'

'Well I'm here now and I'm not going away again.'

'Dad . . .' Jack sounded nervous and Dan dragged his attention from Anne and turned to hear what his son had to say. 'Dad, Colette needs someone to talk things over with and Mam's the ideal person.'

'What about her own mother? Or her grannie for that matter?'

'Remember, Dad, her family live in Omagh.'

'That's not the other side of the world, son. I'm sure her parents would be willing to travel up now and again to make plans. They might even want the wedding to be held in their own parish church in Omagh, for all you know.'

'That's where you're wrong, Dan,' Anne piped in. 'Colette was telling me tonight that her parents don't want her to marry our Jack.'

Colette let out a wail of dismay; she had told Anne this in confidence and now here she was, blabbering her big mouth off already. She cringed as both son and father turned looks of amazement on her.

'Is this true?' Jack managed to gasp.

'No!' The consternation in her voice was acute as she threw Anne a withering glare of pure hatred. 'It's not true! They just want me to wait a year or two in case I change my mind. They think I'm too young and don't know what I'm doing.'

Dan could see how upset she was and turned his wrath on Anne. 'Get out! Go on. Get out of here before I throw you out.'

Anne slowly shrugged into her coat and with an airy wave in the direction of her son and Colette left the house. Dan followed her out on to the pavement, not wanting the others to hear what he had to say.

'If you cause any more mischief I swear I won't rest until I make you pay. That wee girl in there is devastated, so she is. You're nothing but a bloody troublemaker.'

'And whose fault is that?'

His jaw dropped and he asked, 'What do you mean by that? No doubt you're about to lay the blame at my door.'

'It's all your fault! If he had a trade he would be more acceptable to her parents. She has a future in banking ahead of her. What has Jack got? A dead end job. That's what!'

'If she loves him it won't make any difference what he works at.'

'Oh, no? Well that's where you're wrong! Didn't you see the effect it had on him? He was gutted, so he was. And another thing, in case you've forgotten . . . love doesn't pay the bills.'

'And that pleases you, does it? Why did you blurt it out like that? Obviously she hasn't told him how her parents feel.'

'He's better knowing where he stands,' she said stubbornly.

'That's only your opinion, and that doesn't count for much. You had two wages coming in and you still weren't satisfied.'

'Oh, give my head peace. You never did think much of my opinion anyway. Perhaps if you'd paid more attention to how I felt we would still be together today.'

'Perish the thought,' he snarled. 'I know now what a narrow escape I had *and* I'd like a divorce.'

She drew back, eyes widening with surprise. 'Isn't that a bit drastic? Are you going to let me telling Jack the truth separate us for good?'

'No, actually, I had already made up my mind to divorce you before this happened. I can, you know. It was you who walked out on me and ran off with another man leaving a young son behind.'

'It'll not be as easy as you think! I'll fight you every inch of the way. And what about the church? How are you going to reconcile your conscience with that?'

'Don't you worry about me. I'll manage. I just want you out of my life for good.' He turned on his heel, leaving her glaring after him.

Inside, there was no sign of Jack. Colette sat huddled on the edge of the settee, arms clasped around her as if for comfort. Big tear-washed eyes looked at him in bewilderment.

'How could she be so cruel? I spoke to her in confidence. There was no need for Jack to know.'

He sat down beside her, and put an arm across her shoulders. 'So it's true then? They don't want you to marry him?'

She shrugged. 'It doesn't make any difference to me what they want, so I can't see why Jack should be so upset.'

'It's his pride that's hurt. He'll get over it. I think you should give him a chance to cool down, love. So wipe those tears up and get yourself off home. Everything will pan out in due course. Just wait and see.'

Inwardly he wasn't so optimistic. She was very young; would her parents be able to put a stop to her wedding plans? He didn't know how these things worked. Hell roast Anne and her interference. He wished she would go and fall under a bus and give them all some peace of mind. God forbid.

Tess washed the crockery and her mother dried them and put them carefully away. It was she who broke the long, tense silence between them.

'Did you have to bring Agnes home with you, tonight

of all nights?' she asked reproachfully. 'Giving her something to gossip about.'

Angrily Tess rounded on her. 'Why should you care who knows about your *platonic* relationship – as you so nicely put it – with him?'

'Because, although it is innocent, people always think the worst in these situations and we intended to be as discreet as possible.'

'So you intend slinking about as if you're ashamed of being seen together. Is that what you're saying?'

'Actually, I was thinking of you. You seem so concerned about us.'

'I take it he's talked you into seeing him again then?'

'And why not? We both enjoyed this evening very much.'

'That's not the point, Mam. You're forgetting he's a married man!'

'Listen, girl! My conscience is clear and I'm not going to let you or anyone else for that matter dictate terms to me. So there! Now, if you'll excuse me, I don't want to discuss this any further . . . I'm off to bed.'

Tess banked the fire and checked the windows and doors automatically. Easter was fast approaching; perhaps her mother's trip to see Malachy and Rose would give her time to think and maybe see the folly of her ways. But then, that holiday break hadn't been mentioned for some time now. Did her mother not intend going after all?

She wished her Uncle Malachy's phone was sorted out. It had been out of order for some time now, and you'd think with the farm being so isolated the PO would give him some priority. Instead, it seemed it was well down the pecking order for repairs. Tomorrow she would write to him and ask him to somehow get to a phone and ring her mother and persuade her to keep her promise.

Two days after Tess posted the letter the phone rang. It was her uncle calling to tell her that at long last the line had been repaired. 'Rose was sick of running up the lane every time she wanted a word with me, so I gave in and put some pressure on the PO. I didn't think it would do any good, but it must have worked. It was connected again last week. I intended phoning earlier to let you know, but one of the ewes died and we are having to bottle-feed her two lambs. I've been so busy, what with one thing and another, I never got round to it.'

'I'm sorry to hear about the ewe, Uncle Malachy.'

'Oh, well, these things do happen and I'm not complaining. Far from it. Things could be a lot worse. I'm just explaining why I didn't phone sooner.' He lowered his voice and said softly, 'Can I speak freely?'

'Yes. Mam's out at the shops.'

'Your letter has me awfully worried. What on earth's the matter with Alice?'

'She's seeing a married man.' What she considered words of doom produced a great roar of laughter down the line that almost deafened her.

Stifling his mirth, Malachy said, 'Ah now, Tess, what do you think I can do about that?'

'It's wrong, Uncle Malachy! It's a mortal sin, so it is. You'll have to talk some sense into her.'

'Tess . . . love, I must remind you it's the nineteen sixties and things are changing dramatically.'

'I know that! But that doesn't make it right. You know what Mam is like. I don't want her to get hurt.'

'Don't distress yourself so much, Tess. When Alice

comes to visit us at Easter I'll try to broach the subject. I take it you'll not want her to know you've been discussing her affairs with me?'

'Oh, God, no! And thank you for being so understanding. But you see, the problem is, I don't think she intends visiting you at Easter.'

'Oh, but she must!' He sounded aghast. 'Rose will be so disappointed if she doesn't. She has been doing all sorts in preparation for her visit.'

'Tell Rose to phone Mam and insist that she comes to Carlingford. Tell her to put pressure on her and in no circumstances to let her off the hook. Look, I hear Mam at the door now. I'll put her on and you can tell her all the latest country gossip. That'll please her no end,' she informed him, tongue in cheek. 'Don't forget to get Rose to phone!'

Alice paused at the door to shake the rain off her umbrella. Tess hurried forward and took it from her.

'Mam, it's Uncle Malachy on the phone. The lines have been repaired at long last. He wants a word with you.'

Alice walked slowly to the phone. Tess could see her mother was reluctant to speak to her brother. She closed the umbrella and passed along the hall to put it in the kitchen sink to drip dry.

'But now, Malachy, I mightn't be able to come at Easter after all. I've a lot on my plate, you know.'

At these words Tess crossed her fingers and said a quiet prayer. Please, God, let Mam be persuaded to go to Carlingford out of temptation's way.

She reached for the kettle and half filled it with water for a cup of tea. When Alice entered the kitchen she looked at her inquiringly.

'I've told him I can't go, Tess.'

'Why? You were all for it at Christmas, so you were.'

'I know, but talk's cheap. And after all, it was just talk. You know how I hate the countryside.'

'You sounded very sincere about wanting to go, Mam. Besides, it will do you a world of good to get away for a while.'

'You're just saying that hoping that I'll split up with Dan. Isn't that it?'

'That's not true! I was delighted when you told Uncle Malachy and Rose that you'd visit them at Easter. You know that for a fact, and that was long before Dan Thompson arrived on the scene.'

Alice's voice took on a coaxing note. 'Tess . . . I'd much rather stay at home with you.'

'Me? Hah, don't make me laugh.'

'All right. You and Dan.'

'And nothing I can say will make you change your mind?'

'No . . . nothing. My mind's made up,' Alice replied defiantly.

It was Rose who was the deciding factor. She phoned and put the thumbscrews on, lamenting how hard she had worked to get her cottage ready, hoping Alice might stay for a day or two with her before going home. Telling her how she planned to take her new friend round all the local farming community.

'You just have to come, Alice. I would never dream of letting you down if the positions were reversed. Please say you'll come . . . please. I won't be able to show my face round here again if you don't come, not after all I've told them about you and Tess.'

In the face of all this determination how could Alice possibly refuse? She told Dan when she saw him that

Thursday night and was pleased when he agreed with her that it would indeed be very selfish of her not to go, but added that she must spend some extra time with him before she left. Two extra outings were arranged and Alice was inclined to think that everything had worked out for the best.

Chapter Seven

Spy Wednesday dawned wet and miserable. Alice stood at the work room window gazing up at the heavy, dark clouds hanging low over the rooftops. 'You said the weather was going to improve,' she cried plaintively. 'That sky doesn't look very promising to me.'

'Give it a chance, Mam. It's early yet, and the weather forecast did say that it would brighten up later on.'

'I don't know why I let Rose talk me into going to Carlingford,' Alice grumbled. 'I must need my head examining.'

'Because she has obviously gone to a lot of trouble getting everything in order for you coming, that's why! It would have been very unkind to let her down. Besides, a couple of weeks will soon fly in.'

Alice reared back in alarm. 'A couple of weeks? Ah, no. I've told Malachy I'd only be able to stay one week and one week it'll be.'

'We'll see. You might change your mind when you've been there a few days. You might even meet a rich, eligible farmer,' Tess teased, and was rewarded by a dirty look from her mother.

'You make it sound as if I'm on the lookout for the first presentable thing in trousers to come along,' she hissed.

'Well, aren't you?' Tess dared to joke.

'Indeed I am not,' Alice cried indignantly. 'Dan and I are just good friends. As you well know.'

Having used her absence in Carlingford for a week as an excuse for extra outings with Alice, Dan had persuaded her to accompany him to the cinema the previous Saturday night. Not wanting to play gooseberry, Tess had made herself scarce before they returned home. Now, remembering the long silences and low-pitched voices, she was sceptical about their *friendship*. Of course they could have been keeping quiet so as not to awaken her. Chance would be a fine thing, she thought derisively.

'Then two weeks won't do you any harm,' she assured her mother.

'*One* week,' Alice insisted stubbornly.

'All right! One week then. Here's the taxi.'

Tess grabbed her mother's suitcase, leaving her to carry the holdall. This was one of the times she wished she could drive. It was so costly to take taxis everywhere.

'Where to, miss?' the driver inquired.

'The bus station, please,' Tess informed him.

Ten minutes later they were unloading Alice's luggage from the boot. After paying the taxi fare Tess looked round to see where they would have to wait for the bus, but could see no sign with Newry on it. Alice had to get the bus to Newry and then a connection to Carlingford. Leaving her disgruntled mother standing with the luggage at her feet, Tess approached the reception booth. The assistant pointed to a bay where a single-decker bus was parked and Tess hastened back to Alice. 'The bus is here already. It must be early. Come on, hurry up, before it takes off without you.'

'If only,' Alice muttered bad-temperedly.

'What did you say?'

'Nothing.'

'I heard,' Tess ground out between clenched teeth, her own temper flaring. 'How can you be so ungrateful? Everybody is falling over themselves trying to help you.'

'Calm down, Tess. I never asked or wanted anyone to help me. Besides, the driver isn't even in the bus yet. It won't go off on its own, you know. It will probably sit there for another half hour. And mind you, I'm not boarding until it's ready to go.' Alice, trailing behind with the holdall, was irritated at her daughter for rushing her off her feet. In her opinion there was no need for all this haste.

They joined the small queue and, seeing the resentful scowl on her mother's face suddenly change into a wide grin, Tess turned to find out the cause of the sudden transformation. Striding across the depot was Dan Thompson.

'He said he'd come to see me off, but I told him there was no need,' her mother spluttered, pink-cheeked but obviously delighted to see him. And neither was there any need, Tess thought resentfully. As far as she could see, he could only complicate things.

Dan towered smilingly over them. Dressed in his work clothes and cement-splattered boots, he still managed to receive admiring glances from a few of the women in the queue, as they openly appraised him and mentally approved what they saw.

It never ceased to amaze Tess the way he managed to attract women's attention. Oh, he was attractive, as Agnes had rightly pointed out to her. A Cary Grant lookalike. He was a middle-aged man, yet even younger women openly admired him. She herself wouldn't dream of staring at men old enough to be her father. Still, she was inclined to think that he was totally unaware of his magnetism to the opposite sex; couldn't care less what they thought of him.

Except Alice. All of his attention was hers. He locked eyes with her and said softly, 'I couldn't let you go without saying goodbye, Alice.'

'It's very kind of you,' Alice simpered, 'but I told you not to bother.' She was looking at Dan with cow's eyes. That was the only way Tess could describe her mother's demeanour at that moment, and she felt like grabbing her and giving her a good shaking. It disgusted her to see a grown woman like her mother behaving like a young girl. It was totally unbecoming of her!

Now she muttered ungraciously, 'You shouldn't have come, Dan.'

'Why not? I won't see your mother for a whole week.'

'Two weeks, as a matter of fact.'

Dan shot her a startled glance, then turned an inquiring look on Alice. 'Two weeks?'

'She's having you on. I'm only staying one week.' Alice glared at her daughter resentfully and assured him, 'You can count on it, Dan.'

The doors of the bus opened and the queue shuffled forward. Alice hung back, reluctance in her every step. Annoyed, Tess urged her. 'Come on, Mam, if you want to get a decent seat.'

'Leave me alone, Tess. I don't care where I sit,' Alice snapped.

Dan reached for the luggage. 'Look, before you two come to blows, I'll see her on to the bus, Tess. Maybe you'd like to go on home?'

He laughed aloud when she retorted, 'No, thank you. I'll wait and make sure she gets on that bus.'

He shook his head and teased, 'Oh, ye of little faith.'

Aware that the other travellers on the bus were being entertained by the spectacle the trio was creating, Tess muttered in exasperation, 'Never mind! Just get on with it.' Giving her mother a quick hug, she said, 'Don't forget to phone and let me know you've arrived safely.'

It was with a sigh of relief that she at last waved the bus out of sight. 'Thanks for your help, Dan. For a moment there, I thought she was going to renege.'

He silently agreed with her and smiled, knowing full well that it wouldn't have taken much to persuade Alice to change her mind. 'Can I buy you a coffee?'

Tess thought about it. Why not? She wasn't in any hurry to get back home; only cleaning and tidying up awaited her. 'That would be nice, thank you, Dan. But have you not to get back to work?'

'I'm making a late start this morning. In case the bus went out late or something. You know what I mean.'

They debated where to go, but when she suggested the Ulster Milk Bar he demurred and said it was too popular and would be crowded. 'Besides, I couldn't go in there dressed like this.' He gestured to his work clothes. 'I was thinking more along the lines of a working man's café. That is, if you don't mind?'

'The Ulster Milk Bar won't be too busy this early,' she objected. 'And it's really only your boots that look dirty. Please? I love their frothy coffee. My mouth is watering just thinking about it.'

He laughed and gave in gracefully. 'All right, if that's how much it means to you.'

They turned and headed in the direction of Castle Junction, and a short time later they were seated in the Ulster Milk Bar. 'Would you like a cake or a scone, or anything else to eat, Tess?'

'No, thank you, coffee will be fine.'

She watched as he went to the counter and gave their order. The girl behind the bar greeted him with a wide grin, obviously smitten. The girl, or young woman, whom Tess judged to be about thirty, was actually fawning over him. She was attractive in her own right, so why did she get on like that over a middle-aged stranger? Or was he a stranger to her? Was she the reason he didn't want to come here in the first place? Even if she was, what business was it of Tess's whom he chatted up? What a suspicious mind I'm developing, Tess thought, disgusted with herself.

Catching Tess's watchful eye the girl gave her a bright friendly smile and winked at her before turning to serve another customer. Tess looked away in embarrassment. The girl probably thought Dan was her sugar daddy. How did he manage it? It seemed to require no effort at all on his part. And how come Anne had left him and no other woman had managed to hook him since, if he was as wonderful as he seemed? Did he play the field? Was her mother just another conquest for him? All sorts of unsavoury thoughts raced through her troubled mind as she sat watching him.

He set her coffee down in front of her and took a chair facing her. 'Tess, I want to have a chat with you about me and your mother.'

She lifted the cup and tilted it in his direction. 'Thank you.' She eyed him over the rim. 'Fire away.'

He grimaced. 'Imagine, now I have your undivided attention I don't know where to start.'

'Mam always told me the beginning is the best place to start.' She smiled. 'Especially if it is something unpleasant you have to say.'

'Your mother is, of course, quite right. But you see,

I don't really know where it began.' He eyed her intently as he confessed, 'I don't know just when I fell in love with Alice and knew I had to have her for my wife.'

She managed to place the cup carefully back on the saucer without spilling a drop. Straightening her back in the chair, she reminded him, 'You're a married man, remember?'

'That's what I want to talk to you about. If I get a divorce, do you think Alice would consent to marry me in a register office?'

'Never!' The word spat from her mouth with such venom that it startled him. 'She's of the opinion that if Catholics marry outside the church, they aren't married in the eyes of God.'

Regaining his composure he leaned across the table. 'And you, Tess. Is that what you think?' he asked earnestly.

'It's not me you're wanting to marry,' she retaliated softly.

'Ah, I know . . . but if your mother asked for your opinion, what would you say?'

'Look, Dan, I know my mother inside out. If, in a moment of sheer madness, she actually married you in a register office, she would never forgive herself and would regret it till her dying day. I'm sure you'll agree that's no recipe for a happy marriage, but that's the type of woman she is, I'm afraid.'

'So, that means you wouldn't back me, then?'

She shook her head. 'No, I'm afraid not. I wouldn't encourage my mother to do anything that I knew to be against her better principles. It would bring her too much heartache in the long run.' Suddenly suspicious, she asked, 'Have you already discussed this with my mother? Has she said something to give you hope and now you're testing my reaction?'

He shook his head sadly. 'No. I wouldn't dare suggest anything at the moment. I'm afraid she might send me packing.'

'I did warn Mam that there was no future for you two together.'

'Tess, talk's cheap and you can go into something with the best of intentions and still get your fingers burnt. One can't foresee how things will turn out. I'm hoping for a small miracle. I do admit I want your mother for my wife. I wish now I'd given Anne a divorce years ago when she asked for it. At least I'd be a free man today.'

Reaching for her handbag, Tess rose abruptly to her feet. 'Look, Dan, I can't discuss anything like this with you. It's just not right. I don't want to be involved in your private affairs.'

He was on his feet in a flash. 'I'm sorry, Tess. I shouldn't have said that. Please sit down and finish your coffee. We'll talk about something else. All right?'

Slowly she sank down on her chair, still clasping the bag on her lap as if ready for flight at the slightest provocation. She eyed him warily. 'Fair enough.'

He was quiet for some moments, his mind still on Alice. Then, making a great effort, he asked, 'Did you know our Jack will be twenty-one next Thursday?'

She smiled faintly. 'How could I? I've seen very little of him since Colette came along.'

He grimaced. 'I can't seem to say anything to you without putting my big foot in it.'

'Oh, I'm not offended,' she quickly assured him. 'Far from it. That episode in my life is over and done with long ago, I'm happy to say.'

He eyed her intently and saw she meant it. 'I'm glad to hear that, Tess. One of these days you'll meet some nice young lad who'll make you happy.'

'So it is you who's spouting off to Mam about me needing to meet suitable young men?' she accused with a twinkle in her eye.

He had the grace to look ashamed. 'I'll use any argument to win Alice over. So you've been warned, Tess.'

'Dan, I've nothing against you personally. I only want what's best for Mam.'

'I know that, love. And in my heart I don't blame you. But I've promised not to discuss that with you, so to get back to Jack . . . he has always wanted a motorbike so I've bought him one for his birthday. A second-hand one, a 250cc Triumph. It's a couple of years old but in very good nick. The guy who owns the repair shed at the corner of our street has polished and cleaned it and it looks like new. A friend of mine who works in that yard at the bottom of the street – you know, on the bend a couple of doors from us – well, he's keeping it in the yard, out of sight, until the big day. So you see, Jack's in for a big surprise. He knows nothing whatsoever about it.'

Tess had to smile at the enthusiasm in his voice. 'He'll be dead chuffed, so he will,' she said softly.

'I suggested having a bit of a do for him but he wasn't interested, so I'm taking Colette and him out for a meal and he thinks that's his present. I can't wait to see his face next Thursday morning when he sees it sitting outside our front door.'

Tess looked at this kind, thoughtful man and wished he was free to marry her mother. He would make a nice stepdad. But even if he got a divorce from Anne it could never be.

She drained her cup and he said quickly, 'Have another one.'

'I can't, Dan. I have some shopping to do before I go home,' she excused herself.

[143]

He rose and accompanied her outside. Taking her hand between his he bent down and gazed earnestly into her face, saying solemnly, 'I've enjoyed your company, Tess. I always do. I think you and Alice and I could all live very happily together. Think about it, love . . . goodbye for now.'

Tess spent the next hour shopping in High Street and Ann Street before crossing Castle Junction and catching the bus at the bottom of Castle Street. She thought of her mother on her way to Carlingford, resentful and bitter. Had she done the right thing persuading her to go? She knew that Malachy and Rose would see that she enjoyed herself while she was there, and fervently hoped they would be able to persuade her to stay for two weeks. But would it do any good in the long run? Dan was obviously a man on a mission, and by the sound of him would not be deterred. Not by Tess or anyone else for that matter.

She sighed and her mind turned to Jack. So he'd be twenty-one next week! And he would be a married man by the end of the summer. A lot had happened since she had first met him that night at the Rolling Stones concert, but her elusive Mr Right had yet to put in an appearance.

Leaving the bus at the junction of Springfield Road, and crossing over, Tess spotted Agnes coming out of the post office, accompanied by a man Tess did not recognise.

'Hi, Agnes,' she called.

'Tess! Where have you been?' Agnes cried, hurrying to meet her, the stranger following her with long loping strides. 'I've been ringing you all morning.'

'I've been down at the bus station seeing Mam off to

Carlingford. Remember? Why, what's all the fuss?'

'I forgot about your mam going away over Easter. That's great! It means you're free.' She indicated her companion. 'I want you to meet Dominic Sullivan. Remember I told you he was coming home from America to be Dennis's best man?'

'Of course. Pleased to meet you, Dominic.'

Thrusting a hand towards her, he exclaimed in a slow American drawl, 'The pleasure is all mine. Agnes has been telling me all about you, but she didn't say how attractive you are.'

Tess had just been thinking that he was quite handsome in a rugged sort of way and could feel the colour creeping up her neck at the compliment.

Agnes laughed at her embarrassment. 'He's a terrible flirt, Tess. He can't stop the compliments dripping off his tongue. He's even got Mam eating out of his hand. So don't pay any attention to him. The reason I've been trying to get in touch with you is, Dennis and Marie, Joan and her husband and Tony and I are going out for a meal and then round to the Orpheus afterwards on Saturday night. We've booked a table for seven o'clock, and we would like you to join us.'

'Oh, I don't think I'll . . .' Tess flailed about in her mind for the right words.

Softly, in that lovely drawl of his, Dominic interrupted. 'Agnes neglected to say I'm also going and I need a partner, Tess. Please take pity on me. I'd sure be honoured to have you along.' Dominic held her eye and she found herself unable to look away. Her head nodded as if of its own volition and he said, 'Thank you. I look forward to seeing you again.' He turned to Agnes. 'If you'll excuse me, Agnes, I'll leave you two ladies to get on with your business now and push off down town.'

[145]

'Dominic, there is no need for you to rush off. Tess doesn't bite, you know.'

He laughed. 'She can nibble my ear any time she likes. But really, I want to walk into town and have a look round. I've some bits and pieces I need. I'll see you later.' The tousled blond head inclined in their direction and then he headed off down the Falls Road.

They watched him for some moments – tight blue hip-hugging jeans, leather jacket and tan-coloured suede boots – then Agnes turned to her friend. 'Isn't he something else, then?'

'He sure is. He stands out like a sore thumb in those clothes. You'd think he'd just got off the stagecoach.' Tess laughed and hoped Agnes wasn't aware just how much he had affected her. 'Anyway, madam, shouldn't you be at work?'

'I've asked for some time off. I don't go back until Monday week.'

'How did the rehearsal go?'

'Great! Dominic arrived on Sunday and we had the rehearsal on Monday night and everything went smoothly. I bet he'll look great in high hat and tails. I wish you were coming to the reception, Tess. You would be great company for him.'

'I don't think he'll be stuck for company. The girls will be round him like wasps round a jam jar. And don't worry about me not coming to the reception. I'll come down to the church and have a look at all the finery. I hope the weather picks up for you all.'

'So do I.'

'Meanwhile, I must dash. I took down all the heavy curtains to get them dry cleaned and they came back yesterday. I want to hang them all today if possible.'

'I'll come up and give you a hand.'

'Are you sure? Won't you be needed at home?'

'I'm glad to get out for a while, Tess. Roll on Monday! I'll be happy when this wedding is over and done with.'

'If that's the case, I'll certainly be glad of your help. So let's go.'

Tess had shaken out the curtains and spread them over the banister and beds to remove any wrinkles. Four pairs in all to be hung, but undaunted the two girls got stuck in. The curtains were off the biggest windows and very heavy and awkward to control. The matching pelmets were a right pain to work with. Tess was glad that Agnes had offered her assistance. She would never have managed on her own.

Some time later they stepped back, hands on hips, and examined their handiwork. Tess said, 'I think you deserve more than a cup of tea after all that hard work. Will you let me treat you to a fish supper later on?'

'That sounds great. I'll nip home now and meet you on the corner about seven. Will that be all right?'

'Smashing. I'll see you there.'

They decided to go to Johnny Long's, down behind the Ritz cinema, for a change and it was while they were waiting for their order that Tess questioned Agnes. 'Did you know that Jack will be twenty-one next Thursday?'

'Yes, Tony mentioned it. He's surprised Dan isn't having a bit of a do for him.'

'Oh, Dan told me he wanted to throw a party but Jack turned down the idea, so he's bought him a smashing present instead.'

'Oh, what did he buy him?'

'I'm afraid I can't say in case you let it slip to Tony and he tells Jack. You see, it's a surprise. Jack knows nothing about it.'

'I see. I thought perhaps the reason was that Dan was a bit short of cash now he has a woman to spend his money on,' Agnes said slyly.

'If you mean my mam, I wouldn't say he's spending a fortune on her.'

'Ah, but he might be making plans for the future, Tess. He knows your mam would never consider living in Spinner Street.'

'You seem to forget, he's a married man, Agnes.'

'Do you think that really matters in this day and age?'

'Yes. As a matter of fact I do.'

'Ah well, everybody is not as strait-laced as you, Tess. Your mother deserves some happiness. She's been a widow far too long.'

'Do you think I don't know that? I'm sure she could have had many a man while I was growing up, but she didn't seem interested. Her and my dad were very close from what I hear, and I honestly think she wasn't interested in any other men . . . until now, that is! Sometimes I wish I'd never met Jack Thompson, then Mam wouldn't have met Dan. In fact *most* times I wish I'd never met him. He's brought me nothing but misery since day one.'

'Ever heard tell of fate, Tess? If it is meant to be, it was just waiting in the wings to happen, whether or not you had made Jack's acquaintance.'

Their fish suppers arrived and all else was forgotten as they tucked in.

A shadow falling across the table brought raised eyes to rest on Dominic Sullivan. Weighed down with parcels, he stood at their table.

'I was over in the Crown bar to sample their Guinness and then dandered round here to see if this chip shop was still open for business. I couldn't believe my eyes when I popped in and saw you two ladies sitting here.' He gave Agnes a reproachful look. 'You didn't mention you were coming here this evening.'

Agnes shrugged and pointed her fork towards Tess. 'Blame her. She's treating me.' Her voice was abrupt and his eyebrows rose fractionally.

'Mind if I join you?' He kept his gaze on Agnes, waiting for her response, and only when she said 'Be our guest' did he look questioningly at Tess.

She nodded her consent. Dominic tucked his parcels under the table and went to the counter to place his order. Tess looked suspiciously at her friend. 'Do I detect some sort of tension between you two?'

'Don't be silly,' Agnes muttered bad-temperedly.

During the meal, Tess watched them closely, but everything seemed normal. There was lots of banter and laughter and Tess found Dominic very easy to get on with. She put all ideas of animosity between Agnes and him from her mind. Her imagination had been working overtime lately. She would be delighted to accompany this man to the Orpheus on Saturday night.

Still not very happy with her lot, Alice descended from the bus at Carlingford in bad humour to find Malachy and Rose waiting for her. They were so pleased to see her and welcomed her with such warmth that she felt ashamed of her reluctance to visit them.

'I'm preparing lunch in my house. Is that all right with you, Alice?'

'That will be lovely, Rose. Thank you very much.'

A huge grin split Rose's face and she cried merrily, 'Right, Malachy, you see to the baggage and we'll be on our way.'

By the time they climbed into the Land-Rover Alice

was in a happier frame of mind. After all, she consoled herself, a week was no time at all and didn't they say absence made the heart grow fonder?

Rose's home was a whitewashed, two-storey detached house not too far back from the main road. She explained to Alice that her farm was about half a mile further up the lane that ran past the side of the house and that she had very little to do with the running of it these days. Her son and his wife were living there now and although, when necessary, Rose helped out, she now left the actual day to day running of the farm to them, as they would inherit it one day.

'Don't you get lonely living here on your own?' Alice asked tentatively, following her friend through the gate and down the garden path to the front door, while Malachy parked the Land-Rover at the rear of the house.

'Not a bit of it! I enjoy my own company and my two daughters bring their friends to visit the odd week-end when they've nothing better to do. And Malachy, when he's not too busy, comes round for a bit of a chin-wag. There always seems to be something for me to do, so you see I'm never too lonely.'

She led Alice into a big, sprawling, tastefully furnished room that ran the full length of the house. A turf fire burned brightly, throwing out welcome heat, and an open staircase ran up against the opposite wall.

'Oh, this is lovely,' Alice exclaimed.

Rose smiled in appreciation at her genuine praise. 'Thank you. I must confess I *am* proud of it. It wasn't like this when my husband was alive, mind you. More like a hovel, to tell you the truth. I was for ever on to him to get something done to it, so the girls could stay here when they came home from college. The farm-house is a bit on the small side, now they have grown up. However, he wouldn't hear tell of it. Said it would be a waste of good money. Oh dear, here's me rambling on and forgetting all about my guest. You'll be thinking I've no manners whatsoever, Alice. Here, give me your coat and make yourself at home, while I finish off the lunch.'

Alice chose one of the armchairs near the blazing fire, and sinking back into its comfortable depths she had a good old look around the room. The wood block floor was highly polished and good quality rugs were strategically positioned in front of the large sofa and easy chairs. The walls were adorned with watercolour prints, presumably of local sceneries. She recognised one of Carlingford Lough. A Welsh dresser graced the wall to the right of the fireplace and was home to a willow patterned dinner service. Under the staircase stood a large china cabinet. Two shelves displayed a number of beautiful porcelain figurines while the bottom shelf was cluttered with a variety of sporting trophies.

Malachy's voice broke into her musing. 'Rose has this room lovely, hasn't she? She's a real home-maker.'

Alice turned her head to where he stood at the door watching her. 'I didn't know you were there. She certainly has it beautiful. I take it this was once two rooms?' She nodded upwards to where an encased beam ran across the ceiling.

'Correct! Shortly after her husband's death, she got Seamus Corrigan, the local handyman, in. She had the partition wall pulled down, as you can see, and an extension built on at the back for a kitchen and dining room, through there.' He pointed to the door through which Rose had disappeared. 'The new bathroom is above the kitchen. She has been working hard putting the finishing touches to the house for your arrival.'

'It's all very nice. I had pictured you and Rose on adjoining farms.' Alice grimaced slightly, remembering how she was dreading muddy farmyards and yapping dogs.

As if reading her mind, Malachy said, 'Muddy yards and the like, eh, Alice? You'll be surprised when you see my farm. It's been modernised a lot since you last were here. I have only one dog now, Meg, and she's a bit long in the tooth. The worst you'll get from old Meg is a good sniffing.'

Alice grinned. 'We'll see. I'll reserve my opinion till I've run my beady eye over the place.'

Rose popped her head round the kitchen door. 'Lunch is almost ready. Perhaps you would like to freshen up first, Alice?' When Alice nodded, Rose said, 'The bathroom is upstairs at the end of the landing. You can't miss it.'

Alice returned from the very modern bathroom, full of praise. 'You really have a natural talent, Rose. Everything up there is just beautiful.'

'You're very kind, thank you, Alice. Sit here, please.'

Alice seated herself at the big pine table, which was laden with an assortment of dishes. 'There's enough here to feed an army!' She lifted up the lids of a few dishes for a quick peek while Rose's back was turned. 'And don't forget . . . it's a day of fast and abstinence today.'

'Why do you think there's no meat on the table, Alice? Rose is like you and abides strictly by the rules,' Malachy said drily.

The meal consisted of poached salmon, trout with a fine, crispy, golden coating dusted with salt and pepper, green salad and crusty bread, with different sauces and pickles. It was delicious and Alice was sincere when she said, 'That was absolutely mouth-watering, Rose. I really enjoyed it.'

'Those trout were caught early this morning,' her brother informed her.

'I could tell,' Alice assured him. 'I could taste the peaty freshness.'

After lunch they retired to the big room. 'You must have a drink before you go.' Rose sent Malachy an inquiring look. 'I'm afraid I don't have much of a selection. Just white wine and Bristol Cream.'

'White wine will be fine, thank you.'

'Will you pour, Malachy?'

Handing Alice a glass, Malachy laughed softly. 'You must be wondering why Rose is throwing me all sorts of queer looks, Alice. So let me put you in the picture. It's like this . . . she's hoping you'll stay here in the cottage with her for a few days. How do you feel about that?'

Taken unawares, Alice was tongue-tied. She had expected to go to her brother's farm first and after Easter stay with Rose for a couple of days before going home. 'Well now . . .'

Rose quickly came to her rescue. 'It was just a thought, Alice. Don't worry about it. I won't be offended if you don't want to stay.'

'Oh, but I'd love to.' She turned to her brother. 'That's if Malachy doesn't mind.'

'Actually I think it's a great idea. Rose will be able to take you out and about in her car while I'm busy during the day.'

Rose was grinning from ear to ear. 'Good! That's settled then. Would you fetch Alice's luggage and put it in the back bedroom, Malachy? You'll get a better view from there, Alice. Thanks for agreeing to stay. I'll take you in and around the town and show you some of our beauty spots.'

'I have been here before, Rose,' Alice reminded her softly, remembering that in her opinion there hadn't been much to Carlingford.

'Ah, but I know places you've never heard tell of.' Rose hugged her new-found friend close. 'I'm so glad you came.'

Before going into the house that night after work, Dan called in at the yard to have another look at the motor-bike. His friend, Bob Crosby, smiled and patiently closed the big double wooden doors so that there would be no spectators. Then he went to the far end of the yard and flipped the canvas cover from the bike.

The two men stood side by side gazing at the gleaming machine in silent admiration. 'She's a beaut, isn't she, Bob?'

'She certainly is.'

'Old Geordie did a grand job of cleaning it up. It looks almost new. Do you think Jack will like it?'

'He'll be very hard to please if he doesn't. I take it he'll be able to handle it all right?'

'I've no sweat about that. His cousin had an old wreck of a motorbike and they rode about everywhere on it. My heart used to be in my mouth watching them set off. He'll be able to manage this one all right.' Dan helped Bob cover it again and said, 'I'll get away on in now, Bob. Thanks for looking after it for me.'

'Any time, mate. It's no trouble at all.'

Jack was on the early shift and was in the scullery preparing the evening meal when his dad came in.

'Hi, son. How did your day go?'

'Ach, so-so. You know what it's like.'

He sounded so despondent Dan's heart went out to him. 'Hey! Why all the doom and gloom?'

With feet that dragged Jack entered the kitchen. 'Dad, there's something I have to tell you and you're not going to be one bit pleased.'

Dan's brows gathered in a frown. 'It must have something to do with your mother then, if you think I'm not going to like it.'

Jack nodded. 'She wanted to have a bit of a party for my birthday and I knew you wouldn't take kindly to it, so I said no.'

'I see.'

'I explained that you had suggested having a few friends round here for a party but I'd said I'd rather just go out for a meal.'

'And what had she to say about that?'

'It's not what she said . . . it's what she did. She's gone and bought me an expensive present.'

'How do you know?'

'She's given it to me already.'

A ball of anger gathered in Dan's chest. 'Has she forgotten your birthday is not till next Thursday?'

'She wanted me to be able to wear it over Easter, Dad. Please say you don't mind.'

Dan wanted to rant and rave at the way Anne was sticking her oar in and spoiling everything. She must have had a right old laugh at his expense, at the thought of him taking Jack and Colette out for a meal as a twenty-first birthday present. For two pins he'd take his son down to the yard after dinner and show him the motorbike; let him know he had also bought his son something worth talking about. He thought better of it. It was for his twenty-first birthday and that was the day he would first set eyes on it.

Curbing his temper he asked, 'And what is this expensive present she has bought you?'

'A lovely wristwatch, Dad. Would you like to see it?'

'Why not? It's obviously what she had in mind.'

'You're wrong there, Dad. Mam was afraid you might buy me a watch too. That's one of the reasons she gave it to me early. She was relieved when I told her you were just taking Colette and me out for a meal.'

'I'll bet she was,' Dan said sarcastically. 'Well now, where's this watch you're all excited over?'

Going to a drawer in the dresser, Jack removed a small dark blue box and handed it to his father. 'It's a beauty, Dad.'

'It is that, son,' Dan agreed when he opened the box and saw the slim, gold-faced watch with the black leather strap. 'An Avia calendar watch. It must have cost a pretty penny by the looks of it.'

'You won't be offended if I wear it, will you?'

'Not at all, son. I just wish I had thought of buying you something like that.' A smile tugged at Dan's lips when he thought of the treat Jack had in store.

'What are you smiling at?'

Jack's voice was suspicious and Dan hastened to reassure him. 'Nothing, honestly. I was just thinking how pleased your mother must have been when she handed it to you. I hope you and Colette will still come out for a meal with me?'

'Of course we will.' Jack looked embarrassed and muttered, 'That's another thing, Dad. Mam wants to know if she can come along too.'

'I can't believe her cheek,' Dan gasped, shaking his head in bewilderment. 'No! I'm sorry, son, but I must put my foot down. If she wants to take you out another time that's fine by me. I've booked a table for three at the International Hotel and I don't want your mother there. That's final! Now what's that lovely aroma I smell? Can we eat now and forget all about your mother?'

Jack stood gnawing at his bottom lip, at a loss as to how to change his father's mind regarding an invitation for his mother.

'Dad . . .' His voice trailed off. He was aware himself that it would be a disaster if his mother joined them. But what could he tell her? How would he be able to make her understand that he had no say in the matter; that it was his father's treat?

As he passed him in the scullery to wash his hands, Dan noted the strained expression on his son's face. He gave a short laugh. 'Don't worry about it, son. Your mother will understand that I don't want her to come with us. So sit down and enjoy your dinner.'

The meal was eaten in silence. Dan, angry that his wife was managing to take all the pleasure out of his plans, shovelled the food into his mouth. The smoked haddock tasted like cardboard. Jack was pushing his food around the plate and very little of it was reaching his mouth.

Unable to stand it any longer, Dan put down his knife and fork and gave his son a hard look. 'See here, Jack, if you would like your mother to take my place at the International Hotel with you and Colette, I'll understand. I will still pay for the treat, of course.'

Jack looked scandalised. 'You'll do no such thing! Colette would be mad. She still hasn't forgiven Mam for revealing how her parents feel about me.' He nodded his head determinedly. 'I'll just tell Mam she can't come.'

Relieved that his son hadn't jumped at the chance to decide in favour of his mother, Dan said, 'That's settled then. Eat your dinner, son.'

Appetite somewhat recovered, Jack smiled at his father and got stuck in. His mother must be made to understand that she couldn't invite herself along when it suited *her*; that she wasn't always welcome. He was beginning to realise that his father no longer had any future plans that included his wife, so the sooner he got used to the idea the better.

As if to prove him right, Dan said, 'Jack . . . Mrs Maguire is in Carlingford at the moment, but . . . she is expected to return next Wednesday. Would you be upset if I invited her to dine out with us on your birthday?' Jack kept his head down, staring at his plate. Dan hurried on. 'Forget it, son. It's unrealistic of me to expect you to accept Alice. Especially after me rejecting your mother.'

Raising his head, Jack looked him in the eye. 'No, Dad, you're quite right. I've finally accepted that the past is over and done with. By all means invite Mrs Maguire along. I only hope she doesn't hold it against me, after my fling with her daughter.'

Alice had thought that time would drag in Carlingford. Not one bit of it. The first day, taking a packed lunch, they set off early and headed for Omeath and then Newry. When Rose had suggested that they visit these two towns, Alice smothered a grimace of distaste. Hadn't she passed through both many a time and found them boring? How would they get a day in there?

However, under Rose's supervision they visited places Alice had never heard of. As they drove along with the lough shimmering on the right Rose explained that Carlingford was actually at the foot of Slieve Foye, the highest of the Cooley Mountains, and that these mountains were more jagged than the smooth lines of the

Mournes distinctively visible across the lough, the contrast being due to the different rock types that made up the mountains, formed as molten magma cooled down after volcanic eruptions millions of years ago. Alice began to view her surroundings through different eyes. Everywhere it seemed was steeped in history and Rose soon had her asking questions and wanting to learn more about the neighbouring countryside.

Near Newry, situated at the head of Carlingford Lough, they had a picnic close to the historic Gap of the North and as they sat in the warm sun Rose told Alice that in the twelfth century St Malachy had founded an abbey in Newry.

'How come you know so much history?'

'Don't forget I was born and reared here. It's only natural that I should know all about it.'

'You make me feel so ignorant,' Alice complained.

'Ah, now, don't talk like that. I'm sure you know more about Belfast and surrounding areas than I could ever imagine.'

'Well, I suppose you're right. I know this much . . . in future I'll find out all I can about the places I visit.'

Next Rose headed the car in the direction of Warrenpoint. Just before entering the town she turned into a car park so that Alice could visit Narrow Water Castle, built in 1570. Their next port of call was Warrenpoint itself, where they spent some time, and Alice learned a lot more history before they headed home.

They arrived back quite late and after a quick meal relaxed in front of the fire happy and contented, gabbling away as if they had known each other for years. On Friday Rose was surprised when Alice was a bit subdued when she suggested they should go to Dundalk.

'We don't have to go anywhere today if you'd rather stay at home,' she stressed.

'It's not that I don't want to go, Rose. It's just . . . well, it's Good Friday, and I feel I should be going to church to do the Way of the Cross.'

Relieved, Rose quickly reassured her. 'But sure, we can make our own pilgrimage by way of reparation. Believe me, on Good Friday there will be plenty of places to stop and pray.'

So on Friday they headed in the opposite direction, going along the coast and spending some time on a few quiet beaches between Carlingford and Dundalk.

Malachy was right. Alice was surprised and impressed when Rose finally drove her to his farm on Holy Saturday morning. The old ramshackle building nestling at the foot of the hills had been transformed into a pleasant homestead. The yard in front of the whitewashed building had been flagged.

'It is not always as clean as this,' Malachy informed her. 'I've given it a good hosing down so you wouldn't get those pretty boots of yours dirty.'

Just as he had foretold, the old collie, Meg, waddled over to Alice, had a good sniff and returned to her place by the door.

The Cooley Hills rose steep and jagged behind the farm and Alice couldn't believe that she hadn't really noticed them before, they were so majestically over-powering. I must have gone about with my eyes shut in my younger days, she thought, not to have noticed all this beauty.

Saturday had dawned dull and misty and a haze still obscured the Mourne Mountains, but Malachy assured her that this was not unusual and the mist would probably lift later on in the morning. He was right again. After lunch they visited the local market and Alice was amazed at all the wonderful produce on sale. By the end of the afternoon Malachy and Rose were weighed down with all sorts for their respective larders. Alice also bought some jars of pickles and preserves, all made by the farmers' wives, to take home to Belfast.

On Easter Sunday friends of Malachy's were invited to lunch to meet his sister. Everybody was so friendly and they got on so well together that an impromptu musical get-together was arranged for that evening. A buffet was laid on, the farmers brought their fiddles and flutes and they danced until the early hours of the morning. Alice was much in demand as a partner. She really was enjoying herself.

Monday was spent likewise meeting Rose's family and friends in her farmhouse. After all this sociability and activity, Alice had no difficulty in agreeing to extend her visit until Saturday to attend the wedding of a friend's son, which Rose assured her would be worth staying on for. Without hesitation she agreed to tell Dan of her decision when he phoned, as planned, on Tuesday evening.

Tess was delighted when she phoned her mother on Monday evening and discovered her change of plans. Perhaps she was having second thoughts about Dan Thompson after all and she wouldn't have to worry about them living in sin. 'Good God, I'm beginning to sound like my mother,' she thought in shocked dismay.

Chapter Eight

As the weather forecast had predicted the weather in Belfast did get better as Wednesday in Holy Week progressed and it was a dry, cool evening, the stars above sparkling bright against a dark sky, when Agnes, Tess and Dominic at last left Johnny Long's. Drawing in deep breaths of the crisp air, Dominic suggested they walk home.

'Are you not tired?' Tess asked. 'You've been on the go all day. We sat in there yarning so long I was sure Johnny would throw us out.'

'I don't usually like shopping but I enjoyed myself immensely today, trailing round the shops in Belfast, recognising some, unable to find others. It was strange. A lot of the stores have changed hands and a lot of places are missing altogether since I left.' He hoisted the bags up. 'Back home I'm a bit of a miser. All my money goes back into the business. But today I spent a fortune. I came back to Belfast determined to enjoy myself and that's what I'm going to do.'

'I can believe that, looking at all those parcels. You've every right to spoil yourself. But . . . are they heavy? Don't you think we should get a taxi home?'

'Not a bit of it! It's too good an evening to spend cooped up in a car. We'll be home in no time.'

Tess laughed and saluted him. 'If you say so, sir. Anything you say, sir.'

'I say.' He returned the salute with a smile.

One on either side of him, they stepped out smartly up Grosvenor Road. He was a great conversationalist and had them in stitches as he related episodes from the time when he was training to be a chef.

'And now you own your own catering business.' Agnes's voice was full of awe. 'That's some feat.'

'I've been lucky. And mind you, it is only a small establishment mostly catering for the Irish in our community, but I intend branching out. I have met this girl and she is a superb cook.'

'Girl friend, as in courting?' Agnes asked brightly.

He slanted a glance at her. 'Not quite, yet. But who knows what the future has in store.'

'What kind of food does she specialise in?'

'I can truthfully say that she can successfully turn her hand to most dishes. That's why I was able to come home with an easy conscience. She can be depended upon. As for her pastries and desserts, they're mouth-watering.'

'She sounds the ideal partner for you.'

He shrugged. 'Who knows? I always thought when I met the right woman I'd be bowled over. To be truthful, the people I know to have been bowled over by love are few and far between and, sad to say, a couple of the marriages have ended in divorce. So perhaps there is more to marriage than love alone. I suppose I'm just an old romantic fool at heart. Anyhow, who knows, maybe this wedding will put me in the notion and I'll go racing back to the States and fall on my knees and propose to Stella.'

Behind his back Agnes caught Tess's eye and mimed *Stella*.

*   *   *

[163]

A short time later they reached and passed Violet Street, and walked Tess to her front door. Refusing an invitation to come in for a cup of tea, Agnes and Dominic retraced their steps back down to Violet Street, both locked in their own thoughts.

Feeling cheerful, Tess made herself a mug of hot cocoa and, sipping it, slowly climbed the stairs to examine her wardrobe. She was happy to know that Dominic had a woman friend back in America whom he cared enough about to maybe ask to marry him. It put all the silly ideas out of her head. Knowing he was practically spoken for, she could now enjoy herself in his company without any romantic nonsense and take anything that happened with a pinch of salt. There was no way she would ever make a fool of herself over a man again; once bitten, twice shy. But this way, knowing he was practically engaged, she wasn't likely to be tempted. It was nice to be aware from the beginning that he wasn't available. At least she knew where she stood, and wouldn't get any silly ideas as she had where Jack was concerned.

Running her hand along the row of clothes in the wardrobe, she was dismayed. Plenty of suits, skirts and blouses hung there, but precious little else. Well, her social life didn't include dancing, so why should she have any dresses? There was certainly nothing in her wardrobe that would be suitable for a dance at the Orpheus. How on earth could she possibly accompany Dominic Sullivan to the Orpheus in a skirt and blouse? It would be unheard of. Her only two dresses, hanging forlornly on the rail, were well out of fashion. She had made them herself some years ago when Agnes persuaded her to go to a class in Sammy Leckie's to learn ballroom dancing. Her enthusiasm had waned after a time, so no more dresses were made.

Quickly descending the stairs she dialled Agnes's number. She had to let her friend know that she was unavailable, give her a chance to ask someone else. It was a pity but it couldn't be helped. It was Agnes herself who answered the phone.

Without any greeting, Tess blurted out, 'Look, Agnes, I'm sorry, but I'm afraid I can't go to the dance on Saturday night.'

'Why ever not?'

'I haven't anything to wear.'

'Don't be silly, Tess. You have some lovely clothes. Your taste is impeccable.'

'You're wrong. I haven't anything to go dancing in. I have two dresses and they are as old as the hills. Not at all suitable for somewhere like the Orpheus, I can assure you. I'm afraid you'll have to find someone else to round off your numbers.'

'You can go down town tomorrow and treat yourself to a new dress. And don't pretend you can't afford it, Tess. I know you're not short of a bob or two, so I won't take no for an answer.'

'Pay a fortune for a dress I may never wear again? You've got to be joking. I'm sorry, but you'll have to find someone else, Agnes.'

'And just who can I ask at this late stage?'

'I really don't see your problem. Dominic doesn't really need a partner. All the unattached girls will be falling over themselves to get a dance with him and, as we both know, he's not shy. Far from it. For goodness' sake, he'll be in his glory! All that talent to pick from. As for the meal . . . you can say one of your party has taken ill. It happens all the time. Restaurants must surely make allowance for things like that.'

'Look here, Tess Maguire, you promised to come and you can't let me down. You just *can't*! Do you hear me? I'm depending on you, and I'm not taking any of your old excuses. So there!'

Tess heard the dialling tone and taking the receiver away from her ear gazed at it in amazement. Agnes had hung up on her. What cheek! What on earth had got into her? Annoyed, she started to dial again, then thought better of it. She had made her position quite clear and it was now up to Agnes to find someone else to partner Dominic. Perhaps it was all for the best, Tess consoled herself. Dominic was probably a terrific dancer, whereas she had only ever learned the basic steps and would probably trample all over him.

Deciding to have an early night, she checked the doors and windows and climbed the stairs. Her mother had phoned to let her know she had arrived safely and was spending a few days with Rose before moving on to stay at her brother's farm. She had seemed quite contented and Dan Thompson's name had not entered into the conversation.

The house was quiet as a crypt and for the very first time Tess regretted not having a television. Her mother had broached the subject a few times but neither of them was keen enough to rush out and buy one. They were quite expensive, and so they kept putting it off. Perhaps when her mother came back from Carlingford they would go down town and look at some sets.

It seemed strange being alone in the house. This was the first time her mother and she had ever been separated. It was something she was going to have to get used to in the future, if Dan Thompson had anything to do with it.

Now was the opportunity to finish the book she was

reading, she thought. However, the family saga she usually had difficulty putting down tonight failed to grip her attention. After reading the same page three times, she marked her place and rose from the bed. Thrusting her feet into her slippers, she picked up her dressing gown and descended the stairs.

Something was niggling at the back of her mind. The year before, a customer had chosen velvet for her bridesmaid dress and a piece of the material had been surplus to requirements. The girl had insisted it was of no use to her and that Tess must keep it. If she recalled correctly the material wouldn't be big enough for a dress for herself but a long velvet skirt matched to her best blouse might be dressy enough for the occasion.

She was beginning to think she had thrown the material out when at last she discovered it at the bottom of a drawer full of remnants. A rich dark green, it was good quality and not a wrinkle marred its softness. It would be ideal, but holding it against her she confirmed that there would not be enough for a ball dress. A long skirt it would have to be. Spreading it out on the work table, she measured it carefully.

Now if she had wanted one of those skimpy dresses that were all the style at the moment there would be no problem whatsoever. With a bit of care she would certainly be able to make one. But her mother would take a turn in her eye if she dared to wear something revealing. However, her mother wouldn't be here to see her, and what the eye doesn't see the heart doesn't grieve over. So why not? Why not be daring for a change, just for the hell of it? A dress would be so much more suitable than a skirt and blouse!

Tomorrow morning she would go down to Anderson & McAuley's and get a pattern. She would be sure to get one of the very latest designs there. She would also let Agnes know that she had changed her mind . . . again.

Dominic and Agnes walked the short distance to her home in silence. He kept throwing sideways glances at her, aware that she was in an unhappy frame of mind but at a loss to understand why.

'Have you not enjoyed yourself tonight, Agnes?'

'Of course I have! The crack was great.'

They lapsed into silence again but when they arrived at the house and she made to open the door, with a hand on her arm he stopped her. 'Agnes, have I done something to offend you?'

She reared back like a startled deer, and gazed at him apprehensively. 'No! What gives you that idea?'

'When I first met you last Monday you were like a breath of spring, laughing and happy. The loveliest girl I've ever clapped eyes on. But since then, whenever we happen to be alone you go all quiet and moody. I feel I must have done or said something that has offended you. If I have . . . I can honestly say it was unintentional. I know I do sometimes say things without thinking how they might sound to others, but I certainly never meant you any offence.'

She clutched at his arm and shook it roughly. 'Don't you dare think like that, Dominic Sullivan. You're one of the nicest people I have ever met and I like you very much.' She shrugged and made futile gestures with her hands as if trying to shoo off a fly. 'It's this wedding. It's all we seem to talk about these days, morning, noon and night, wedding, wedding, wedding! I'll be glad when it's all over and the household can get back to some state of normality.'

'Then you'll have your own wedding to prepare for,' he reminded her gently.

She waved this idea aside. 'That's away in the future. I'll have plenty of time to get used to the idea.'

Her smile was tremulous and he felt sad. Surely a wedding was something to plan for joyously? Not an idea to get used to, he thought.

'Are you very much in love with Tony?' he asked softly.

She blinked in confusion at the question. 'Of course I am. Look, we'd better go in now. I'm sure Dennis will be anxious to get home. He has to get up early in the morning for work. So has Tony for that matter. I didn't think we'd be this late or I'd have told him to go on home straight from work.'

Slowly he released her arm and she opened the door, bewildered and confused by the emotion his touch had awakened in her. Thank God he had a girl waiting for him in America!

Tony came into the hall to meet her. He stopped abruptly when he saw Dominic. 'I was worried about you. I didn't realise you two were together.'

She smiled brightly. 'Tess and I went down to Johnny Long's for a supper and would you believe it?' She nodded behind her. 'We bumped into this fellow.'

May came into the hall. 'Would you like a sandwich, or perhaps something else to eat, Dominic?'

'No thank you, Mrs Quinn, I've already eaten.'

'A cup of tea then?'

Dennis's voice reached them from the living room. 'Dominic can have a cup of tea at home, Mrs Quinn. I've waited long enough for him.'

'I'm sorry if I'm annoying you, Dennis,' Dominic shouted back. 'But it was you who suggested that I call in here and walk home with you.'

Dennis came into the hall. 'I'm not disputing it. I just didn't realise you'd be this late. So let's get a move on. I'm whacked.' He lovingly took Marie into his arms. 'It's getting a bit crowded in here. Let's say good night outside, love. Give us a couple of minutes, Dominic. I haven't had a good kiss with Marie for a couple of days. She'll be leaving me standing at the altar if I'm not careful.' With these words he grabbed his coat off the hallstand and ushered Marie out the door, pulling it shut after them.

As she made to enter the living room Tony drew Agnes aside. 'Let's go into the sitting room, love.'

'Why?'

He lowered his voice, a frown gathering on his brow. 'Surely it's obvious . . . just to be alone for a while with you. Is that asking too much?'

'We've got company, Tony. It would be bad manners to take ourselves off.'

'Your mam and dad are in there. I'm sure Dominic won't mind. He, apparently, has had your company all evening by the sound of things.'

In spite of Tony's low tone, Dominic heard every word. 'Don't worry about me. I'll be going home in a minute or two.'

Disgruntled, Agnes let Tony urge her into the sitting room and, when the door closed on them, rounded on him angrily. 'Don't you ever speak to me in company like that again. You're acting as if you own me.'

He drew her into his arms. 'Hold on, Agnes. I just wanted some time alone with you.'

She shrugged herself free from his embrace. 'I'm tired, Tony. There will be plenty of time for this kind of thing later on.'

Tight lipped he faced her, eyes filled with distaste.

[170]

'Will there, Agnes? Sometimes I doubt that.'

'And just what do you mean by that?'

'I'm worried about you. You seem to have ice in your veins.'

He turned on his heel and left the room. She heard him call out 'Good night, everyone' and the outer door close after him. Immediately contrite, she rushed to stop him. How could she treat him like that? She was behaving like a spoiled child.

In the hall she stopped abruptly. Dominic was coming out of the living room and said with a smile, 'I think Dennis has had enough time to say good night to Marie, don't you?' He peered intently at her. 'Are you all right? You look a bit pale.'

She started retreating into the shadows of the sitting room again, to escape his penetrating look. 'I'm fine. Good night, Dominic.'

He followed her, pausing in the doorway. 'If you don't mind me saying so, you don't look fine to me.'

Tears threatened. With a wave of the hand she motioned him out of the room but instead he came further in, closing the door. 'Have you and Tony quarrelled?'

The tears spilled over and ran down her cheeks. 'Just a silly little lover's tiff, that's all.'

He produced a handkerchief and moved closer. Gratefully she grabbed it and dabbed at her eyes. 'Thank you. It was all my fault. I'm treating Tony terrible of late. He must have the patience of a saint to put up with me the way he does.'

'He loves you, that's why.'

'I know he does and I'm not worthy of him. Everything he does is for our future and all I do is find fault.' A sob caught in her throat.

Dominic drew her into his arms and patted her on the back, just as he would comfort a child. 'There now, don't get all upset. All courting couples quarrel now and again. It will all work out all right in the long run.'

A sigh escaped her lips and putting a finger under her chin he tilted her face up towards his. 'It will be all right,' he stressed. 'You'll see.'

She smiled and looked so forlorn that without further ado he kissed her. He caught himself on immediately and quickly released her. 'I'm sorry. I'd no right to do that.' For the life of him he couldn't understand what had possessed him, kissing his brother's future sister-in-law like that and her engaged to another man. One thing he did know, he hadn't wanted to stop. She had felt comfortable in his arms and her lips had been soft and responsive.

'It's all right, Dominic. I know you only meant to be kind. I'm fine now. Thank you.'

Resisting the urge to gather her close again, he said, 'Then I'll be off. Good night, Agnes.'

The phone rang as she passed through the hall and she lifted the receiver. 'Hello.'

It was Tess saying she couldn't go out with them on Saturday night. After a brief, bitter discussion, Agnes hung up on her friend. She was at the end of her tether. What else could go wrong? Weren't troubles supposed to come in threes? Tears blinding her, she called out good night to her parents and once in the privacy of her own room threw herself on the bed and gave way to her emotions.

The dress was beautiful! Daring but beautiful. It looked so small lying on the bed she found it hard to believe it would actually fit her. But it did. She had been careful to try it on step by step as she went along, and it fitted her . . . just!

She stood by the bed in her black satin waist slip and sheer black nylon stockings and gazed in awe at her creation. Then, gently lifting the dress, she stepped into it and eased it up over her hips, wiggling it into position and securing it at the waist where it fitted snugly. Then lifting the two front panels up over her bare breasts she secured them at the back of her neck.

It fitted like a glove. The front dipped low and for the first time in her life she realised just what a cleavage meant. Her firm breasts pushed at the material and looked larger than they actually were, and a mole high on the left one tantalisingly caught the eye when she moved. Her skin gleamed translucently above the rich colour of the dress and her eyes looked enormous and glowed like emeralds. She twisted to see the back of the dress and was glad her skin was free of blemishes as it was exposed to the waist.

She stood open mouthed at the creature reflected in the mirror. Surely this couldn't be prim and proper Tess Maguire. Could it?

It was indeed! She looked and felt wonderful. But there was no way she could possibly go out in this creation! What would people think? Distractedly her mind roved over all alternatives in her wardrobe and nothing else would do. She must wear this dress or stay at home. The door bell startled her into action. A glance at the clock showed her that Dominic, Brian and Joan, whom she was travelling down with, were early. She couldn't back out now. Not with the car at the door. With one last look at her reflection she shrugged into her coat and grabbing the small suede black bag that matched her court shoes she headed for the stairs.

Agnes would soon let her know if she looked out of place.

A table was booked at the Steak House on Wellington Place and the others were already waiting outside. Tess tumbled out of the car with Joan and Dominic and Brian went to find a parking spot while the rest of them entered the building.

Tess was dismayed when the women all removed their coats. She had thought she could remain covered up until they went to the Orpheus, but Dominic was gesturing for her coat to hang on the stand and reluctantly she slipped it off and handed it to him. Her transformation was not wasted on Dominic. He hesitated so long to examine her that the others caught on that something was afoot, and all eyes turned in her direction.

Becoming aware of her embarrassment, Dominic apologised and pulled her chair away from the table for her. Thankfully she sat down. Taking his place beside her he murmured, 'You look fantastic.'

'Thank you. The dress isn't a bit over the top, then?'

He laughed. 'Just the opposite! It's way below it.' Her colour deepened and he said, reassuringly, 'It's perfect.'

Dennis caught her eye across the table and winked and Agnes gave her the thumbs up sign. Tess relaxed and determined to enjoy herself.

In the Orpheus cloakroom Agnes delayed after Marie and Joan had left them. Those two hadn't even noticed the change in Tess, so wrapped up were they in plans for the wedding. This evening was supposed to be a break away from anything to do with the wedding, but no, that pair couldn't relax for even a couple of hours. Eyeing her friend from head to toe, Agnes said sincerely,

'You look lovely.' She had managed to stamp down the jealous pangs that reared their ugly head as she watched Dominic practically drool over Tess in the Steak House, reminding herself she was engaged to Tony.

With her friend's approval, Tess was content. She must look all right. However, Agnes couldn't resist teasing her. 'I don't know whether or not your mother would approve, mind.'

Tess grimaced. 'I can imagine her reaction, but if I have my way Mam will never set eyes on this dress.'

'If you are ever giving it away, remember we wear the same size,' Agnes remarked casually.

'I'll certainly bear that in mind,' Tess assured her. 'Though I can't see your mam being any more tolerant than mine. But thanks for your vote of confidence. I was feeling a bit overdressed.'

Agnes laughed aloud. 'In that skimpy outfit?'

Nudging her with her elbow, Tess retorted, 'You know what I mean. Shall we join the others?'

'Yes, let's.'

The evening proved to be the most memorable of Tess's young life. The dance floor was so crowded it wasn't important whether or not you knew the proper dance steps. Held clasped to Dominic's chest she relaxed and gave herself up to the rhythm of the music, swaying in perfect unison with his body.

At one point she became aware of her partner's close scrutiny and following the direction of his gaze realised he was examining the mole on her breast. Defensively her hand moved to try to cover the offending spot with some of the dress material. He caught her hand and, holding it tight in his, apologised.

'I'm sorry. But it is very eye catching, you know. Is it real?'

Her eyes widened and she gazed at him, uncompre-hending.

He laughed and whispered in her ear, 'I can see that it must be. I should have known you wouldn't seek to attract attention by false means.'

Totally bewildered, she said, 'I don't know what you're talking about, Dominic.'

He sighed. 'I can see that. Don't ever let anyone take advantage of your honesty and charm, Tess. Would you like to sit this one out while I fetch you a drink?'

'That would be nice, thank you.'

Leading her back to the table, he excused himself and headed for the bar where soft drinks were served. She watched heads turn as he made his way round the edge of the dance floor and was not surprised at the atten-tion he received. He would stand out in any crowd. He was also the nicest man she had ever met. This girl back in Florida was very lucky. Very lucky indeed.

A breathless Agnes joined her at that moment and with a nod in Tess's direction Tony followed Dominic to the bar. 'I've been watching you,' Agnes said accus-ingly. 'You're having the time of your life.'

Confused, Tess asked, 'Are you not enjoying your-self?'

'It's run of the mill for me now with Tony. I've danced so often with him it doesn't excite me any more.'

Tess wanted to question her friend, ask if it had ever excited her, but bit back the words. This was neither the time nor the place to probe. 'I think anyone would enjoy dancing with Dominic.'

Agnes grinned but Tess thought it looked contrived. 'He's not just dancing with you. He's drooling all over you.'

'Don't be silly!'

'Are you saying he doesn't excite you?'

Tess gave this some consideration and smiled. 'I must admit I find him very attractive. In fact, I have to keep reminding myself he has a girl back in Florida.'

'You like him that much?' Agnes gasped.

Tess smiled and reassured her. 'Don't worry. Once bitten twice shy. Believe me, I'll keep control of my emotions.'

After a cool drink and a lot of enjoyable conversation Dominic asked Agnes to dance with him. As they moved on to the floor Tony gave a slight bow and invited Tess to follow them.

He smiled down at her. 'You look very attractive in that dress, Tess.'

'Thank you, kind sir.'

'Dominic is obviously smitten with you.'

'Well now, since he has a girlfriend back home and I think him a gentleman, I'll ignore that remark.'

'Oh . . . is he engaged, then?'

'I don't think he's actually engaged, as far as a ring is concerned, but he has a close friend.'

'Agnes never mentioned it.'

'Why should she? She probably thinks you wouldn't be interested.'

For some moments Dominic and Agnes danced in silence. He was marvelling at the blonde halo of hair around a pert, exquisite face. He loved the feel of her in his arms; the closeness of her body. The tantalising memory of her lips under his. He was determined to hold her as far away as possible so she wouldn't realise the effect she was having on him. He didn't think she would take kindly to it, her being engaged to another man. Tony Burke was a very lucky fellow.

Agnes felt affronted, remembering how he had talked and laughed and drooled all over Tess. Why wasn't he talking to her? Did he dislike dancing with her that much? With Tess he had seemed so relaxed, whilst now he was stiff and unbending. Deciding to try to find out why, she broke the silence.

Looking up at him through long silky lashes, she asked softly, 'Am I boring you, Dominic?'

'No. Not in the slightest.'

Hmm! That bit of conversation didn't lead to anything, she thought. Changing tack, she said, 'Perhaps I should warn you that Tess has had a nasty experience with a boy. It took her a while getting over it. You'll be careful of her feelings, won't you?'

He looked down at her through narrowed lids. 'Tess doesn't appear to be nursing a broken heart as far as I can see.'

'No, not any more she's not. But do be careful, won't you? Remember, you're not a free agent.'

'Are you warning me off?' he muttered incredulously. 'Surely Tess can look after herself?'

'Of course she can!'

'Then why the concern?'

'Because I don't want her to be hurt again.'

He swung her round in a reverse turn to face the opposite direction. 'Can you see Tony and Tess from here?'

'Yes, I can. Do you think I'm blind?'

'And you can see that Tess is laughing and talking to Tony, just like she behaves with me?'

Agnes nodded, at a loss to understand what he was implying.

'Does that not tell you anything, Agnes?'

'No. Should it?'

'That's the first time tonight I've seen Tony look happy and relaxed. You and he dance round the floor as if you have been married about twenty years.'

Tight lipped, she glared at him. 'Remember, I was brought up never to be a temptation to the opposite sex. No long kisses or close embracing. Surely you were taught the same, Dominic? Surely the Christian brothers were as strict as the nuns where morality is concerned? Tony was reared the same as me, and we are saving ourselves for after our marriage.' She was so angry she almost stamped her foot. He might have lived in America for a long time but he grew up on the Springfield Road just as she had.

'Oh, yes. The brothers were very strict but us lads were not as easily influenced as you girls. Are you saying Tony has agreed to all this waiting?'

Now she was really angry. 'Yes, he has!' she hissed.

'Then he is a bigger fool than I thought he was.'

'He respects me.'

He changed course. 'All right. What about Tess? Does she not agree with what the nuns preached?'

'Huh! Even more so than me.'

'You wouldn't think it, to look at her. She's so relaxed and normal.'

'Are you insinuating that there is something wrong with me?'

'No . . .'

'You sound dubious.'

He shrugged. 'I just don't understand you.'

'Fortunately you don't have to.'

'No.' He sounded sad and her eyes questioned him. 'So long as Tony does. Does it not worry you that he dances so close with Tess?'

'Why should it? I trust him.'

'Are you not afraid that all kinds of thoughts may be going on in that head of his while he gazes down at that neckline?'

'The way they do when you dance with her, you mean?' she asked sarcastically.

He smiled. 'Mm. Maybe.'

She gave a very definite shake of the head. 'Tony isn't anything like you! He wouldn't ever think like that about Tess, or any woman, for that matter.'

'Hah! So it's a saint you're engaged to? Or are you implying that Tess Maguire isn't attractive enough to interest the opposite sex?'

'No! I'm not implying anything of the sort. She's lovely! Especially in that dress.'

'But you don't think Tony may be tempted by her closeness? Remember, he's holding her much closer than he holds you.'

Agnes twisted round to have another look at the other couple. She could see nothing untoward. Dominic watched her with laughing eyes. He was enjoying teasing Agnes; she was so uptight about everything. Then she flashed him a look of complete bewilderment and he caught a glimpse of the misery shadowed in her eyes, and shame smote him. 'I'm sorry, Agnes. I'm only teasing. I always seem to rub you up the wrong way.'

'No,' she said sadly. 'No, it's me. I don't seem to have a sense of humour where you're concerned.'

Annoyed at himself for having upset her, he apologised. 'I'm sorry. Really sorry. I don't know what gets into me when I'm with you.' The dance was drawing to an end and she twisted from his hold and headed for the table. He followed her and once she was seated he excused himself and left the room.

He was disgusted with himself. Why did he let her

get to him like this? Tormenting her like that on the dance floor. Ridiculing her choice of husband. Laughing at her morals. It was cruel! He ought to be horse-whipped. What did it matter to him that she was an ice queen? It was Tony she was going to marry. It was some time before he felt enough in control to return to the ballroom and face her. He had decided to ask her to dance with him again and try to put things right between them. But he warned himself not to be surprised if she refused.

Disgruntled, Agnes watched him go. What did Dominic have against her? She just wanted him to be her friend. Treat her like he treated Tess. As if she had summoned her, a breathless Tess sank down on to the chair next to hers. 'Where's Dominic? Surely you can't have lost him already.'

Agnes looked at her glowing features and said sourly, 'How do I know where he is? I'm not his keeper. And I wish you would try to look intelligent for a change, Tess. You've been acting like the laughing cavalier all evening.'

'Agnes!' Tony cried, aghast. 'What's got into you?'

Tess looked stunned. 'What on earth do you mean?'

Throwing an apologetic glance in her friend's direction, Agnes muttered, 'I'm sorry. Please forgive me, Tess. And will you both excuse me?' Grabbing hold of her handbag she literally ran from the table.

Tony rose to his feet but Tess motioned him to sit down again. She nodded reassuringly at him. 'Don't worry. I'll see what ails her.' She followed Agnes to the cloakroom, where she discovered Marie and Joan, whom they had seen little of all evening as they had spent most of the time in a corner with their partners going over wedding details, hovering around Agnes trying to find out what had upset her.

'I was just overcome with the heat! That's all. Nothing to worry about.'

Tess stood to one side for some moments and silently watched the trio. She could understand why the others were anxious, Agnes was as white as a sheet and trembling slightly. What on earth had affected her so?

Stepping forward she said, 'You girls go back to the lads. They'll be wondering what's happening. I'll look after Agnes.'

'Are you sure, Tess?' Marie turned gratefully to her and then back to her sister. 'If you want to go home, Agnes, let me know and I'll get Dennis to fetch the car,' she volunteered.

'I feel fine now. Just leave me be. Go on, leave me alone.'

The others reluctantly withdrew and Tess hovered solicitously over her friend. 'What on earth happened?'

'Nothing!'

'Come off it, Agnes, you're not in this state over nothing. Did Dominic say something to offend you?'

'No. He didn't say anything.' Heading for a cubicle, Agnes said, 'Look, Tess, do you mind? I'd really like to be alone for a few minutes. I'll come back to the table presently.'

'All right, but don't be too long or I'll come looking for you.'

'I won't. I promise.' Agnes smiled but the misery reflected in her eyes tore at her friend's heart. What could have happened, to affect her so?

Back at the table there was still no sign of Dominic. When he saw her, Tony bounded to his feet and came hurriedly to meet her. 'Where's Agnes? Is she all right?'

Tess nodded. 'She'll be here in a few minutes. I think the heat got to her.'

Dominic arrived on Tess's heels and was relieved to find that he had been reprieved and didn't have to face Agnes just yet. 'Would anyone like a drink?' he asked. He looked pale and worried and Tess decided to find out just what was going on.

'You wait here for Agnes, Tony. I'll go to the bar with Dominic.' She was determined to get to the bottom of this; Dominic had yet to look her straight in the eye and as they waited to be served she asked directly, 'What happened back there?'

'Nothing. No matter what I say, I seem to rub Agnes up the wrong way. She's a very prickly person. Has no sense of humour whatsoever.'

'On the contrary, her sense of humour is above reproach. I think it's all this talk about weddings that's getting her down.'

'I don't buy that. She's not even excited about her own wedding.'

'I know that. But then, it might never happen.'

Suddenly she had all his attention. 'Why do you say that?'

'She only got engaged to Tony because he produced the ring and asked her to marry him in front of a lot of people. Otherwise I'm sure she would have put him off.'

He sounded bemused. 'No wonder she seems indifferent to him.' Sensing Tess's surprise, he added, 'And here I am teasing her. Still, she should loosen up a bit. She takes life far too seriously.'

Determined to defend her friend, Tess said, 'It was the heat! She was too hot and that's why she left the dance floor.'

'No, I was teasing the life out of her and she couldn't take it. I wish now I'd minded my own business. I deliberately pointed out to her how relaxed Tony was with you. When they dance together they're like an old married couple.'

Whilst silently agreeing with him that all was not well with her friend's relationship, Tess nevertheless did not want to discuss Agnes's engagement with him. She shrugged. 'We're all different. Have different ways of showing affection.' Didn't she know how different? Suddenly startled, she cried, 'Look! Agnes and Tony have just left the room and she has her coat on. They must be going home.'

She started to cross the room but with a hand on her arm Dominic stopped her. 'Let her go.'

'She might need me.'

'For heaven's sake catch yourself on! She's with Tony. Why would she want you?'

His voice was so sharp she drew back and gaped at him. 'She's my best friend, so she is! I worry about her.'

He released his hold on her. 'I'm sorry. By all means go after her. I don't know when to keep my big mouth shut.'

Tess dithered. Dominic was right. Agnes was with Tony; the man she was betrothed to. She hadn't even bothered to say good night to them. 'You're right. I don't know why I feel so protective of her.'

There were still a few people ahead of them waiting to be served and he turned to her. 'Are you very thirsty? Shall we forget about these drinks and dance the night away?'

She nodded and willingly entered his arms. This was her night and nothing and nobody must be allowed to spoil it.

*   *   *

The rest of the evening passed in a whirl. Dominic was a wonderful companion, teasing and flirting with her. She thought him delightful. How come Agnes couldn't get on with him?

It was with reluctance that she sought out Joan at the end of the evening to go to the cloakroom to collect their coats.

She found Joan very subdued. 'Why so quiet? Did you and Brian not enjoy yourselves?'

'To be truthful, Marie and I are worried about Agnes. Marie was surprised when Tony came and asked if they could go home early. It's not like Agnes to want to leave anywhere early. Do you think she's sickening for something?'

Tess was immediately concerned. She had not considered a physical cause for her friend's apparent illness. Not wanting to involve Dominic, she said apprehensively, 'I hope not, with the wedding so near. No, I think it was just the heat getting to her.'

'I hope you're right.' Joan didn't sound in the least confident.

Collecting their coats they made their way outside to where the others were waiting to walk them to the car park.

Outside her home Dominic insisted on leaving the car and escorting her to the door. She smiled up at him. 'Thank you for a marvellous evening. I've never enjoyed myself so much.'

'The pleasure was all mine. Listen, I've persuaded Dennis to let me have the loan of the car tomorrow. Will you come out for a run along the coast with me?'

'That sounds wonderful. I'll get in touch with Agnes in the morning and see if she is well enough to come.'

'No. Let Agnes and Tony have some time together. I've been thinking that maybe I've been crowding her and Tony doesn't like it. I don't want to be a bone of contention between them. I want you to come out alone with me. I promise not to tease or do anything to annoy you. Cross my heart and hope to die.' He made a big cross on his chest and she laughed.

'Hah! Tease all you like. I think I'll be able to handle you.'

Cupping her face in his hands he whispered, 'You're so sweet . . . I wish . . .'

What he wished she wasn't to hear. With a light kiss on the lips, he said, 'Good night. I'll ring you in the morning,' and joined the others in the car. She stayed at the door and waved as it drew away from the kerb and headed up the road, before she entered the house.

Hugging herself with happiness, she waltzed down the hall and around the kitchen. She could become very fond of Dominic Sullivan if she wasn't careful. Was he really serious about this girl, Stella? Behave yourself, Tess warned. Remember you vowed you would enjoy whatever came, no strings attached. Roll on tomorrow.

Early on Sunday morning Tess rang Agnes to inquire how she felt. It was Mrs Quinn who answered the phone.

'She's still in bed, Tess. Do you want me to give her a shout?'

'No, it is quite early. I'll ring later on. How is she?'

'She went straight to bed when she came home from the dance last night, saying she had a headache. Other than that she seemed all right to me.' Worry crept into her voice. 'Is there anything I should know?'

'No. No, she left the dance early and I just wanted to make sure she was all right.'

'I'll get her to give you a ring when she gets up, Tess. Okay?'

'That will be great, Mrs Quinn. A happy Easter to you and the family.'

'Thank you. And the same to you, Tess. Goodbye, love.'

A couple of hours later Agnes still hadn't rung. Not wishing to interfere, Tess resisted the impulse to call her again. She didn't want Mrs Quinn to start questioning her daughter.

She would have to be patient and wait until Agnes got in touch with her.

Chapter Nine

There was a great big bubble of anticipation in Tess's heart as she prepared for twelve o'clock Mass in Clonard Monastery. It was another sunny day with bright blue skies and just a hint of a breeze and she knew a lot of the outfits and children's clothes that she had made would be on parade this Easter day. She always got the satisfied feeling of a job well done on these occasions, as she watched her handiwork pass up and down the aisles. Afterwards, Dominic was picking her up to go for a drive along the Antrim coast and she had prepared a picnic lunch to take along. She couldn't contain her excitement; at this moment in time life couldn't be any better.

As she mingled with the congregation leaving the church after Mass, exchanging greetings, a familiar face caught her eye. Theresa Cunningham, the young woman who had trained her in the Belart factory, was coming towards her. Tess had heard that Theresa had bought a house further up the Springfield Road a couple of years ago but this was the first time she had run into her. Theresa met her gaze and a pleasant smile relaxed her rather stern features.

They greeted each other and fell into step along Dunmore Street. 'It's a long time since I last saw you,

Tess Maguire, but I've been hearing all sorts of good reports about your factory.'

'Ah, dear God, surely they're not calling my work room a factory?' Tess laughed. 'I work from home, Theresa.'

'I know you do, but people do tend to exaggerate. Especially if they like you and you're doing well. Mind you, any reports I hear about your work are all good.'

'Thank God for that at least. Mam and I aren't doing too badly at the moment. In fact we were thinking of taking on a trainee stitcher,' Tess couldn't help boasting proudly. 'What about you? Are you still in the Belart?'

'No. I had to leave work some months ago. After me breaking out and investing in a more upmarket house. You see my mother fell ill and can't be left on her own for long periods. I don't want to put her into a nursing home. Not unless it becomes absolutely necessary. But it was either that or leave the Belart.' She sighed. 'I chose the latter.'

In times past Tess had met Mrs Cunningham in town when she was out with her daughter and had thought her a nice person. 'I'm sorry to hear that, Theresa. Give her my regards, won't you? Do you like living on the Springfield Road?'

'I must confess I do. In spite of everything, I'm glad I moved when I had the opportunity.'

They had reached the corner of Dunmore Street, from where Tess would go down Springfield Road and Theresa in the opposite direction.

'Goodbye, then. It was nice seeing you again.' Tess made to leave, but Theresa hesitated and Tess paused to hear what she had to say.

'You say you are taking on a trainee stitcher?'

Mystified at her interest, Tess said, 'Well . . . I've been

threatening to do so for some time now, but it's getting the right person. I will eventually get round to it. Why? Do you know anyone suitable?'

'Would you not be better taking on a qualified stitcher? Someone who knows all the ropes?'

'I wish I could. But unfortunately I can't afford anyone like that. We wouldn't have enough work in at any one time to justify taking on a trained stitcher.'

'Would you consider taking me on . . . on a part-time basis, that is, say a couple of afternoons a week? I wouldn't expect top wages, but a small steady income would augment the money me and Mam have coming in weekly. It would also protect the savings I have salted away for a rainy day. And, as you know, I'm more than capable of doing any job you'd give me.'

Tess studied her for a moment. 'But what about your mother?'

'I'd be all right as far as that's concerned. A friend comes to visit her two or three afternoons a week so there would be no problem me getting away. In fact they'd be glad to get rid of me for a while. And I'd only be down the road if I was needed in a hurry. You are on the phone, aren't you, Tess?'

Caught on the hop, Tess was looking at her, tongue-tied. Embarrassment brought extra colour to Theresa's face. 'Look, Tess, I'm sorry for putting you on the spot like this.' She hastened to add, 'What if I give you my telephone number and if you think it would work out, you could give me a ring. If I don't hear from you, I'll understand. Okay? There will be no hard feelings.'

Tess was in a quandary. Theresa had trained her in her first two years in the Belart factory. How would she cope with being on the other side of the fence; taking orders from Tess? 'Tell you what . . . I'll talk it over with

Mam. She's in Carlingford at the moment, but I'll let you know next week what we decide, one way or the other.'

Theresa rummaged in her bag and produced a pen and an old envelope. 'Thanks, Tess. And remember, I'll understand no matter how you decide.' Quickly jotting down her telephone number she handed it to Tess and with a final farewell hurried away.

Dominic was so easy to talk to that Tess found herself confiding in him about her conversation with Theresa.

'You know this lady?' he asked gravely.

'Yes. She taught me everything I know about the rag trade.'

He sat in thought for some moments. 'If I were going to start someone new in my kitchen, I'd prefer a mature person who knows all the ropes, and would be willing to work part time say two, maybe three days a week, to having the bother of training a greenhorn. That's just my opinion, of course. You see, while you're training a new hand to your procedures you're not doing any real constructive work yourself, and as there's only your mother and yourself in the business you could soon find yourself falling behind in your work programme. I am assuming of course that you do work to a planned schedule. You see what I'm getting at? You'll find your-self spending too much valuable time with the trainee or watching every move she makes. In no time at all you'll let some customer down and that could cost you dearly in the long run. You might make the excuse that it's only one customer. So what? But that could be a very big mistake to make; the turning point in a success-ful business. That disgruntled customer will tell another of your customers, there's no doubt whatsoever about

that, and it will soon snowball. If you're not very careful, you could soon find yourself facing bankruptcy. I'm
not telling you any old cock and bull story, Tess. I've
seen it happen before in the States and it will happen
again, so be very careful and give it a lot of thought
before coming to a decision.'

Tess sat through this lecture in silence taking in every
single word, occasionally nodding in agreement. 'Phew!
That was certainly laying it on the line. I was thinking
along those lines myself, actually. Not in such depth,
though. Nevertheless you have made me aware of the
pitfalls I could face if I took on a trainee. I'll see what
Mam has to say when she returns. Thanks for lending
me your ear – I'll give it back to you tomorrow – and
thanks for your valued advice.'

'Any time, Tess . . . What are you going to give me
back tomorrow?'

'It was a joke.'

The outing along the Antrim coast was a great success.
They had their picnic on Fair Head at Ballycastle over-
looking the sea towards Rathlin Island. They sat in a
sheltered spot and as he viewed the lush green grass
and gently swaying bushes around them, and the
choppy blue-green waters below, Dominic confided
wistfully, 'I really miss Ireland, you know, Tess.'

'Why did you leave?'

'Oh, me and Dad had a big row. He had all these
grand ideas for his eldest son but I didn't want my life
laid out for me by someone else. He thought he knew
best and wouldn't listen to reason, so I made my own
plans on the QT and when I had everything arranged
I announced I was going to America to work. You can
imagine the reception that got. I was called all sorts of

unrepeatable names and warned never to come back. That's why I've never been home before. I was surprised when our Dennis wrote and asked me to be best man. He said my dad had no objections, so here I am.'

'But now you're here, why not stay? Have your parents forgiven you?'

'I think so. I know Mam is happy enough and would be glad if I stayed, but Dad is another matter. I think he's having me stay on sufferance to please Mam and Dennis, who is now his blue-eyed boy.'

'If you stayed here, I'm sure he'd come round in time to your way of thinking, and surely with all your experience you could open your own restaurant here?'

'Yes, that would be no problem. And I know I'd have no trouble selling my business in America, but . . .'

'You're thinking of Stella,' Tess guessed. 'Would she not agree to coming over here to live?'

'No. I'm afraid she wouldn't.' He turned a mischievous smile on her. 'I've a confession to make as far as Stella is concerned. You see, I failed to mention that she is happily married to a friend of mine.'

Tess blinked in confusion. 'But . . . but why didn't you say?' Comprehension dawned and she gasped, 'I know why! You don't want any romantic complications here in Belfast. Isn't that it?'

'No. You're wrong. You and Agnes assumed I was committed to Stella so I let you believe it. After all, what difference does it make?' Tess sat silent and he said, 'You're not annoyed at me, surely?'

'No. I just can't understand your reasoning. Were you afraid someone might make a pass at you? Try to get you to stay?'

He gazed across the water. 'On the contrary, I was big-headed enough to think perhaps I'd fall in love with an Irish colleen, sweep my heart's desire off her feet, and take her back to Florida with me. However, it's not to be. It would cause a terrible upheaval. Remember, I told you I was an old romantic at heart? Well, I really am. And I don't want to cause any bother to anybody. So far everyone I've met is very committed to their families and careers and that's the way it should be. I doubt if anyone would consider leaving this beautiful country, and to be truthful I don't blame them.'

Tess wished he would make himself a bit clearer. Had he a particular girl in mind? He sounded as if he had met someone he could care for. Could it possibly be her? Hadn't he told her just last night how sweet he thought her? Did he think she wouldn't leave her mother and her wee business? Well, he was right on that count. That was something she would be very reluctant to do. But hadn't he just implied that he missed his homeland and would like to come back?

He saw her bewilderment and reached for her hand. 'Tess, don't worry your head about me, I'm a survivor. I have however decided not to prolong the agony. I intend cutting short my holiday. I'll only be staying one month instead of two, as I had intended.'

She turned her head away so that he wouldn't see her disappointment. 'I'm sorry to hear that, Dominic. I'll miss you.'

Hand under her chin, he turned her face towards him. 'Let's not spoil our day out.' His lips met hers and she responded to them willingly. It was a tender kiss but when she would have moved closer he gently released her and rising to his feet assisted her up. 'Well, where do we go from here?'

She knew he wasn't alluding to the kiss but to the next stage of their journey and said, 'Let's have a look at that map.' After all, she still had over two weeks to get him to change his mind.

Tess opened her eyes to bright sunlight streaming in through her bedroom window and thanked God for another lovely day.

It was Easter Monday and she dressed with care to go down to St Paul's Church to the Nuptial Mass and to see all the wedding finery. From now on she would be out to make a big impression on Dominic every chance she got. To this end her make-up took much longer than usual to apply, and she fussed over her hair before settling the small close-fitting hat on the bright curls until everything was to her complete satisfaction. After a final look in the full length mirror and a pleased smile at her reflection, she made a final unnecessary adjustment to her skirt and left the house.

She was glad her mother was away from home or she would have smelt a rat long ago and known a man must be involved. How she now wished she was going to the reception. She was convinced that all the single girls would be attracted to Dominic. How could they help it? As far as she was concerned he was the bee's knees.

Arriving at the church early, Tess chose a pew at the front of the left hand aisle where she would have a clear view of the centre altar where the ceremony would be performed. Dennis, looking nervous, was already seated. Dominic in the role of best man was whispering in Dennis's ear, obviously reassuring his brother. Tess wanted to feast her eyes on Dominic without his being aware that she was there and this was the ideal spot for doing so.

Marie seemed to float up the aisle, hand resting lightly on her father's arm. She looked like a fairy tale princess, her face shining luminously through the fine veil, and Tess thought how beautiful she looked. Her shimmering white silk, figure-hugging dress had a long train that swept out in her wake. She carried a bouquet of roses and lilies of the valley, and young Amy walked in front looking like a small replica of the bride, scattering flower petals as she went. Behind the bride came Agnes and Joan, their dresses a warm shade of primrose.

Agnes had failed to get in touch with Tess the day before and she, taking umbrage, had made no further attempt to break the silence between them. She sorely regretted this when she saw her friend. Agnes looked so pale and fragile Tess's heart went out to her. Perhaps Joan was right and she really was sickening for something. Turning to enter the front centre pew Agnes caught Tess's eye and gave her a nervous smile. Anxious to make amends, Tess mouthed the words *See you outside* and received a nod in reply.

Throughout the service Tess found her eyes returning again and again to Dominic. He stood a head above everyone nearby, and was a commanding figure in his grey morning suit, snowy white shirt and silver cravat. The ceremony was conducted with great sincerity and the mothers of both bride and groom were in tears. Tess had a lump in her own throat as she watched them and was glad when the bridal group finally disappeared into the vestry to sign the register.

Wishing to catch Agnes before she got caught up in the taking of photographs, Tess hurried outside to wait at the church doors for the wedding group to come out. She also wanted to convey her best wishes to the bride and groom. As her eyes ranged over the crowd milling about she noted that quite a few of the wedding guests were young, attractive women and her heart sank. She could only hope that most of them were married.

Dominic spotted her immediately and, ignoring those who were seeking his attention, came to her side. She glowed with pride, glad she had worn her pale green tailored suit and close-fitting hat as his eyes swept over her from head to toes.

'You look lovely,' he greeted her. Leaning closer he whispered, 'I can't understand why you weren't invited to the reception. I'll miss you.'

'It, as you well know, is being held in Belfast Castle and will cost a fortune, and' – she nodded to the crowd milling about – 'you'll soon find consolation.'

'One more guest wouldn't have broken them, I'm sure.'

She shrugged. 'One has to draw the line somewhere, Dominic.'

They were calling for him to come over for the photographs. He sighed. 'I hate getting my photo taken. I feel such a fool in this gear.'

She wanted to tell him that he looked just wonderful but thought he was already well aware of the fact. 'You're keeping everybody waiting. You'd better get yourself over and into that group,' she said, giving him a slight push in the right direction.

St Paul's Church, being situated on the junction of the Falls Road and Cavendish Street, had no suitable background for photographs so only a few were snapped at the church doors before the group broke up and piled into the waiting limousines to go to Belfast Castle and its beautiful grounds to continue the photography session in more picturesque surroundings.

Before leaving, Agnes hurried over to Tess. 'I'm sorry about the way I've been behaving. I would have phoned Sunday afternoon but Joan told me you were away for a run in the car with Dominic. Where did you go? Did you have a nice time?'

'Along the Antrim coast, and we had a marvellous day. Dominic certainly knows how to treat a woman.' A frown puckered her brow. 'I can't understand why you've gone off him, Agnes. It's not like you. What on earth did he say to offend you?'

'I haven't gone off him,' Agnes hastened to assure her. 'I think he's great. It was all a silly misunderstanding. I'll ring you tomorrow. Okay?

With that Tess had to be content but she was still worried about her friend, she looked so pale and tense.

Dan found the time dragging without his dates with Alice. He had been a loner before but all that had changed since Alice had come into his life. If only he were free. He wished Anne would conveniently fall under a bus or something. He immediately asked God's forgiveness for such dark thoughts. It was because he was afraid of losing Alice. She was a very attractive woman, after all, and he was inclined to think that some of the locals in Carlingford would indeed be paying her attention. And why not? How could they help it? Had she already met someone else? Perhaps some guy who wasn't short of a bob or two. A man who would be able to give her the kind of life she deserved. He thought he'd go crazy thinking about it.

But no matter, he decided. First things first. All his attention must be given to making his son's twenty-first birthday a time to remember. Nothing must be allowed to spoil Jack's great day. Dan would concentrate on that; push all else to the back of his mind. He had the motorbike, a table booked for a meal, in the International Hotel no less, so that much was settled. Now he must buy a helmet and gauntlets. He intended letting Jack pick his own leathers but a helmet was essential because it was only to be expected that Jack would want to go for a run on the bike right away. Colette would probably accompany him so he would have to splash out on two helmets.

His shopping didn't take up too much time and Easter passed quietly as far as he was concerned. Colette and Jack had packed haversacks and a tent and gone to Bray Head for the long weekend. Dan spent most of his time alone, thinking about and longing for Alice.

On Tuesday on his way home from work he went to the public phone in the Clock Bar and, as promised, rang Alice. He was all keyed up, had been thinking all day about seeing her tomorrow; planning how he would ask her to accompany them to the International Hotel. Would she agree to come, after all the hurt Jack had caused her daughter?

He was gobsmacked when Alice informed him that she intended staying on an extra few days. It was like a betrayal, after the fuss she had made about going in the first place. She explained that she was staying to please her friend Rose as she had asked her to accompany her to a wedding.

Dan's heart sank. He couldn't believe that Alice was putting Rose in front of him. Were his fears to be realised? Was there some old fellow lurking in the background plying her with compliments and gifts?

'I see,' he said, at a loss for words.

'I'll come home Saturday,' Alice promised, and paused, expecting him to say he would be at the station to meet her. To her surprise he made no such offer. 'Are you still there, Dan?'

'Yes, I'm still here. Forgive me, but I never dreamt

you'd stay on.' He wanted to add that he missed her sorely but refrained. Obviously she wasn't missing him. 'I'll see you sometime on Saturday, Alice. That is if you're not too tired. Goodbye for now, dear.'

Crushed with disappointment, he went to the bar and ordered a double Black Bush. Downing it in two gulps, he was about to order the same again but, realising the futility of it, left the bar and headed back to his empty house.

To his surprise Anne waylaid him on the way down Spinner Street. He was so deep in thought that he didn't see her until it was too late to avoid contact. She was hovering in the doorway of Lily Brady's house and as he passed by a hand shot out and grabbed his arm. 'A word, please, Dan.'

He glanced at his watch. 'It had better be a quick one. It's my turn to make the tea and I'm running late as it is.'

'Right. I'll make it as short as possible. Unless . . . would you be agreeable to my making the tea for you and Jack tonight? We could talk as I cook.'

'No, thank you. I'm not that desperate.'

'You're a hard man, Dan Thompson.'

'Not really. Not with everyone. Just those I don't have any time for.'

She bit nervously on her lip. He certainly didn't pull his punches. She forced herself not to retaliate. This was important to her. 'Dan, I think you're being very mean not allowing me to come to my own son's birthday dinner. After all, he only comes of age once and it should be a family affair.'

He looked down his nose and examined her through narrowed lids. 'Should it, now?'

'Yes, it should. You know quite well he wants me to

be there. Why, he was so embarrassed when he explained you didn't want me to come, I felt heartsore for him.'

'Did he also tell you that I offered to let you take my place? Still my treat, mind you, but he refused to consider it?'

'No. No, he didn't say.'

'It's true. You see, Anne, you offended Colette when you broke her confidence. That's not something she'll willingly forgive.'

'What do you mean? Colette and I have spoken since that episode. She has forgiven me.'

'Forgiven? Oh, yes, I can imagine her pretending to forgive you for the sake of peace. But somehow or other I don't think she'll go out of her way to seek your company ever again.'

'So that's a definite no, then?'

'Very much so, I'm afraid.'

'Tell me, Dan. Have you met someone who is really special to you? I've been told that you haven't bothered with another woman all these years.'

'Now I wonder who told you that? Lily Brady, I suppose. And how would she know? Eh? Just because I don't bring women home with me doesn't mean I'm not seeing them. As for whether or not I've met someone special, well, that's none of your business. Anyway, why the sudden interest?'

She leaned closer. 'Because if you have met someone and she doesn't come up to scratch, remember I still think we could make a go of it. I made you happy once and I can do it again.'

His head swayed from side to side and he smiled mockingly. 'Do you know something, Anne? I wish you had never come back into our lives. No one wants you about here.'

'Jack does! Only he doesn't want to offend you. But I'll continue to work on him and see what happens. I might not be at his twenty-first birthday dinner, but you mark my words, Dan Thompson! I'll certainly be at his wedding. And there is damned little you can do about it.'

'Over my dead body,' he muttered as he turned away.

'Stranger things have happened,' she hissed after him.

Bob Crosby had been decent enough in his offer to come in to work early Thursday morning so that Dan could get into the yard for the bike before Jack awoke for his breakfast. Between them they decorated the bike with balloons and a huge birthday card saying 'Happy 21st Birthday' and wheeled it along the pavement to set it outside Dan's door.

'Thanks, Bob. I owe you a pint . . . or two. I can't wait to see Jack's face when he sees it.'

'To be truthful, neither can I.'

'I'll give you a shout.'

'No need to do that. I'll be watching out for him,' Bob laughed.

Jack awoke, stretched, looked at his bedside clock and snuggled back down under the blankets again with a contented sigh. It was his birthday, he had two days off work, and he could have a lie in. At least that was his intention. The noise coming from downstairs was enough to waken the dead. What on earth was his dad up to so early in the morning?

Pulling on an old pair of jeans and a pullover, Jack descended the stairs, hair tousled and still half asleep. He was surprised to see his father sitting at the table eating his breakfast.

'What on earth are you doing? I thought you were

taking a day off work and we'd have a lie in. And what was all that noise about?'

'I couldn't sleep, son. It was those ones out there that were kicking up a racket.' Dan stabbed his fork in the direction of the front window and managed to hide a smile as Jack went to investigate.

Dan heard his gasp of surprise and joined him at the window. 'Well, say something! Do you like it or not?'

'You mean it's really mine?' The words came out on a shrill, high-pitched note and Dan put an arm round his son's shoulders.

'It's really yours, son. Happy birthday.'

Jack headed for the door but Dan stopped him. 'You don't want to go out looking like that. I've boiled a kettle of water. Away and clean yourself up and put on some decent clothes.'

After a hurried wash and shave and a change of clothes, Jack went outside and walked round and round the bike, giving it a good examination. Tears pricked his eyes when he at last turned to his father.

'Thanks, Dad. It's beautiful. If you'd asked me what I wanted for my twenty-first, and money no object, I'd have chosen a Triumph motorbike.'

'You're welcome, son. I'm glad you like it. Hold on a minute.' Dan entered the house and came out holding the biker's helmet and gauntlets. 'I'll buy you the leathers at the weekend. I want you to pick your own.'

Carefully, Jack secured the helmet on his head. 'It's a perfect fit. You've thought of everything. Thanks, Dad.'

'Well then, let's see what you look like on it.'

Dan removed the decorations and Jack swung his leg over the bike and kicked the engine into life. It fired at the first attempt. When he twisted the throttle the engine responded with a healthy roar. As if summoned, Bob immediately came from the yard followed by his two workers, and Colette and her grannie appeared at their door in their dressing gowns and just stood there gawking.

Slowly Colette approached the bike and Jack cried, 'Get your clothes on, girl, and we'll go for a spin.'

Still she stood as if mesmerised. 'Is it yours?'

'Yes.' Jack grinned at his father. 'Dad's been spending all his savings on me.'

He sounded so pleased, Dan flushed with pleasure. 'You only come of age once, son,' he said gruffly.

Bob Crosby said, 'She's a good 'un, son. You should be proud to own her.'

'Oh, I am. I am. Believe me, Bob, I'll treasure it and look after it. I can't thank you enough, Dad.'

'Any time the yard is open you can keep it there at night, but I've a feeling we'll close too early to suit you.'

'Thanks for the offer, Bob, but I've already had a word with wee Mrs McAnulty.' Dan nodded to the end house on the other side of the street whose yard was covered in and had a large wooden gate for access. 'She has agreed to let him have a key to her yard.'

Bob saluted him. 'That's good thinking, Dan. Meanwhile, if you ever need me you know where I am. Come on, lads, no more skiving. Back to work.'

During this discourse Colette had disappeared indoors. Now she came out in warm clothes with a scarf around her head to protect it from the wind.

'Climb on, love, and let's see how fast we can go.' Jack couldn't keep the happy grin off his face. Seeing his mother slowly approaching, he waved excitedly. 'Mam, see what Dad bought me for my birthday.'

Anne came to a halt beside the machine, unable to hide the resentment on her face. 'It's just as well I bought you that watch, otherwise you'd never have received such a wonderful present from your dad,' she replied sarcastically.

Dan heard these words as he came from the house with the other safety helmet for Colette. 'If he has any doubts, Jack has just to ask Bob Crosby how long the motorbike has been in his yard. Long before you had any notion of buying him anything.'

'Please, you two. Can we call a truce for today at least? Look, Mam, I'll pick you up at Lily Brady's at eleven tomorrow morning and take you for a run, okay? Let's go, Colette.'

Climbing on to the pillion seat, Colette put her arms round Jack's waist. 'Thanks a million for the helmet, Mr Thompson.' Without so much as a glance in Anne's direction she added, 'I'm ready, Jack.'

'Take care now, Jack. Don't go mad,' Dan warned.

'Don't worry, Dad. I'll just be feeling my way at first, until I get used to the feel of her. See you later.'

They shot off up the street as Dan yelled, 'Don't forget we're going out tonight.' Ignoring Anne completely he entered the house and closed the door before his wife had a chance to open her big trap again and take all the pleasure out of the occasion. And she was the one who could do just that.

Chapter Ten

On that Thursday night of Easter week a lot of wine was supped at the International Hotel with the appetising four-course gourmet dinner. They dallied over the meal, delighting in every delicious morsel, before retiring to the lounge for coffee and brandies. The evening that stretched before them proved to be a terrific success and Dan admitted to himself that he had been wrong in thinking that Tess would have been a more suitable partner for his son. Jack and Colette were obviously made for each other. He remembered his mother saying in the old days about apparently suited couples, 'When God made them, He matched them.'

It was a very merry trio that eventually arrived back at Spinner Street. As they stood giggling on the pavement outside Dan's door while he tried, unsuccessfully, with an unsteady hand, to find the keyhole, Mrs Burns opened her door and beckoned them in. A widow in her early seventies, she rarely left the house because of arthritis but liked dabbling about in the kitchen. She delighted in providing delicious dishes for her granddaughter and her friends. Now she pointed to the table on which stood a beautifully decorated birthday cake complete with twenty-one candles.

'Happy birthday, Jack.' She smiled happily at him.

Jack, who had adopted her as his grannie, carefully, so as not to cause her swollen joints any pain, lifted the small figure gently in his arms and kissed her tenderly on the cheek. 'Thanks, Grannie. It's beautiful. It was very thoughtful of you to bake it.'

An embarrassed smile crossed her face and she said gruffly, 'Put me down, you big fool, and I'll put the teapot on.'

'You'll do no such thing, Grannie!' Releasing her, Jack led her to the sofa. 'You sit yourself down there and I'll look after the tea.'

Colette had already beaten him to it. He followed her into the scullery and they grinned happily at each other as they waited for the kettle to boil.

Standing on tiptoe, Colette kissed him. 'Gran has been working on that cake all week. It's lovely, isn't it?'

'It's a work of art. Seems a shame to cut it. All those decorations must have taken hours. And I'm sure it will taste lovely too.'

Looking pleased at his praise, Colette agreed. 'You can be sure of that.'

'Your grannie is a wonderful wee woman.'

'Yes, she is. It's been a great night altogether, hasn't it?'

'It has,' Jack agreed. Gathering her close he wheedled, 'I don't suppose you'd agree to make it even better if I stayed behind when your gran retires to bed and Dad goes home?'

'Now you know my views on that, Jack Thompson! You'll have to hold yourself in check for another few months.'

'Oh, I suppose so. You're the boss. It's just I have this terrible fear that you'll meet someone else. Someone with a bit of money. You meet so many men through your work at the bank.'

Placing her hands against his chest, she gazed earnestly up at him. 'I love you, Jack Thompson. You're in my heart and in my mind. No one or nothing is going to change that. Money or no money. Now get that into your big thick skull.'

He still looked unconvinced. 'I love you so much. I can't believe you could possibly love me in return. I don't know what you see in someone like me.' They kissed again and not wanting to overstep the mark he fought down his rising passion and changed the subject. He hadn't given up hope, though. Perhaps she would change her mind later when they were alone. 'I hope this tea sobers me up a bit. I feel quite tipsy,' he confessed.

'So do I and I didn't drink half as much as you.'

Jack wagged a finger at her. 'Ah, but then, it's *my* birthday, and . . . I haven't to go to work in the morning,' he finished smugly.

She gave him a push. 'You lucky devil! Get out of my way and let me get the cups down. Away in and talk to your dad and my grannie.'

Dan had always found Mrs Burns a good conversationalist and Jack discovered them deep into current affairs. The escalation of American involvement in Vietnam was the topic of conversation so he sat down and listened.

The tea was poured and the cake cut and as they gathered around the table the troubles in south-east Asia were quickly forgotten.

Jack raised his cup. 'A toast to the three people who have made this such a wonderful day for me.' They all drank to that and then Dan went next door to fetch the beer and whiskey he had left in to finish off the celebrations.

*   *   *

Both father and son consumed too much that night, and as a result were nursing throbbing heads the following morning.

'I wish I hadn't told Mam I'd take her for a ride on my motorbike this morning.'

'I'd forgotten all about that. You'd be as well putting her off, son. Make another date. She'll understand.' Under his breath Dan muttered, 'Maybe.'

'Ah, Dad, I can't do that. She'll be ready and waiting. I can't let her down. You know what she's like.'

Dan rose to his feet, screwing his eyes closed and wincing as the sudden movement sent pain shooting through his head. 'I'll go up to Lily Brady's and explain to your mother . . .'

'No, Dad, please don't. She has missed out on so much, I feel sorry for her. I want to take her for a ride. I won't go far, I promise. Besides, I can't wait to get back on that bike. It's brilliant, so it is.'

'Do you feel well enough to go out on it? My head's throbbing. I certainly wouldn't fancy riding on a motorbike this morning, in my condition.'

'I don't think I'm quite as bad as you, Dad. My head's clearing already. But then, I didn't touch the whiskey and I have a cooked breakfast inside me. That's two things in my favour. Shall I phone work and explain you're feeling under the weather?'

'And have them all laughing up their sleeves at me? You'll do no such thing! A couple of aspirins and a mug of strong tea and I'll be as right as rain.'

'You really should eat that fry I've ready for you.'

'I couldn't face it, son. I believe aspirin and strong tea are the cure for a hangover. They've always worked for me in the past.'

With concern, Jack watched his father down some

aspirin tablets and drink a mug of strong tea before leaving the house, declaring himself fit and raring to go. In Jack's opinion he still looked a bit drunk.

Jack found that dunking his head under the cold water tap worked wonders at clearing the remaining cobwebs of his hangover. Once washed and shaved he was in fine fettle and ready for the road. Crossing the street, he opened the high wooden gate to Mrs McAnulty's yard and wheeled the bike outside, thrilled to the core to be the owner of such a fine machine.

Anne was ready and waiting and he was glad he hadn't put her off. 'How did your birthday treat go?'

'It was great, Mam. I'm sorry you couldn't be there.'

'Are you? I very much doubt that. I think with a little persuasion you could have gotten me invited,' she grunted sarcastically.

'That's not true, Mam! You know I wanted you there, but it was awkward. I wish things could be different, but I can't do anything about it.'

'You can.'

He looked bewildered. 'How?'

'Let's you and me find a flat where we can live together until your wedding. I know more about weddings than your dad ever could and with Colette's parents not wanting to be involved my experience could prove very helpful.'

'Colette's parents will be involved. They have agreed to accept me.'

'Is that good enough for you, son? To be accepted? To be tolerated!'

'Mam . . . as long as Colette loves me, that's all that matters. And anyway we don't see much of her family these days.' He was beginning to get a bit annoyed at her attitude. 'Are you coming for a ride or do you just want to stand there arguing?' She shrugged her shoulders and he handed her Colette's helmet.

She waved it away. 'I'm not going to wear that thing. It will ruin my new hair-do.'

He shrugged. 'Suit yourself. But we're not going anywhere unless you put it on.'

Reluctantly she donned the helmet and climbed on to the bike behind him.

'Hold on tight. Anywhere in particular you want to go?'

'No. I'm just happy to be with you, son,' she said, wishing to make amends for her bad behaviour.

'Okay, let's head up the Glen Road then. It's a long time since I've been up there. An old pal lives there near St Teresa's and I want to show off my new bike, if he's about. Right. Hang on, Mam. Here we go.'

Working automatically, Dan managed somehow to get through the morning, glad that he could almost do his job with his eyes shut. By lunch time his headache had subsided and, having skipped breakfast, he began to feel the pangs of hunger. Having neglected to bring any sandwiches with him, he went to the mobile cafe that parked outside the building site every work day and purchased a couple of bacon rolls and a mug of tea.

Choosing to sit a short distance from his noisy mates, who had been ribbing him all morning about his hangover, he was just finishing the last of his rolls and feeling much better for the nourishment when he saw Billy Robson, the foreman, leave the site office and walk towards the workers. Only then did he notice the police car parked in front of the office and a terrible premonition descended on him. A cold tremor went through his whole body. He knew it was bad news; just knew it!

Silence fell as Billy passed the rest of the gang. Followed by questioning stares and concerned looks, he continued to where Dan sat alone. When the foreman stopped in front of him and said, 'I'm sorry, Dan . . .' the howl that escaped Dan's lips and rent the air was almost inhuman.

The men were all on their feet, staring over, embarrassed, not knowing what was going on, not knowing what to say or do; how to be of help.

Billy patted his arm in futile comfort. 'The police want a word with you, Dan.'

'Is he . . . dead, Billy?'

'I don't know. They wouldn't tell me anything. Just said that your son's motorbike had been involved in an accident and they needed to speak to you.'

'Oh, my God. Oh, my God,' Dan whimpered, his mind spinning uncontrollably. He was afraid to rise, sure that his legs wouldn't support his large frame.

Holding out a helping hand, Billy said, 'Come on, Dan. They're waiting for you. You'll have to speak to them.'

Gripping the proffered hand, Dan allowed himself to be hauled up. He was glad to find that once upright he was steady enough on his feet, though somewhat shaky. 'Thanks, Billy.'

The police were very sympathetic and polite, explaining that no other vehicle was involved in the accident. Apparently, on the journey up the Glen Road, a dog had run out in front of the bike and Jack had swerved to avoid it. He lost control of the motorcycle and crashed head on into a stone wall. When the ambulance arrived he was declared dead at the scene but Dan's wife had survived, although she was in a critical condition in hospital.

'Have you any transport, Mr Thompson?' At his shake of the head the police offered to take him to the hospital where he would be required to formally identify his son's body.

He sat with his head buried in his large hands in the back of the police car beside the younger of the two constables, feeling as if he had fallen into a great chasm and couldn't get out. Surely he would wake up soon and discover it was all a bad dream. Suddenly Colette entered his head. 'Has Jack's girlfriend been notified?'

'I'm afraid we wouldn't know of any girlfriend, Mr Thompson. We were only told to contact you, being the next of kin,' was the polite reply.

'I understand.' Dan glanced at his watch. 'She will still be at work at the Northern Bank in the town centre. We can't have her finding out by herself. Will it be on the radio, do you think?'

'Most certainly, but your son's name will not be released until all the relatives have been informed.'

'But she will guess. You see, he only got the bike yesterday for his twenty-first birthday. She knows he's taking his mother for a spin on it today.'

The young constable looked aghast. What a tragedy! 'I'll radio in to the station and see if they can get some-one to pick her up from the bank. Will we have them bring her to the hospital?'

'Yes, please.' Where else could she go? If she landed in on her grannie with this terrible news, the poor old dear might have a heart attack. She was so fond of Jack.

Dan was taken to the City Hospital. He had always hated the disinfectant smell that seemed to permeate all hospitals, but today it really turned his stomach and he had to fight down the bile that rose in his throat as the constable led him down some stairs and along a corridor until they were standing outside the mortuary door.

'Are you ready, sir?'

Drawing a deep breath, Dan nodded. 'As ready as I'll ever be.'

Inside there were banks of what looked like large stainless steel filing cabinets. An attendant stood by one of the cabinets, his hand poised over the handle, and waited for the constable to give the go-ahead nod before slowly pulling on the drawer. It slid out effortlessly and almost silently, befitting the atmosphere in the room, to its full extent. A sheet covered the body that rested within.

The sheet was solemnly drawn back and Dan, gripping the drawer tightly with both hands as if to support himself, gazed in sorrow on his only son. There wasn't a mark or cut to be seen on his face. Dan had been worried in case Jack was so badly damaged he would be unable to recognise him. His shoulders slumped as he relaxed a little. 'That's him. That's my Jack,' he managed to mumble.

He swayed slightly and the constable quickly stepped forward and gripped his arm to steady him. Dan's other hand locked in a vice-like grip on the young man's arm. 'He doesn't look dead!' he cried shrilly. 'Are you sure? How did he die?'

It was the mortuary attendant who answered him. 'We're quite sure, sir. It was probably a broken neck, but the post-mortem will show the cause. If it's any consolation, sir, death would have been instantaneous. He wouldn't have suffered.'

The police had been quick picking Colette up and she was sitting in the corridor, hands on her lap, twisting nervously at her handkerchief. She gazed with dread at Dan as he approached. 'It's true then? It really is Jack? I kept hoping that it was some terrible mistake.' She started to sob uncontrollably.

Dan nodded speechlessly. He knew what she meant. Hadn't he felt the same?

'Can I see him?'

Dan looked askance at the constable. He answered the mute question. 'If you think it's wise, sir.'

Dan turned to Colette. 'He's not marked. Not even a single bruise. You'd think he was just lying there sleeping. I think you'd be as well seeing him, love, or you won't be able to believe he's dead. I'll wait here for you.'

Fifteen minutes later Colette returned to the corridor as white as a sheet, tears pouring down her face, her mascara, usually so attractive, now a complete mess of black smudges and streaks as she dabbed at her eyes with her already tear-soaked hankie. Dan gathered her close, comforting her as best he could.

A hand on his shoulder brought him back to attention. 'Would you like to see your wife now, sir?'

Colette pulled away from Dan, gaping at him in horror. 'Is *she* still alive?'

He nodded. 'Would you like to come with me?'

'No! No, I wouldn't. It's not fair! How come *she* survived?'

'Hush now, love. The constable will think you don't like Anne. Will you wait for me?'

The policeman interrupted. 'We'll see her home, if you like, Mr Thompson.'

Colette would like! 'That will be great, thank you.' Colette quickly accepted the offer before Dan could intervene. How could she pretend she was glad that *that* woman was still alive, when her beloved Jack was dead?

She just couldn't do it. 'I'll see you later, Mr Thompson.' She wanted to be alone in the privacy of her own home, to try to come to terms with this nightmare, but she dreaded breaking the news to her grannie.

Anne lay in the high hospital bed looking small and vulnerable. Behind the oxygen mask that covered the lower part of her face, Dan could see that she was badly marked. Her hair was scraped back from her forehead and stitches ran from the corner of one eye and down the side of her left cheek. She had two black eyes and looked battered, as if she had just gone fifteen rounds with Cassius Clay.

'She's sedated,' the nurse explained.

'How bad are her injuries?'

'A broken wrist, two broken ribs and a badly bruised sternum, which is making breathing difficult for her at the minute. She has to go back to the operating theatre for exploratory surgery, to see if there is any internal damage to the chest cavity. She did get the worst of the impact.'

Dan rounded on her in a fury. 'Are you daft, woman? She's *alive*! My son is *dead*, for God's sake.'

The nurse drew back alarmed in the face of such venom. 'I was only explaining her condition, Mr Thompson, like you asked. I think you'd be as well going home for a rest and coming back later. It's been a harrowing morning for you. If we need you, you'll be notified.'

Dan had every intention of going home. Anne was not his problem. He had a son to bury. He never stopped to wonder just whose problem Anne would be. The nurse looked after him in bewilderment. He had hardly looked at his wife! Hadn't even touched her hand as any normal husband would surely do. But then, he was probably in a state of shock, poor man. After all wasn't his son lying down in the morgue?

When Colette broke the news to Mrs Burns the small woman collapsed in a heap, sending her granddaughter into a state of sheer panic. She made to dash next door to get Dan's assistance but remembered in time that he wasn't there. She knew a doctor must be called out immediately, but how? She couldn't leave her grannie alone for any length of time. She saw Mrs McAnulty leave her house, and hailed her.

Once put in the picture wee Molly took control. 'Who's her doctor?'

'Dr Giles.'

'Same as myself. Look, love, Mrs Madden up the street has a phone. I'll get her to send for him.'

Dan arrived home in time to see Mrs Burns being stretchered into an ambulance and Colette clambering in after her.

He hurried forward. 'What's happened? Is Mrs Burns all right? Do you want me to come along, Colette?' The questions poured from his mouth.

'No, Mr Thompson, you have things to see to. I'll call in and see you when I get back. I'll tell you all about it then.'

Inside the house Dan sought the remains of the whiskey and poured himself a stiff drink before climbing the stairs. Colette was right, he had things to do. People to see. From the top of the wardrobe he removed an old battered shoe box and placed it on the bed. One by one he removed documents from it. When he came to his marriage certificate he paused, fighting the urge to rip it to shreds, but these were things you were supposed to keep safe so he set it down. Finding what he was looking for he put it to one side and, replacing the other documents, closed the box and put it back on top of the wardrobe.

Downstairs he smoothed out the Britannic insurance policy on the kitchen table. Would there be enough to bury Jack? He doubted it. No matter. Jack would go out in style, he'd make sure of that, should he have to beg, borrow or steal any extra money that may be required. Having settled that in his mind he cradled his head on his hands and gave way to his grief, great sobs ripping him apart and a sea of tears streaming from his eyes. How would he be able to bear this terrible tragedy? What had he done to deserve it?

He was awakened by a loud knocking on the door and the arrival of Bob Crosby and his workers to offer their condolences. He beckoned them in; offered them a drink which they declined, and thanked them for their trouble.

'If there's anything at all we can do, you know you only have to say the word. You know that, don't you, Dan?'

'I'll remember that, Bob.'

'Well then, we'll get back to work and leave you in peace. You look absolutely shattered, Dan, if you don't mind me saying so.'

'I am a bit tired. Thanks . . . lads, for coming over.'

They had no sooner gone than there was another knock on the door. This time it was Lily Brady.

'Dan, I've just heard the bad news. I'm so sorry.' She stood on the doorstep wringing her hands in despair. He reached for them and drew her into the house.

'Thanks, Lily. I don't how I'm going to manage, but I will . . . somehow.'

She waited, gazing speechlessly at him, obviously

expecting something more. He dithered, not knowing what she expected of him.

After a pause she blurted out, 'What about Anne? Wasn't she with him?'

He thumped his head with his fist. 'Good God! I'd completely forgotten about Anne. She's badly wounded, but I think they expect her to recover.'

Lily couldn't believe her ears. He sounded so indifferent. Didn't he care at all about the fate of his wife? 'Will they let me in to see her, do you think?'

'I don't see why not. And I'd be grateful if you would go. She's in the City Hospital. Awkward to get to from here. Will that be a problem, Lily?'

'No. My brother has a car; I'll get him to run me over after tea.' Lily continued to stare at him as if he had two heads. This man had been married to Anne and had lived with her here in this very house for twelve years and they had appeared happy enough at the time. Then to everybody's surprise Anne ran off with that guy from work. Now Dan didn't seem to care whether she lived or died. He was one hard-hearted bastard. 'Goodbye, Dan. I'll see myself out.' Poor Anne. Poor lonely Anne. What would become of her?

After Lily, a long string of friends, both Jack's and his, came to the door. The continual flow of people, the talk and reminiscing, lifted Dan's mind, helping him blank out his grief for the time being.

Colette returned from the hospital with the bad news that her grannie had had a slight heart attack and they were keeping her in for a couple of days for observation.

She looked at the stacks of dirty cups and glasses scattered about and cried in amazement, 'Did no one offer to wash these?'

[219]

'They did. But I wouldn't let them.'

She sighed. 'Right. First let's get these dishes cleared up and then I'll make us something to eat.'

Dan looked at her as if she had just uttered a string of obscenities. 'Are you mad? I couldn't eat a thing. Food would only choke me.'

'Mr Thompson, you're not the only one grieving,' she retorted sharply. 'I loved Jack too. I was going to marry him, remember. And I thought I was going to lose my grannie as well. In fact I might still lose her. But life goes on and we have a funeral to arrange. We must eat to keep up our strength.'

Seeing her point of view, he backed down. 'You're right. Of course you're right. But don't make too much, eh? Just scramble a couple of eggs.'

'If that's what you want. I take it you've been in touch with the undertaker?'

He shook his head. 'Not yet.'

She glanced at the clock. 'It's too late now. But first thing in the morning you must start to make arrangements, and don't forget the parish priest while you're at it. Right. I'll scramble some eggs and toast a bit of bread, then we'll clear up this mess.' She had no intention of letting him wallow in self-pity. He must be kept alert.

In the privacy of the scullery Colette buried her face in her hands and fought for control. She must be strong! Mr Thompson obviously didn't know whether he was coming or going. She had him and her grannie to think about. She would grieve later.

Friends and neighbours continued to call during the evening and Colette acted as hostess, making tea and trying to make things easier for Dan. About midnight they closed the door on the last visitor and Colette, who had managed to keep Dan away from the bottle most of the evening, relented and poured him a large Jameson's, courtesy of one of the callers. She poured one for herself as well and sat down. She intended staying to see he retired to bed, didn't sit boozing all night.

He sat on the settee and she sat near the fire watching him. Great tears rolled down his face. Unable to contain her own sorrow, she joined him on the settee and they cried together, united in grief.

Easter week was a time of joy for Tess. Dennis let Dominic have the loan of his car while he was on honeymoon and on Tuesday morning when Dominic phoned and asked Tess out for the day she at first demurred, saying that Tony would be returning to work that day and she had half promised Agnes that they would go out somewhere together. She confided in him that she was worried about her friend and didn't want to leave her to brood on her own.

Reluctantly he agreed that she could ask Agnes to come along but warned her that if Agnes refused, Tess must still come out with him.

Agnes was only too happy to agree. She wanted to make amends to Dominic for her bad manners towards him.

They all met in Tess's house and Dominic confided, 'I've been thinking. Why don't we go down south this time. Say maybe as far as Galway? What do you think?'

The girls looked at each other. It was Agnes who spoke. 'It's a long way to travel. We'd be no sooner there than we'd have to turn back.'

'Oh, how stupid of me. I didn't think of that,' Dominic lamented.

He looked so disappointed that Tess suggested, 'We

could of course take our night things and toothbrushes and stay overnight – or even two nights, for that matter. It would be a nice wee break. There's plenty of bed and breakfast places down south and they all have a good name.'

'That sounds like a smashing idea to me,' he agreed happily.

Realising that Agnes hadn't commented, they both looked at her for her reaction. She grimaced. 'I'm afraid you will have to go without me. Tony wouldn't be too pleased if I tagged along.'

'Sorry, Agnes,' Tess exclaimed. 'I wasn't thinking straight. Can we go somewhere else, Dominic? Somewhere closer to home?'

He paid her little attention. His eyes held Agnes's, intent and probing. Suddenly, as if they had discussed it telepathically, she said, 'I'll come. I'll leave a note for Tony.'

'Good girl! That's settled then. Tess, while you pack your bits and pieces, I'll run Agnes down to pack hers and come back for you. May as well pack your little green number, in case we go somewhere special while we're down there.'

Tess hesitated. She didn't want to cause any trouble between Agnes and Tony.

As if guessing her thoughts Dominic said, 'Come on, Tess, get a move on. It wasn't your decision, after all.'

Without another word she rushed upstairs. Dominic eyed Agnes. 'Are you sure this is what you want to do?'

Without removing her gaze from his, she whispered, 'More than anything else in the world.' Without giving it any thought she knew that she just wanted to please him.

He reached for her, but what might have happened

she would never know, because at that moment Tess suddenly reappeared to inquire if one dress would be enough, and the spell was broken. However, in the car going back home Agnes was aware of a lovely warm feeling around her heart. Surely not just because she was going to Galway? Feeling Dominic's gaze on her she turned and met his eyes. No! Definitely not because she was going to Galway.

They returned to pick up Tess and then went to collect some toiletries and extra clothes for Dominic. The girls waited outside the Sullivans' house on Mackie's Height and Tess, still worried about Tony's reaction when he discovered Agnes had gone on holiday without him, asked tentatively, 'Do you think Tony will be very upset?'

'At the moment I couldn't care one way or the other. I'm fed up bending over backwards to please everybody. I need this break to sort myself out.'

'Just so long as you know what you're doing.'

'I don't really, but for the first time in my life I'm willing to take the chance.'

The journey down through the towns, big and small, was a pleasure. Even when they passed through heavy showers and the rain beat mercilessly down on the car and Dominic had to stop because it was obscuring their vision, they were at peace with the world. After all, it was April, one had to expect showers of some sort, and they were on their way to Galway.

For part of the journey Tess sat in the front of the car with Dominic. They stopped in Cavan for lunch and afterwards Tess changed seats with Agnes. Glad that she and Dominic were friends again, Agnes covertly watched him as she sat up front, admiring his strong hands on the wheel. She began to fantasise about him, something she had never done about anyone in her life before, imagining him touching her. Wondering what it would be like to be kissed properly by him; not the friendly peck he had given her before, but a full-blooded kiss filled with passion! She laughed secretly, deriding herself. What did she know about passion? This thought caused her to brood on the word, analyse it. How come there was no passion in her relationship with Tony? That was her own fault. She never gave Tony a chance to get started; but then, she never had the desire to.

Dominic caught her eye in his peripheral vision and she blushed with shame. Could he possibly guess what she was thinking? For the rest of the journey she kept her eyes on the road and engaged Tess in small talk about the passing scenery to keep her mind from running amok again.

Dominic smiled, a secret smile. He was getting through to her. At last she was coming round to his way of thinking; he was in with a chance.

After a while the girls' chatter lapsed into silence. He brought her attention back to him.

'Are you all right, Agnes?'

Startled, she swung towards him. 'Of course. Why shouldn't I be?'

'You're not worrying about Tony, are you?'

Truthfully she answered him, 'No. But I do feel mean, taking off like this. I'm sure he will understand when I explain that I just had to get away for a while.'

Dominic looked sceptical but she had to have a show-down with Tony, clear the air once and for all.

'What about you, Tess? Are you all right back there?'

No answer. A quick glance in the driving mirror confirmed that Tess was asleep. Without further ado, Dominic caught hold of Agnes's hand and kissing the palm he closed her fingers round it. 'Keep that for me. I'll get it back when you're ready.'

Agnes nodded slowly, her brow puckered. When she was ready? What did he mean?

Dominic insisted that they do it in style, his treat. He booked them into the Warwick Hotel, in Salthill on the outskirts of Galway, for bed and breakfast and inquired about entertainment. He was informed that there was no entertainment in the hotel on a Tuesday night but that dances were held regularly in a hall further up the road.

They decided that they would have a short rest and freshen up before going out for a meal and later to the dance. The girls were sharing a room and when they had each had a bath and were preparing for their evening out, Tess confided in Agnes. 'I'm glad you and Dominic are friends again. He really is a nice person.'

Suddenly apprehensive, Agnes asked, 'You haven't gone and fallen for him, have you?'

Remembering the hurt caused by Jack Thompson, Tess was cautious. 'Not really. I'm very fond of him, mind, and he has hinted that he would like to remain in Ireland, so who knows how things might turn out?'

Agnes concentrated on her eye make-up. She should have known that Tess was likely to fall for Dominic. What difference did it make, anyway? She was engaged to Tony. However, she discovered that it certainly did make one hell of a difference. The idea of Dominic maybe one day marrying her best friend devastated her. Why? She hadn't been in the least annoyed when Tess was falling for Jack Thompson.

It was raining when they joined Dominic in the lounge. A perusal of the dinner menu made them decide to remain in the hotel for their meal and avoid getting wet before going to the dance. The dance hall was packed and Tess caused a stir in her green dress. Once the local men became aware that she was unattached, she wasn't short of partners and Dominic was free to dance a lot of the time with Agnes.

Agnes dared to tease him. 'You'll be sorry you asked me along.'

'Why?'

'I'm keeping you from dancing with Tess.'

'If I wanted to dance more with Tess I'd ask her before anyone else had the chance. Am I monopolising you? Perhaps you'd rather dance with some of the local talent?'

'No,' she whispered, her voice husky. 'I'd rather be with you.'

He held her closer and was content when she didn't draw away. He was making headway.

Tess was having the time of her life as she twirled around the floor in the arms of numerous men. She could see it was giving her friend and Dominic a chance to get over their differences and was pleased. They danced until the early hours of the morning and returned exhausted but happy to the hotel.

They spent Wednesday exploring Galway and the surrounding countryside and returned to the hotel for dinner. Afterwards, in the lounge Tess slipped off her shoes and rubbed her hot, weary feet. 'I think I'll retire early. You two look quite fresh, but I feel completely whacked. Do you mind if I leave you?'

'Not at all. Will you have another drink before you go up?'

'No, thank you, Dominic. I think I'll have a hot bath

and go straight to bed. Good night, Agnes, Dominic. See you both in the morning.'

'I'll be very quiet when I come up and try not to disturb you.'

'Be as noisy as you want, Agnes. As long as I'm in bed you won't annoy me.'

At the door of the lounge she waved and they returned her salute. Slowly Dominic turned his gaze on Agnes. 'Have you ever watched the sun go down on Galway Bay?'

She laughed. 'No. I'm afraid that is something I've never managed to do.'

'I can't go back to Florida and say I was in Galway and didn't see the sun go down on the bay. I'd never hear the end of it.' He raised a brow at her.

'No. That is something you'll have to do,' she agreed solemnly.

'Will you join me?'

'I'd love to.'

'Then you will have to wrap up warmly. It gets chilly late on.'

Tess was surprised to see her friend so soon. 'I didn't expect you to be up for another hour or so.'

Agnes explained Dominic's desire to see the sun go down on the bay.

'I wish he had said sooner. I've a bath running or I'd come with you.'

Agnes hesitated, undecided. Without understanding why, she found herself praying that Tess wouldn't decide to join them. She breathed a sigh of relief when Tess said, 'I think I'll just stay here in our room. I really am very tired.'

'See you later, then.' Grabbing her coat and scarf, Agnes was out of the door before her friend could change her mind, leaving Tess staring at it, a perplexed frown on her brow.

They left the hotel and Dominic drew her arm through his and pressed it close to his side. This was an unexpected chance to make her aware of him as a man; not just Dennis's brother. She was completely unawakened. She thought that she and Tony were on the right track for marriage. Who knows, perhaps she was right. He only knew that from the moment he first set eyes on her he had wanted her for his wife.

They watched in awe as the sun slowly appeared to sink into the bay, lighting up the sky in a blazing, golden backdrop. It was an experience that Dominic would never forget.

Cuddling even closer to him, Agnes whispered, 'Wasn't that beautiful?'

He held her against his body. 'It still is.'

She lifted her face to his and nodded. With a finger he tilted her face until he had a clear route to her mouth, and then he fastened his lips on hers. She returned kiss for kiss, caress for caress. They stayed locked together for some time until he sighed and put her gently from him.

'It's time we were getting back to the hotel.' An arm across her shoulders, he led her away from the darkening horizon. 'What did you think of that, then?'

'It was wonderful.'

'It wasn't the sunset I was talking about.'

'I know,' she whispered, as if afraid to admit the effect he had had on her. 'You are wonderful.'

He sighed contentedly. 'You know now you're engaged to the wrong man, don't you?'

'Yes. But it's much too late for us. I couldn't do anything to hurt Tony. He has been so patient and kind to me.'

Dominic couldn't believe his ears. He gripped her by the shoulders. 'What about me? Don't I come into this anywhere?' She looked so bewildered, he released her. He had no intention of trying to coerce her. She must come off her own bat or not at all. 'I've shown you how I feel about you. I'm returning to Florida sooner than planned. If you care about me you must break off with Tony and come to Florida with me. The choice is yours.'

Agnes was in a state of confusion. When she dwelt on thoughts of Dominic, the happiness she felt was new to her. She had never known anything like it. However, Tony was the stumbling block. How could she do anything that would hurt him? It was on the journey home, when they had stopped once again in Cavan and got out to stretch their legs with a short stroll down the main street and then back to the same restaurant for lunch, that Agnes had a rude awakening.

She and Tess were in the cloakroom of the restaurant, refreshing themselves before continuing the journey, when Tess smiled happily at her and said, 'I'm delighted you and Dominic are friends again. Now if he decides to stay in Ireland, which I hope he does, I can pursue him with a happy frame of mind.'

Agnes turned a startled look on her. 'You mean you really do fancy him?'

'Yes. I wasn't going to tell you after all those shenanigans with Jack Thompson but I feel quite confident that Dominic likes me too.'

'Why, has he said anything?'

'Not outright, but I do know he has met someone he can care for . . . and if not me, who else? He hasn't bothered with anyone else that I know of.'

'Would you be willing to go to Florida with him?'

'Oh, no. I couldn't leave Mam, but he has implied that he would like to stay here in Ireland.'

Agnes was confused. Had she picked Dominic up wrong? Probably. After all, he had been talking in riddles as far as she was concerned. He had kissed her, and that had knocked all sensible reasoning out of her head. What kind of mind games was he playing at?

Dominic noticed the difference in Agnes's attitude towards him during the rest of the journey and could not account for it. When he dropped her off at her door a grim-faced Tony came out to meet her. A cup of tea was politely declined. Dominic tried to catch Agnes's eye but she avoided contact, so wishing them both good night he drove off.

'I wouldn't have minded a nice cup of tea,' Tess said plaintively. She was annoyed at not being given the chance to accept.

'Oh, Tess, I do apologise. That look on Tony's face put me right off,' he lied blithely. If Agnes had been more forthcoming he would have ignored Tony's attitude.

'You're right. I do hope Agnes doesn't grovel to him. Just because they are engaged to be married doesn't mean he owns her. She's too soft where he's concerned.'

Dominic agreed wholeheartedly. Had he shown his hand too soon? Would Agnes be strong enough to break off with Tony? Would she realise that they were soulmates? Or was it all only in his head? Only time would tell.

Chapter Eleven

They were home so late on Thursday that Tess was glad her mother had decided to stay on in Carlingford until Saturday. It would give her a chance to tidy up the house on Friday, get in the groceries and hide the little green dress somewhere her mother wouldn't come across it. These last few days had been so happy she was still floating on cloud nine. As far as she was concerned, life had never been so exciting.

On Friday evening she was in the work room getting everything ready for her return to the grindstone the following week when she saw Tony and Agnes approach the house. They saw her, waved, and waited to be admitted.

'This is a nice surprise,' she greeted them. 'I was just about to make a cup of tea. Will you join me?' They both looked pale and strained and this worried Tess. She wondered if Tony was still annoyed at Agnes for going to Galway without him. She supposed he had cause to be disgruntled, but surely he wouldn't continue to hold a grudge if he really loved Agnes.

To Tess's bewilderment, without as much as a hello or anything, Agnes took her by the arm, and, leading her into the living room, pushed her gently down on to a chair. 'We have some bad news, I'm afraid.'

Tess's thoughts immediately flew to Alice. 'Is it my mam? Has something happened to her?' It would be just like Malachy to try to soften the blow by phoning Agnes and asking her to break any bad news in person.

'No. Relax. Your mam is okay. At least, we haven't heard anything to the contrary.' Agnes paused and bit hard on her lip before blurting out, 'I'm afraid it's Jack. He was killed today on his new motorbike.'

Tess sat stunned, remembering Dan's excitement at buying the motorcycle. He had been absolutely over the moon about it.

Her silence worried Agnes and she asked anxiously, 'Are you all right, Tess? Can I get you a drink or something?'

'No. No, I'm fine. I just can't take it in. Mr Thompson must be in an awful state. He bought Jack that bike for his twenty-first birthday. He will be blaming himself. And poor Colette. She must be absolutely devastated.'

Glad that her friend's thoughts were all for others with no obvious signs of distress for herself, Agnes's shoulders rose and fell in a sigh of relief and she slipped off her coat. 'You stay there and I'll put the kettle on for that cup of tea.'

While Agnes was in the kitchen, Tess questioned Tony. 'When did you say it happened?'

'Early today.'

'How did you find out about it?'

'It was on the radio at lunch time but I didn't twig. You see, no names were mentioned. They just said that a man and woman were involved in a fatal motorcycle accident but names were being withheld until the relatives had been notified. I didn't know anything about the bike so I didn't give it a second thought. Then one of the lads went out for cigarettes and said he had heard

Jack Thompson's name mentioned in the newsagent's. That's when I learned who it was.'

'A man and woman?' Tess latched on to this piece of information. 'Was Colette with him?'

Tony shook his head. 'Apparently he had been taking his mother for a ride.'

'Is Anne dead too?'

'No, but I hear she is badly injured. They took her to the City Hospital.'

'Wait until my mam hears about this. She'll be gutted.'

'When is she due home?'

'Tomorrow morning. Have you been down to see Dan?'

'Yes, but I just stayed a few minutes. The house was packed and I didn't like to ask any questions about what happened. Dan's in an awful state. And to crown it all, Colette's grannie collapsed when she heard about it and she was rushed to the Royal. Agnes and I will call down in the morning and see if we can be of any help.'

'Poor Colette. Poor Mrs Burns! God, it never rains but it pours. I'd come with you but I've to meet Mam at the station. I'll see what she wants to do.' Tess shook her head. 'It's so hard to take in, that Jack is dead. I can't believe it. I'll go and give Agnes a hand with the tea, Tony.'

Agnes was pouring water into the teapot and eyed Tess keenly when she entered the kitchen. 'I was very worried when I heard about Jack. About how the news would affect you, that is. I didn't know how you'd take it.'

'No need to worry about me. I got over Jack some time ago. It's poor Colette I'm worried about. She must be heartbroken.'

'And Dan! How must he feel, having bought Jack the

bike? Eh? I must admit I'm not looking forward to seeing him tomorrow.'

Tess lifted the now laden tray. 'Let's take this into the living room.' She paused and lowered her voice. 'Is Tony all right about you going to Galway without any warning?'

Agnes shrugged. 'There's nothing he can do about it. I'm my own boss.'

'But . . . is the engagement still on?'

Agnes nodded despondently. If only it wasn't, she lamented inwardly. 'Oh, yes. It will take more than that to separate us.'

Dominic phoned later that night to invite Tess out for a meal and on to the cinema the following day. Tess explained the circumstances and reminded him that her mother was returning home tomorrow morning. 'She's bound to be upset and I don't know whether I'll be able to leave her on her own and come out with you.'

'Tell you what, I'll drive you to the bus station in the morning and we'll take it from there, okay?'

'That would be wonderful. Thank you very much, Dominic.' A time was arranged for him to pick her up, and when she placed the receiver back in the cradle she felt a sudden surge of guilt. She was happy that she would be seeing Dominic, when poor Jack was lying in the mortuary, dead.

Tess was apprehensive as she waited at the station next morning, with Dominic, for her mother's return from Carlingford. 'Do you think I should tell her straight away or wait until we get home?'

'Does it make any difference? I mean, will she be very upset? Was your mother very fond of this lad?'

'No, I wouldn't go so far as to say that. Quite the

opposite in fact. You see, Jack dated me a few times and I was upset when he dropped me and started going out with another girl. Mam foolishly held it against him. Although it didn't stop her becoming friendly with his father,' she added drily.

'Ah, now I understand. So this Jack Thompson is the lad Agnes was telling me about? The one who broke your heart?'

Tess's mouth gaped slightly at these revelations. 'Why did she tell you that? She had no right to discuss my affairs with you.'

'She was warning me off. Said you were still fragile and I must be careful not to give you any wrong ideas.'

'And were you careful not to give me any wrong ideas?'

'I hope I made my intentions quite clear to you. I certainly didn't want to cause any concern.'

He was saved from further questions as the bus pulled into the bay where they waited and Tess caught sight of her mother and waved.

Alice left the bus and stood waiting for an introduction to the handsome young man accompanying her daughter.

'Mam, this is Dennis Sullivan's brother. He came home from Florida to be best man at the wedding. He was kind enough to offer me a lift down to meet you.'

'That was very kind of him.'

Dominic gripped her hand and, flirtatious as usual, said, 'I'm very pleased to meet you, Mrs Maguire. Tess neglected to mention how lovely you are. And, by the way, my name is Dominic.'

Tess suppressed a smile as her mother preened herself and said graciously, 'I'm pleased to meet you too, Dominic.'

Introductions over, Alice let her gaze scan the bus

station. 'I thought Dan might have been with you.'

'Mam, I've some bad news.'

'About Dan?' She was alert at once. 'Has he gone back to his wife?'

Tess never ceased to wonder how everyone first jumped to the conclusion that might affect *them*. 'No, it's Jack. Did you know he was twenty-one last Thursday?'

Alice shook her head. 'No. Dan never mentioned it.'

'Well, Dan bought Jack a motorbike for his birthday and he crashed on it yesterday morning and was killed.'

'Oh, my God.' Alice's hand covered her mouth and she whispered behind it. 'Sweet Jesus have mercy on his soul. Dan must be in an awful state. I must go to him immediately.'

'Would you not be better going home first and freshening up?'

'No. Dan might need me.'

Tess glanced at Dominic and he responded immediately. Reaching for Alice's luggage he said, 'Give me directions and I'll take you both there.'

'Thank you.'

They found Dan's house locked up and the window blind down. Colette came from next door and beckoned them in. 'Mr Thompson has gone to the undertakers to make arrangements for the funeral.' She was pale and red-eyed from lack of sleep and crying.

Tess immediately put her arms round Colette and held her close, rocking her gently to and fro. 'I'm so sorry for you. So very, very sorry.'

The women were in tears and, embarrassed, Dominic moved restlessly, shuffling from one foot to the other.

Wiping her eyes, Tess said, 'Forgive me. My manners

are terrible. Colette, this is Dominic Sullivan, Dennis's brother.'

Dominic gripped her small hand. 'Sorry we couldn't meet in happier circumstances. If there's anything at all I can do, please let me know. Now I know you don't know me, but I really mean that.'

'Thanks.'

'Has Dan been gone long?'

'Here he is now,' Colette said, as she recognised Dan's step in the hall. With a light tap on the door he entered the room.

He stopped abruptly when he saw Alice. She went to him and slowly – almost reluctantly, it seemed – he opened his arms to embrace her. He released her at once, and nodded a greeting to Tess. A bit put out, Alice said, 'I'm sorry I wasn't here, Dan.'

'Don't be. After all, you had better things to do, Alice.'

Alice couldn't hide her hurt surprise at his words and curt tone of voice. To cover her mother's confusion, Tess introduced Dominic and offered her condolences.

'Mam is just off the bus from Carlingford. I'm sure she's tired, so we will leave you for now, Dan, and come back later on today or tomorrow morning. Okay?'

'Yes, Alice will be tired after her extended holiday,' Dan agreed. 'Don't worry about coming back. There will be plenty of people here over the next few days. Excuse me, please.' With these words he passed through the scullery and out into the yard, leaving a stunned silence behind.

At a loss for words and close to tears, Alice looked beseechingly at Tess. 'I think we'd better go.'

'Of course, Mam. Sorry to rush away like this, Colette, but whether Dan likes it or not we will be back.'

'I'd wait until tomorrow if I were you, Tess,' Colette

advised. 'The mood he's in at the moment, he's not very sociable.'

'That's probably good advice. We'll see you tomorrow, then.'

Dan stood in the yard and berated himself. What on earth had gotten into him? Imagine speaking to Alice like that. And in front of a stranger too. Still, if she had returned on Wednesday as planned she would have been here when he most needed her and perhaps he wouldn't now feel so steeped in guilt. He'd had no one to turn to. Well, that wasn't unusual, he reminded himself. After all, he had managed on his own all these years, so why should he need a woman now?

His guilt had stemmed from his evil thoughts. He had wished Anne would fall under a bus, God forgive him. But it had backfired. Instead he had lost his only son.

He delayed for a while outside and when he eventually returned indoors, the others had gone and Lily Brady was sitting there talking to Colette. He nodded to Lily in acknowledgement and would have passed outside to go home, but she rose to her feet. 'Dan, I must speak to you.'

Realising that he had forgotten to inquire after his wife's health, he said, 'Did you see Anne last night?' She nodded and he continued, 'How is she?'

'That's what I want to talk to you about.'

He felt apprehensive. 'Anne is no concern of mine any more, Lily. Hasn't been for the last nine years.'

'I'm afraid you're going to have to take some kind of responsibility for her, Dan. You're all she has, you know.'

Dan frowned, and Lily rushed on. 'They will let her out in a few days, so long as she has somewhere to go and someone to keep an eye on her.'

'Isn't she living with you?'

'Dan, as you well know, I've two sons. They share the second bedroom. Bill is away on a course and decided to stay with friends over Easter. Tom offered to sleep on the settee and let Anne have the bedroom for the holiday period. But in a few days' time Bill will be home and I'll have no room for Anne. She understands that. I made it crystal clear when she first came to me that it would be for a short time only.' Her hands spread in a futile gesture. 'But then this happened.'

'And what did Anne intend doing when Bill came home? She must have had some plans.'

Lily looked shame-faced. 'She had hoped that she would have persuaded Jack to set up house with her by then.'

Dan was dazed. Had he not enough on his plate without worrying about Anne? 'I've nowhere to put her,' he said curtly.

'Ah, come on now, Dan. There's two bedrooms in all these houses.' Annoyed at his callousness, Lily cried bitterly, 'Jack won't need his any more, after all.'

White with fury, Dan pointed to the door. 'How dare you. Get out! Go on, get out. Anne is not going to have Jack's room.'

Lily stepped towards the door but stopped. 'I've a message from Anne. She says to tell you that Jimmy settled a generous allowance on her when they split up and she wants to contribute to the funeral costs.'

'You tell her to stick it! I don't need or want her money.'

'And will you take her in?'

'I will not! And you can tell her that too. If she hadn't been trying to come between me and my son she'd have had a place of her own by now. And, God knows, this might never have happened. So, tough, if she has nowhere to go!'

Lily slammed the door on her way out and Dan turned to where Colette sat, wide eyed, listening to his ranting. 'Sorry about that, love.'

'I hope you don't mind my saying so, Dan, but it looks as if you will have no other option than to take Anne in for a while. She is still your wife, after all, even if in name only. You can't just abandon her.'

'She abandoned me, and Jack! I feel nothing for her. Nothing! I applied for a divorce just last week and if we live under the same roof it will only slow up the proceedings.'

Colette shrugged. She had nothing to be grateful to Anne for. She was just trying to be charitable. 'If you happen to be looking for me later on, Dan, I'll be out for a while. I'm going to the hospital to see Grannie.'

Dan's expression softened. 'Give her my regards, won't you? But hold on a minute. Will you take a look at these first, and tell me what you think?'

He took some sheets of paper from his pocket and spread them on the table. They were pictures of coffins and accessories. 'I chose this one and these handles and a crucifix for the lid. What do you think?'

Colette noted that he had chosen the most expensive items. She said, tentatively, 'Can you afford these? Everything doesn't have to be the dearest, you know. No one is going to be examining them. I think you should pick something a little less expensive, Mr Thompson.'

'Only the best will do for my son. As well as the hearse there will be two limousines. Will that be enough, do you think?'

Colette nodded silently; tears, already so close to the surface, were ready to fall again.

Dan took her gently in his arms but she pushed him roughly away. 'Leave me alone. I'll be all right! I forgot to tell you, Mam is coming tomorrow and staying for the funeral. When is Jack being buried?'

'I haven't seen the priest yet.' At her look of amazement he hurriedly gathered up the papers and turned to the door. 'I'm on my way down to St Peter's right now.'

Once he'd gone Colette closed and locked the outer door and curled up on the settee. She was exhausted; needed a good rest, needed some time to herself. If Grannie's health permitted, she would go back to Omagh with her parents. Not something she wanted to do, but there was nothing left for her here, now that Jack was gone. She dozed on and off for an hour and then, still dopey from lack of sleep, prepared to visit her grannie.

Tess invited Dominic in for a bite to eat when he dropped them off, but he had had enough of weeping women for one day and gracefully declined. 'I'll give you a ring tomorrow and perhaps we will be able to arrange something for during the week,' he suggested, placing Alice's luggage in the hallway.

'That would be nice. Thanks for everything, Dominic.'

Alice was sitting on the edge of a chair hugging herself as if for comfort. 'Did you hear the way Dan spoke to me back there?'

'Now, Mam, he's not himself. He has a lot on his plate with Jack dead and Anne in hospital and all the arrangements to make. He must be out of his mind with worry.'

Wild eyed, Alice's fear came to the surface again. 'Do you think he will have her back?'

At her wits' end as to how to reason with her mother, Tess said, 'Even if he doesn't, Mam, it will make no difference. They're still married.'

'Oh, I wish she had died instead of Jack. That would have solved all our problems.'

'Mam! Listen to yourself. How can you even think such a thing?'

'Because these past ten days away have shown me how much I love Dan Thompson, that's how! I can't picture life without him any more. We were getting on so well together and now there seems to be a great rift between us and I can't get through to him. I wish I hadn't let myself be persuaded to go to Carlingford.'

Although unspoken, the words 'It's all your fault' hung in the air. Tess was annoyed and it showed in the look she bestowed on her mother. She retaliated quickly. 'Then why didn't you come home on Wednesday as planned? Eh? To be truthful I thought someone else had caught your fancy. Perhaps Dan thought so too.'

'No one I met could hold a candle to Dan Thompson. When Rose asked me to stay over for a few extra days, I suppose I agreed because I was trying to make Dan jealous; make him realise that he really cared for me. Instead I seem to have given him the wrong impression. I've implied that I don't care for him enough. It will be all my fault if he takes Anne back.' Her body was racked by harsh sobs.

Tess knelt beside her mother and held her close. 'Forget about Anne Thompson for the time being. It might never happen. We must wait and see what *does* happen. We'll wait until tomorrow and after Mass in the morning we'll both go down and offer our assistance. Dan will have had a chance to collect his thoughts and I'm sure he will be glad of our help around the house, looking after his visitors.'

*   *   *

She was wrong. Next morning when once again they arrived at his house on their errand of mercy, Dan showed no inclination to accept their help, insisting that everything was being taken care of. Worried, Tess took Colette to one side. 'Is Dan managing okay?'

Colette shrugged. 'He's locking all his grief up inside himself. He doesn't say much to me.'

'When's the funeral?'

'Tomorrow, after Requiem Mass in St Peter's. The Mass is at eleven o'clock. That much I do know.'

'Won't some of the mourners be invited back to the house afterwards? Who's going to make the tea and sandwiches and all that? You can't possibly manage all on your own, Colette.'

'I've questioned him till I'm blue in the face, but he says I'm not to worry my head about anything. Just look after my mother and father when they arrive.'

'They're coming for the funeral?'

'Yes. They arrive today and go back Tuesday.'

'What will you do, Colette?'

'I'll stay until my grannie is well enough to look after herself, and then I suppose I'll go back home. There's nothing for me here any more.'

Although Tess and Alice were the only visitors, after a curt greeting in their direction Dan kept his distance, leaving Colette to entertain them.

While Tess and Colette were talking, Alice waited her chance to have a quiet word alone with Dan. Determined to get to the bottom of his obvious animosity towards her, she followed him when he muttered something and restlessly went into the scullery. Pausing on the threshold, she pleaded, 'Don't do this to me, Dan.'

She moved closer and to her relief he didn't back

away and seek refuge in the yard. 'I don't know what you mean,' he blustered.

'I think you do. You're blaming me. You're acting as if I were the cause of the accident because I stayed over an extra three days. That's the only reason I can think of for your present behaviour.'

Suddenly he gripped her by the shoulders. 'Look, Alice, I admit that at first I was annoyed at you for staying away longer than planned. Annoyed? I was consumed with jealousy, thinking you had met someone else. But perhaps it was all for the best. I treated Jack and Colette to a slap-up meal in the International Hotel on Thursday night as part of his birthday present and I wanted you to be there. I wanted you to get to know him better. See what a fine lad he is . . . was.'

'You should have said before I went away. I would certainly have come.'

He shrugged. 'I never thought for one minute you'd stay longer than planned. I couldn't have stayed away from you if the circumstances had been reversed.'

'I know. I was foolishly trying to make you jealous.'

'Ah, Alice. Well, you certainly succeeded. But that's all water under the bridge. Now I'm just keeping my distance because I know there's no hope for us. I don't want you to get caught up in anything that you might later regret.'

'Don't be silly. As far as I'm concerned, nothing has changed. We can still be friends, can't we?'

He shook his head in sorrow. 'That's not good enough for me any more. I love you, Alice. And because I love you, I did a terrible thing! I wished Anne would fall under a bus. Imagine wishing that on your own wife, just so you could be free to marry someone else. I didn't really mean it, of course. But the thought was there.

[244]

Well, I certainly received an answer to my wish. Jack was taken from me.'

Appalled at his revelations, Alice whispered furiously, 'Now you're talking rubbish and you know it.'

'Listen to me, Alice! Anne has nowhere to go. I might be forced to bring her here to stay until she recovers.'

These words floored Alice. Was her worst fear to be realised? 'Can't she go to one of her friends?'

'She hasn't any, I'm afraid. She severed all her connections round here when she left me and Jack.'

'Where was she living?'

'With a woman up the street, but she was only staying there over the Easter holidays. Lily Brady has been to see me and says she needs Anne's room back as her sons will be back in the house next week. So Anne has nowhere else to go. Now do you understand?'

He gazed at the sadness in her eyes and, drawing her further into the scullery, against his better judgement he roughly gathered her close and kissed her trembling lips. Alice hungrily responded. Slowly, he released her. 'Why did this have to happen, Alice? I had such high hopes for us. I had applied for a divorce, hoping to persuade you to marry me in a register office, but that's all hit on the head now.'

These words salved Alice's wounded pride. Register office? What did it matter. He had admitted that he loved her and wanted to marry her.

From her seat near the fireside, Tess could not see Dan, just her mother near the entrance to the scullery. When Dan's hands came into view and gripped her mother's shoulders, Tess moved to the edge of her chair, ready to intervene if anything started in there. She had to fight hard to control her impulse to interfere. Alice wouldn't thank her for it, but neither had she any intention of letting Dan hurt her mother.

At the same time, if Alice was making a fool of herself, Tess was the one who would have to be around to pick up the pieces and live with the results. She dragged her mind back to what Colette was saying.

'He assures me the catering has been arranged and a wreath ordered. This is my first funeral, Tess. Is there anything else I should be reminding him of?'

'I don't know. I was too young when my father died to pay much attention to what was going on. I'm more into weddings than anything else. I'll ask Mam . . . that is, if she can manage to tear herself out of that scullery.'

As if she had heard her, Alice entered the kitchen. She was pale and had obviously been crying, but looked more relaxed than she had previously. Dan followed her to the settee and they sat close together.

'Mam, have you and Dan been discussing the funeral arrangements?' It was obvious from their guilty expressions that they hadn't. Tess turned her attention to Dan. 'Look, I'm not being nosy, Dan, I just want to make sure everything is under control and you haven't forgotten anything.'

Dan spread one hand out and ticked off the items on his fingers. 'First, I've been to the undertaker and arranged for a new grave to be opened in Milltown Cemetery. Second, I've ordered the cars and picked a coffin. And last but not least I've seen the priest. Jack's body will be received into the church tonight at seven o'clock and he will be buried tomorrow after eleven o'clock Mass.' His eyes passed from one to the other of them questioningly. 'Have I forgotten anything?'

It was Alice who spoke next. 'Are you not bringing him home, then?'

'No, it would break my heart to have him lying here

for all and sundry to gawk at. It's much better this way.'

'Have you put a notice in the newspapers to let people know when the funeral is taking place?' Tess asked. It was a bit late thinking of that now, but better late than never. At least it could be in tomorrow's *Irish News*.

'To be truthful, I'd forgotten all about that.' He caught and held Colette's eye. 'I can't remember whether or not I mentioned to you about the newspapers on Friday night, Colette. Everything was such a blur then.' Tight lipped, she shook her head as if in anger. He apologised quickly. 'Sorry about that, but if I recall correctly, I was quite drunk at the time.' A brow was raised in Colette's direction. He received another curt angry nod. 'Anyhow, I called into the Silk & Rayon on Friday afternoon to let Jack's boss know what had happened, but he already knew about the accident. It was him who mentioned the newspapers. When I admitted I hadn't given it a thought, he kindly offered to see to it for me. We wrote out all the details between us and it was in yesterday's *Irish News* and last night's *Telegraph*. Luckily, Father McAleese later fell in with all my wishes regarding the time of admittance to church on Sunday night and the Requiem Mass at eleven on Monday.'

'Thank God for that!' Tess exclaimed. 'That only leaves the catering. Agnes has offered to help us three with that, if you will allow us.'

'There's no need. That is also taken care of. Mrs McAnulty and a few other neighbours are looking after that for me, so you see' – he spread his hands wide – 'like I said, it's all under control.'

They were all looking at him, flabbergasted. He wearily washed his hands over his face. 'I've surprised you, haven't I? Seeing to all these arrangements is what has kept me sane this past couple of days,' he admitted.

Reaching for his hand Alice clasped it and moved closer to him. He returned her grip like a dying man grasping at a straw. With one accord Tess and Colette rose to their feet.

'Mam, I'll go in next door with Colette for a while. I'll be back for you in half an hour or so, okay?'

An absentminded nod was all the reply she received and the girls left the house, closing the outer door behind them.

'I don't know what is to become of those two,' Tess confided in Colette. 'Is it all right if I come in with you for a while?'

'Of course it is. I'll be only too glad of your company. You can talk to me, take my mind off things, while I prepare something for Mam coming. I envy Dan having your mother to turn to. They can at least comfort each other. I feel so alone and empty. It would be different if Grannie were here; she's great company.'

'I'm glad your parents are coming for the funeral. They'll be there to support you.'

'Yes. I suppose I shouldn't say this, but I bet Mam's relieved that the wedding will not now take place.' Colette choked back a sob at this confession.

At a loss for words of comfort, Tess cried, 'Oh, I'm sure you're wrong.'

'You don't know my mother.'

'Colette, I know we never got the chance to become friends the way things happened, but I do like you and, if you ever need someone to talk to, I'll be here for you.'

'Thanks, Tess. I'll remember that.' Colette raised her head and peered through the net curtains. 'Here's Mam now.'

Tess rose hurriedly to her feet. 'I'm sure you'll have

a lot to talk about so I'll go now and let you get on with it.'

'You'll do nothing of the kind. You'll stay and have a cup of tea with us. You told your mam you'd come for her in half an hour or so. That was only ten minutes ago.'

Colette listened for the car door to slam and then went out to greet her parents. Colette's mother was tall and elegant. The man who followed her through the doorway was grey-haired and distinguished looking.

'Tess . . . this is my mother and stepfather. Betty and Stan. Tess is a friend of mine.'

'This is a terrible situation, isn't it?' Betty lamented. 'Such a loss of a young life.'

'At least the wedding will not now take place.'

'Now, now, Colette . . . no need to speak to your mother like that. Obviously these things are laid out for us. It wasn't meant to be.'

'Do you really believe that, Stan?'

'Yes. As a matter of fact I do. I've seen it happen time and time again. It is known as fate.'

'You mean . . . in your opinion, if I hadn't met Jack and planned to marry him, he'd still be alive today. You're talking through your hat.'

With a quick glance in Tess's direction, Stan said warningly, 'Now, Colette, let's not start any of that old nonsense.'

She looked at her mother's face, taut with anger, and relented. 'All right. I'm sorry, Mam. Everyone to their own way of thinking. I've prepared some sandwiches. I'll just go and put the teapot on.'

Dominic had obviously been kept up to date with events and phoned to ask if the Maguires needed a lift down to St Peter's that evening. Gratefully, they accepted his offer and at five minutes to seven they joined the other mourners at the back of the church to await the arrival of the coffin.

The service was brief, the eloquent words of the priest about the loss of such a young man bringing tears to all present. As the congregation shuffled out of the church afterwards, Dan remained behind, by the side of the coffin that reposed before the high altar, shoulders slumped and head bowed in grief.

Alice waited at the back of the church with her daughter, undecided what to do. It was Tess who made up her mind for her. 'Go to him, Mam. He'll be there all night if you don't.'

It was as Tess left the church that she caught sight of Anne, supported by a man and a woman. She was in great distress and beckoned Tess over. 'Is Dan avoiding me?'

'I don't think so. I don't think he knows you're here.' Pity wrung Tess's heart at the change in the woman's appearance. Black eyes, bruised face and stitched brow made her a sorry-looking sight indeed. 'How are you faring, Anne?'

'I'm not so bad. At least they've discovered there is nothing seriously wrong with my chest, which is a relief. I couldn't bear it if I had to stay in that hospital for any length of time.'

'I'm glad to hear that. All the same, I'm surprised they let you out so soon.'

'I signed myself out.' She nodded towards the woman. 'Lily is putting me up until her son comes back.' Her head inclined towards the man. 'Her brother very kindly gave us a lift down tonight. Dan never thought to let me know anything at all about the funeral arrangements.

It's as if I didn't exist. But I do! And I must speak with him. Is he still in there?'

'Yes. I'll let him know you're here. I won't be a minute.'

Dan and her mother were sitting in a pew near the coffin. Tess approached quietly and addressed them. 'Dan, your wife is in the porch. She wishes to speak with you.'

Alice visibly paled. Dan gasped aloud. 'Anne's here?'

'It's only to be expected,' Tess said reprovingly. 'Someone called Lily has brought her along. She says she needs to speak with you. Come on, Mam, let's get you home.'

Blindly Alice grasped at her daughter's arm. Dan's voice stayed her. 'I'll see you later, Alice.'

'In the morning, Dan. We'll see you then,' Tess informed him and gently led her mother down the aisle.

Tess was apprehensive as they entered the church porch, wondering how her mother would react when she saw Anne. She needn't have worried. Pity and compassion immediately wiped out any ill feelings Alice might be harbouring, when she saw the state Anne was in. Going to her she gathered her close. 'You poor, poor dear, how you must be suffering.'

Tears fell afresh at this unexpected show of sympathy. 'Oh, I am! But nobody cares. I'm just Jack's mother, after all. I've lost my only child and my husband won't even speak to me. Let me know what's going on.'

'He will. He's coming now. I'll see you at the funeral tomorrow, Anne.'

'Thanks, Alice. It's nice to know someone understands how I feel.'

When Dan appeared, Lily's brother gave him a look of utter contempt and followed Tess and her mother outside. Lily slowly relaxed the hold she had on Anne's waist and said, 'You'd better support her or she'll fall.'

'There's no need for you to leave, Lily. This won't take long.' Dan was startled at the state of his wife but he had no intention of being influenced. Nine years was a long time and this woman was like a stranger to him now.

Lily gave him a look that was positively venomous. 'Anne wants to speak alone with you. I'll be waiting outside.'

Anne put a hand against the wall for support and Dan slipped his arm round her waist. 'Let's get you inside. We may as well sit down. Why didn't you stay inside and wait for me?'

'I was afraid of you giving me the slip,' she said simply.

'Surely you don't really think I'd do a thing like that?'

'Why not?' Her voice rose shrilly and with an apprehensive glance towards the coffin he hushed her. She wanted to mock him, ask if he thought Jack could hear them . . . fighting, as usual. However, she was well aware that, if provoked, Dan could very easily storm off leaving her on her own; then what would she do? She lowered her voice and continued, 'Why wouldn't you avoid me? You're a cruel bugger, Dan Thompson. You've kept me in the dark about everything, but you're still my husband in the eyes of the law, remember, and that's my son lying up there. I intend being at his funeral, in spite of you! And afterwards, well, I've nowhere to go. What are you going to do about that?'

Dan held a tight rein on his temper. This woman always brought out the worst in him. 'You seem to forget, Anne, that you're not my responsibility any more. What about this Jimmy fellow? Are you out of touch with him completely? Won't he take you in?'

'Look, Dan.' She made a sweeping gesture with her

hands, palms down, dismissing Jimmy. 'That's all in the past. I've left all that behind me.'

'Huh! Like you left me and Jack?' Dan scoffed.

Ignoring him, Anne continued. 'Meanwhile, Bill Brady is due home on Wednesday. Lily has been kindness itself to me but she needs time to get the room ready for his return. If I stay there a couple of nights, will you put me up from Tuesday onwards? Just until I'm well enough to look for a flat.'

He wanted to argue with her; tell her to go to hell. Tell her that what she was asking was out of the question, but decided it would be useless. The cards were stacked against him. She was, after all, Jack's mother and in dire need of help. And he was the only one who could help her.

'All right. I'll see what I can do. But don't take too long finding somewhere else to live. I won't put you up indefinitely. Is Lily waiting to take you home?'

'Yes.'

'Then let's get you out of here.'

It was raining early Monday morning, dark clouds hanging low over the rooftops. By mid-morning the rain had petered out and a weak watery sun showed signs of breaking through the grey clouds. Dan didn't know whether to be glad or sad. To him it seemed fitting that his son's body should be put into the earth in bad weather. He had always felt this way about funerals. He thought it better to leave the world behind in drabness, but if Jack had been attending a funeral he had always liked the sun to shine; said it made him feel hopeful that there really was life after death.

The funeral service was, as usual, a solemn affair. Dan broke down when he did one of the readings and

Colette's stepfather, after some hesitation and a nod from the priest, took over. By the time the Requiem Mass had finished and the coffin was carried from the church, the sun was shining brightly. Dan, after conferring with the undertakers, had asked that the coffin be carried up the Falls Road, past Spinner Street and Waterford Street, before being put into the hearse. A large crowd of mourners had turned out so the lifting would be no problem. There were plenty of friends and sympathisers to lend a shoulder when required.

Dan, Tony, Bob Crosby and Colette's father took the first lift. After that friends and neighbours and workmates of both Jack and Dan took turns until Leeson Street was reached. Here the coffin was placed on Dan's shoulder again and the burden was shared by Tony and two of Jack's workmates from Silk & Rayon. They continued slowly along the road and paused at the top of Spinner Street where a crowd of neighbours had gathered as a sign of respect, and also at the bottom of Waterford Street where it seemed as if the rest of the Silk & Rayon employees had assembled. At the Springfield Road junction the coffin was put in the hearse and mourners got into the limousines and other cars that had joined the funeral cortège and rolled slowly towards Milltown Cemetery.

Chapter Twelve

As the funeral procession paused at Spinner Street, Anne, who stood, supported by Colette and Tess, at the corner, collapsed and hung heavily in their arms. Distressed, they looked frantically around for assistance. Fearing it would prove too much for her, they had tried to persuade Anne to remain indoors, but she had insisted that, since Dan had forbidden her to go to the cemetery, she must at least see her son's remains pass by his street. It would be the last she would ever see of him in this world. Compassion overcame common sense and they had agreed to accompany her to the top of the street. And this was the outcome.

The two men who worked for Bob Crosby were standing, caps in hand, close by as the cortège passed and became aware of their plight. They immediately went to the girls' rescue. The younger man swept Anne's limp figure up in his strong arms and at a nod from Tess followed her down the street to Dan's house.

Inside the house Tess asked him to lay Anne on the settee and, thanking them for their trouble, offered them a drink.

'Better not, miss. We've got work to do.' It was the older man who answered with a wistful look.

It was Colette who twigged. 'Perhaps later?' she suggested.

'That would be lovely, miss. See you after work?'

'Any time at all. You just come along when you're free, and thanks for all your help.'

He touched his forelock. 'No problem, miss.'

When the door closed on them, Colette turned to Tess in despair. 'What are we going to do with her? She can't lie there all day. The mourners will be coming back soon.'

Tess bent low and examined Anne closely. 'Do you think she needs a doctor?'

'No. I doubt it. I think she just went into a cold faint.'

'Let's get her upstairs to bed then.'

'I wouldn't dare,' Colette retorted. 'You weren't here when Lily Brady suggested that Anne could have Jack's room. Dan was furious and ordered her out of the house. He vowed Anne would never sleep in Jack's bed. He was livid, so he was. So in no circumstances would I dare risk putting her in Jack's bed. And to put her in Dan's? That would be unthinkable.'

An angry twitch warned them that Anne wasn't as unconscious as she was leading them to believe. With a wink at Colette, Tess said, 'Well then, we'll just have to get her awake and settled in that chair over there, out of everybody's way. There's nothing else for it.'

Anne's eyes shot open and she let out an exaggerated groan as she swung her feet to the floor. 'Don't talk about me as if I'm not here. And thanks for all your sympathy.'

'Oh, a fox's doze, was it?' Colette asked in an inno-cent voice. 'Let me tell you something, Mrs Thompson. You're not the only one who needs a bit of sympathy round here. You lost a son you walked out on nine years ago . . . I lost my future husband.'

Colette received a look of pure venom, but Anne was saved by the bell, as it were. There was a light knock on the door and Mrs McAnulty stepped into the room. 'Just popped over to make sure you were satisfied with the spread.' She nodded to the long, narrow tables borrowed from neighbours and covered in white sheets, along one wall. They were laden with sandwiches, savoury pies and plates of cooked ham and chicken.

'Everything is marvellous, Mrs McAnulty. You and your friends have done a great job there. Can I coax you to stay and help with the making of the tea and serving it?'

'I'd be delighted.' Without further ado the small woman removed her coat and disappeared into the scullery.

Colette turned her attention to Anne. 'If you will kindly move into that chair over there I'll fetch you a cup of tea when it's ready. Tess, here's the crowd that was at the corner. Will you let them in and I'll give Mrs McAnulty a hand?'

Tess went to this brave girl who was putting on such a show of courage. 'You have my deepest admiration, Colette. I couldn't have done it if I were in your shoes.'

Tears came to Colette's eyes at this unexpected praise. 'Everyone seems to forget about me. I'm grieving too.' Her eyes strayed to the door as the mourners began filing in. 'Here's Mam and Stan. At least I've now got someone of my own to support me.'

That was the start of the visitors. There was a constant flow of people: relatives, neighbours, workmates and just about anybody who happened to be passing by, it seemed. 'Just dropping in to offer my condolences, can't stay too long. Oh all right then, if you insist. I'll just have the one thank you and then I'll be on my way' appeared to be more or less the formula on most visitors' lips. And so it continued till the early hours of the morning.

The women left around midnight. Dominic, after paying his respects, had left in the afternoon but had promised to return about twelve for Tess, Alice, Tony and Agnes to taxi them home. This he did, dropping Agnes and Tony at her house before continuing up Springfield Road with Alice and Tess.

Weary and exhausted, Alice thanked him, and climbed the stairs to go to bed straight away, for once not worrying her head about what her daughter might get up to with the handsome American, as Alice called him.

'Can I offer you a drink, Dominic?'

'I've already had a couple of beers, Tess, and I'm driving. Any chance of a nice cup of tea?'

'Ah, a man after my own heart. Make yourself comfortable. I won't be long.'

Delighted at the prospect of having him all to herself for a while, Tess made some sandwiches and a pot of tea. Dominic relieved her of the tray and put it on a small table which he had placed ready in front of the settee. 'You look all in. Sit down here and I'll pour.'

Tess thankfully curled up on one end of the settee and watched him. He handed her a plate with some sandwiches and a cup of tea. After helping himself, he sat down beside her.

She feasted her eyes on him. He really was very handsome. 'Thanks very much. You're spoiling me.'

His eyes were affectionate and warm. 'I couldn't spoil a nicer person, Tess,' he assured her.

She laughed and wagged a finger at him. 'Now you're

flirting again,' she warned. Becoming subdued, she said, 'It hasn't been much of a holiday for you, Dominic. Running us about to the church and the funeral. Not to mention collecting Mam from the bus station. You should start up a wee taxi service while you're here. You'd make a bomb at it.'

He shrugged. 'To be truthful, I'd nothing better to do.'

'You must be bored stiff. Do you still intend returning to Florida at the end of next week?'

A nod was her answer as he bit into a sandwich.

'There's no chance of you staying on here, is there?'

'No.'

'Then you haven't met that lovely Irish colleen you were hoping to sweep off her feet and take back with you?'

'Well now . . . I have and I haven't.'

Tess had been moodily contemplating her cup, as if expecting some foreign object to float to the surface. Now her head jerked up. 'You have?'

He frowned. 'I thought you understood that?'

'No, but then there is a lot I don't understand about you, Dominic Sullivan. You're an enigma. You talk in riddles most of the time. For instance, I thought if you met someone special you intended staying in Ireland.'

'No. That was just a foolish dream of mine. My home is in America. I can see that now. And it would cause too much of an upheaval for anyone to return there with me. So it looks like I shall be going back alone, more's the pity.'

Tess turned these words over in her mind and said tentatively, 'But surely if a woman cared enough . . . could she not follow you out at a later date?'

'Perhaps. The question is, *does* she care enough?'

Exasperated, she cried, 'Why don't you ask her, then?'

'I intend to, but not until the last minute. I would like her to be prepared to drop everything and return with me. Cut all her ties completely.'

'That's expecting a lot, Dominic. What if she hasn't got a valid passport?'

'She has. I know that for a fact.'

Tess recalled how, last week, before Jack was killed, Dominic had suggested that perhaps she and he could make up a foursome with Tony and Agnes and go over to Paris for a few days. That is, if they all had passports, which they all assured him they had.

With Jack's death, the idea had been shelved. But had that been Dominic's way of finding out if she had a passport? Could she just up and go as he seemed to be suggesting? No, of course she couldn't. And surely even he wouldn't expect her to. What about her mother? Their dressmaking business? Maybe he thought if a woman really loved a man, that was the way she could prove it to him.

Perhaps she could show him in her own way how much she cared. She swung her legs off the settee and, placing her plate and cup on the table, moved closer. They were thigh to thigh and knee to knee. She thought the pressure of his leg against hers would make her swoon. Never had she felt such strong vibrations because of another person's nearness. It was like an electric current coursing through her entire being. She willed him to put an arm round her and pressed closer still, trying to encourage him.

Dominic sat still, watching all these manoeuvres as though mesmerised. What on earth was she playing at? Suddenly it dawned on him. Good Lord! Tess thought he was propositioning her. Wanted her to throw caution to the wind and go to Florida with him. How on earth had he managed to put that notion into her head? He thought he had made it quite plain that someone else was involved. How had he got himself into this pickle? He had always thought he was being above board with Tess but somehow he had managed to get it all wrong. Now he saw little chance of getting out of this mess without hurting this sweet, kind girl.

Tess was an attractive girl and he was no saint. The closeness, warmth, and pressure of her body; the faint fragrance of her perfume – her very willingness was arousing him. He squirmed, not wanting his body to betray him. In no circumstances must he lose control. Tess was too nice a person to be taken advantage of. He was fighting a losing battle and knew he must get away, and pronto.

Placing a hand on his thigh, she whispered reassuringly, 'It's all right, Dominic. I understand. I feel the same way too.'

He was on his feet in a flash, gazing down at her in dismay. 'Tess, this is all wrong. I'll have to go now before we do something we'll both later regret. I'll give you a ring tomorrow.'

She sat in stunned silence until she heard the outer door close and the car pull away from the footpath. Bewildered, she went back over in her mind everything that had been said. Could she possibly have picked him up wrong? Surely not. There was no other woman that she could think of in the reckoning. All she could do was wait and see what developed, now she had admitted she cared deeply for him. Tired though she was, she tossed and turned all night long, and dawn was pushing weak skeletal fingers of light across her bed before she at long last fell into a restless doze.

*   *   *

The rest of the week passed slowly. Alice was in constant tears wondering how Dan was coping with Anne. He had promised to phone and let her know how things went. The call never materialised and she was too proud to troop down to Spinner Street to find out how he was getting on. Tess, in a similar position to her mother, also waited in vain for the phone to ring. Surely never before was a phone so stubbornly silent!

Alice seemed disinclined to start back to work. Tess, finishing the alterations to two skirts, decided it was time to broach the subject of Theresa Cunningham. 'Mam, look, we will have to get to work on the first Communion dresses and boys' suits as soon as possible. You know we never have enough time and always finish up rushed off our feet at the last minute, so I have a suggestion to make. Remember Theresa Cunningham?'

A blank face was turned to her and a slow shake of the head denied all knowledge of anyone called Theresa Cunningham. 'Of course you remember her,' Tess insisted. 'You met her a couple of times. She trained me in the Belart.'

At last the penny dropped and she had her mother's attention. 'Ah, yes. Theresa was a nice girl, so she was.'

'Come on, Mam. Snap out of it. She still is! I was talking to her outside the monastery on Easter Sunday. Her mother is poorly and Theresa has had to give up her job in the Belart to look after her.'

'Oh, I'm sorry to hear that.'

'She congratulated me, saying she had heard how well we are doing, and we got talking about work. I'm afraid I got carried away with my own importance and bragged a bit. I said we were thinking of taking on a trainee stitcher. She thought I was looking for someone right away and suggested we take her on for a couple of after-noons a week instead.'

'Can we afford her?'

'She wouldn't expect top wages and she certainly knows all about children's fashions. She'd be an asset to us, so she would. I think we should give her a try.'

Alice sat in thought for some moments. 'As you say, we could certainly sell more first Communion clothes if we had them. No matter how early we start we never manage to make enough. Would she come for a trial period, say for a month?'

'I think she would be willing to do that. I'll give her a ring and ask her to call in and see us. What day would be most suitable for you?'

'Any day,' Alice said despondently. 'No one seems to want to be bothered with us. What's happened to that friend of yours? You know, the American.'

'Mam, Dominic is on holiday. He knows it's back to porridge for me this week, so he'll want to get out and about during the day.' Why was she making excuses for Dominic's absence? His neglecting to phone and his continued absence was bothering her. Surely he wasn't ashamed to face her? Wanting to get away from her mother's penetrating stare, she said brightly, 'I'll give Theresa a ring now.'

Theresa was relieved and delighted to hear from her. She agreed to come and see them the following day. Tess replaced the receiver and stood with one hand still resting on it, gazing at it for some moments as if willing it to ring. It remained mute, however, as if mocking her with its continued silence.

It was seven o'clock that evening when Dan arrived at the door. Alice answered his knock and he asked her if she would go to the Broadway picture house with him.

He looked so haggard that she drew him into the hall and hugged him. 'Would you not rather stay here for a few hours and rest?'

He shook his head. 'I need to get out for a while before I go mad or something. Could we go for a walk, Alice?'

'What's it like outside?'

'Not too bad, but better put on a warm coat in case it gets cold later on.'

Grabbing her coat from the hall stand, Alice shrugged her arms into it and belted it round her waist. Wrapping a head scarf round her head and knotting it under her chin, she glanced to where Tess stood watching. 'I've my key with me, love, so don't be afraid to go out if you feel like it.'

'Chance would be a fine thing. Good night, Dan. On the other hand . . . perhaps it's not good night. Maybe I'll see you later. Feel free to come back for a bit of supper.'

'Thanks, Tess. I might just take you up on that.'

Tess stood at the door and gazed after them in amazement. It was the only time she could ever remember her mother leaving the house without first checking her appearance in the hall mirror. It must really be love. Wonders would never cease.

Dan strode purposefully along and Alice had difficulty keeping up with him.

'Hold your horses there, Dan,' she chided gently. 'You're running me off my poor old feet.'

He slowed down immediately and gave her all his attention. 'I'm sorry, love. I don't know what I'm doing half the time.'

Slipping her hand under his elbow, Alice said, 'It must

have been difficult for you these past few days, with Anne living under the same roof.'

'That's what I want to talk to you about.'

Fear clutched at Alice's heart. Had Anne wormed her way back into his affections? Was he about to tell her they were going to try for a reconciliation? She held back her fears and asked gently, 'What is it you want to tell me?'

'I want to ask your advice. As you already know, Lily Brady needed the bedroom Anne was using, for her sons, so she moved in with me on Tuesday.'

'And how's it going?' Alice asked with trepidation; perhaps she would be better off not knowing.

'Bloody awful. She never shuts up about the past and how happy we used to be. She must be looking back through rose-tinted glasses. She insists we can make a go of it again.'

'And has she managed to convince you?'

'No! She hasn't swayed me one wee bit. Maybe if I hadn't met and fallen in love with you, I might have been persuaded to give it another try, just to get some peace of mind.'

Alice was in turmoil. What could she say? If Dan's marriage could be saved she should be urging him to try to save it. It was the decent thing to do. After all, while Anne was alive he would never be free to marry anyone else in the eyes of God, so why try to keep them apart?

But she couldn't bring herself to nudge him in that direction, and didn't want to sever all connections with him. She compromised. 'What do you want to do?'

'I thought that was obvious. I want to marry you.'

'But you know that can never be, Dan.'

'It could! If only you would put your scruples to one

side. I've applied for a divorce, you know, and I only hope that Anne and I being under the same roof won't jeopardise my case. If it does come through would you be willing to marry me in a register office?'

'I . . . I don't know about that, Dan. It's against everything I believe in.'

'I know that, Alice. But would you at least consider it?'

'Well . . . now . . .'

'Please, Alice. Give me some hope. Just say you'll consider it.'

Unwilling to commit herself to such a promise, Alice remained silent. It was a lonely stretch of road and Dan stopped suddenly. Gripping Alice by the shoulders he gazed deeply into her eyes.

'Alice, I'm at my wits' end. I can't live under the same roof as that woman and I can't put her out. So what am I to do? Can you give me any advice?'

Tentatively, Alice asked, 'Has she managed to get into your bed?' A blush suffused her cheeks at the very idea of it. She had no right to question him like this. After all, Anne was still his wife and, by the sound of it, would be more than willing to oblige him in that department, given half a chance.

Dan glowered at her. 'How can you even think like that?'

Relieved, Alice relaxed against him. 'I'm sorry. I should know better. Well then, you'll have to move out of the house for a time until Anne finds somewhere else to live. To be truthful I can't bear the thought of you two being under the same roof.'

'Ah, Alice, my love.' He kissed her gently on the eyes, the cheeks, the lips, longing in every touch, before replying. 'And where do you suggest I go?'

Mesmerised by his kisses she replied without stopping to think of the consequences. 'There's plenty of room in our house. You could stay with us.'

The minute the words were out of her mouth she regretted them. What on earth would Tess say? She would never agree to a man's living with them.

'Is there any chance of that?'

'Of course I'd have to talk it over with Tess first. See what she has to say about it.'

He smiled wryly. 'I can't see her agreeing. Can you?'

'It is my house, you know, Dan.'

'I know that. But I would never forgive myself if I was to cause any friction between you and your daughter.'

Suddenly in command, Alice broke away from him and turned back down the road. 'Right! Let's go back for some supper and if I get a chance I'll put it to Tess. The decision will be hers. Okay?'

On their return, leaving Dan seated in the living room where a fire burned brightly in the modern grate, Alice manoeuvred Tess into the sitting room. 'I've a big favour to ask of you, my dear.'

She knew she was about to put her daughter on a sticky spot and had difficulty framing the right words to soften the impact of her proposal. She dithered so long that Tess cried out in exasperation. 'Well, get on with it. What has you in such a quandary? You're never usually at a loss for words where I'm concerned.'

The words came out in a gush. 'Can Dan stay here till Anne finds a place of her own?'

Tess staggered back, eyes almost popping out of their sockets at her mother's gumption. 'You mean . . . you and he share a room?'

Alice's jaw dropped slightly. 'Catch yourself on, Tess.

Of course not! I'm surprised at you, so I am. I thought he might have the attic bedroom. That is, if you have no objections.'

'Why all the embarrassment then? You mean can he stay as a *paying* lodger?'

Alice smiled. 'To be truthful, money wasn't mentioned. I just suggested that he might be able to stay until Anne finds a place of her own. If you were willing, of course,' she added hastily.

'Mam, you saw the state of Anne. She won't want to show her face outside for some time to come. She is sitting there rent free with an estranged husband who supposedly hates her guts, and probably thinks she can eventually win him over. I think Dan will be here for some time to come, so he'll have to pay his way. We're not running a charity shop, you know, and the sooner he learns that the better.'

'Thanks, Tess. I'm sure he will agree to anything you say.' Alice was so relieved to think she was going to prise Dan away from his wife's clutches that she impulsively hugged her daughter.

The following day, Friday, Dominic rang and asked Tess if she would like to go to the pictures with him on Saturday night, adding that they could make up a foursome with Agnes and Tony if she wanted.

Tess bit down on her bottom lip for some moments before answering sweetly, 'You don't have to bring your chaperons along, Dominic. I can assure you that I've no intention of jumping on you at the first opportunity.'

Obviously in the dark as to what she meant he said hesitantly, 'Does that mean you'll come?'

'Only if you feel safe enough with me sitting beside you in a darkened cinema.'

He laughed, but was clearly still somewhat perplexed. 'I'll pick you up at half six then. Bye for now.'

The doorbell rang as she was about to leave the hall, heralding the arrival of Theresa Cunningham.

'Come in, Theresa. Mam has just popped out for a minute or two. She won't be too long.'

They were passing the work room and Tess said, 'Would you like to take a look around? This is where we work. It's not very big for three people to work in comfort, I'm afraid, but I think Mam would be more than willing to do her work in the sitting room when necessary.'

Theresa's eyes ranged over the room. 'It's smashing, Tess. The layout's great and you have a good stock of material by the looks of things. And *two* sewing machines! I was wondering about that.'

'Yes, that one was going at a bargain price when that factory on Donegal Road was closing down last year. It was practically new, so I jumped at the chance to buy it, hoping that we might eventually expand.'

'You're obviously a good businesswoman as well as everything else. And it takes you to have your head screwed on these days. Plan ahead, that's what I say.'

'We don't do too badly, and in a way it's all due to you. You taught me all I know about this trade, Theresa.'

'I only did what I was paid to do. The talent has to be there in the first instance for you to be able to succeed. And you have, Tess. I'm very proud to be associated with you.'

She sounded so sincere that Tess was grinning from ear to ear and red with embarrassment. 'Here's Mam now,' she said with relief when the outer door slammed shut.

Alice was accompanied by Dan carrying a couple of large suitcases.

'Hello, Theresa. It's lovely to see you again.' Alice proffered her cheek for a kiss and then introduced Dan. 'This is a friend of mine, Dan Thompson. He'll be staying with us for a while. I'll show you where to put your cases, Dan. Excuse me, Theresa. I won't be a minute; then we can sit down and have that talk.'

While they waited, Theresa confided in Tess that she would be delighted to work on these premises and sincerely hoped they could come to an amicable arrangement. She need not have worried. After a short interview, throughout which Tess let her mother do most of the talking, terms were offered and accepted.

Theresa refused a drink or a cup of tea on the grounds that her mother would be waiting impatiently to hear the good news, and left, saying she looked forward to seeing them on Monday afternoon.

The outing to the cinema wasn't much of a success. The film, advertised as an exciting spy thriller, turned out to be a mediocre affair, and so it was a glum foursome that headed up Grosvenor Road to where the car was parked in a side street. Tess had to admit to herself that if Dominic had acted a bit more friendly towards her, her attitude would have probably been very different and she wouldn't have cared one way or the other about the film.

But it annoyed her that Dominic seemed to be distancing himself from her; hadn't even held her hand during the show as he had done during their previous visit to the pictures. Did he really think she was out to get him at any cost? He should know her better than that. Shrugging off her misery, Tess tried to lift the gloom that was hanging over them like a black cloud. 'All right then, let's brighten up a bit, lads! Even a visit to the graveyard would be a lot more cheerful than this. So where do we go from here?'

Agnes looked daggers at her friend. 'That's not a very nice thing to say. After all, *they* didn't choose which picture house we should go to. In fact, if I remember correctly it was you who suggested going to the Ritz.'

'Go on now! Put the blame on me! It was supposed to be a good thriller, according to the write-up in the papers.'

'Well you're the one complaining.'

'Hey, hold on a minute, girls,' Dominic interrupted. 'Let's not start a slanging match in public. So it wasn't a great film, so what? It's not the end of the world, after all. Can I suggest that, since Johnny Long's is nearby, we go round there for a fish supper or something. I don't know about you lot, but I'm a little bit peckish.'

'Sounds good to me,' Tess agreed, turning in that direction.

As usual the succulent, crispy cod and golden chips were delicious and lifted them out of their doldrums. 'Dennis is due home tomorrow so let's make the most of having the use of his car tonight,' Dominic declared. 'Any suggestions, folks?'

'Let's take a run down to Bangor. That would be a pleasant change, and it's a nice run and not too far away.' Tony surprised them all by making a decision.

Agnes flashed him a pleasant look of surprise. He usually asked her opinion first and then fell in with her wishes. Perhaps he wasn't such a dull person after all, she thought. Maybe they *could* make a go of it once Dominic's overpowering influence was removed from the scene. Another week to go. She had been dismayed when she learned that he was shortening his holiday;

had experienced a great sense of loss which she couldn't understand. However, after some consideration she decided it was all for the best. Once she and Tony were married she would soon forget all about Dominic. Tony was a quiet, reliable man. She would be safe with him.

Dominic had never again referred to her going to Florida with him and she had mixed feelings about that. She had actually given consideration to his proposal; had in her mind's eye pictured herself running off with him, and the idea of living in a warm climate had appealed to her. Since he hadn't mentioned it again he obviously had changed his mind about her. He had been making a fool of her and she was glad she hadn't rushed in head over heels and made a fool of herself into the bargain. Mind you, at the time, after viewing that magical sunset and the wonderful joy of his kisses, the idea had been very tempting indeed; then Tess began to talk as if she had some claim on him. Was he making a pass at both of them as a bit of warped humour on his part? Something to boast about when he got back to the States?

To be truthful, she would be glad to see the back of him, then everything could get back to normal. His constant presence filled her with urges she couldn't control; she was afraid to catch his eye unexpectedly, when in his company, in case any of the others noticed the effect he had on her. It wasn't natural to feel the way she did about someone she hardly knew and it disturbed her immensely.

Without the desires she felt when in his presence, he wouldn't be haunting her dreams. Tony was the man for her. Married life with him should prove rewarding. Wasn't he willing to wait until after marriage? In truth, she couldn't see what all the fuss was about; why couples risked pregnancy by behaving immorally before taking their marriage vows and ended up getting married too young and before they were ready. More times than she cared to remember these shotgun marriages didn't last. It was a source of wonder to her.

When they left the car park at Bangor, Agnes slipped her arm through Tony's and hugged it tightly; a possessive gesture that caught Dominic's attention.

Dominic gave her a long searching look and received a defiant tilt of the chin in return. He turned his attention to Tess. 'Which direction do you want to go, Tess?'

'What about a stroll along the promenade?'

Without another word he placed an arm across her shoulders and led her away. With an apprehensive glance in the direction of their companions, Tess asked, 'What's wrong, Dominic? Did I miss something there?'

'I think they deserve some time alone. In fact I'm beginning to think they deserve each other,' he added grimly.

Shrugging his arm off her shoulders, Tess said drily, 'How thoughtful of you. I wish you were just as considerate towards *me*.'

'Ah, Tess. Don't be like that. I never meant to offend you.'

'Who's offended? I'm just the stupid eejit who went along with everything you said. You didn't even phone me when you promised you would. Why didn't you?'

'I didn't know what to say. I didn't even think you cared. You could easily have hung up on me and then what would I have done? Can't we remain friends, Tess? I value your friendship a lot.'

Friendship! He was offering her bloody *friendship*. Still, it was so uncharacteristic of arrogant, confident Dominic to be so humble, she felt her bad humour evaporate.

At least he hadn't let her make a fool of herself that night on the settee. She could still face him without feeling ashamed. Now she admitted, 'I'm afraid I over-reacted a bit. Sorry.'

'You have nothing to apologise for. This is all my fault. I should have made my intentions crystal clear.'

'No! You made no promises. It was my fault. I got the wrong end of the stick . . . as usual. For a while there I actually thought you fancied me,' she confessed in a small voice.

'You're a wonderful person, Tess. I wish things could be different.'

'There's nothing you can do about it, Dominic. Always the bridesmaid, never the bride. Good old Tess. That's me!'

'Oh, you'll marry one day, Tess. You're too nice a girl to be passed over. I only hope you get someone worthy of you. Don't you ever settle for anything less.'

She looked up at him. 'I wish you'd confide in me who this mysterious girl is. I've racked my brains and can't, for the life of me, think who it could be. Unless you've been seeing someone on the sly.'

He hesitated, undecided, and she urged him, 'Go on! Tell me.'

'If I tell you, will you promise not to say a word to anyone? Especially not to Agnes?'

She nodded her head excitedly, and vowed, 'I promise. Scout's honour.'

'It's Agnes.'

If he'd smacked her full on the nose with his fist, she wouldn't have been any more shocked. She stood stock still as if pinned to the spot, and gasped, 'What? You're having me on. Aren't you?'

'Don't sound so surprised. I fell for her the moment

I clapped eyes on her. She's beautiful and sweet and Tony doesn't deserve her.'

'That's as may be, but she did choose to get engaged to Tony. Does she know you fancy her?'

'Well . . . I did tell her in a roundabout way that she was the one for me, but obviously she didn't believe me. Maybe she thought I was pulling her leg.'

'Huh! You told her in a roundabout way? I'm sure it was as clear as mud to her. Even when you think you're being straightforward, you're very vague. You talk in riddles at the best of times. Did you know that?'

'I'll try and put it into words you'll understand, Tess, and maybe you'll be able to advise me. Remember the night in Galway when Agnes and I went to watch the sun set on the bay?' Tess nodded and he continued. 'It was a wonderful experience, watching that great ball of fire slowly sink out of sight. It seemed the natural thing to do, that we kiss. And she enjoyed it, mind you. I know she did. I got the impression that Tony didn't kiss her like that. But when I suggested she was engaged to the wrong man, and she must break off with him and return to Florida with me, she said Tony was very good to her and she could never do anything that would hurt him.'

Tess wagged her head. 'That's Agnes for you. And what did you say to that?'

'Well, I had no intention of trying to force her. If love isn't spontaneous it's not the real thing as far as I'm concerned. So I told her the decision was hers. I know she's very reserved, but she has to care enough to throw caution to the winds and come away with me. Make a complete break of it.'

'And?'

'And nothing. She hasn't given me any signs that she's

even thinking about it. In fact she was so cool on the journey home from Galway, I thought she had already made up her mind to stay with Tony. I haven't had the chance to talk to her since.'

Tess recalled the conversation she had had with Agnes in the restaurant in Cavan. She groaned aloud.

'What?' he asked urgently. 'You've thought of something, haven't you?'

'Yes, I have, and it might have some bearing on your predicament. On our way home from Galway I implied that you were interested in me and wanted to stay in Ireland.'

'Ah, I see.'

'Well, you can't blame me for thinking like that! It's your talking in riddles again.'

'Probably. What did she say?'

'She asked me if I had fallen for you . . . and I admitted that I had. So there you are! I bet it's me she won't risk hurting. Not after Jack Thompson dropping me for another girl.' They strolled along in silence for some moments, gazing unseeingly at the numerous yachts bobbing on the swell. 'We'll have to do something about it, Dominic.'

'You think I might still stand a chance with her?'

'Not if you keep on the way you're going. Do what you vowed you'd do. Sweep her off her feet! Take her back to Florida with you. Above all else, speak in a language she can understand, not your usual double Dutch. Make it as simple as possible. That way there can be no misunderstandings.'

Tony and Agnes were already back at the car when they eventually returned. Tess looked at her friend with new eyes. She'd always known that Agnes was a stunner. Short, natural blonde hair, sparkling blue eyes and good figure. With looks like that, how could she be otherwise? Tony was the obstacle. If only Agnes hadn't allowed him to coerce her into an engagement. If she were free, everything would be hunky-dory. She caught Agnes's eye and before her friend could look away Tess detected a hint of what could possibly be jealousy in its depths.

Annoyed at herself for worrying what Dominic and Tess might have been getting up to, Agnes sat trying to come to terms with her misery. She sat apart from Tony, incurring anxious glances from him. An uneasy silence encompassed them on the drive back to Belfast. After dropping Agnes and Tony off, Dominic stopped the car outside Tess's house.

'It's too late to ask you in, Dominic. I forgot to mention that Dan Thompson is lodging with us at the minute. Mam and him will be in bed by now – separate beds that is. But then, how do I know what they get up to when I'm out? Good heavens, would you listen to me. I'm beginning to sound like Mam when she is worrying about me. Still, I don't want to disturb them. I want to have a private chat with you.'

Dominic turned sideways in the driving seat and eyed her. 'What about?'

'You and Agnes. Now that I've gotten over the shock, I think you two would make ideal partners.'

'You're such a good person, Tess, and fun to be with. You never cease to amaze me. I'm so sorry I'm not the one for you, but I know you *will* find your Mr Right one day.'

'That's okay, Dominic.' She smiled wryly. 'Mind you, you are going to have one hell of a job persuading her to break off with Tony. You see, she's the old-fashioned type. She'll worry about leaving him to face the music on his lonesome. Nevertheless, let's see if I can be of some assistance. Let's put our heads together and see what we come up with.'

'Right!'

'When do you leave for America?'

'I leave Aldergrove for Shannon on Sunday night, and my connection to Florida leaves Monday evening.'

'That doesn't give us much time, so let's put some plans together. And the sooner the better.'

'I think I had better mention that my parents are throwing a party for me. Just at home, like, with relatives and close friends.'

'When will that be?'

'Friday night.'

'Oh, dear, we'd better get a move on. What if we . . .'

A plan was concocted. Whether or not it would succeed was another matter.

Chapter Thirteen

Agnes was concerned to find that Dominic and Tess seemed to be closer than ever. What if he changed his mind and remained in Belfast; could she live with that? Tony was also aware of the covert looks exchanged by the pair when they were together, and thought that, with a bit of luck, they might get engaged. He would certainly be glad to get Dominic out of his hair once and for all, one way or the other. It worried him that Agnes got all uptight when the guy was around.

They had decided to cram as much action into Dominic's last few days as possible and were constantly on the go. Dennis had obligingly let his brother have the loan of the car for the remainder of his stay and on Sunday they spent the day at Newcastle. On Monday they took a drive to Portrush.

Tess cried off going anywhere on Tuesday, her excuse being that she needed to work and put in some over-time to justify taking on Theresa Cunningham who had started work on Monday afternoon. Dominic also pleaded a prior engagement and they made plans for the four of them to meet up again on Thursday for a final fling, Dominic saying he wasn't sure what was happening on Wednesday.

As the car pulled away from her doorway on Monday

night, Agnes muttered, 'I feel sure those two have made their own plans for tomorrow night. They just don't want us with them.'

Putting his arms round her, Tony said gently, 'Dominic hasn't much time left. Perhaps they want to be alone for a change.'

'Why? Do you think they've fallen in love?' She managed to keep the horror of this idea from her voice.

Unaware of her misery, Tony shrugged. 'It's not impossible. After all, they're both free to do as they please. So why not?'

'I can't see Tess leaving her mother to go and live in Florida, can you? They're as thick as thieves, those two. No, I can't see it.'

'Maybe Dominic will go back to America and settle his affairs and come back here to live. I don't think he would expect Tess to give up her business and all. If he sold up, he would have plenty of cash to start up a restaurant over here.'

Appalled at the very idea, Agnes wriggled herself free of Tony's arms. 'It's getting late, Tony, and I'm very tired. Do you mind if I don't ask you in?'

Tony did mind. He minded very much, in fact, but knew from past experience it would be useless to argue with her. Agnes always got her own way. Why did he put up with it? Because he loved her and it would be all so different once they were married. Or would it? He was beginning to have his doubts. Would he always be henpecked?

Agnes was surprised when her mother shouted upstairs at tea time the following night and said Tess wanted to speak to her on the phone. Skipping lightly down the stairs, she lifted the receiver to her ear. 'I thought you and Dominic were going it alone tonight?'

'What gave you that idea? I told you I was working late. We need a couple of Communion dresses and a boy's suit for display purposes. That way potential customers can see what they're getting for their money before placing their orders. Theresa made the boy's suit yesterday afternoon and it's beautiful. She's a great seamstress. I have a long and a short Communion dress almost ready and I want to finish them off tonight.'

'Huh! If I were to believe that I'd believe anything.'

'Do I detect a note of jealousy in your voice, Agnes Quinn?'

'You've got to be joking. What have I got to be jealous about?'

'Perhaps because you like Dominic more than you're letting on, and you're picturing me and him off somewhere on our own, having a cosy wee cuddle. Could that be the reason for your jealousy?'

Glad that her friend couldn't see her blazing face – for hadn't she been harbouring just such thoughts about Tess and Dominic? – Agnes muttered, 'Catch yourself on! Anyway, to get back to business, why did you phone?'

'I was wondering if you were seeing Tony tonight?'

'No . . . like you, he feels the need to work some overtime.'

'The reason I phoned is because I need some advice, Agnes. Will you come up here and listen to my tale of woe?'

'Now? Can't it wait till tomorrow?'

'I need your opinion as soon as possible.'

'Does it concern Dominic?'

'In a way, yes, it does. I'll explain when I see you. Bye for now.' Tess hung up before her friend could ask any more questions. Replacing the receiver in its cradle, she turned and faced Dominic. 'Well, she's coming, so be ready to get her into the car and take off.'

'What if she won't come with me?'

'Dominic! For heaven's sake think positive. If you can't persuade her into the car to go for a drive with you, you may as well forget all about whisking her off to America in a plane.'

He headed for the door. 'Wish me luck, Tess. I hope she doesn't take too long getting here or I might get cold feet and do a runner.'

'Good luck, Dominic. I've a gut feeling that this is going to work out okay.'

When the door closed on him she stood for some moments gazing blindly at it. Why was she being so helpful? Because Dominic would be of no use to her while he was in love with Agnes. It was as simple as that. Going into the work room she pulled a chair up close to the window. It could be some time before Agnes arrived, but Tess intended keeping a lookout to make sure her friend didn't run off when Dominic invited her to go for a drive. The way things stood at the moment, Agnes would probably imagine it was like being invited to go on a drive with the devil.

It was a half hour later that Agnes dandered up the road at her leisure. A frown plucked at her brow when she saw Dennis's car parked in front of Tess's house. Tess hadn't mentioned that Dominic was going to be there. Had he come unexpectedly? Would she be interrupting anything? Should she go back home? In a dither she squinted closely at the car through narrowed eyelids. Surely there was someone sitting in it.

A bundle of nerves after sitting in the car so long,

Dominic watched her approach in the mirror. When she hesitated, he quickly got out of the car and stood waiting for her.

'What's going on? Tess said she wanted to talk to me about something.'

'No, *I* want to talk to you.' His hands rested lightly on her shoulders, in case she turned tail and ran back down the road. 'I want you to come for a drive with me, without Tony waiting patiently in the background. I want to have a good long chat with you without any interference.'

Head high, she looked disdainfully down her nose at him. 'You make patience sound like a curse instead of a blessing.'

'No, you're wrong. Patience is a great virtue, but mine is stretched to the limit at the minute. There isn't much time left and I need to talk to you before I go back to Florida. Will you come for a drive with me? Please?'

Her eyes scanned the bay window. There wasn't a light in the room but she had a feeling that Tess was there, watching them, although everything was obscured by the street light reflecting on the glass.

'All right. Let's go.' If Tess had anything to do with this, God knows what Dominic was about to confide to her. She had better prepare herself for the worst. Her heart was thumping like a trip-hammer as she got into the car.

Tess watched the meeting take place. She saw Agnes glance towards the window and willed herself to remain motionless. After what seemed like ages, Dominic led Agnes round to the passenger side of the car. She climbed in and off they went. Where would he take her, Tess wondered. They needed to be completely alone, without any interruptions. Probably up past Whiterock Road into the countryside. Oh, to be alone in a car with Dominic and him intent on making her feel loved. Tears pricked at her eyes. For a while there she had thought Dominic was her Mr Right. Would she ever meet someone she really cared for and have those feelings reciprocated?

Stretching her cramped limbs, she squared her shoulders and entered the living room. She found her mother and Dan seated either side of the hearth like an old married couple. Dan had certainly made himself at home in their house. If at times Tess was annoyed at the intrusion into her organised life she managed to hide her feelings. After all, he had only been here a short time and it wouldn't be for ever, she consoled herself. Or would it? Her mother was waiting on him hand and foot, so why should he be in a hurry to get back to that drab house in Spinner Street, where he had to cook for himself and do the washing up and all the other housework that required doing. He knew when he was well off. 'Have you seen any sign of Anne since you moved in here?'

Dan hesitated. A quick glance in Alice's direction and a brief nod was Tess's answer. Her mother's chin rose a fraction and there was a slight tightening of her lips. Obviously he hadn't mentioned to her that he had visited his estranged wife.

Determined to get a positive answer, Tess said, 'How is she managing on her own with a broken wrist?'

'She seems to be coping okay. You'll never believe it, but remember Lily Brady's brother Pat? The one who brought her down to the church that night in the car? Well, I've since found out that he's a bachelor and a bit sweet on Anne. With a bit of luck the two of them might just hit it off together. So who knows . . . perhaps he'll take her off my hands, once and for all.'

Vexation oozing from her every movement, Alice rose and left the room in a huff. They heard her climb the stairs and a bedroom door close none too gently.

'In future, if I were you, Dan, I'd keep Mam up to date on your meetings with Anne. She has every right to know what's going on. If you've nothing to hide there shouldn't be a problem.'

'Tess, believe me . . . there's nothing going on. As I've just said, maybe this Pat fellow will talk Anne into going to live with him. I certainly hope so.'

'And what good will that do, pray tell me? You will still be a married man. I'm warning you, Dan Thompson, don't trifle with my mother's affections, or you'll have me to answer to. She's too good to be hurt by the likes of you.'

With these words, Tess rose abruptly and left the room. He followed her into the kitchen. The dinner dishes were still soaking and as she angrily thumped them about with unnecessary vigour, he lifted a glass cloth and started drying the plates.

'That is something else you could do more often,' Tess said, thumping another plate on to the stainless steel drainer. If they were chipped she would have no one to blame but herself. She was angry and intended getting all the aggression off her chest while she had the chance. 'I'm sure you had to share the chores with Jack while he was alive. So you'd better pull your weight while you're staying in our house. I for one will not become a skivvy just because a man has come to stay. *And* I certainly won't stand by any longer while you sit in there on that big fat arse of yours, and watch Mam wait on you hand and foot. So you'd better pay heed if you know what's good for you.'

Putting the last dish on the draining board she

flounced from the kitchen, throwing over her shoulder, 'And you can do the worktops while you're at it.'

His voice stayed her. 'Tess . . . I *have* offered, you know. Honestly! But your mother won't let me do any housework.'

Tess knew this to be true and it rankled. 'Ignore her! Or so help me, if you don't get your finger out, you'll be looking for somewhere else to live.'

'I'll do my best,' he promised. 'And listen, Tess, if you're not too busy could you nip down and see Colette some time? It was her I called to see, when Anne collared me. Colette's grannie is still in hospital and the poor wee dear hasn't a minute to herself. No sooner is she home from work than she's off again to the hospital. That girl's run off her feet. She can't even find the time to cook a proper meal. She deserves a medal, so she does. Anne says she's tried to help, but Colette won't have anything to do with her. Won't even come in for a cuppa or a drink or even a wee chat. For that matter, she won't have anything to do with me either. You'd think I'd offended her in some way. When I ask how she's coping she just says she's managing very well thank you, and that I'm to leave her alone and not annoy her.'

Tess was overcome with remorse. She had meant to keep in touch with Colette and encourage her to get out and about, and not to dwell on the past. But all that fuss with Dominic and Agnes had driven the girl completely from her thoughts. 'I'll go down now, Dan. It was very inconsiderate of me. I should have gone down sooner.'

'Thanks, Tess. You're an angel. And by the way . . . have I really got a big fat backside? Are you suggesting that I'm putting on weight?'

He grinned at her and she laughed at the very idea of her rude remarks as she headed for the stairs. 'Yes!'

Tess found Colette looking wan and miserable when she answered her knock. She followed the girl into the kitchen and, full of compassion, gathered her close and rocked her gently in her arms.

'Colette, I'm so sorry for neglecting you. I should have come down sooner.'

Colette sniffed loudly, tears brimming. But she remained in the comfort of Tess's embrace, glad of human contact. 'Don't be silly, I'm not your problem. But thanks all the same for thinking of me.'

Sobs began to shudder through the girl's frail body and Tess wondered what to do. 'Don't, love, don't upset yourself so. Can I get you anything?'

Easing herself from Tess's arms, Colette sat down on the settee and wiped her eyes with the back of her hand. 'You'll have to forgive me, Tess. I'm just back from the Royal. Grannie's getting home tomorrow.'

'Why, that's wonderful news,' Tess cried, at a loss as to why Colette appeared so despondent. 'I suppose it's the relief of knowing she's better that has you in this state,' she chided her. 'You'll be soon back to normal, once she's home. You'll see.'

But Colette's head was slowly shaking from side to side in sorrow, as more tears fell. 'She's not going to get better. They've given her a month at the most.'

'Oh, my God.' Tess, always the practical one, let her thoughts race ahead of her. 'Will you be able to get the time off work to look after her?'

'I don't know, but if the bank won't give me compassionate leave I'll have to give up my job. It's as simple as that. The hospital offered to put Grannie in a nursing home, but I wouldn't hear tell of it. I won't have her looked after by strangers when I'm capable of doing it myself. A nurse will call in twice daily, morning and evening, to help me bathe her and move her about to prevent her getting bedsores.'

'You've my admiration, Colette. You're a very brave girl. But if there's anything – anything at all – my mam or I can do to help, you have only to ask.'

'Thanks.'

Tess smiled wryly. 'I suppose you're taking that with a pinch of salt considering how I've been neglecting you lately. You'll be thinking, as soon as I'm out of that door it's the last you'll see of me. But I do sincerely mean it. Honest!'

To divert Colette's troubled mind away from thoughts of her grannie, Tess confided her reason for not keeping in touch with her. After all, she could trust Colette to keep her own counsel, and giving her thoughts a new direction was more important than keeping a secret that would be resolved one way or the other in a few days' time in any case. She told Colette how for a second time she had thought that perhaps fate was smiling on her at last and she had met her Mr Right, only to discover she had got it all wrong . . . again. Colette sat enthralled as Tess related how she had misread all the signs. She had thought that Dominic was wooing her, only to find out that all the while he was in love with her best friend, Agnes, and hoped to take her back to Florida with him. 'How could I have been so blind, I ask you?' she finished.

Now the consoler, Colette patted Tess's knee in a comforting gesture. 'I'm sorry to hear that. You must be so disappointed.'

'Oh, I'll get over it. I'm only too glad I didn't make

a fool of myself. This is my second disappointment, remember. Maybe third time lucky.'

'What about Tony?' Colette asked quietly.

'He'll just have to be like me. Grin and bear it. Agnes should never have gotten engaged to him in the first place.'

'Still, she did agree to marry him.'

'Under duress.'

'Poor Tony. He'll be heartbroken. There is more to him than meets the eye, you know. I got to know him quite well when I was going out with Jack. He's very obliging and wouldn't hurt a fly.'

For the first time Tess considered Tony's position in all this. So far, in her estimation he had just been one pain in the neck; hadn't deserved any sympathy. But she admitted that he did, in his own quiet way, love Agnes. Of that there could be no doubt, so of course he'd be devastated. She silently seconded Colette's words. Poor Tony. Well, I'm losing Dominic, she reminded herself. Only, to be truthful, it wasn't the same thing, now was it? Dominic had not committed himself to her. It was all a big misunderstanding on her part. Tony's case was a different kettle of fish altogether.

She rose to her feet. 'Now I've told you all my little secrets, I'll have to be getting back home.'

'Thanks for calling down, Tess. Realising other people besides myself have their own troubles has lifted my spirits a lot.'

'Your troubles are more horrendous. Nevertheless, I'll be back to keep you up to date on the saga of the yank and Agnes. Will she or won't she? Watch out for next week's episode.' She laughed, heading for the door.

Slowly, Colette followed her, a look of consternation on her face. 'I hope Agnes opts to stay with Tony.'

Tess was amazed that Colette could think along those lines. 'Do you?' she gasped. 'Why?'

'Well, it seems to me that Dominic has a lot going for him in America. He'll have so many things to occupy his mind and will soon get over his disappointment. Whereas if Agnes leaves Tony . . . he may never get over the loss of her.'

'You know, I never thought of that. You're a very wise person, Colette.'

'No, I'm not!'

'Oh, but yes you are! You've set me thinking. Look, I must run. If it's all right with you, I'll nip down tomorrow for a short time and meet your grannie.'

'Make it the afternoon. She won't be home until about three.'

'Right, afternoon it is. Bye for now.'

Agnes sat silent as the car sped up Springfield Road. She had convinced herself that Dominic was going to apologise for pretending he cared for her. She wanted to be able to assure him that it didn't matter in the slightest. That she would be only too glad to see him and Tess hitting it off and, maybe, him settling down in Belfast.

She clasped her hands so tightly in her lap that her knuckles were white, as she tried to compose herself. Would she be able to carry it off? As usual, when in his company, she was restless. Hurry up, she willed him silently. Hurry up and get it over with.

Dominic watched her from the corner of his eye. He could almost feel the tension that surrounded her; could see the different emotions flicker across her face. This was all one big mistake. He had been wrong to lure her to meet him. She would never agree to anything he proposed; never relax enough for him to talk her round to his way of thinking.

Up in the countryside, on a lonely stretch of road, he drew the car to a stop in the entrance to a field and sat gathering his thoughts. Should he turn round and take her home?

'Would you mind getting on with it? I haven't all night, you know.'

Startled by her tone of voice, he turned in his seat and faced her. She was staring straight ahead, ignoring him completely. 'Excuse me? Did you speak?'

'Yes! I said get on with it. What do you want to talk about?'

'I'm not sure that it's such a good idea now.'

'If it was important enough for you to practically kidnap me and drive me away up here, it must be important enough to talk about. Shall I make it easier for you?'

Grim faced, he nodded. 'Yes, you do that.'

'You want to apologise for making a pass at me in Galway. Right? I understand perfectly, Dominic. It was the romantic atmosphere. The setting of the sun on the bay was enough to bring out the romance in anyone.' How she wished she could forget that night. She had tried, but it haunted her dreams, filling her with longings she had no control over. In an unsteady voice she continued. 'There's no need for you to explain anything, or apologise. No need whatsoever. I felt the magic of it too. And it takes two consenting people to enjoy it. So don't go blaming yourself.'

'But I asked you a question that night, and you didn't give me an answer, Agnes.'

'Why should I? It was all make believe on your part, after all. Wasn't it? Tess made it quite clear the next day in Cavan that you were interested in her. You'd have got one heck of a shock had I pretended to have fancied you.'

'That's a laugh! You wouldn't have fooled me for one minute. The only one you're fooling is yourself. It never ceases to amaze me the way you stick to Tony like a bloody sticking plaster every time we all go out together. It must be damned uncomfortable at times, trying to drag yourself away from him.'

The air in the car was so charged with electricity that Dominic felt a flick of a switch would spark off an explosion, blowing them both to smithereens. He could see she was crying, but hardened his heart. He had come to the conclusion that he was flogging a dead horse. She wasn't in the least bit interested in him at all. Her only interest was in good old boring Tony. What an exciting life lay ahead of her.

He turned the key in the ignition. 'I apologise for wasting your precious time. I'll take you back.'

He was reversing out on to the road when he brought the car to an abrupt halt and drove forward again. 'I imagine I'll get a cursory peck on the cheek as my farewell kiss at the weekend, before I leave. So if you don't mind I'll say goodbye now.'

Aware of her blotched face and swollen eyes she made to get out of the car, away from his penetrating gaze. 'Leave me alone.'

Gently he pulled her into his arms and sank his face in her hair. 'I'm sorry, love. I really am sorry. Please forgive me. I wouldn't hurt you for the world. Can I have one kiss? Just one.'

Lifting her head she nodded and his mouth closed over hers. He seemed to draw all the breath from her body. Limp as a rag she clung to him and the kiss went on, and on, and on. His hand hovered over her breast but having got this far he had no intention of taking any chances that might go frightening her off. He drew back and gazed into her eyes, silently seeking permission. Eyes swimming in love gazed back at him, bringing a surge of tenderness to his heart. With a nod she gave her permission.

This was frustrating. There wasn't enough room; steering wheel, gear stick, hand brake and just about everything else that could get in the way was getting in the way. He didn't dare suggest they move to the back seat. That would only break the magic spell. To his astonishment, as if she had read his mind, the next time they came up for air she said, 'Wouldn't we be more comfortable in the back?'

With a sigh of relief, he assured her, 'We certainly would.'

Much, much later they became aware that dusk was falling around them. The long grass in the field in front of them had turned from forty shades of green to a dark mass swaying gently in the light breeze.

Dominic laughed. 'You know something? I didn't even notice how lush that grass was, when we first arrived.'

'Neither did I,' Agnes confessed. 'I was so worried that you were about to confess your love for Tess. I was such a bundle of nerves about how I'd hide my feelings for you that everything else was just a blank.'

Her honesty touched his heart. 'You do realise now that I was never interested in Tess?'

'I do now . . . but does she? I thought she really cared for you.'

'It was her who convinced me that I might stand a chance with you. To be truthful, I was going to return to Florida nursing a broken heart.'

'Would you just listen to yourself,' she chided gently. 'You'd have found someone else over there and I'd soon become a passing memory.'

'It's you I want.'

She laughed. 'Prove it.'

He reached for her again and there was no shyness in her response; no holding back. She returned kiss for kiss, caress for caress.

It was dark when he eventually stopped the car at her door. 'Do you want me to come in with you?'

'No. Tony will probably be in there waiting for me. He'll be wondering where I am. I think it would be better if I faced him alone. I won't break the news to anyone else until tomorrow.'

'Promise me you won't renege?'

She lightly trailed the contours of his face with her fingers. 'Do you think I could live without you now?'

Standing on the pavement she watched him drive away, a great well of love engulfing her heart. The hall door opened and Tony was there waiting for her. Good, kind, dependable Tony. How could she ever justify what she was about to do? Head up, shoulders squared, like a soldier going to war she went in to drop her bomb-shell.

Alice accompanied Tess when she went to visit Mrs Burns next day. She had an ulterior motive for visiting Spinner Street. She hoped to see Anne and have a chat with her; find out all she could about this new man Dan had mentioned. It bothered her that Anne might still win Dan over. Nevertheless, she was sincere in her offer to be of any help to Colette.

Dan had made his peace with Alice the previous night, explaining it was Colette he was worried about and that he had called in to see how she was faring, and how Anne had collared him as he was leaving Colette's house and asked him to open a can for her.

Bearing in mind that she had a broken wrist, he had felt obliged to enter the house and give her some assistance. He assured Alice he had not dallied and a few minutes later had seen him on his way. Anne had told him she also was worried about Colette, hence his asking Tess to visit her. It was all above board, he assured her.

Mrs Burns, looking very frail, was propped up on white pillows, her transparent skin rivalling them in colour.

Colette introduced them. 'Grannie, this is Tess; you've heard me speak of her?' A nod from her grannie confirmed it. 'And this is Mrs Maguire, Tess's mother.'

Mrs Burns greeted them in a husky whisper. 'It's good of you to come and see me. Now that I'm home, away from that hospital, I'll be back to porridge in no time.'

Alice bent low over the bed and gently lifted the skeletal hand, the skin stretched like parchment over the old bones, the joints swollen with rheumatism. 'Of course you will. I bet you have more work left in you than the rest of us put together. I've brought you some grapes. Not everybody likes them, I know, but it seems the expected thing to do.'

The little woman smiled and whispered, 'Actually, I love grapes. Thank you.'

Tess came forward holding out a spray of roses. 'I hope you like flowers too.'

'I do. Very much, and roses are my favourite. They're beautiful. Thank you.'

'I'll put them in some water for you.' Colette relieved Tess of the flowers and said gently, 'We'll leave you to rest for a while, Grannie. I think you've talked long enough.'

In the scullery, Tess watched Colette arrange the flowers. 'She's very frail, isn't she?'

Tears ran down Colette's face and dripped unheeded on to the roses. 'She's so weak. I can't see her lasting a month.'

Tess silently agreed with her. 'Now you listen to me, Colette. We're only a stone's throw away. Any time you need us, get a neighbour to phone. Day or night. Okay?' She wrote down her number on an old envelope and gave it to Colette.

'Thank you. Mind you, I may have to hold you to that. I've no one else to turn to in an emergency.'

'We'll be glad to help. But what about your mother? Would she not come and stay? Be here with you, keep you company during the night and be with you at the end?'

'We aren't on speaking terms at the moment. You see, after Jack died Mam wanted me to go back to Omagh with her and she's very annoyed that I didn't fall in with her wishes. It didn't matter to her that Grannie was lying in the Royal and needed someone to visit her. She'd condemn Grannie to a nursing home tomorrow without giving it a second thought.'

'What about your father? Surely he will want to come when he finds out how little time his mother has left?'

'I've tried to get in touch with him, but it's hopeless. He's been gone so long, moved about so often, no one knows where he is now.'

Alice said, 'Why don't you get Dan to try and find him? I know he'd be delighted to be able to help. After all, he was almost your father-in-law. He might know someone who knows about tracking down missing persons.'

To Tess's surprise, Colette's lip curled with scorn. 'Let's leave him out of this. I don't want any help from *him*.

Will you both excuse me, please? The nurse will be here soon and I've things to get ready for her arrival.'

Tess and her mother exchanged an inquiring glance. They knew when they were being dismissed. Tess said, 'I'll call down again tomorrow, Colette. In the meantime, if you need us, you know what to do.'

'Thank you. I'll be pleased to see you.'

'Outside, Alice turned to her daughter. 'I wonder what Dan did to offend her?'

'I was thinking the same thing myself. Whatever it is he appears to be totally unaware of it. Surely she's not blaming him for Jack's death, just because he bought the motorbike?'

'If she is, she can't blame him any more than he blames himself. Sometimes he is so engulfed in guilt that I can't get through to him no matter what I do.'

'Poor Dan. Poor Colette, for that matter.'

'Let's not go all maudlin. Since we're down here, I think it would be neighbourly to call on Anne and see how she is faring. Don't you?'

'Not really, but it's obviously what you intend doing.'

Anne answered their knock, but did not invite them in. She raised an inquiring brow at them.

'We were in visiting Mrs Burns and thought we'd call and see how you are,' Alice explained.

'Oh, never felt better,' was her sarky reply. 'Sorry I can't invite you in but I've got company.' Careful application of make-up covered her bruises and the pucker of stitches was stretching and fading.

Glad that she seemed on the mend, Alice retorted, 'Oh, excuse me for interrupting.' She was not to be deterred. If Anne wanted to discuss her affairs on the doorstep that suited her fine. 'Have you found alternative accommodation yet?' she asked sweetly.

'I beg your pardon? I can't see how that is any business of yours.'

'Oh, but it is very much my business. You see, when the divorce comes through, Dan and I will be getting married and we intend living here. I know there's a lot of work to be done to the interior, so the sooner Dan and I get started on it the better.'

Anne looked stunned. 'So you're the *other woman*?' she gasped, her surprise transparent. 'Well, well, well, what do you know! I would never have dreamt it. I'm sorry, but no, I haven't found anywhere else yet. Tell Dan he'll be the first to know as soon as I do.' The door closed on them with a decisive click.

Turning away, Alice clucked her tongue. 'Don't look at me like that, Tess.'

'What way am I looking at you? As if you've lost your marbles, Mam? Well, have you? Has Dan convinced you it is all right to live in sin after all?'

'No, of course not! He knows nothing about this. I wanted to shake her up a bit, that's all. Remind her that it's not her home any more. Do you think the boyfriend is in there with her?'

'Mam, it's none of our business who her visitor is.'

'It is, if she's carrying on under Dan's roof.'

Tess stopped and gazed in horror at her mother. She was carrying things just a little too far.

Alice threw back her head and laughed aloud. 'I wish I had my camera with me. You should see your face, Tess. I'm only pulling your leg, love. And I've no intention of marrying Dan. At least not at the moment. I think I'll just be his live-in lover. After all, it's the done thing now.' She went into another kink of laughter at her own wit, making Tess shake her head in frustration.

'Come on, Mam. Let's get you home before they cart you off to the laughing house.'

Tess received a phone call from Dominic early Wednesday morning. He sounded jubilant and thanked her for all her help in bringing him and Agnes together.

'Am I to take it that she has agreed to go to Florida with you?'

'You can. We are going down today to try and get her on the same flight as myself. She doesn't fancy travelling alone. I don't think there will be any problem. I can't believe she's coming with me. And I can't thank you enough for all your help, Tess.'

'Does Tony know yet?'

'Well, he should by now. She was to break the bad news to him last night. She wouldn't let me go in with her. Said she wanted to do it on her own. I never thought I'd say this but I actually feel sorry for the guy.'

'Never you worry about him. Agnes must really love you or she wouldn't be willing to take off with you, just like that. Tony and her wouldn't have been happy together. It's obvious, now, they weren't meant for each other.'

'That's true, but I still feel guilty. I only hope he doesn't take a swing at me. I wouldn't have the heart to retaliate.'

'And Mr and Mrs Quinn, how do they feel about it?'

'We have decided not to tell them or anyone else for that matter – yourself excluded of course – until the flight and all is arranged. Is it all right if Agnes and I call up to see you tonight? She's worried about how all this will affect you. You know what I mean.'

'Tell her not to worry, that I'll be only too happy to see you both.'

*　　*　　*

[299]

They arrived around seven o'clock brandishing a bottle of wine. One look at them and Tess sighed inwardly. Oh to be in love. They simply oozed happiness.

She fetched three glasses and a corkscrew and Dominic opened the bottle. He nodded at the glasses. 'Won't your mother and Dan join us?'

'They're away out to the pictures. Mam's favourite actor, Glenn Ford, is on in the Broadway.' She raised her glass. 'To both of you. May your happiness last for ever.'

'Thank you, Tess. Your help was invaluable.'

'You *will* be my bridesmaid, won't you, Tess?'

Flustered, Tess said, 'Well now, I don't know about that. America is a long way off.'

'Oh, but you must, Tess!' Dominic looked fondly at Agnes. 'She could easily back out, you know, if you refuse.'

'I don't think there's any sweat about that,' Tess replied wryly.

'I'll send you the air tickets.'

Tess laughed. 'Well that certainly simplify matters, but it would depend on when you intended getting married.' She shot an inquiring glance from one to the other.

Agnes answered. 'Dominic wants to get married as soon as possible.'

'And why not?' Dominic retorted.

'I see.' Tess thought for a moment. 'Let me know as soon as you set the date, and I'll see how things go. Meanwhile, tell me, Agnes. Did you manage to get booked on the same flight?'

'I did, yes, and for that I'm grateful. I can't picture myself travelling all the way to America on my own.'

'Have you told your mam and dad yet?'

'No. When we leave here we're going to tell them and then go up and break the news to the Sullivans.'

'It will be one hell of a shock for them all.'

'I know.' Agnes's voice trembled.

Dominic interrupted. 'They will still give us their blessing. I'm sure of it.'

'I don't know about that. Mam has grown very fond of Tony. We'll just have to wait and see.' Agnes looked at Tess and sighed. 'I'm afraid we've blown it as far as a final fling goes. We can't very well go out without Tony. It would be the final insult. As if I was thumbing my nose at him.'

'Ah, well! That's the way the cookie crumbles.' Tess raised her glass once again. 'To both of you.'

There was a strange atmosphere at the party on Friday night. A feeling of disbelief permeated the air as everyone gazed in wonderment at the happy couple. It had come as a terrific shock to both families, but they agreed the pair were well matched and obviously in love, which was all that really mattered.

Tony was noticeable by his absence. Tess didn't blame him. If the crowd had been aware of her designs on Dominic, she wouldn't have had the gall to show her face either. Everybody avoided mentioning his name. It was as if he had never been. Agnes had confided in her the night before how badly he had taken it.

'Do you know something, Tess? I can't see Dominic and me being happy ever after – as the saying goes – when we have inflicted so much misery on another person.'

'I know this sounds trite, Agnes, but he'll get over it, so he will. So don't you go worrying yourself over him. Didn't I get over Jack Thompson?'

'And what about Dominic? Did you really care for him?'

'No. I must admit that for a time I did have high hopes about him, but deep down I didn't really think they would come to anything. So you can rest assured, I'm not nursing a broken heart . . . and I have no intention of jumping off the Queen's Bridge when he leaves.'

Agnes laughed outright. 'You would never be that foolish, no matter what the circumstances.'

'Oh, I don't know about that now, but you're probably right. I'm too big a coward.'

'I'm going to miss you, Tess.'

'Catch yourself on. Dominic will make sure you haven't any time to mope about thinking of me or anyone else for that matter.' They were in each other's arms, tears mingling. 'You're a very lucky girl, Agnes.'

'I know! I can't believe that I almost lost him.'

They separated as the kitchen door opened and Dominic breezed in carrying some empty glasses. 'You two have been in here long enough,' he admonished. 'You're supposed to be bringing in those trays of sandwiches, in case you didn't know.' He looked more closely at them now. 'Is that tears I see?'

Putting down the glasses, he took Agnes in his arms. She melted against him and they didn't even notice Tess slip from the kitchen. How come she hadn't made the connection before, she mused. Surely there must have been some outward indication of how they felt towards each other.

Chapter Fourteen

Mrs Burns didn't last the month. Two weeks from the day she left hospital, she died peacefully in her sleep, in the early hours of the morning. The doctor had warned Colette earlier that day that death was imminent and afterwards Father McAleese had given her the last rites of the church. Tess and Alice kept a vigil with Colette during the night until her grannie slipped quietly from this world.

As she breathed her last few breaths and the death rattle was in her throat, Colette fell to her knees beside the bed, and reaching for her hand grasped it tightly.

Alice placed a warning hand on the young girl's shoulder. 'Don't call her back, love. She's on her way to heaven, I'm sure.'

'I know! I know one shouldn't call a soul back. It's just that . . . I don't want to let her go. I love her! She's all I really have.'

'And what would you be condemning her to? Eh? To lie there unable to help herself. Ah, love, she would be praying that God would release her from her agony.' Alice leaned closer to the little figure on the bed, then gently lowered the eyelids. She made the sign of the cross and said, 'She's away, love. God rest her soul.'

A mournful wail left Colette's lips. 'I wish I had done more for her when she was alive. She hasn't had much happiness since Grandfather died. I'll never forgive my father for not keeping in touch with her.'

'She had you, love. And I'm sure you were a great source of joy and comfort to her. Let's all say a wee prayer for her, then Tess can go and catch a few hours' sleep before getting back to work. Later on she'll notify the doctor of your grannie's death. No need to call him out in the middle of the night, but he'll have to come later on and sign the death certificate.'

Alice helped Colette wash her grannie's body to get it ready for the undertaker. It was as they gently moved her about that they discovered an envelope under the pillows. Colette's name was scrawled across it in her grannie's spidery handwriting. When she opened it Colette found it contained her grannie's last will and testament. The typed will was signed by a member of a firm of solicitors in the city centre, Frank Hanna and Co., and witnessed by two hospital orderlies. It confirmed that Mrs Burns had left all her worldly possessions to her granddaughter, Colette. There was also a second letter enclosed, stating that Miss Colette Burns should make an appointment at their office, at her earliest convenience, to learn exactly what she had inherited. It was signed Matthew McIlroy. In the same envelope there was a Liverpool Victoria insurance policy covering the funeral expenses.

Colette wept when she read it. 'Grannie was always so good to me. And now even in death she hasn't left me any debts to pay off.'

Alice examined the expensive looking letterhead from the solicitors and said, 'There just might be something worthwhile here. On the other hand don't build your hopes too high, Colette. The chances of your grannie having much to leave are slim.'

[304]

Colette rounded on her in anger, which quickly evaporated when Alice drew back in dismay. Quickly Colette apologised. 'I'm sorry, Mrs Maguire. But you see I don't expect her to have much to leave. It's the fact that even at the end she was thinking of me, and went to all this trouble.'

Colette decided to keep the funeral a quiet affair and three days later, with just a handful of friends present, Mrs Burns was laid to rest in her husband's grave in Milltown Cemetery. It was in a sheltered corner of the cemetery, and the sun shone high above as her coffin was lowered into the ground.

Her only son knew nothing of her demise and, in private, Colette used some choice words to describe just what she thought of this man who had walked away from all his responsibilities years ago. But then, she reminded herself, she must bear in mind that her mother had put him out of the house. She had been too young at the time to understand the ins and outs of it; could barely remember him; had no real feelings towards him, the way a daughter should have for her father. But still, no matter the differences between him and his wife, he should have kept in touch with his own mother. Then again, who knows? Perhaps the poor bugger was dead.

Her mother and Stan came to the funeral but departed shortly afterwards, explaining that they were too busy to stay any longer. They tried again to persuade Colette to return to Omagh with them but she refused. She intended to remain in her grannie's house as long as the landlord would let her, and until she decided what to do with her life. It would also give her a chance to save some money. Her grannie had some fine pieces of furniture which looked quite valuable. What would become of them, she wondered.

Tess suggested that Colette should try to get her name put on the rent book and then she would be free to stay there as long as she cared to. Taking her advice Colette called into the rent office. She was informed that her name had been on the rent book for the last four months. Mrs Burns had insisted that she needed her granddaughter to remain with her and her name should be in the book. If money had changed hands no one mentioned it.

A week later Colette presented herself at the offices of Frank Hanna and was shown into an elegant wood-panelled office.

A small elderly man with stooped shoulders, a thatch of snow white hair and bright blue eyes behind rimless glasses rose from behind a highly polished desk and came to greet her. He gripped her hand tightly in his own smooth, well manicured one and spoke in a modulated voice. 'My name is Matthew McIlroy and I am pleased to meet you, Miss Burns. May I offer my condolences on the death of your grandmother? She was a grand lady and it was my great pleasure to make her acquaintance. She was admired by all who got to know her here in the office, before it became too difficult for her to travel. But then, that was all while you were still a young schoolgirl.'

Tess was bemused. Her grandmother had been in the habit of dealing with these people, in these very offices? She had certainly kept that quiet.

He gestured to a leather chair in front of the desk. 'Please take a seat.' When she was seated, he asked, 'Would you like a cup of coffee or tea?' A shake of the head rejected his offer. Colette couldn't imagine herself drinking tea or coffee comfortably in these plush surroundings; she would be sure to spill it. But somehow or other she had no difficulty picturing her grannie sitting here, at ease in this chair, sipping coffee and conversing with Mr McIlroy. The solicitor was continuing and she brought her mind back to attention. 'Now let me acquaint you of your inheritance, my dear.'

Colette sat primly on the edge of the chair, knees close together and hands clasped tightly in her lap. She felt intimidated by all this grandeur and was anxious to get the meeting over and done with as quickly as possible. A file sitting precisely in front of the man was opened by long slender fingers and Matthew McIlroy smiled at Colette before beginning to read. 'It is short and to the point,' he said, patting the file with the flat of his hand. 'First let me inform you that you are the sole beneficiary of this will.'

His gaze returned to the papers in front of him. 'I the undersigned, Margaret Emily Burns, being of sound mind, do hereby bequeath all my worldly goods solely to my granddaughter Colette Mary Burns.' The small man raised his eyes and she thought she detected a mischievous twinkle in their depths. 'I think you are in for a nice surprise, Miss Burns. Your grandmother has left you, after all expenses have been settled, just over ten thousand pounds. She also bequeaths a few pieces of jewellery which are in safe keeping at her bank, and the contents of the house in which she resided.' Once more he glanced in her direction, preparing to deliver another bombshell. 'If I remember correctly the pieces of jewellery are very valuable. Your grandfather, not wanting all his eggs in one basket, invested in gold.' He sat back in his chair with his fingers steepled in his lap, a satisfied smile on his face.

However, one glance across the desk and he was on his feet immediately and scurrying round it, bending in concern over Colette. 'Are you all right, my dear?'

Colette willed herself not to pass out. This man would think her such a fool. Ten thousand pounds would probably seem nothing to him but to her it was a fortune; a fantastic amount of money. She couldn't take it in. Perhaps she had picked him up wrong. He pressed a bell on the desk and a girl immediately answered its summons. 'Doris, please fetch Miss Burns a glass of water.' When Doris returned with the water, he said, tersely, 'Bring some coffee too, will you, please? I think this young lady is in shock. It's all been too much for her.'

A few sips of the cold water revived Colette to some extent and she smiled weakly at the solicitor. 'Did I hear you right, Mr McIlroy? Did you say *ten thousand pounds*?'

'Yes. You heard me right.' The coffee arrived and, more at ease now, Colette sat back in her chair. She had to; she was afraid of tumbling off it. She was trembling all over and felt light headed, her mind racing in all directions. Matthew poured the coffee into fine china cups. 'Sugar and milk, my dear?'

'Yes, please. One spoonful.'

Handing her the cup, he said, 'Drink that up. Let's get some colour back into those cheeks of yours.'

Colette sipped at the coffee. It was delicious. Not any old coffee here. 'I'm all right now, thank you, Mr McIlroy. I've gotten over the initial shock. I just can't understand how my grannie came by all that money.' Struck by a thought, she cried in alarm, 'There's no mistake, is there? You are reading the right will?'

He smiled benevolently at her. 'I can assure you, my dear, there is no mistake.'

Bewildered, she repeated, 'How on earth did Grannie come by all that money?'

'We have handled your grandparents' affairs for a number of years and I can tell you that your grandfather was a very shrewd man where the stock market was concerned. He left your grandmother comfortably off when he died. However, without his expertise, she wasn't willing to risk what she had and the money has been lying in the building society gathering interest over the years. I think she had your future welfare in mind even then. She always mentioned your name in the course of any conversation with us. She was very proud of you.'

'She was a wonderful woman. I still can't take it in.' Her eyes widened in wonder. 'I'm rich.'

'It's a lot of money, yes, but I'm sure you'll handle it sensibly. If you ever need advice or decide to invest it, or indeed part of it, I would be only too delighted to be of service to you.'

Colette walked about the town in a daze. If only Jack were still alive! The plans they would be making now. They wouldn't have to count the pennies. They would be able to buy a house, have a big wedding and an expensive honeymoon. Restless, she felt the need to share her news with someone. Talk about her good fortune. Tess was the closest she had to a friend and catching a bus up Grosvenor Road she travelled on up the Springfield Road to the stop nearest Tess's house.

Tess and Theresa were sewing away in the work room and were surprised to see Colette. As a rule, friends knew better than to visit during working hours. 'Is anything wrong?' Tess asked anxiously.

'No. Far from it. The very opposite in fact. I'm sorry

for interrupting you at your work. I never thought. I just had to talk to someone.'

Sensing that whatever Colette wanted to talk about was meant for Tess's ears only, Theresa suggested, 'It's time for a break anyway, Tess. Why don't you make the tea?'

'Good idea, Theresa. I'll bring you in a cuppa.'

In the kitchen Colette revealed her good news. 'You're having me on!' Tess gasped. 'Aren't you?'

Delighted at her friend's response, Colette assured her, 'It's true. I can't take it in myself.'

'I'm very happy for you, Colette. You deserve it. You were devoted to your grannie. She knew you loved her dearly.'

'I don't want everyone to know. That's why I didn't say anything in front of Theresa. I want to have a good think about it. Decide what I want to do. But meanwhile, let's celebrate, eh? Let's go out on Saturday night and paint the town red.'

'I'm all for that!' Tess hesitated, wondering if what she was about to suggest was the right thing. 'I wonder . . .'

'Come on, out with it,' Colette prompted.

'Would you mind inviting Tony along? He's not exactly the best of company since Agnes left, but if we can persuade him to join us it might cheer him up.'

Colette agreed willingly. 'Will you ask him or shall I?'

'I'll probably see him before you do, so leave it to me.'

Tess was already regretting her impulsive suggestion. Tony was making a nuisance of himself hanging about the road outside the house, waylaying her whenever possible. He might put a damper on their night out. He seemed to imagine that he and she should be crying on each other's shoulder, whereas Tess was just happy that things were apparently working out so well for Agnes and Dominic. The letters she received from her friend simply glowed with happiness. Dominic had bought a house and they were in the process of decorating it. Stella who managed the restaurant in Dominic's absence and Agnes got on together like a house on fire. Last but not least they hoped to marry in August. Tess was glad for her friend but wanted to get on with her own life. Meanwhile Tony was still wallowing in self-pity.

'I'd better take this cup in to Theresa, or she'll think we've forgotten all about her. Mam is at the shops and she'll be back soon. I take it you won't want her to know either?'

'Not at the moment, Tess, if you don't mind. It's too much to take in all at once. As I said, I need some time to think it over. Let it sink in.'

Tony said he would be delighted to join the girls on Saturday night, which left Tess feeling somewhat guilty. Perhaps she should have encouraged him more. He had asked her out a few times but she was afraid of giving him the wrong impression. She had no interest whatsoever in Tony Burke.

Struck by a sudden thought, she recalled how Colette had championed Tony when she learned that Agnes might return his ring. Was there a chance that these two could help each other recover from their respective losses? Maybe even find romance together? Tess thought it was indeed a possibility and vowed to do all in her power to help it along.

Saturday evening was a great success. Tony determinedly shrugged off his gloom and was, on the whole, quite good company. With Colette not wanting anyone else to know about her inheritance they had difficulty persuading him to let her foot the bill. He said it was only fair that he paid his own way. In fact, he had a bit saved and would be only too happy to treat them. At this Colette relented a bit and said her grannie had left her a few hundred pounds and she wanted to treat him and Tess. He eventually agreed on condition that he treated them the following Saturday night.

Thus it became a habit, the three of them going out together once a week, but although Tess left them in each other's company whenever possible, romance didn't blossom between Colette and Tony. They remained just good friends.

The orders were rolling in for first Communion outfits and Tess and Theresa got on famously, working happily together while Alice made the headdresses in the back room.

The only cloud on Tess's horizon was Dan Thompson. It looked as if he was going to become a permanent feature about the house. Anne had really settled into his house and showed no signs of budging in the foreseeable future. They eventually heard that her friend Pat had moved in with her.

Waiting until her mother was out of the room, Tess confronted Dan. 'Look here, Dan, I don't mind you staying here, but don't you think you should be making a bigger effort to get Anne and her boyfriend out of your house?'

'I didn't say anything to your mother, Tess, but I have tried. Anne is claiming squatter's rights. Whether or not she can get away with it I don't know. As for her friend . . . he's proving to be one awkward customer, so he is.'

'Well, you can't live here for ever! So what are you going to do about it?'

He shrugged his shoulders and just sat staring at her. Tess turned away in disgust. In her eyes he was proving to be an unsavoury customer too, living here for next to nothing. Her mother could find no fault in him, so Tess's hands, and indeed her tongue, were tied. When she had tried to talk to her mother about the situation, Alice had implied that her daughter would find any man difficult to live with and that she had all the makings of a spinster. This had rankled within Tess, and made her question her own lifestyle. Working five, sometimes six days a week with hardly any social life, what chance had she of meeting a suitable man? But, she vowed, if married life meant buckling down to the demands of some lazy bugger like Dan Thompson, she would be better off single.

As first Communion time approached the outfits were selling like hot cakes. Theresa surprised her one day as they sewed away. 'Tess, there's a shop down the road, you know the one near the corner that sells children's clothes? Well, it's up for sale. Would you not be interested in branching out?'

Tess had indeed noticed the For Sale sign above the shop and the idea had crossed her mind only to be pushed aside. Now she voiced her thoughts. 'Where on earth would I get that kind of money?'

'Actually, I was thinking of us entering into a partnership. I've a bit salted away and I imagine you've some savings too?'

Tess sat thinking for some time. 'It's a big step to take, Theresa.'

'Not really. It's already well established as a children's clothier and we've got the ability to make a go of it. The two spinster ladies who own it are retiring to Carrickfergus. It's still a going concern so of course we would also have to buy the goodwill.'

Her description of the owners cut Tess to the bone. Is that how she and Theresa would be known in years to come? Spinster ladies? 'Have you any idea how much they are looking for?'

'No, but if you're interested we can find out. And the sooner the better. It won't be on the market much longer. It's sure to be snapped up.'

'I'll talk it over with Mam and let you know. Okay?'

'Fine. But I must warn you, I've given this a lot of thought. I'm really interested in it. If you find you can't see your way to taking a risk, I won't hold it against you, but I'll be looking for a partner elsewhere. I think it's the chance of a lifetime. Maybe the only one I'll ever get, and it's too good an opportunity to miss.'

They had become good friends; got on so well together at work that the thought of losing Theresa spurred Tess on. Knowing she would have difficulty holding a private conversation with her mother once Dan came home from work, she broached the subject as soon as Theresa had left for the day.

'Mam, did you notice that shop at the bottom of the road is up for sale?'

'Which shop's that?'

'The one that sells all those lovely children's clothes.'

'No I didn't. I'm surprised to hear it's in trouble. It seems to do a roaring trade.'

'As far as I know it isn't in trouble and is being sold as a going concern. The two ladies who run it are retiring.'

'Mm, I suppose they are getting on a bit.' Her glance sharpened. 'Where's all this leading, Tess?'

'Theresa has suggested we join resources and put in an offer for it.'

'Has she indeed! It could be quite costly.'

'Theresa has some money saved; whether or not I can match it is another matter. But it won't cost anything to find out just how much is involved. The question is, how do you feel about it?'

'Huh! For a minute there I thought I didn't count.'

'Ah, Mam! You know you and I are partners. And always will be.'

'I'm glad to hear that. Let me mull it over in my mind for a while, will you?'

'I need to let Theresa know as soon as possible. She'll be looking elsewhere for a partner if I'm not interested.'

'Is she threatening to leave?'

'It's not a threat, Mam. Just good business sense. Like myself, she's a single girl, and has to look to the future.'

'She is quite a bit older than you, Tess. But no matter, I'll let you know tomorrow morning. Is that soon enough?'

A bit peeved, Tess nodded. For the life of her she couldn't understand what her mother had to think over. All she had to do was agree or disagree. Unless of course she wanted to talk it over with Dan.

Tess didn't have to wait until the next morning for her mother's reply. Dan retired early that night, much to Tess's surprise, and obviously at her mother's instigation, strengthening the feeling that indeed her business had been discussed with him. Usually he sat her out these nights and she had little time alone with her mother. She didn't like the idea that their business had been mulled over, as her mother put it, with Dan, but what could she do about it?

Alice broached the subject directly. 'I've been thinking over what you said about that shop, Tess, and I think it would be a good investment.'

[315]

Pleased, Tess replied, 'You think we should go for it then?'

'Why not? As you are well aware, you'll be twenty-one in July . . .'

'You won't believe me, Mam, but I'd forgotten all about that.'

'Well, when you were born your father and I took out a small endowment policy on you. Nothing big, mind you. Just a few shillings a month. We had planned to bump it up, but somehow or other it was pushed into the background. Then when your dad died I never got round to it. Careless of me,' she admitted sadly. 'Just last week I received a letter from the Prudential reminding me that the policy would mature at the beginning of August.'

Tess watched her mother wide eyed, hanging on her every word, not knowing what was coming next.

'And what do you know?' Alice continued. 'With final bonuses they reckon it will be worth somewhere in the region of twelve hundred pounds.'

Tess sat in stunned silence, trying to take in what her mother was saying. 'You mean . . .' Her voice trailed off; she was afraid to put her thoughts into words in case she was wrong.

'I intended using some of the money to throw a surprise birthday party in your honour, but I think the money itself would be more beneficial to you, if you're interested in purchasing this shop. So as soon as the cheque comes I'll give it to you.'

'Ah, Mam, what can I say?'

'Don't say anything. Just be sure you're not throwing good money away.'

'Never you fear! Theresa and I will go into it very thoroughly. She has a very shrewd business mind and is also quite competent at ordering goods and the like. She looked after the books and all at Belart for a time, so I have every confidence in her. She certainly won't let anyone pull the wool over her eyes, that's for sure.' Going to her mother, Tess fell to her knees beside the chair and gripped her hands tightly. 'You're a wonderful woman, Mam. I'll never be able to thank you enough.'

Alice cupped her daughter's face in her hands. 'I don't want any thanks. You've been a good daughter to me. I'm just glad the money is coming at the right time and will be there when you need it.'

The excitement proved too much for Tess. She didn't sleep a wink that night. She was downstairs twice during the night making cups of tea and wandering about the house, cup in hand, her mind in turmoil with the possibility of being part owner of the shop. In her mind's eye she could envisage the name over the shop: *Maguire & Cunningham – Children's Outfitter*. It was during her second rambling that she first learned that Dan was sharing her mother's room. She was shocked to the very core. Her mother was such a puritan, had questioned everybody else's morals, and here she was, cavorting with a married man. How long had it been going on? Sleep was completely out of the question after that discovery. Tess's mind swung between the excitement of buying the shop and her mother's fall from grace. She kept telling herself it was none of her business; nevertheless she had difficulty hiding her feelings at breakfast next morning. No wonder they acted like an old married couple. There would be no rush to get married now, and *he* would certainly be in no rush to get back to his own home.

Why should he leave a nice comfortable house where he was lifted and laid to return to a cold, dingy house in Spinner Street?

She phoned Theresa and told her the deal was on. Where did they go from here?

'Our first call will be to the estate agents. Once I get Mam settled I'll ask a neighbour to sit with her and I'll pick you up at . . . say eleven?'

'I'll be ready and waiting,' Tess promised.

Theresa parked her car outside the estate agents in Lower Donegall Street. She warned Tess not to appear too enthusiastic. They would pretend it was a casual inquiry and that they had other property to view.

The young man in charge of the agency introduced himself as Barry McGuinness and was full of praise for the premises on Springfield Road. Sadly, he informed them that an offer had already been made for it.

Disappointed, Tess remained silent, having been told to follow Theresa's lead. Theresa had done her home-work well. She knew there was an empty shop on the Falls Road with a different agency. Now she said sweetly, 'Thank you for your attention, Mr McGuinness.' She headed for the door. 'I guess we will just have to have another look at that shop near Waterford Street, Tess. It should prove to be cheaper, as it's been empty quite a while.'

'Just a minute, Mrs . . . Oh dear, I'm afraid I've forgot-ten your names already.'

'It's *Miss* Cunningham, and you never asked for our names, which was very remiss of you. This is Miss Maguire. I think perhaps we should speak to your supe-rior. When would that be possible?'

Thoroughly flustered now, the young man apologised profusely and pulling two chairs away from a desk said, 'If you will take a seat, please, I'll show you what we have on our books.'

'We're only interested in the clothes shop near the corner of Springfield Road,' Theresa warned. 'So don't think you can dump anything else on us. You'd be wasting your time.'

Barry opened a cabinet, took a file from it, and spread it out on the desk. 'I was telling the truth when I said an offer has been made for it . . . but well below the asking price.'

Theresa leaned forward, elbows on the table. 'Someone you know? Is that why you were reluctant to tell us about it?' Barry's face blazed with colour but she let him off the hook. 'Okay, let's hear about this offer you've received.'

They discussed all the details. At last Theresa seemed satisfied and rose to her feet. 'We'll be in touch with you, Mr McGuinness. Thank you for all your help.'

Outside, Tess looked in bewilderment at Theresa. 'Even at more than they were offered it still sounded good to me. Less than we expected it to be. Wasn't it?'

'Trust me, Tess. Whoever put that offer in was chancing their arm. They will be willing to go higher. Much higher, if I'm not mistaken.'

'Does that mean we're out of the running?'

'No. We're going to visit the two ladies who run the shop. Find out how much they want for the goodwill.'

'Goodwill?'

'Names, addresses, contact numbers for their clients.'

'Does that matter?'

'Oh, yes. It matters very much. They might also have

some stock on their hands we could get at a bargain price.'

Tess was beginning to realise there was more to buying a property than she had ever imagined. She was glad Theresa was in control.

It turned out that the two elderly ladies, one thin as a whippet and the other plump and jolly, were sisters. When the bell above the door tinkled, the thin one bustled out from a room at the back of the shop and came to the counter.

'Can I be of any assistance, ladies?'

'Yes. We are interested in buying these premises and would like to speak to the owner.'

After giving them a considering look and obviously deeming them trustworthy, the woman lifted the flap at the end of the counter that gave access to the rest of the shop, shouting over her shoulder, 'Mary, there are two young ladies inquiring about the shop. Just go on through there,' she instructed. 'I'll close up for a short while.'

A small plump woman came forward to meet them at the entrance to the back room. Thrusting her hand towards Theresa, she introduced herself. 'My name is Mary Donnelly, and' – she nodded to the thin woman – 'that's my sister Cissie. Just what is it you'd like to know?'

'Well, first of all, what do you think of the offer that has already been submitted to the estate agent?'

Mary's chin lifted in the air and her nostrils flared in anger. 'Insulting! That's what we think.'

'Is the goodwill included in your asking price?'

Sensing that this was a genuine inquiry and not just someone being nosy, Mary led them through to yet another room, comfortably furnished, and nodded to a small settee. 'Let's sit in here and discuss this in comfort. Would you like a wee cup of tea, my dears?'

An hour later they all stood on the threshold of the shop and exchanged handshakes.

'We will need to arrange a loan from the bank,' Theresa said. 'But there will be no problems there, we can assure you. Meanwhile, you say you will turn down the offer already made?'

'You can count on that,' the sisters chorused.

'What if they come up with a better one?' Tess voiced her worry.

'We are more than happy with your offer,' Cissie assured her. 'And we are so glad that you will continue to sell children's clothes. We spent years building up this wee business and are glad to know it won't become an electrical goods shop, which is what the other client intended.'

'We shall submit a written offer first thing tomorrow morning and make an appointment to see about a loan from the bank. I'm glad we called to see you person-ally. It was a pleasure meeting you. You've been a wealth of information.'

'We'll keep in touch. Anything you want to know about suppliers and buyers, you only have to ask.'

Goodbyes were said all round and Theresa and Tess headed to where the car was parked in McQuillan Street. At the corner of the Falls Road they stopped and faced each other.

'Well? What do you think?' a breathless Theresa asked.

'I think, if it all goes through without a hitch, we're getting a smashing bargain,' Tess enthused.

'So do I. We will have to go to the bank first thing tomorrow morning and see about a loan.'

'I'll phone Colette. I'm almost sure she works in the department that deals with business loans. Do you think we'll have any trouble getting one?'

'Of course not. We only need a small loan to let us retain some of our savings as security against the unexpected.'

As soon as she got home Tess phoned the bank and asked to speak to Colette. As she had hoped, her friend did indeed work in the business loans department and immediately made an appointment with her superior.

That evening she called in on Tess and surprised her by offering to lend her the money personally, interest free.

'Oh, but I couldn't take your money,' Tess exclaimed, profoundly touched by her generosity.

'Of course you can. I trust you. How much do you need?'

'It's not just for me, Colette. Sit down and I'll tell you all about it.'

Colette listened as Tess related how Theresa had suggested they go into partnership and put in an offer on the shop, and how they had gone down to see the estate agent and then up to the shop in question and the agreement they had struck with the two sisters.

'Wow! You certainly hit it lucky there, getting Theresa as a partner. It sounds as if she knows her onions all right. You will definitely make a go of it. Both of you are such hard workers, it's bound to be a success.'

'Thanks, Colette. We can only give it our best shot.'

'I've been a bit busy myself lately,' Colette confided. 'I wrote to my friend in Canada and I got a reply from her yesterday. She's going to try and get me fixed up with a job out there. She said that with my banking experience I'm more or less guaranteed a job. It will be a complete change for me and I'm looking forward to it. I'm all excited.'

'I'm sure you are. It's a great opportunity for you. Too good to miss.' Tess felt a twinge of sadness; she had become very attached to this young girl. 'I'll miss you, so I will.'

'Not a bit of it! You'll be too busy making your fortune to notice my absence. I'd better run. I let Tony talk me into going for a walk up the mountain loney.'

Tess's eyes widened and she said, 'Why, that's wonderful news.'

'It's not, you know. All he'll do is talk about *you*. But it will get me out of the house for a couple of hours. Here, did I tell you I've been to the Ulster Bank and had a look at the jewellery Grannie left me?' At Tess's shake of the head she continued with a huge smile on her face. 'Six pieces in all and worth, I've been assured, at least another five thousand pounds. They are absolutely gorgeous. I don't know what to do about them.'

'Oh, you lucky devil! You're set for life.'

'And all because of my grannie, God bless her. Look, I'd better run on or Tony will think I've stood him up. Don't forget my offer of the loan. I'm dead serious about it, Tess. I mightn't see you at the bank in the morning – you'll be interviewed in one of the private rooms – but if not, I'll see you Saturday night as usual.'

On Saturday night the trio went to the Carlton steak house and then on to the Hippodrome. Although everything appeared all right on the surface, Tess sensed that Colette was worried about something. Knowing that she didn't like her affairs discussed in front of anyone else, not even Tony, she held her tongue but had every intention of finding out what was worrying her friend.

With this in mind Tess called down to see Colette on Sunday afternoon. As she awaited an answer to her knock, she let her eyes roam over Dan's house, noting that the door had been freshly painted and crisp white net curtains hung at the windows. Anne was certainly making herself at home.

She was turning to leave, thinking that Colette must be out, when the door opened just a fraction and Colette peered out. 'I'm not very good company at the moment, Tess. Could you come back later?'

Tess dithered. Had Colette someone with her and didn't want Tess to know? She looked closer and was concerned to note that her friend had been crying. 'Are you sure you wouldn't like someone to talk to? It was obvious to me last night that you were unhappy. That's why I'm here now. To see if I can be of any use.'

Slowly the gap in the doorway widened enough for Tess to enter and Colette confessed, 'I'm in a quandary. Don't know where to turn. You see, once I speak about it, there'll be no turning back.'

They sat together on the settee. 'Let me guess. Your friend in Canada has changed her mind and doesn't want you to go out there now. Am I right? Is that why you're so down in the mouth?'

'Far from it. That might set me back a bit but it would be the least of my worries right now.'

Intrigued, Tess insisted, 'Trust me, Colette. You know I can keep my big trap shut when I have to.'

Colette covered her face with her hands. 'I'm so ashamed. But it won't go away, so I suppose I may as well tell you. You'll know soon enough anyhow. Everyone will. *I'm pregnant!*'

You could have knocked Tess down with a feather. This was the last thing in the world she would have expected to hear. At last she got her breath back. 'Has Tony . . .'

A bewildered frown gathered on Colette's brow. 'Tony? Of course not! You've got it all wrong. When I missed my first period I thought it was the upheaval of Jack's death, but when I missed the second one I realised I was expecting a baby. Oh, Tess, what am I going to do?'

Tess could only guess at her friend's predicament. Wasn't she herself gobsmacked at the news? Colette had been so happy, looking forward to a new life in Canada . . . and now this. 'As you say . . . this is something that can't be kept a secret very long. Your mother will have to be told—'

'*Never!* Do you hear me? I'm trusting you to keep your mouth shut like you promised. I'll think of something. I just haven't got my mind round it yet. But I won't give my mother the satisfaction of saying, "Didn't I tell you so?"'

Remembering Colette's intention of going down the aisle a virgin, Tess was sad. If only she had persevered. But these things do happen in the heat of the moment. 'Whatever you decide to do, I'll back you all the way,' she promised.

'I don't want this baby.' At Tess's startled look, Colette cried, 'Oh, I'm not thinking of an abortion! But I won't keep it! I will get it adopted.'

'It's early days, Colette. Let's get used to the idea first and then we'll put our heads together and see what we can come up with. Remember, I'll help you all I can.'

'I feel a great deal better already. Just having someone to talk to makes all the difference. I thought I'd go away in the head this past few days. Thanks, Tess. Thanks for being so understanding.'

'That's what friends are for. But never you fear. Between us we'll sort something out.' Tess sounded confident but for the life of her she couldn't see any way out of this dilemma without involving Colette's mother.

Chapter Fifteen

After a few minor hiccups, everything went smoothly regarding the purchase of the shop. They had been invited to examine the premises, so on the advice of their bank had hired an assessor to do it on a professional basis. When they got his favourable report they put down a deposit as a token gesture of good faith to show their intentions as genuine buyers. The sisters had kept the shop in a good state of repair and would be vacating it at the beginning of August. The girls would be able to move in straight away. Tess and Theresa proudly had cards printed and sent out to their regular customers informing them of their new business address. The future was beginning to look rosy indeed.

They had sold far more first Communion outfits than they normally did. They had also worked hard finishing off two wedding outfits at the end of June. On the whole, a good few months' hard graft had reaped substantial dividends. Theresa was overjoyed with the bonus she received for all her hard work, happy in the knowledge that her trial period was over. She was now part owner in a small but going concern.

Alice advised them to take a break during the Twelfth fortnight as she would be around to collect the weekly payments from their regular tick customers. The girls readily agreed that this was a good idea indeed as, with most firms closing down for two weeks in July, a lot of families chose this time to take their annual holidays and there would be few orders coming in. August and September would see them working on the wedding outfits already in their order books for the autumn, and then there would be Christmas dresses and children's party dresses, so now was certainly the time for a well earned holiday. Theresa happily began making plans to take her mother away to visit a cousin in Bundoran for a week; she had a lot of boasting to do about her new status in life.

Tess's thoughts flew to Carlingford. Her Uncle Malachy had phoned a few times reminding her of her promise to visit him, but she had thought it unlikely that she would be able to get away due to pressure of work. However, the employment of Theresa had changed all that and now she decided she would give him a ring and make arrangements to visit the farm for a week or two.

As yet unaware that Tess knew she was sharing her bed with Dan, her mother was in her element, looking forward to having the house all to herself and the love of her life. Tess could not deny that her mother looked fulfilled and happy, wandering about the place with a perpetual smile on her face, but for the life of her Tess couldn't get it out of her head that Dan wasn't a free agent. Would it all end in tears? Still, as she kept reminding herself, it was none of her business. Since her confrontation with him, Dan was contributing more money for his keep and generally pulling his weight about the house. Nevertheless, Tess missed her own privacy. Things were a lot different with a man, practically a stranger, around the house.

Before getting in touch with Malachy, she decided she would endeavour to persuade Colette to accompany her to Carlingford. Tess had kept in close contact with Colette over the past weeks, ever ready with an attentive ear or a sympathetic shoulder to cry on. As yet her friend had not come up with any concrete plans for the immediate future, saying there was plenty of time as she wasn't even showing yet. Perhaps if Tess could get her away from Belfast for a while to the peace and tranquillity of Malachy's farm she would be able to talk her round to her own way of thinking. At the moment Colette was adamant that she would not keep the child and that her mother must never know about the pickle she had landed herself in. Betty seemed to worry Colette more than anything else and Tess thought it tragic that one couldn't turn to one's own mother in such circumstances. It seemed such a pity that the baby would go to complete strangers and might never know its natural grandparents, one at least of whom would lavish it with love.

Now, when the proposition of a holiday was put to her, Colette shook her head determinedly and said, 'I can't go to Carlingford with you, Tess. I'd be a wet blanket, always moaning and groaning about one thing or another. I'd only spoil your holiday and you'd end up wishing you'd never invited me along in the first place. Thanks anyway for asking, but . . . no thanks.'

'Look, Colette, you need to get away for a while. Give yourself a break, a chance to think things through more rationally in the quiet of the countryside.'

'I've already thought it through. I've turned it over in my mind time after time after time and always come up with the same answer. I'll work as long as I can and then I'll go away somewhere and have the baby.'

'Huh! Just like that?'

'And why not? Other girls have done it. I'll get in touch with one of those homes for unmarried mothers where I'll stay until the baby is born. Afterwards, the authorities will find a good home for it, someone who'll love it more than I ever could. No one need be any the wiser. Thanks to Grannie, money won't be a problem.'

All this sounded so cold and calculated and not one bit like the Colette Tess had grown to like and respect. A perplexed frown on her brow, Tess asked tentatively, 'I know you must feel very bitter about Jack leaving you in this predicament, but after the birth you might feel different. They say that once you hold your baby in your arms, you don't want to let go. Don't you think you should at least tell Dan you are expecting his grand-child? It seems only fair that he should know about it. In fact, he would be the ideal person to rear the child and Mam would be only too delighted to help him. I mean, they're still quite young and I'd also be there to give a hand when needed. You wouldn't have to go away to have it, and I'm sure your friend in Canada wouldn't mind waiting a bit longer for your company. Everybody would understand the circumstances and the child would be here if you should ever change your mind. Think about it, Colette. It's the sensible thing to do.'

'Look, Tess, I know you mean well, and I wish things could be different, but they can't. Meanwhile, I don't want anybody to know I'm pregnant. No one. Do you understand? So don't you dare break your promise . . . please.'

Feeling as if she had come in in the middle of a play and had missed the beginning of the plot, Tess vowed, 'Colette, unless you give me permission, I will never utter a single word about it to anyone. But you can't blame me for speaking my thoughts to you; giving you my opinion. Don't deny the child its family connections.'

'Look, Tess, this is getting us nowhere fast. Could we change the subject, please?'

Noting the stress lines on her friend's face, Tess quietly agreed. 'All right. But you do need a holiday, you know. Can you get two weeks off in July?'

'Yes, but—'

'No buts about it! You look as if you could do with a good rest. And you know what they say . . . a change is as good as a tonic.'

Colette could see the logic in her friend's words and admitted, 'You're right. I'm not getting much sleep these nights. I'd love to come to Carlingford with you. That is, if your Uncle Malachy doesn't object.'

Malachy was delighted to receive Tess's phone call. He had given up all hope of seeing her this side of Christmas. 'Of course you must bring Colette along. Wait until I tell Rose,' he cried. 'She'll be over the moon. And Tess, since you're coming down here I'll be able to give you your birthday present in person.'

'That sounds intriguing. Can I ask what it is?'

'You certainly can, but that's as far as it goes. It's my big secret and will remain so until you get here. But I know you'll be delighted with it.'

'Well, if you're not going to tell me, I'll just have to wait then, won't I?'

'I'm afraid so. I'm glad you're bringing a friend along. Rose and I will do all we can to see you enjoy your stay. I'll call her when you hang up and tell her the good news. Bye for now. See you soon.'

*　　*　　*

Alice couldn't contain her excitement at the idea of having Dan all to herself for two whole, uninterrupted weeks. No having to slip out of each other's bedrooms in the wee small hours, in case Tess guessed what was going on. No keeping their hands to themselves when they were alone. Although she admitted to herself that the need for secrecy added spice to their affair.

She often pondered on how she had managed to end up in this glorified lust; how she, above all people, had managed to suppress her conscience enough to cohabit with Dan. He on the other hand wanted her to look out for a place of their own where they could live together openly. She had soon put that idea out of his head. *Openly in sin?* How could he even contemplate it? What would people think of the high and mighty Alice Maguire's fall from grace? She was totally mortified at the very thought of it. Why, she would never be able to hold her head up in public again.

Dan was also off work for two weeks and she couldn't get Tess out of the way quickly enough. It would be marvellous being in the house all alone with him. Just like being on her honeymoon. The first night she intended making a special meal and a bottle of champagne was hidden at the back of the fridge.

The Twelfth of July fell on a Monday this year and Saturday morning the tenth saw Tess packed and rarin' to go. As Alice hovered about impatiently waiting to say her goodbyes the taxi arrived, and Tess couldn't help taking the opportunity to tease her mother.

'Mam, I think perhaps we should wait and travel down tomorrow morning. The roads won't be so busy then. What do you think?'

'But . . . what about your taxi? It's sitting outside waiting for you.'

'I can always send it away.'

Seeing all her plans evaporating into thin air Alice cried, 'And what about Colette? Won't she be expecting you to pick her up soon? She'll be sitting there all packed and ready to go. You can't let her down.' Tess's eyes twinkled and Alice realised she was pulling her leg. 'You're having me on, aren't you?'

'Do you think I don't know about all your shenanigans with Dan?' She watched the blood creep up her mother's neck. 'Ah, Mam! I've got eyes in my head. I've known for some time how it is between you two.' She wanted to add, 'How could you?' but didn't. Why spoil things for her mother with snide remarks? It certainly wouldn't stop her carry-ons.

To her surprise Alice said sadly, 'I know what you must be thinking and I don't blame you, love. I don't know where it all started. I've always been so bloody sanctimonious. But it's too late now. I just can't help myself.'

'Mam, I understand. I'm a big girl, you know. He *is* handsome . . . in fact Agnes Quinn thinks he's the spittin' image of Cary Grant.'

'Does she?' Alice's face brightened as she gave it some thought, and with a wag of the head she conceded, 'She does have a point.'

'And we must remember you're a very attractive woman. If he was free, there would be no problem whatsoever.'

Dan, descending the stairs, put an end to their little *tête-à-tête*. 'So you'll be off soon then, Tess? See and enjoy yourself. I'm glad Colette is going with you. She needs a break too.'

Tess allowed him to peck at her cheek. 'My taxi's sitting outside.'

Dan lifted the two suitcases. 'I'll carry these out.'

Tess wrapped her arms around her mother in a bear hug. 'No use telling you to be good, but at least be careful. If he ever hurts you, I swear I'll swing for him. And you tell him that. Goodbye, Mam.'

'Goodbye, love. And I know *you* will be good. See you when you get back.'

Tess laughed at the very idea. 'I don't think there will be any chance to be otherwise. From what I hear all the farmers' sons and daughters are spoken for practically from birth.'

'Well then, don't you go upsetting the apple-cart by catching some lad's eye,' Alice warned, with a twinkle in her own. 'Enjoy yourself, love.'

When Tess arrived in the taxi to pick her up, Colette greeted her friend eagerly. 'You know, I didn't think I could get excited over this holiday . . . but I am!'

'Oh, I'm so pleased to hear you say that. Just forget all your troubles and woes and let's enjoy ourselves for the next two weeks, eh?'

'I'm all for it!'

The warmth of their welcome at Carlingford nearly brought tears to Colette's eyes. Once introductions were made, she was hugged and kissed as if she were the prodigal daughter. Old Meg had died and Malachy had acquired a new Border collie to take her place. He had named her Florrie and she frisked around them, running back and forth between the girls and a shed close to the house.

'She wants you to go and look at her litter,' Malachy explained.

'A litter already? Impossible!' Tess exclaimed.

'I took her off a friend's hands when he realised she

[334]

had been playing around. Luckily, as it turned out, it was another Border collie she was having fun with. I shouldn't have any bother getting homes for her six pups.'

Colette was enthralled with the wiggling bundles of fur. 'I've always wanted a dog,' she said, cradling one of the pups against her cheek.

'No problem. I'll be only too glad to let you take one home with you. Take your pick. Mind you, they need plenty of exercise,' Malachy warned.

Colette flashed a startled glance at Tess. 'Well now . . . I . . . I don't know about that,' she spluttered. 'I might be going away in the near future.'

Before Tess could intervene on her behalf, Malachy said, 'No sweat, Colette. I'll not force you to take one. Think it over. The decision's all yours.'

While Malachy worked in the fields by day, Rose took them for drives to the outlying villages and Colette was enchanted. In the evenings, weather permitting, Malachy took them further afield.

'I could stay here for ever.' Colette confided. 'You never told me how beautiful it was, Tess.'

'And spoil your first impression of it?'

'There is still so much to see.'

'Well, we have another week and by the sound of things it's going to be a hectic one. For instance, Malachy is throwing a small party to celebrate my twenty-first birthday on Saturday night.'

'He's very fond of you, Tess. You're very lucky to have relatives who truly care for you.'

'I know. Everybody needs someone close that they can discuss their troubles with. And remember, I'm here for you, Colette.' Always ready to press a point home, she asked tentatively, 'Have you changed your mind at all about the baby?'

'Now Tess . . . behave yourself. Please?'

'All right! All right, I'll not say another word.'

Saturday started off damp and miserable. 'I hope it's not going to rain today of all days. It will spoil all my carefully laid plans,' Malachy moaned. The two girls were spending a few days at Rose's home, and today Malachy had been invited to join them. As they ate breakfast at the big table in Rose's kitchen he gazed dolefully out over the wet hedges and fields at the blanket of mist hanging over the mountain tops.

'The forecast for today is good, actually,' Rose informed him.

'Ach! They're not always right. Far from it,' he said pessimistically.

'What's so important that a little rain will spoil it?' Tess queried.

'Tonight I want everything to be just perfect. First we are going for a meal in that new restaurant near Dundalk and then we're coming back here to meet a small gathering of friends. All in honour of your twenty-first. I know your big day isn't till the end of the month, but I do want to be there when you see your present. It's a bit large to send in the post.' He caught Rose's eye and they shared a secret smile.

Looking from one to the other, Tess said, 'Ah! The plot thickens! I can't wait to see this mysterious present, whatever it is.'

Rose nodded her head sagely. 'You won't be disappointed. I can understand Malachy not wanting it to be raining.' She too peered out at the mist and drizzle. 'But with those dark clouds scudding overhead, I can understand his misgivings.'

'I'm looking forward to this evening, Uncle Malachy.

We'll enjoy ourselves no matter what the weather is like,' Tess assured him.

'Of course we will,' Rose agreed. 'Meanwhile, I want to take you girls to the market today. So while the bathroom is free, you two get cleaned up and I'll clear up in the kitchen, all right?'

'No it's not all right. We'll help you in the kitchen before we get ready to go out,' Tess declared.

'She sounds determined, Rose. Better let them help out.' With a wide grin on his face, Malachy headed for the stairs. 'Besides, the bathroom won't be empty much longer.'

By mid-morning the sun had broken through the now thinning clouds, and the girls left for the market in a happy frame of mind. It was going to be a fine day after all. As they drove along the road they saw Malachy in the distance and pointing to the sky he gave them the thumbs up.

'You know, I can't help wondering about this mysterious present Uncle Malachy has bought for me.' Tess slanted her eyes at Rose. 'I don't suppose you'd give me a clue, would you?'

Rose gazed at her in amazement. 'I wouldn't dare! Malachy would murder me if I said a single word about it. So I'm afraid you'll just have to contain your curiosity a little longer, my dear.' Her smile was full of mischief. 'But I can assure you, it's worth waiting for. You won't be disappointed.'

They spent hours wandering about the open-air market. There were stalls offering all sorts of wares – 'You can get anything here from a needle to an anchor,' as Rose had so aptly put it. Tess was pleased to find beautiful hand-painted vases for her mother and Theresa, a leather belt with his name etched into it for Dan, and a pale blue mohair wrap for Theresa's mother to match her still sapphire eyes. Colette bought some small ornaments for workmates and they ended the afternoon having tea and cream scones in the big marquee erected for that purpose, before returning to Rose's house to prepare for their night out.

The restaurant near Dundalk stood in its own grounds; acres of lawns and gardens, and a small lake that was home to a pair of majestic swans. Before entering the magnificent building, they took a leisurely walk in the gardens admiring the colourful display of flowers and shrubs.

Indoors they were led by the head waiter to a table reserved in a spacious booth. The booths were in an alcove to one side of the room and each was overlooked by a high window. 'I'll send the wine waiter over, shall I, sir?'

'Please do.'

When he came over Malachy ordered two bottles of medium dry white wine.

As Tess sank down on to a plush velvet-covered seat she muttered to Colette, 'This must be costing Uncle Malachy a bomb.'

Rose heard her and whispered, 'It is! But you only come of age once and he regards you as the daughter he never had.' She hesitated before adding, 'Malachy did invite your mother and Dan, you know, but Alice said they were busy making their own plans for your birthday. She wished us all the best.'

Not wanting Alice to appear uncaring, Tess assured her, 'Mam has been very generous too.' She went on to explain about the endowment policy and how she would be able to buy her share in the shop with it. 'Besides, I know why they didn't want to come,' she added with a twinkle in her eye.

As the waiter poured the drinks they perused the menu and chose their starters, of which there was a long intriguing list. Each ordered something different, something they had never heard of before, so that they could find out just what some of the mysterious names actually were.

While they waited for the starters, Rose looked inquiringly at Malachy. He gave a little nod and delving into her handbag she retrieved a small parcel. Reaching across, she placed it in front of Tess, who smothered a secret smile. Too big to send through the post, eh?

'Happy birthday, Tess.'

'Thank you.' Tess carefully removed the silver wrapping paper to display a jeweller's box. Inside nestled a watch with a fine mesh gold strap, obviously expensive, and a card bearing the greeting, 'To my friend Tess. From Rose, Happy Birthday.'

'Oh, Rose . . . this is far too expensive! I can't possibly accept it.'

'Tess, Malachy talks so much about you I feel as if you are already family. And since—'

She stopped abruptly and shot Malachy a guilty look. He spread his hands wide and shrugged. 'Trust a woman not to be able to keep a secret. Go on, you may as well tell them.' Although he pretended to be annoyed, the girls could see he was pleased and rather chuffed.

'Malachy has, in fact, persuaded me to become part of the family. We are getting married next spring. He's right, it's a bit early to be talking about it, but I'm hoping you'll make my wedding suit for me, Tess.'

Tess left her chair and going to Rose kissed and

[339]

hugged her. 'Oh, I'm so pleased for you, and thank you for this beautiful watch. It's gorgeous! And of course I'll make your suit.'

Before returning to her chair she hugged Malachy. 'Rose is a lovely person and I'm so happy for you. I hope you will have many years together. Can I tell Mam? She'll be delighted.'

Colette offered her congratulations, then she too produced a small parcel and gave it to Tess, saying shyly, 'Happy birthday, Tess. I know it's a week early, but I hope you like it.'

Colette's present was a small gold crucifix on a chain. Tears in her eyes, Tess said, 'Oh, Colette. It's beautiful. Thank you very much.' Reaching for her friend's hand she squeezed it tightly. 'I don't deserve such expensive presents.'

'You've been a good, loyal friend to me, Tess, when I really needed one. I couldn't have coped without you since Jack died.'

The three women were almost in tears and an embarrassed Malachy was glad when the waiter arrived with their starters.

The meal was delicious, from the unusual starters and main courses to the mouth-watering desserts. A sated, happy party retired to the lounge for coffee and mints prior to returning to Rose's house to have a bit of a do with the neighbours. Just as they were finishing a waiter approached Malachy and whispered in his ear. A grin split his face and he rose quickly to his feet, offering his arm to Tess. 'Please accompany me, madam. Your transport has arrived.'

A puzzled frown puckering her brow, Tess looked to Rose for support. Rose gave her a confident nod and, gathering her and Tess's belongings, signalled for Colette to accompany them outside.

Striding forth in a grand manner Malachy led his bemused niece out of the lounge, across the foyer and through the revolving doors. He came to a halt outside and turned to watch Tess's reaction.

She couldn't believe her eyes. Parked outside the main entrance was a gleaming, bright red Austin Mini, sporting a large placard saying 'Happy Birthday Tess. From Uncle Malachy.' It sat in full glory, the chrome trimmings glistening in the late sunshine.

Her reaction was more than Malachy could have hoped for. She took a startled step backwards and her enormous green eyes looked as if they were about to pop out of her head. Her mouth hung open in astonishment. Closing it with a gulp, she turned a stupefied gaze on her uncle and managed to splutter, 'Is it really mine?'

'It's really yours,' he assured her solemnly.

Throwing herself into his arms she hugged him tightly, tears pouring down her face. 'Oh, it's wonderful! I'll never be able to thank you enough, Uncle Mal.'

'I've been keeping in touch with Theresa Cunningham and she assures me you drive her car like an old hand.'

'And she never said a word,' Tess exclaimed. 'Although, mind you, I did wonder why she insisted that I learn to drive her car. It seemed such a waste of time since I thought it would be years before I could afford one of my own. And now this! My very own car. I can't believe it. I just can't believe it.'

'Mind you, it's not brand new, but it had just one careful owner.' Malachy handed Tess the keys with a flourish. 'In you go. Let's see you drive it to the car park at the rear while I settle the bill. That wee waiter is watching us like a hawk. I imagine he thinks we're about to do a runner.'

Nervously, Tess glanced at Rose and Colette, who were standing silently in the background. They each gave her a nod of approval and timidly she turned the key in the lock and for the first time got into her very own car. She felt at home almost immediately. Adjusting the seat and driving mirror, she started the engine, and confidently drove the car round and round the building before expertly reversing into a parking space at the rear.

'Well . . . what do you think of it?' Rose asked, peering in at her.

'It's absolutely out of this world, so it is.' Tess got out of the car and walked slowly round it, her hand trailing admiringly along its smooth bodywork as she went.

'I told you it was worth waiting for, didn't I?' Rose said coyly.

'And it certainly was, Rose. I would never have guessed Uncle Mal would have bought me a car. It's breathtaking, so it is! I'm not surprised that he couldn't post it to me,' she joked.

Returning from the restaurant Malachy waved her back into the car. 'In you go, girl! You're driving home.'

'But . . . I'm not insured.'

'Oh, yes, you are. This car comes with six months' insurance and road tax.' Seeing tears about to fall, he added sternly, 'And no more tears. Do you hear me? Good God, girl, you're supposed to be happy.'

'Oh, I am. I am!' Tess sniffled and clambered back into the driving seat.

With Rose and Colette leading the way in the Land-Rover, and Malachy in the passenger seat of the Mini, Tess drove all the way back to Carlingford. Her uncle nodded approvingly as she turned into the driveway and smoothly pulled up outside the house. 'Theresa was right. You're a natural driver, Tess.'

'Ah, Uncle Malachy, thank you! Thank you very much. This has been the happiest day of my life.'

'Just one of many, Tess, I hope. And it's not over yet,' he added, as with a fanfare of sound and a blaze of light the front door burst open and friends and neighbours came pouring out to congratulate her.

After another hectic week, the girls decided to have a quiet night in before returning to Belfast on Saturday morning. Tess elected to take an early bath and disappeared upstairs. Saying she wouldn't be long, Rose nipped over to Malachy's with some freshly baked soda farls.

It was a beautiful evening with just a nip in the air and, left to her own devices, Colette took a stroll down towards the lough. Choosing a spot close to the shore she sat on a bench and watched the stars reflecting on the smooth water. It was lovely and peaceful here. If only they could stay a little while longer, but duty called and it was back to porridge in the morning.

She was surprised at how smoothly her pregnancy was progressing. No morning sickness and just a slight thickening of the waist. No one would ever dream that she was carrying a child. Of course she was aware that this state of affairs could not last much longer. She would soon be obliged to see a doctor and then what? The idea of applying to one of those homes for unmarried mothers was abhorrent to her. She pretended to Tess that she was tough, but deep down she was scared stiff. What was going to become of her? She suddenly felt very frightened and alone.

Rose studied Colette's still figure from a distance. In repose the young girl looked so sad. She left the road and slipped down on to the bench beside her before Colette was aware of her presence.

'Are you saying your goodbyes to Carlingford?' she asked gently.

Sadness dispelled, a smile transformed Colette's features. 'Something like that. It's a beautiful spot you live in here, so close to the Cooley Mountains. You don't realise how lucky you are. All this peace and tranquillity. Thank you for having me here this past two weeks.'

'It's been our pleasure having you.' Silence reigned for some moments and Rose broke it by asking tentatively, 'Have you made any plans for the future?'

'Well, a friend in Canada has been asking me to join her for some time now. She says I'd have no trouble at all getting a job there. There was a time when I wouldn't have been able to afford to go, but my grannie made that all possible by leaving me a large sum of money. So now I hope to eventually emigrate to Canada.'

A bewildered frown appeared on Rose's brow. 'But what about the baby? Do you intend taking it with you?'

Colette cringed away from her. 'Tess promised never to mention that to anyone,' she wailed.

Gripping her hand, Rose gave it a slight tug. 'Listen to me, Colette. Tess never said a word about you being pregnant.'

Slowly Colette relaxed and looked in confusion at Rose. 'Then how did you know? I never told anyone else.'

'I'm a country woman, remember, Colette. The signs are obvious to me. I'm sorry if I startled you, but . . . it isn't something you can hide for ever.'

'I know,' she replied sadly.

'Why are you keeping it such a big secret then? Don't you want Jack's child?'

'It's a long story, Rose. When Jack died I was devastated. I was so low that I even contemplated suicide. If Tess hadn't come into my life then, I'd probably not be here today. Tess doesn't know about this, so I'd appreciate you not mentioning it to her. Well, after a while I got my mind straightened out and began planning a new life for myself. Unfortunately the planning stage was as far as I got, due to an acute shortage of finances. Then when Grannie left me the money my dream of getting away from it all became a real possibility. I was in a position to go to Canada to start a new life. And then . . . . I discovered I was pregnant. It was a terrible shock, I can tell you.'

'And now you've gotten over the shock what do you intend to do?'

'I don't know. I honestly don't know. I feel I must be some kind of monster not to want my own baby.' She turned towards Rose and gripped her arm. 'But I don't want it! I honestly don't!'

Putting an arm round her shoulders, Rose soothed her as best she could. 'Let's get you indoors and we can discuss it further, over a nice wee cup of tea.'

Walking back to the house, Rose said, 'What about your mother? She's the obvious one to help you. Won't she be annoyed when she finds out you've kept her in the dark all this time?'

'She's the last one I'd turn to. A child born out of wedlock? She would run a mile. She'd disown me.'

Rose smiled slightly. 'I think you're wrong there. Most mothers threaten dire penalties to try to protect their offspring, but if something happens they rally to the cause. It's only natural.'

'Believe you me, my mother is not in that category.'

At the finality in her voice Rose did not pursue the subject any further.

It was chilly, and when they entered the house Rose went straight to the grate and put a light to the fire that was already laid. They sat either side of the hearth and suddenly Colette leaned across and gripped this kind woman's hands. 'Rose, I'm not really a monster, you know.' Her voice pleaded for understanding.

'I know you're not. I find you a very kind and caring person, Colette.'

'If you only knew how much I regretted that night. I'm so ashamed every time I think of it. One night when I wasn't in full control of my senses and my life is ruined for ever.'

'I think you're being a little harsh on yourself. When you're in love these things happen quite naturally, no matter how good your intentions are.'

'But you don't understand! It should never have happened. I'll regret it till my dying day, so I will.'

Rose roughly shook her hands. 'Now you listen to me, Colette Burns. Regrets are futile. Many a time I've said *If only . . . What if?* But it does no good. You just have to put whatever it is behind you and get on with your life.' Colette opened her mouth to dispute this. How could you put the imminent birth of a child behind you? Rose forestalled her. 'I know your problem seems insurmountable, but it's a case of finding the right solution. Trust me. Things will work out somehow. They always do.'

Tess descended the stairs in her dressing gown, towelling her wet hair. 'My, but you two look solemn,' she said, joining them by the fire.

Wanting to leave the friends alone so that Tess could

be brought up to date on affairs, Rose volunteered, 'I'll put the teapot on, shall I?'

'That would be lovely,' Colette readily agreed, glad of the respite.

At the huskiness in her voice Tess peered closer and saw the signs of recent tears. Concerned, she sat close to her friend. 'What's wrong?'

'Rose knows I'm pregnant.'

Immediately, Tess straightened her back. 'I swear I never said a word. Honest!'

'I know you didn't. She read all the signs.'

'Of course, I should have known. She's a country woman, isn't she? But I do know this much. You can trust her. If you ask her to keep her mouth shut she will.'

'I've been waiting for you to come down, so we can discuss it. See what options I have, before it drives me round the bend with worry.'

Tess breathed a sigh of relief; her prayers had been answered. Now there were two of them to persuade Colette to keep the baby.

Rose returned with a tray laden with teapot, milk, sugar and a plate of still hot soda farls dripping with butter. Setting it down on a coffee table she went back to the kitchen for the cups and saucers. They ate in silence, each buried in her own thoughts. It was Rose who finally spoke.

'When is the baby due?'

'January.'

'You must have some idea what you intend doing?'

'I was thinking that I'd write to one of these homes for unmarried mothers and when the baby is born have it adopted.'

Rose gnawed at her bottom lip for some seconds,

while Tess willed her to come up with some pearls of wisdom. But Rose's argument was the same as hers. 'Do you not think Dan would be happy to take responsibility for the baby? After all, it's his grandchild.'

'No. No, I don't think that would be a good idea.'

'Why not?'

'Because then everybody would have to know.'

'Has the doctor given you an approximate date?'

'I haven't been to the doctor yet.'

Rose nodded her head. 'I thought as much. Perhaps that's a good thing. While I was making the tea I was trying out ideas in my head. Shall I tell you what I came up with?'

They both nodded eagerly and Rose continued. 'You'll be able to work for another couple of months. Right?' A nod from Colette confirmed it. 'What if I arrange for my doctor to look after you?'

'I don't see how that could help, Rose. Remember I live in Belfast.'

'I don't want you to rush into anything, Colette, but I'm going to make a suggestion and I want you to give it some careful consideration before you answer, okay?'

'Okay.'

'When you feel the need to leave work, why not come here and live with me? After all, you did say what a lovely spot this is. I'd be glad of your company and my doctor is a very understanding man. He would look after your welfare while you were staying here. I would tell him you're a young friend in trouble. He would understand and wouldn't ask any awkward questions.'

Tess couldn't believe her ears. Here was her future aunt offering her friend a solution to her immediate troubles. Her prayers had indeed been answered. She looked expectantly at Colette and was dismayed to see her sadly shake her head.

'Thank you, Rose. You're very kind. But you see I want to go away so no one in Belfast need ever know the truth. What you're suggesting wouldn't remain a secret for very long.' She glanced towards Tess. 'For instance, Mrs Maguire would know and through her Mr Thompson. And then he would start pestering me regarding the baby's future.' The head shake became more definite. 'No, this way it wouldn't work out.'

Tess had been taking all this in and turning it over in her mind, quickly coming to a decision. Now she interrupted. 'Mam wouldn't necessarily have to know. When the time comes that you have to leave work you could suddenly get the chance to go to Canada to see how you feel about working over there on a permanent basis, and not have time to say goodbye. No one else connected with the family, except Uncle Malachy of course, need ever know you're here. I think it's a great idea. It could work out for the best, Colette.'

'Do you think it possible? It would be lovely to come here instead of being away among a lot of strangers. I really do love Carlingford. Everyone I've met has been so nice and friendly towards me.'

'With a bit of careful planning it can be managed,' Tess assured her. 'I'll keep your secret no matter what. Trust me!'

'Mind you, I'd still want the baby adopted.'

Tess and Rose stared at each other and a silent pact was made. They had plenty of time to persuade Colette to change her mind.

Chapter Sixteen

Next day Tess drove proudly home in her new Austin Mini. She left Colette, much relieved now that a decision had been made about her immediate future, on Spinner Street and proceeded up the Falls Road to Springfield Road. She had phoned her mother and told her about all her presents, especially the car, and now she sat outside her home expecting Alice and Dan to come rushing out and fawn all over it. Not a bit of it!

No sign of life at all. Such a difference from Carlingford. And to crown it all, today – the 24th – was her actual birthday. Feeling desolate, Tess got out of the car and unlocking the boot proceeded to unload her suitcases and parcels. Just what had she expected? Was her mother going to be awkward about the car? Did she resent Uncle Malachy's buying it for Tess, as she had with the Christmas present he had given her? Surely not. She had sounded so pleased on the phone when Tess told her all about it. Had insisted on talking to her brother and thanking him for his generosity. But the reception here in Belfast was one big disappointment.

Her reverie was broken by the sound of the front door opening and her mother, followed closely by Dan, Theresa and a few other friends, clattered down the steps to greet her. Alice hugged her as she wished her a happy birthday. 'Sorry it took us so long coming out,' she apologised. 'We've been on the lookout for you all day and then, wouldn't you know, as soon as we turned our backs you arrived at the door. Something came up at the last minute to distract us. But you'll hear all about that soon enough.' She turned her attention to the car. 'Oh, my, but isn't that car one wee beaut. I love that colour.'

Pleased at her reaction, Tess watched closely, but her mother seemed genuinely sincere in her admiration. Dan was also giving the Mini the once over. 'It certainly is. It's a grand wee car. Happy birthday, Tess. Here, give us a hug.'

Theresa was tugging at her sleeve. 'Let them drool over your lovely car all they want, but you must come inside, Tess. There's a load of presents to be opened.'

'If I could just give you mine now, Tess. I have to rush off.' Tony Burke thrust a parcel into her arms and pecked her on the cheek. 'Happy birthday. I'll see you tomorrow.'

Theresa grabbed his arm. 'What about dinner tonight?'

Gently he released her hold. 'I don't think so. Bye for now, Tess. Have a nice time tonight.'

'Bye, Tony, and thanks for the present.' She looked in bewilderment at Theresa. 'What on earth's up with him? And what's all this dinner business?' she asked.

'If you'll just come inside I'll explain.'

'Dan, can I leave you to look after my cases?'

'No sweat, Tess. Away you go.'

When she entered the hall a whiff of remembered perfume hung in the air. Alerted, she quickly entered the sitting room only to come to an abrupt halt and stand gaping speechlessly. There, looking like a million dollars in a suit that fitted like a glove, stood a smiling Agnes Quinn, her arms held out wide to embrace her best friend.

'When did *you* get here?' Tess managed to splutter.

'Just before you. That's why they were so slow at going to the door.'

'Where's Dominic?'

'He couldn't afford to leave the business again so soon, so he arranged all this behind my back. I didn't know I was coming until yesterday. It was a last minute rush. So you can guess I've hardly any clothes with me.'

'I don't believe that for one second. Anyway, how long are you home for?'

'Just a week. It was a cancellation so Dominic got it cheap.'

They were wrapped in each other's arms, hugging and kissing, tears mingling as if they hadn't seen each other for years. 'Oh, I'm so glad to see you again, Agnes. This is the best birthday I've ever had.'

Agnes pointed to a large box on the table. 'That's my present. It arrived long before me, since I didn't know I was coming. I'm afraid it's a winter jacket. But then I didn't know you'd be the proud owner of a car. It's lovely, by the way. I had a wee peek at it from behind the curtains. Imagine you being able to drive, eh, Tess? Wonders will never cease!'

Tearing off the wrapping paper and opening the box, Tess exclaimed with pleasure when she saw the dark green ski-type jacket. She slipped it on and examined herself in the mirror. 'Oh, it's lovely! And as you well know, a winter coat will never go to waste over here, Agnes.'

'I suppose not. It goes with your eyes. I'm glad you like it.' Agnes nodded to where Theresa stood beaming at them. 'I believe you are also part owner in a shop now?'

'Yes. Isn't it wonderful? I take it you've already met Theresa? Me and her get on like a house on fire.'

'I'm pleased to hear that, Tess. I hope I meet someone like her out in America. At the moment it's a bit lonely over there as I hardly know anybody, but Dominic takes me round introducing me to his friends every chance he gets.'

'Here's your mam and Dan coming in now,' Theresa exclaimed. 'Let's move into the living room. There's a bottle of champagne waiting to be opened. My mam is in there too, patiently waiting to give you your present.'

Linking her arm through Agnes's as she always did, Tess happily led the way. What a lovely homecoming it had turned out to be, and there's her thinking that everyone had forgotten her big day. She gave an involuntary sniffle at the thought. The twenty-fourth of July was going to be a great day. Apparently a table had been booked at the Royal Avenue Hotel for eight o'clock that night. Her best friend was home for a week. Life couldn't be better. The only fly in the ointment was Tony. She would phone later that afternoon and thank him for the perfume he had bought her, and perhaps she would be able to persuade him to join them for dinner. Did he still care so much for Agnes that he couldn't bear to be in the same room as her? He would have to get her out of his system, or he would end up a grumpy old bachelor.

The weekend was an exciting time for Tess, the dinner and subsequent birthday party going with a swing. The cheque from her mother was gratefully received and was now deposited in the business account of Maguire & Cunningham.

Agnes willingly spent some of her holiday helping the girls clean and polish the shop fittings, in preparation for the big opening day. Theresa listened raptly in the background while the two friends babbled away, exchanging bits of gossip as Tess brought Agnes up to date on all the latest news and scandals. It was during one of these conversations that she discovered that Tony and Agnes had been engaged. She surmised this to be the reason why Tony had refused to come out with them on Saturday night. It surprised her, as she had been inclined to think he was very interested in Tess.

Soon Tess was saying a tearful goodbye once more to Agnes, amidst promises of going out to Florida to be her bridesmaid when a definite date had been set. When Agnes had departed it was no holds barred as, with final papers signed, she and Theresa began moving into their new work premises and shop. They had all agreed that it would be best if Alice were to continue working at home.

A lot of thought was put into the window display. The public were used to seeing children's clothes in this shop window. Tess and Theresa didn't want to appear as if they would be dealing only in children's wear, so a bridal ensemble took up the centre of the display, complemented by a variety of outfits for children. Having bought all the previous owners' stock they had plenty of autumn wear for sale and were free to start working on bridal wear and Christmas dresses.

Tess, Tony and Colette still had their Saturday night outings together and Tess was surprised at how well her friend managed to hide her pregnancy with loose clothes as autumn approached. After Theresa left for the day, Colette spent a lot of evenings in the shop, sewing on buttons or pressing or assisting with anything else that didn't require too much expertise.

On these occasions she could relax and discuss any problems she might have with Tess. It was late September when she handed in her notice at the bank and Tess began to drop hints to her mother and Dan about Colette's wanting to go to Canada for a trial period.

Dan was the first to voice his objections. 'What does she want to go to Canada for?'

'To get away from all the memories around here, that's what. There are good opportunities out there for someone with Colette's experience. Besides, if she doesn't like what she sees, she can always come home.'

'What has her mother got to say about that?' Alice queried.

'I couldn't say. She never discusses her family with me.'

'Talk her out of it, Tess.' Dan sounded disturbed. 'She was almost my daughter-in-law. I feel I should be keeping an eye on her for Jack's sake.'

Tess flashed him a look of derision. 'Hah! That's the best gag I ever heard! Just what have you done for her since Jack died? Go on . . . tell me!'

Dan held up his hands in defence. 'All right! All right! So I haven't done very much. I admit that. However, it wasn't for the sake of trying. She just kept giving me the brush-off. But I always listen whenever you talk about her. I know she's doing all right. If there was ever a hint of trouble I'd be the first one in there fighting the good cause. You've got to believe that, Tess. I feel a good deal of responsibility where she is concerned.'

Tess could see he really was perturbed. Amazed at

how smoothly the lies rolled off her lips, she said, 'Perhaps nothing will come of it. It's all talk at the moment. But, Dan . . . if she does decide to go . . . if I were you I wouldn't interfere. She won't thank you for it.'

'Oh, won't she? Well, I can't see me just standing around holding my tongue.'

'Let's just wait and see what happens and not go flying off the handle, eh? As I said, she might change her mind.'

Two weeks later Tess drove Colette to Great Victoria Street station and put her on the train to Newry. Malachy would be there to pick her up. That night Tess broke the news to her mother and Dan that Colette had left for Canada.

'She's away and all?' Dan exclaimed. 'And you never said a word about it?'

'Here, hold on a minute. I didn't know.' Tess lied through her teeth. 'It was all arranged from Canada. Her friend persuaded Colette to go and see what it was like out there. She arranged it all.'

Dan shook his head in disbelief. 'And she hadn't even time to say goodbye?'

'She didn't want a lot of goodbyes. She said goodbyes always made her weepy.'

'Did you drive her to the airport?'

This was the snag as far as Tess was concerned. She was the obvious one to have driven Colette to the airport, but she hadn't been away from home long enough for that.

More lies came to her lips. 'No. One of the managers from the bank was going to a conference down south and gave her a lift to Shannon.'

Both Alice and Dan still looked unconvinced and, flustered, Tess cried, 'I don't know what all the fuss is about. You hardly ever see her anyhow, so what difference will it make? Even if she decides to make her home in Canada she'll be back to settle her affairs and say her farewells. Anyway, it's none of our business what she does.'

'Still, I wish I'd known. I could have perhaps talked her out of it.'

Dan left the room and they heard him climb the stairs. With a reproving glance at her daughter, Alice followed him.

Dismayed, Tess wondered just what she had got herself into. Letters would be expected from Canada over the next couple of months. What excuse would she give when they failed to arrive? She would have to play it by ear. At least Colette was in safe hands, not away somewhere surrounded by strangers, and that was Tess's primary consideration at the moment. Dan's hurt feelings didn't enter into it as far as she was concerned.

To Tess's surprise, Tony showed no great interest in Colette's departure. When Theresa heard about it she smiled and said, 'I bet Tony is delighted. I think he thought her a bit of a gooseberry.'

'What do you mean?'

'It's obvious he fancies you, and now with Colette out of the picture he will feel free to show his interest. You mark my words, Tess.'

'Tony . . . fancy me? Don't be silly. We're just good friends.'

Theresa laughed outright. 'Just you wait and see.'

'I hope you're wrong. Because believe you me, I am not in the least bit interested in Tony Burke.'

*   *   *

As expected, questions *were* asked about the absence of letters from Canada, or any other communication for that matter. It was a Sunday afternoon and Tess and Alice – Dan having gone for a walk – were having a cup of tea and catching up on each other's news when, taking Tess unawares, Alice wondered aloud about Colette's welfare. Absentmindedly Tess almost assured her that she was doing well and everything was under control. The words were on the tip of her tongue and just in time she swallowed them and muttered, 'It would be nice to know.' She was very annoyed with herself, realising how close she had come to letting the cat out of the bag. So easily done! Exasperated, she cried, 'Mam, if Colette wants us to know her business she'll write in her own good time! Okay? Meanwhile, I wish you and Dan would stop pestering me about her. What makes you think I know any more than you do?'

At her daughter's tone of voice, Alice drew back affronted. 'You can't blame Dan for being worried, Tess.'

'Actually, Mam, I can and I do blame him. He should have been more attentive when she was here and maybe she wouldn't have gone off in the first place.'

'He tried. You heard him. But she wouldn't let him help her.'

'We've only his word for that, Mam. Colette certainly never spoke to me of him offering any help. And anyway, it's none of Dan's business what Colette does or doesn't do.'

Alice rounded on her in anger. 'Are you saying he lied?' she cried indignantly.

'No, Mam, I'm not. What I am saying is that if she didn't want his help before, she won't want it now, so let's forget about Colette for a while. I've more important things on my plate at the moment. If I do get any news you'll be the first to know. Okay? After all, Colette and I weren't exactly bosom pals.'

With a look of disdain, Alice lifted her cup and left the room. Tess buried her face in her hands; so much for a quiet chat over a cup of tea! She prayed she would be able to keep up this deception. At least it was near the end of November; not all that much longer to go now. According to Rose, Colette was still talking about adoption and wanted Rose to get in touch with the proper authorities on her behalf. A distracted Rose informed Tess that if they couldn't change her mind she really would put the baby up for adoption and go off to Canada.

Every Wednesday after closing the shop for the day Tess would settle down and have a good old chin-wag with Rose and Colette before going home, to find out how things were going. They assured her that so far everything was fine and Colette always reminded Tess not to drop her guard and let anyone know where she was.

Christmas day fell on a Saturday this year and the girls were closing shop from Wednesday night for the Christmas break. On Tuesday night Rose rang Tess at home, something she had never done before. It was Alice who answered the phone, and after a short conversation with Rose she called Tess into the hall. 'It's Rose. Something about a pattern for her wedding suit,' she explained.

It was so unlike Rose, to phone out of the blue to discuss her suit, that Tess had a premonition that something awful had happened. Gingerly picking up the receiver, she delayed as long as she could before saying softly, 'Hello, Rose.'

Quick on the uptake, Rose whispered, 'I take it it's not safe to talk at the moment?'

'Not really.'

'I'm sorry. But I couldn't wait any longer. I just had to let you know. Colette has had a baby boy, and I'm afraid of her doing something rash. She wants to see you as soon as possible. Is there any chance of you getting down here tomorrow?' She sounded really worried.

'Why, that's wonderful! Yes, I think I could get down some time tomorrow to have a look at it. It would be a pity to let such a piece of material pass you by as you seem to have your heart set on it. I'll ask Mam if she will help out in the shop.'

Alice was sitting with her ears pricked when Tess put her head round the living room door. 'Mam, Rose has the chance of a beautiful piece of worsted material for her wedding suit,' she lied glibly. 'Is it all right if I go down tomorrow after the shop closes and stay overnight? Or better still, could you possibly help Theresa in the shop tomorrow and let me get away early? We shouldn't be too busy. Just a couple of customers are working and can't pick up their orders until the last minute, so it means keeping the shop open. It's not fair to leave Theresa on her own.'

Alice pulled a wry face. 'Can Rose not hang on to the material until after Christmas? I've to go down to the market tomorrow for my turkey and fresh vegetables. I daren't leave it till Christmas Eve. It'll be murder then.'

'Tell you what, Mam. You get your veg down the road and I'll ask Uncle Malachy to get us a turkey. He should be able to get us a nice one down there.'

Alice pondered for a moment. 'All right. I suppose that's fair enough.'

Tess ran back to the phone. 'Hello? Are you still there, Rose?'

'Of course I am.'

'I can be in Carlingford early tomorrow. Mam will help Theresa in the shop and we're closed on Thursday so I'll be able to stay overnight if that's all right with you? And, Rose . . . would you ask Uncle Malachy to get me a turkey, please?'

'Of course you can stay as long as you like. The turkey will be no problem. I'll see you tomorrow then, Tess. Bye for now.'

On the journey down to Carlingford. Tess said over and over to herself, 'A boy. A little boy.' She wished she knew more about it but her mam would have been suspicious if she and Rose had started whispering on the phone the night before. Not that Alice would ever have guessed the truth, but she would have known that something was going on and would have tried to find out what. That was something they could do without while the baby's fate hung in the balance.

When she got out of the car, Rose quickly left the house, closing the door behind her.

'Oh, I'm so glad to see you, Tess. Colette's in an awful state. She will hardly look at the child and he's absolutely gorgeous. I hope you can talk some sense into her.'

'So do I! What weight was he?'

'Just over seven pounds. It's obvious she wants to hold him but is afraid of getting too attached to him. She's still determined to go to Canada. I don't think we'll be able to put her off that idea.'

'The baby's early, isn't it?'

'Early *and* quick! She went into labour at about seven o'clock yesterday evening. I thought it would take hours and I delayed sending for the doctor. He came in as I was delivering it myself around nine o'clock. I thought I'd wait until you closed for Christmas before letting you know but Colette wouldn't wait. That's why I rang you last night. I'm sorry I put you on the spot, but I couldn't do anything else. She wants to talk to you on your own. So up you go.'

Still Tess dithered. 'I don't mean to sound suspicious . . . but did the doctor say anything about it arriving early?'

Rose stared intently at her. 'No, but then he wouldn't. If Colette told him anything in confidence he wouldn't break that confidence. Just what are you implying, Tess? Do you think maybe it isn't Jack's child?'

A bewildered shake of the head was her answer. 'I honestly don't know. I'll go up now and see her. We'll have a chat later.'

Colette was in despair as she awaited the arrival of Tess, torn by thoughts of her son and how he had come to be conceived. Would Tess understand and lend a sympathetic ear, or would she be disgusted with her friend's despicable behaviour? Heaven knows, she couldn't be any more disgusted than she herself was right now. How she regretted that night. She had thought of little else since it had happened. Jack just a few hours dead and she had betrayed him! If only she could turn back the clock.

In all honesty she hadn't realised Dan was so drunk. As for herself . . . unused to strong alcohol, it had not only deadened the pain of the loss of her beloved Jack, it had lulled her into a sense of false security. When Dan's comforting pats had become sensual caresses she had swayed with the wind as it were, willingly gratifying her desires, urging him on, wanting to blank out reality. It had seemed so right at the time! And she was honest enough to admit to herself that, in her drunken state, she had even enjoyed it. However, it was all over in a very short space of time and she was horrified when the enormity of what she had done hit her. Her great worry was having to face Dan again.

She had tried to waken him but he was dead to the world. Throwing a blanket over his prone form she skulked from the house, engulfed in shame.

The next morning she had waited in trepidation for Dan to come and apologise. She waited in vain. When he did eventually arrive to discuss the funeral arrangements with her, she was dismayed that he did not mention what had taken place between them. Not a word. In fact he appeared to be unaware that anything *had* happened.

At first she couldn't believe that Dan didn't remember what had taken place between them the previous night; had thought he was being evasive about the whole matter. However, it soon became clear to her that he had no recollection whatsoever of their encounter. He had either erased it from his mind or perhaps convinced himself it was all a dream. Either way he had shown no outward sign that anything had occurred between them. How she wished that she could do likewise, but she would never forget that night and the deep shame she felt would stay with her till her dying day.

As time passed she was glad that he did not remember. It meant that she could put it behind her and no one need be any the wiser. By the time she discovered that she was pregnant it was too late to confront Dan about it. Even if she had picked up the courage to do so, would Dan have believed her? She very much doubted it. It was obvious by then that he had eyes only for Alice Maguire. The only solution she could see open to her was to have the baby adopted, but now that she had seen her beautiful son there was no way she could ever give him up. Hearing footsteps on the stairs she closed her eyes and tried to arrange her thoughts. The time of reckoning had arrived and she must confess her guilty secret to Tess.

Tess quietly entered the bedroom and at a glance saw that Colette was sleeping. Her thoughts were in turmoil. Did she really think that Colette had been stringing them along pretending the baby was Jack's? Tiptoeing over to the cot in the corner, she gazed down in wonder on the sleeping child. He was indeed beautiful, with a mane of jet black hair and small perfect features. Whether it was because she wanted it to be so, she didn't know, but she thought he resembled the Thompsons. Not Jack, no, but to her he was the spitting image of his grandfather.

Colette's voice brought her back to reality. 'He's lovely, isn't he?'

Tess glanced towards the bed and big dark haunted eyes gazed back at her. 'He certainly is.'

'Thanks for coming so quickly.' Pushing herself painfully into a sitting position, Colette patted the bedclothes and said, 'Come and sit here. I want to talk to you.'

Hesitantly Tess approached the bed and stood gazing at Colette in concern. 'Are you all right? Do you feel up to talking? I'm staying overnight. We can talk later if you like, after you've had a good rest. I'm sure you're exhausted.'

'I'm fine. Just the stitches are a bit sore when I move.

Please sit down. We mightn't get another opportunity to speak in private.'

Reluctantly Tess sank down on to the bed. She didn't want to know if Colette had been playing around whilst engaged to Jack. She felt betrayed that her friend had used Rose and her to cover up her deceit.

Determinedly, Colette held Tess's eye. 'I've a confession to make, and it isn't pleasant listening. Jack is not the baby's father.'

Even although she was already thinking along these very same lines, Tess couldn't hide the shock and distaste that coursed through her.

'Don't look like that, Tess! Why do you think I was so ashamed when I discovered I was pregnant? If it had been Jack's I'd have been over the moon. But it isn't! And that's why I wanted to get it adopted. The only snag is that now I've seen him I've changed my mind. I certainly don't want him to go to some strangers.'

Tess's thoughts had gone into overdrive. If Jack wasn't the culprit, then who was? Only one other person came to mind.

She voiced her shocked thoughts. 'Is it Tony Burke's?'

Colette smiled sadly. 'I wish it was. But do you think if it had been Tony's I'd have been afraid to tell him? Even if he was engaged to Agnes at that time, Tony is a very responsible person. He would have taken care of me, no matter what.'

'Then *who*?' Tess cried in exasperation. 'Who were you afraid to tell? What bad bastard left you in the lurch? Was it someone at work?'

'No. No, nothing like that. Look, I don't know how to put this into words, so I suppose I'll just have to tell you as simply as I can.' Hands clasped tightly in front of her, Colette continued in a monotone. 'Do you remember when Jack died and Grannie was taken into hospital?'

At a nod from Tess she went on. 'I was distracted. Completely at my wits' end. I didn't know you very well then, and had no one to turn to. That night, after everyone else had gone, dreading going into an empty house, I stayed behind to comfort Dan . . . and, I suppose, to get comfort in return. He holds his drink so well I didn't realise he was already drunk and I poured us both a large whiskey. I hate the stuff, but I made myself drink it hoping it would deaden the awful pain inside me. And it did!' Tears trickled down Colette's cheeks and dripped unheeded on to her nightie.

Having an inkling where all this was leading, Tess reached for Colette's hands and gripped them tightly. 'Don't upset yourself so.'

'I have to tell you, Tess. You see, you're the only one I can really trust. You're my best friend. And . . . you'll know what to do.'

'Me?' Tess squeaked in dismay.

'Yes, you. The whiskey, and I suppose the grief, had taken its toll on me. At first I didn't realise Dan's comforting pats had become sexual pawing.' Her eyes begged Tess to understand. 'It was such a comfort to be wanted.' Tears fell faster at the recollection of it. 'I didn't even try to prevent it happening. You've got to believe me, Tess, when I tell you it seemed the most natural thing in the world. It's the God's honest truth, so it is.'

Tightening her grip on Colette's trembling hands, Tess gasped, 'Are you telling me that Dan Thompson took advantage of you?'

Colette looked blankly at her. 'I suppose he did. I never thought of it like that. I was so confused by my actions, especially as I had refused Jack the night before.'

'What did Dan have to say about it?'

'That's just it! I was afraid to look at him the next day, but he seemed unaware that anything had happened. I thought he was putting on an act and inwardly called him all the bad names I could think of, and some more. However, as time went by he seemed so caring I believed he really had completely blanked it from his mind. So, although I wanted nothing at all to do with him, I was at least glad to be able to put the episode behind me.'

'And when you discovered you were pregnant?'

'I'll never forget it! I nearly went out of my mind. It's awful, you know, to be in my position and have no one to turn to.'

'Why not me? We were friends by then.'

'Come on now, Tess. Be honest about it. Could I have told you? Dan and your mother were becoming so close I didn't know what kind of reception I would get, and I didn't want to lose your friendship. You were the only person I could talk to about being pregnant. Of course I couldn't tell you it was Dan's. I was too afraid of losing you.'

'Oh, God. This is awful. Imagine you having to rely on the likes of me. It's not right! Dan mustn't be allowed to get away with it! He must be made to face up to his responsibilities.'

'That's why I want to talk to you. What happens next will depend entirely on you.'

'Me? I don't understand. What have I got to do with it?'

Leaning closer, Colette said urgently, 'Think of the scandal if I speak out now, Tess. The whispers and the gossip. The people that would get hurt. Your mother for one. And the finger of shame would always be pointed at that poor innocent baby. Think about it!'

'But . . . you've got to agree, Colette, Dan Thompson must be made to pay for his part in this. Why, you could have had him up for rape if you had spoken out sooner. He took advantage of you, the dirty bastard!'

'No! No, Tess, you're wrong. I was a willing partner. But if it became common knowledge, it could be misconstrued. Is that what you want? The man your mother appears to love, being branded a rapist? If it got out of hand it would probably be spread across the front of the local papers, you know. He might even go to jail. Is that really what you want?'

'It doesn't matter about that. Mam would never condone anything like this. She would want to see him pay the penalty for his sin.'

Colette looked sceptical. 'Maybe . . . but would she be grateful to us for opening her eyes? Let's face it, Tess. It was a one off! It's not something that is likely to happen again. And think of Anne! She'd have a field day. Do you want to put your mother through all that humiliation?'

Before Tess could answer, the baby whimpered and she made to go to him. With a hand on her arm, Colette stopped her. 'Don't get too fond of him until we get this sorted out between us.'

'Surely you can't consider letting him go to strangers now. He's beautiful.'

'No. Rose has offered to look after him for me and she says Malachy is more than willing. But it's not the ideal situation. Her son's wife is expecting a baby in March and I don't want his nose put out of joint.' Tess still looked stunned and Colette added sadly, 'I know how you feel. I've been awake all night thinking about it. One thing I do know, I will not have him adopted. Not now.'

'Thank God for that at least! You're not going away then?'

'Oh yes, I'm still going to Canada. Do you think I could look at that wee child's face every day and not remember that I had betrayed my beloved Jack? And with his father of all people? I just couldn't do it, Tess.'

Tess gazed at her in confusion. 'But you didn't really betray Jack. You were drunk and vulnerable, remember. Oh, I wish I could get my mind round this. Just what do you intend doing?'

'I have a suggestion to make, Tess. It all depends on you. You could take the child home with you tomorrow and introduce him as either Dan's son or his grandson. The choice is yours. As Dan's son . . . he will cause a lot of unhappiness and misery, although I don't doubt for one minute that Dan will take on the responsibility of rearing him, even if it means losing your mother's friendship. As Dan's grandson, he will be greeted with delight by all concerned.'

'And what about Rose? How much does she know?'

'She knows nothing. She still thinks it's Jack's. Everyone else will think so too, unless you say otherwise.'

'But why tell me?'

'Because you're my friend and you have been good to me. Your mother's happiness is at stake here. To be truthful, it's not just your mother I'm thinking of. I myself don't relish the scandal that will erupt if the truth is told. They will say terrible things about me as well, you know, but I'll be going far away where it won't hurt me. Where no one will be any the wiser.'

The baby cried out, louder this time, and there was

a tap on the door. Rose's head appeared round it. Her eyes took in the two tense figures on the bed, and she made to withdraw then paused to say, 'Sorry for interrupting. I was just going to take him downstairs and change his nappy. If that's all right?'

'Thanks, Rose. You do that, please.'

When the door closed on Rose, Colette advised, 'Sleep on it, Tess. The decision is yours. And please don't think me awful for wanting to get away. I'll go nuts if I stay in Belfast and live a lie for the rest of my life.'

Reaching for her, Tess gathered her close. 'You poor, poor dear. What you've come through is nobody's business. You must have felt so isolated. I think you're a very brave girl, so I do. I'll go downstairs now. I can't wait to hold that wee fellow. Have you thought of a name for him yet?'

Colette smiled. 'No matter which way it goes, I think Jack will be the most appropriate name. Don't you?'

'You're right there! Jack it will be.'

Downstairs, as she crooned over the baby, Tess could feel Rose watching her covertly, but as yet there was nothing she could tell her.

'Colette is going to name him Jack,' she volunteered.

'And do you still think it might not be Jack's baby?'

'Oh, he's a Thompson all right. The minute I set eyes on him I could see that,' she said convincingly.

'I don't want to appear nosy, but has she said what she intends doing?'

'Rose . . . after all you've done? You could never appear nosy in my book. She wants me to take him back with me tomorrow and introduce him to Dan.' But in what capacity? What a decision to have to make.

'And are you going to do that?'

'Yes, I think he has the right to know about the baby. And I'm sure when he hears that Colette still intends going to Canada he will want to make himself responsible for his upbringing.' She glanced sadly at Rose. 'You must feel let down. Colette says you offered to take him.'

'Don't worry about me! My son's wife is expecting a baby in March. I can spoil that rotten. I just wanted to ease Colette's mind; to let her know that I'd be here if she needed me.'

'You're such a good person, Rose. I hope Uncle Malachy appreciates what he is getting.'

'Don't you worry about that. I'll make sure he does!'

The journey back to Belfast the next day was a different kettle of fish from the one to the farm. Then she had thought that Colette had played the dirty on her and Rose. Had used them. Now she knew the whole sordid story and the part she was required to play in it. From time to time she glanced at the baby's carrycot strapped securely on the passenger seat beside her. Her mother would delight in helping to rear him. And it would also be a blessing in disguise. With Dan out at work every day Tess felt her mother resented working in the house alone while she and Theresa worked in the shop. With a baby to look after she would be happy and contented with her lot.

But could she deceive her mother on such a serious issue? After all, as Colette had pointed out before she left, one way or the other the child would be Dan's responsibility. She would have to play it by ear. See if Dan showed any signs of guilt. If he did, it would mean that he remembered the part he had played in the baby's conception. Even though he had been unaware of the consequences, in that case Tess could not see herself being able to hold her tongue.

One thing was certain. Whatever decision she made today, she would have to stick by it. There could be no turning back.

Drawing the car up to the front of the house she quickly got out and, checking the baby was all right, closed the door.

Dan came out as she opened the boot. 'Your mother asked me to make sure you have a turkey back with you.' He stood gazing in amazement at the variety of baby stuff packed in the boot. 'In the name of God, what's all this? I know it's Christmas, but this is ridiculous.'

'The turkey's in that box.' She indicated a cardboard carton. 'Would you take it in along with my case, Dan? I'll explain everything inside.'

Alice came out in a rush. 'Dan says you've a lot of baby stuff home with you. Who's it for?' Her eyes searched Tess's face. 'You're not . . . Are you?'

Tess smiled at the very idea that she might be pregnant. 'No, Mam, I'm not.'

'Theresa then?'

'Wrong again, Mam. Come and see.'

Tess opened the car door just as Dan returned. Alice gaped in wonder at the sleeping child. Her head swivelled towards Tess. 'It can't be Rose's, surely.'

'Mam, will you stop making these stupid guesses. Dan, will you carry the cot inside, please. Mam, you help me empty the boot.'

Dan had placed the cot on the settee and was gazing intently at it. When Tess came into the room she watched him very closely. He looked totally relaxed. No sign of tension.

Still keeping a close eye on him, she announced, 'Colette gave birth to that child two days ago in Carlingford.'

Dan swung round and his eyes were blazing. 'You mean to tell me that Colette was in Carlingford expecting my grandchild and all along I was led to believe she was in Canada? And no one thought fit to tell me?' He turned on Alice. 'Did you know anything about this?'

'No, I honestly didn't know a thing. I thought she was in Canada too.' She looked accusingly at her daughter. 'Why all the secrecy, Tess?'

'She still intends going to Canada, and actually she was going to have him adopted and not say a word about it.'

'She was going to have my grandchild adopted without my permission?'

'She didn't need your permission, Dan . . . Or did she?' she added slyly, still very attentive to his reactions.

'As a grandfather I must have some rights. Why did she do this, Tess? How could she be so cruel?'

She could see he was completely bewildered. No sign of guilt or evasion. If he was putting on an act, he deserved an Oscar. She stood in thought for some moments before moving to the next scene in the saga. 'When some women are pregnant they get all mixed up. She thought you'd object to her still wanting to start a new life in Canada. Thank God she changed her mind about the adoption. She wants you to take care of him. What about it, Mam? Would you be willing to help Dan? It's a big step to take at your age.'

Alice had lifted the child into her arms and was crooning softly to him. 'Don't be silly! I'm not over the hill yet, girl. It would be the nicest thing that could possibly happen to me. He's the picture of his grandfather. But what about baby food? Shouldn't Colette be breast-feeding him?'

Tess held her breath, but there was still no reaction

from Dan at this allusion to whom the baby resembled. 'Dan? What about it? Are you willing to take on the responsibility? Colette doesn't want to become too attached to her son, so the doctor advised Rose what milk to start him off on. The baby clinic will advise you later on.'

'Willing? To bring up my own grandson? My own flesh and blood? Why, it would be as if Alice and I were rearing our very own son.'

Tess's eyes examined his face once more. Was he being sarky? No, there were no innuendos there. She took the final plunge. 'Well then, meet your grandson. Colette has named him Jack. She'll be coming up to say good-bye to him and the rest of us before going off to Canada. And please be kind to her when she gets here. She's been through the mill these last lot of months.'

Gently, Dan took the tiny infant in his arms, his face wreathed in smiles. 'Of course I will. And I'll love this wee lad as if he was my own son. What a lovely Christmas present, eh, Alice?'

'The nicest ever.'

Such a happy picture they make, Tess thought. But . . . only time would tell if she had made the right decision.

Mary A. Larkin would like to hear from her readers.
You are very welcome to visit her at:
www.marylarkin.co.uk